Michael Baldwin lived in South-West France, and based his last novel *The Rape of Oc* there. He also celebrated the region in *King Horn*, a volume of poetry which gained him a Cholmondeley Award. He has won the Rediffusion Prize and a Japan Award for his work in documentary television.

On his drive South he frequently stayed overnight in Blois and Orléans, his imagination teased by the ghosts of William and Annette, and then again in the mists of early morning by those of William and Michel Beaupuy, indefatigable walkers and talkers both, as he motored through the wilderness of the Salogne.

GW00690794

books by Michael Baldwin include

poetry
KING HORN
THE BURIED GOD
DEATH ON A LIVE WIRE
HOW CHAS EGGET LOST HIS WAY IN A CREATION MYTH
HOB
SNOOK

autobiography
GRANDAD WITH SNAILS
IN STEP WITH A GOAT

fiction
MIRACLEJACK
THE GAMECOCK
THE GREAT CHAM
THE CELLAR
A WORLD OF MEN
THERE'S A WAR ON
EXIT WOUNDS
HOLOFERNES
RATGAME
SEBASTIAN (short stories)
UNDERNEATH (short stories)
THE RAPE OF OC

For Peter

The First

Mrs WORDSWORTH

Michael Baldwin

Michael Baldwin

(a book to bring on

sleep!)

ABACUS

An *Abacus* Book

First published in Great Britain in 1996
by Little, Brown and Company

This edition published by Abacus in 1997

A CIP catalogue record for this book
is available from the British Library.

ISBN 0 349 10817 X

Typeset in Bembo by M Rules
Printed and bound in Great Britain by
Clays Ltd, St Ives plc

UK companies, institutions and other organisations wishing
to make bulk purchases of this or any other book
published by Little, Brown should contact their local
bookshop or the special sales department at the address below.
Tel 0171 911 8000. Fax 0171 911 8100.

Abacus
A Division of
Little, Brown and Company (UK)
Brettenham House
Lancaster Place
London WC2E 7EN

For
Gillian and Joel

Qui finem quaeris amoris
cedit amor rebus . . .

You who look for an end of love
Keep yourself busy . . .

OVID: Remedies of Love

I do not say I weep –
I wept not then – but tears have dimmed my sight
In memory of the farewells of that time . . .

WILLIAM WORDSWORTH: *The Prelude, Book IX*

BOOK ONE:

THE CALENDAR

ORLEANS.
TUESDAY THE SIXTH DAY OF
DECEMBER, 1791
(By Some Called The Third Year Of
Liberty)

'I think our stepfather has instructed you to marry me off!'

Annette had never seen so many young men of quality seated together in a room before, though it struck her with some amusement that the brilliance of their uniforms and the width of their epaulettes made them seem twice as numerous as they were.

Her brother led her through the double doors at the top of the stairway, then forward to meet them. She felt as if she were a horse about to confront its buyers at an auction.

They were much too polite to leave her with a poor opinion of themselves. A dozen of them leapt from their card tables by the fire and rushed to be introduced to her.

'It's true what he tells us,' one of them called from the back. 'Our lawyer friend has found himself a pretty sister!'

There was enchantment in a cavalry officer's uniform, and well they knew it. They had the colour and the glitter, and the way their buckles and breast straps made them hold themselves upright and gaze down their noses as if everything serious was a long way beneath them, as it probably was. Best was the richness of their cloth, and its scent neither of horse nor man but of being sponged with perfumed water in the mornings and taken away by servants to be brushed and hung among pomanders at night.

She was in a strange town, and the ways of the military were in general unknown to her, so she let them greet her as they wanted, some with an elaborate bow, most by taking her fingers and kissing her glove. She spoke to them one by one and realized when she did so that she could remember the names of none of them.

Her brother Paul Vallon left her to make small talk for a minute or two longer, then caught her by the hand and drew her towards an inside window. 'Marry you off? Old Vergez never asked me to do any such thing,' he said. 'He has neither the interest in us nor the wit. We must make our own weddings, sister – believe me – and this is not the place.' He raised his voice to say, 'Noble hussars below the rank of colonel of regiment never marry. Or not until they hang up their swords and return to their estates. By then, they're generally short of a limb or two, and have spots on their hands from going green about the liver.'

Annette laughed at this. So did some of the officers standing nearest, especially those who weren't hussars but belonged to some other order of horseman. She and Paul were surgeons' children and stepchildren, and allowed themselves the frankness of detail that comes from being descended from generations of sawbones.

Paul Vallon was quick-tongued on any subject. Wit seemed to have grown on him since he came to Orléans to be a lawyer, and he worked hard at being liked.

These young aristocrats of the cavalry certainly loved him. Once they had greeted Annette they gathered round him, asking for news of the revolutionary courts, whistling at what he told them, hating to look grave at his fragments of gossip from the prisons, so turning everything into a joke.

They wanted him to join them at cards. When he excused himself because of his sister, they bowed and again pressed her fingers, then went back to their tables and pears pickled in wine. Annette took this to be a messy dish, and silly too, since she never saw the point of drinking while pretending to eat.

'At least they're Christians and loyal,' she murmured to Paul. 'They swear by the Pope and King Louis. I'll never marry anyone in a church of the Constitution, and nor will our family let me!'

'Not even one of these, little sister? Not even *all* of them?'

'Not even all of them with a squadron of horse.'

'Well, I'm glad. Because I didn't stop us by to discuss weddings, whatever you say. I brought you here for your distraction. And your entertainment today is to be shown a madman who will shortly get his head chopped off, if he doesn't fit a ratchet to his tongue.'

'And who is he, pray?' Annette had only just arrived in Orléans from the family home in Blois. Her brother had promised her the place was full of marvels, but so far she hadn't seen any.

'He's the owner of this lodging, and of the workshop downstairs. He's in need of a wife as it happens, having just buried one.'

'Then you'd better fetch our sisters to look at him. Or our mother, next time round. A man must be unspoiled to be any good to me, as fresh as the first skimming of cream.'

Just then a voice sounded through the doorway, echoing up the stairs like a blast on a trumpet. '*Idiots!*' it yelled, '*eeee – dee – ohh!*' It was raucous and round, and obviously started from a full nest of teeth. Otherwise there wasn't much to be said for it. It came from the street at the bottom of the stairs, and possibly from a fair way along the street as well, though it grew nearer and louder, becoming more and more distorted the closer it came, and tearful too, as embarrassing as a drunkard's who's losing control of his dogs. '*Idiots! idiots! –idiots!*' Then still shouting *idiots* it was on its way upstairs.

Annette gazed at her brother questioningly.

'The madman I spoke of. Monsieur Gellet-Duvivier who owns this establishment.'

A young captain of hussars walked towards them from the card tables. He carried a jar of syrup and two glasses half filled with wine. There were no servants to be seen.

Annette took her wine without syrup, and heard him amuse himself by saying, 'As you will have noticed from his sign downstairs, our patron is both a hosier and a hatter. He sells stockings and fancy hats.' Then with a wink at Paul, he added, 'If you think of stockings first, then hats, you'll have a wonderfully exact picture of Master Gellet-Duvivier. There's a deal of him missing between!'

A gaily dressed man came panting in through the doors, turning to slam them behind him, as if disappointed to find them open and wasting the fire. Having made his point and his entrance he spun about and faced the room. His mouth hung ajar and his eyes were bloodshot from shouting, but he twirled the lace on his cuffs and advanced a very pretty shoe buckle to bow towards Annette, then listened to the card players' hoot of amusement and ribald comments as if to a special kind of applause.

Although it wasn't easy to compare colour and cloth in a room full of cavalrymen, he struck Annette as a parrot showing off to peacocks. As her mother would say, he was dressed in a deal of money but very little taste. Her mother had an eye for such matters, and an appropriate circle of acquaintances to exercise it among.

'*Idiots!*' he called again, as soon as he'd got his breath back.

In her mother's circle it wasn't done to say the same thing twice, unless someone asked you to repeat yourself. Then her mother's circle included, or was included by, most of the Montlivault family and even the Comte and Comtesse of Cheverny, all of whom were elegant of gossip and handled their cards discreetly or to music. Such people were a cut above the Gellet-Duviviers, and probably everyone else in the room, in spite of their family estates and parental quarterings.

'The world is full of idiots, patron – and Orléans has its share of them, without a doubt.'

A hand placed a playing card on top of another, and a mouth said, 'It takes one to know one.'

'One, yes. One.' Gellet-Duvivier seemed puzzled for a moment, as if so small a number was beneath him. Then he brightened and said, 'Ah, so you heard my little discussion in the street, my lords and gentlemen. That was with Besserve, the apothecary.'

It was a peculiarity of the language that '*idiot*' sounds the same as '*idiots*', and of Gellet-Duvivier's wrath that everyone who heard him assumed he spoke in plurals.

'He and his forefathers have poisoned our bellies for gener-ations,' the Madman exclaimed. 'Now he is dispensing republicanism and polluting the people's minds.'

'Indeed.'

'It's a sad thing when a member of the mercantile, not to say *professional*, class deals in placebos like Constitution, Equality, and Revolution. I wouldn't use such rubbish to pack a wig – no, not even to line a shoe!'

'That's a truth, sir. But, like most of its kind, a man can only yawn over it.'

The company yawned, noisily and together, as if in despair at the tedium of it all.

'My lords and young gentlemen have their mouths open. They must be in need of wine.' He clapped his hands and shouted downstairs.

After a minute or so, three young women appeared, carrying jugs. They came hot-bodied from the workroom, their fingers red from stitching.

Soon they were hot-faced as well, their cheeks even brighter than their needle fingers.

Annette began to understand why there was a shortage of ser-vants up here. It wasn't the madness of the master they feared so much as the eccentricities of his guests, these commissioned noblemen of title. The seamstresses were pretty much her own age, but the cavalry officers who had treated her so politely mauled them contemptuously, grabbing them by the breasts, pinching their bottoms with hands that went beneath their clothing and loitered inside. Her own presence there did noth-ing to restrain them. Several of them grinned at her, as if encouraging her to stand closer.

'They want our stepfather here to teach them anatomy,' Paul said. 'Then they wouldn't need to keep on discovering where everything is for themselves.'

'It's the same as with horses,' someone laughed, while strug-gling with a young woman who wriggled to escape from him. 'You check their condition by more than their teeth.'

'You've been galloping your string too hard, patron. Water and hay is what this one needs.'

'Then lash her up tight in a blanket!'

The women broke free at last, abandoning their jugs of wine, and leaving them unpoured in their hurry to reach the door.

'That little one with the tooth – I'd like to visit her in her stable. She knows she's for it when I'm around. Always last in and first out.'

'I wouldn't mind grooming our patron's daughter. Or having her groom me!'

'She's only thirteen or so!'

'Or Vallon's sister!'

Somebody laughed. Somebody tutted for silence. Annette pretended she hadn't heard, and turned closely against her brother, hoping he'd feel they'd overstayed their welcome.

The hubbub increased, but there still wasn't enough of it for Monsieur Gellet-Duvivier. Perhaps he knew that when the nobility run wild it's safest to run with them. He dashed among the card tables, selected a pickling pot, toasted the people all about him, and began to drink from it noisily, gulping down wine, cloves, shreds of nutmeg, and pears, everything, till his cheeks swelled disgustingly with more than he could swallow, and the veins almost burst from his throat. Annette was glad her mother wasn't here to see this, or her sisters to giggle. The juice trickled over his chin, sleeve and neckcloth, then to the floor, making him look like a crow in a puddle of fresh meat.

The card players had been entertained by his antics before. They expected something like this from him, and had been waiting for it. They threw down their cards and beat on the tables, spilling score-pegs, tapers and coins. The Madman tossed the emptied pot in the fire and whirled about, receiving applause.

Annette saw no need to join in. Paul tried to whisper something to her, but his comments were interrupted by the madman shouting, 'Swallowing their ears will be as easy, I promise you – their ears and the pips from their dirty little necks!'

The officers groaned and jeered and went on jeering, till one of them decided to cheer instead, and they all discovered that the wine tasted better for it, so the shouts of approval rose to an impossible crescendo.

'Thank you, my young lords and gentlemen. I'd let you off

rent for a twelvemonth, even those of you who lodge here, if only I could find another year in the calendar.'

More thumping on tables.

'Seventeen ninety-two promises me well, just the same. None of these Year Fours – God didn't rewrite the almanac when He let them set fire to the Bastille! So no more Calendars of Liberty!'

The cheering grew a trifle ragged; they were easily bored after so many generations of practice. The Madman noticed the change of mood and was bold enough to say, 'Once Christmas is through, I'll take you young fellows of the blood to greet King Louis in Paris. We shall kiss him together, however much these idiots leave of him. Then we'll set about hanging said idiots up by the neck.'

'Which idiots are we quarrelling with this time?' Annette was surprised to hear a woman's voice among all this riot, till it struck her she was the only woman here, and the voice must be her own.

Monsieur Gellet-Duvivier squinneyed his mad eyes towards her and hissed, 'Is this woman married, or just standing idle? She's old enough to be married.'

'She's his sister. She's the clerk's sister.'

'She's my sister, sir.'

'Then she should be stalwart for the Crown.'

Annette saw no need to discuss matters so delicate. She smiled and said, 'We were going to hang idiots together, you and I, Monsieur Gellet-Duvivier. I think you should tell me which idiots they are.'

'Republicans, young madame – republicans and constitution-alists,' he shouted, circling the room with that birdlike walk of his, confident that here in his upstairs salon over the Coin Maugas of the Rue Royale there could be no such person. 'The rogues who are muddling the nation!'

He reached an outer window in the room's lesser quarter, a window set in the more austere side of the house above the Rue du Tabour, and stood glaring down into the darkness of the scantily lit street. It was here they swarmed, and in the lampless alleys beyond that the mob was waiting for its chance to be king.

A stone struck the pane by his face – Annette supposed a

stone, something sharp and hard that splintered against the glass.

Nothing broke. The panes were as thick as the base of a demijohn, denser than an acid jar. It was typical of the fool that his shutters should be flung back all evening to let out the candle-light and proclaim what a good time his guests were having. Paul had assured her that no one in Orléans was starving this winter, unlike the last. It was simply, as he put it, that 'there are a good many hundred poor folk here with not enough to eat!' The Madman seemed perfectly happy to provoke all these, as well as brawl with republicans of his own class, men like the apothecary Besserve he had just been shouting at.

Another stone, followed by a curse.

Several hussars leapt up at this and crowded behind the patron, but only a single voice had been uplifted, and once it had drawn attention to itself that was the end of the matter, though a strange sense of menace had been planted among them, and every further noise in the two streets seemed to add to it.

'Constitutionalists and republicans, and fools who throw stones against my glass,' Gellet-Duvivier droned on, still gazing downwards, and still with a sniff to his voice, as if inspecting a festering wound. 'Not everyone down there's a constitutionalist, and I dare say there's some of you up here who are. It's these so-called "*Friends* of the Constitution" I can't stand. There's a club of them up the street, and that lot are republicans to the last man.' He wheeled about to snap, 'Hang them I say.'

'There's rather too many of them to hang, I fancy,' the captain of hussars put in.

'It would need too much rope,' the Madman conceded, 'in spite of my acknowledged cunning with the knots. But I shall surprise them all. I shall hang them in their own neckscarves, or else by the sleeves of their shirts – what do you say to that, sirs?'

'Provided it's not their trousers,' Paul Vallon hooted, then recovered himself to add, 'That would be too cruel a death.'

Gellet-Duvivier gazed at him, then looked aside to mutter, 'They don't all wear trousers, and that's the wickedness of it. Half of the fools are women, and some are too poor to get dressed. We won't find enough trousers between them to hang up a quarter of them.'

Sums always kill a fantasy, sums or the mention of women. Annette sensed a further chill in the room, as if the mobs that rushed like a recurring dream about Paris with their womenfolk leading them on were surging towards these havens of privilege on the Loire. Those stones were perhaps the first signal, and now here they were with their fish-gutting knives, their mattocks and saws, and the heads of people they disliked carried on steaming poles.

The nightmare wasn't helped by the bobbing, wine-streaked face and throat of Gellet-Duvivier. Its grin seemed to float disembodied through the blur of the room like one of those selfsame heads on its spike. She remembered Paul's description of him: 'a madman who will have his head chopped off if he doesn't fit a ratchet to his tongue!' There was no sign of a ratchet tonight. He seemed as mad as a Spring hare.

Gellet-Duvivier reinforced this impression by groaning aloud and knocking several times upon his own chin as if to close a drawbridge. 'I knew it!' he cried. 'And fool that I am I've forgotten it.'

'Forgotten what, sir?'

'I've forgotten my new lodger.'

A sigh ran round the card tables. Hands were slapped down, games broken off, some abruptly ended. Several men groaned or gasped out loud. Annette had seen enough of them to know it was their fashion to make trifles of France's largest events, and treat trifles as if they were universal catastrophes. The Madman had at last provided them with a topic tiny enough to take their attention.

'By God!' one of them cried. 'So you've done it at last, sir. You've actually chosen your new lodger! You should have consulted us first, patron!'

'That's right,' Paul said. 'Put the matter to the vote. It's all the fashion in Paris.'

Everybody laughed. 'And up the street,' one agreed. The buzz of excitement seemed genuine. Her mother's circle in Blois, and their offspring and servants all together, couldn't have pretended a greater show of interest, not even in a game of make-believe at Christmas. A new lodger, *the anticipated new lodger*, at the Coin

Maugas was clearly a major topic, and likely to last them for at least a minute.

Already someone was yawning.

People who sell fashionable clothes have to be performers in their way. Monsieur Gellet-Duvivier was such a one, even if his talents were limited to stockings and fancy hats.

Earlier he'd held their attention by right. Now he did so merely by proxy, but he was in no hurry to relinquish it. So he had left someone waiting unattended for a whole quarter of an hour! He took a step towards the doors of the room, held out his hand as if to open them ten paces off, then halted. The time was not yet. There were more things to say. The company needed to be prepared for the new arrival.

'Is it to be the King?' Paul asked him. 'Is the King coming to live here? Or the Queen with her pretty basket and her pinafore of little princes?'

A moment's silence followed this. The idea that it might be a woman held a terrible fascination for some of them.

'It's only His Majesty,' Annette's captain of hussars said sadly. 'He's in need of somewhere grand now the fishwives have taken his palace.'

'My new lodger's a gentleman,' the Madman explained. 'Or I take that to be his title.' He circled the carpet as if he deserved applause even for his quarter hour of forgetfulness. 'The poor fellow is waiting outside. He's standing there bag in hand – if he hasn't been murdered for his new suit, which I must say is substantial.' He approached Annette, as being someone who would appreciate this sort of detail. 'He's just taken the rest of this floor, unseen, for thirty livres a month. A good man, too, though foreign. He's paid me two months in advance, and for his board at another fifty.'

'I suspect that two months in advance,' one of the cardplayers called from behind him. 'I suspect any gentlemen who's ahead with his money.'

'And I suspect foreigners even more,' his partner added. 'Not one of your damned republican spies, is he?'

'Not he,' Gellet-Duvivier crowed. 'He's an Englishman. There are no republicans in England. They've only got kings over there.'

He went skipping through the doorway, leaving Annette to wonder what the Englishman had been doing during his long wait, and whether he had been out there while the Madman was shouting in the street, and if so what he would make of the sight of his landlord's appearance now he had pear juice clogged in his nostrils and running down his chin, and a sticky marinade spattered round the rest of him.

Gellet-Duvivier reappeared with the customary crashing of doors, and set about producing his Englishman with a flourish. 'Monsieur Wodswod,' he announced.

The young Englishman wasn't the man for flourishes. He kept closely behind Gellet-Duvivier, which was not at all where that gentleman expected him to be, then took a single pace to the left and stood absolutely still while introductions were made. These didn't last long, because without being in the least bit offensive, Monsieur Wodswod neither bowed nor smiled, but simply acknowledged the seated card players with a slight nod of the head and a level gaze. If he spoke any words of greeting, Annette did not hear them. These were men of rank the patron presented him to. Perhaps he did not know this, though there was something in his manner that suggested he did not greatly care. He seemed indifferent to cards and to the junior aristocracy in equal measure. Cards were all very well in their place, his gaze seemed to imply; so were these cavalry officers who had nothing better to do than yawn at him. But a moment's consideration had already told him their place was with one another and quite certainly nothing to do with him.

Since nobody rose to greet him, let alone talk to him, and their mad patron kept on skipping about, Annette was at first uncertain of the Englishman's height. There was clearly enough of him, but his body seemed mostly legs, with a strange stoop to the rest of it. What struck her most was the extraordinary elegance of his suit. No wonder the Madman had noticed it. It was cut from grey woollen cloth with a bluish bloom in the nap. There was nothing like this in France. And nothing quite like his shoes, which were entirely wrong for a gentleman. They were undoubtedly of the finest leather but, like his legs, there was altogether too much of them. They weren't in the least bit townish, though the stitching was elegant enough.

It was his footwear that took the cavalrymen's attention.

'He stands like a gentleman. He gazes down his nose like a gentleman. He *dresses* like a gentleman – except for the feet.'

'He's got footsoldier's feet. Look at his shoes. He's shod like a carthorse.'

'Nailed into the quick. The smith has nailed him to the quick. What do you say to his shoes, Monsieur Vallon?'

'I wonder does he take them off in bed?' Paul answered. 'And does he have heels inside them or a hoof?'

'That's for the ladies to tell us.'

Annette decided to smile at this. 'I expect the gentleman has heels, but I doubt if they're for dancing.'

'Did I hear you say you took the diligence from Rouen to Paris, monsieur?' Annette's captain asked.

The Englishman seemed to search his memory for some time before saying, 'I believe you did.'

'Did you pull it all the way by yourself?'

'Monsieur is extremely pleasant.'

The captain was probably a count. He would need to have some title or other before being granted a commission. Being dismissed as a monsieur made him grow petulant. 'He's got a damned foreign way of talking,' he snapped. 'He sounds like a spy. Are you a spy, monsieur?'

'Monsieur is dressed like a soldier. Are you a soldier, monsieur? If you are, you'll soon have enemies enough, without imagining you've found one in me.'

As dangerous to call a hussar a soldier as address a nobleman as if he were a bourgeois, yet there was probably no offence in it.

Unfortunately the newcomer's French was spoken slowly, and sounded over-deliberate as a result. Annette allowed herself another smile, and the company at large took its cue from her, gasping out something between a tut and a chuckle, which may have been no more than the renewed slap of coins upon cards. The fellow was a foreigner, and the foreigner an Englishman, and therefore as ill-matched to the occasion as was his suit to his ridiculous shoes.

He seemed to be trying to say something else.

Annette moved towards him, taking Paul with her. His first speech had been reckless enough, but Monsieur Wodswod's pronunciation was execrable and his grammar worse. She could not believe the quarrel would be over so simply if she allowed him to add any more words to it. The card players seemed to have been drinking all day, perhaps for ever. One of them might feel insulted to find a stranger prepared to stand his ground with him.

'What are you doing in Orléans at such a time, Monsieur Wodswod?'

'The time is chiefly why I have come here. In addition I am looking for someone to teach me some French, madame.'

'If you know enough of our language to ask for such a thing, then I fear there's very little left for anyone to teach you.'

'Nouns, madame. I am hungry for the names of things. I don't know enough of them to recognize what anyone is saying. And as for your verbs, I see no way to make them behave. So how can I say anything on my own account?'

'You must try singing it, sir. They say singing loosens the tongue.'

'Or mime your message,' Paul put in. 'You have the limbs for a dumb show.'

'Mr Wodswod, your French serves you well enough as it is,' Annette said. 'Besides I suspect — I have an instinct for such matters — suspect you find it easier to be free with words in our tongue than you can ever be in your own.'

'I'm comfortable enough with silence in any language.' He smiled at her. 'I shall continue my quest for a teacher just the same.'

His smile seemed condescending, perhaps because she gave herself time to realize he was considerably taller than she was.

'*You* teach him, sister. It will occupy your stay here. Silence is well within your abilities.'

'Would you, madame? I'm afraid I can offer little in the way of salary.'

'"Madame" is inappropriate. I am neither married nor ancient.'

He didn't blush at her reproof, simply drew himself away as if it would be the end of their talking together.

A loud cheer from the card tables punctuated her annoyance. Monsieur Gellet-Duvivier must have left the room for a moment or two, for here he was back again having changed his costume. This time he was wearing uniform. He was parading himself in the powder blue three-quarter coat and crossed sashes of the National Guard, with royal white leggings and tunic. The Madman was only a ranker, a grenadier or some such: he clearly lacked enough quarters of nobility in his arms to qualify for a commission. Never to be outshone, he'd obviously had his out-fit run up in his own workroom and fussed over his needlewomen every stitch of the way, and not just when they fashioned the stockings and the tricorne hat. His coat was cut fit for a king, and his trousers even sweeter, though no king could condescend to wear them. There wasn't a better dressed general in the entire royal army. Lafayette himself would have looked a scarecrow by comparison.

He strutted to and fro in this finery, and the landed gentlemen of the cavalry applauded him as if he were a bear being lugged before them on its nose-pole and encouraged to dance by the whip and the drum. Poor little man, he was much too bright for a bear, too lively of eye and deft of head. As he bounced to and fro, he looked even more like a parrot than earlier in the evening.

'There are guardsmen and guardsmen,' he cried.

The applause was prolonged. No one was in any doubt what sort of guardsman he was.

'There are guardsmen who are for His Majesty King Louis—'

'So there are, patron. So there are.'

'And there are guardsmen who'll give their oath to those idiots without trousers, and if there's one thing above all else that makes an idiot an idiot it's being without trousers.'

The applause continued. A nobleman of the cavalry might have little enough time for politics, but the Madman's politics were of a kind impossible to ignore. 'Fishwives are another case,' he roared. 'Fishwives taken singly, and fishwives in a rabble. Fishwives are a species of idiot I insist I'll have none of.' He seized the young Englishman warmly by the hand, and shook it.

'If I ever take hold of any such a person in the way I salute you now, any such person – or any other Friend of the Constitution, with or without trousers – you can cut me down the middle, Monsieur Wodswod, and throw my right half on the dunghill.'

The company clapped its hands and rattled its tables in a surge of approval that clearly included Mr Wodswod. The Englishman himself smiled only wanly, as if he was having difficulty with the language. Not in this case, surely? Annette thought anyone who'd spent half a day in Paris would have heard of the trouser-less ones and the fish women. They were the rabble's darlings. They were themselves the mob.

Then she had another thought. Surely the Englishman could-n't side with revolutionaries and against Europe's kings and his own class? This was hardly the way for an Englishman to behave. She'd heard the English had packed off all such people to the Americas.

She found herself drawing closer to him again, horrified at her suspicions. She must help him free his hand from Monsieur Gellet-Duvivier, who was still pounding it up and down as if it was the handle to a water pump.

'Monsieur Wodswod,' she said firmly, 'I shall teach you my language as you request.'

The Madman was not without manners. He could not persist in a handshake across a resumed conversation of such earnestness.

'I shall teach you, Wodswod,' she repeated, as the Madman at last let go of his hand.

The Englishman straightened his fingers and flexed them. When he spoke it came as a shock to hear him say, 'My name, mademoiselle, is something you must first learn from me.'

This was gross of him. She found herself snapping, 'My own name, sir, is something you haven't yet asked for.'

'No doubt you'll part with it when it suits you.'

Again she was in a fury. She didn't know whether it was the young man's air of condescension, Paul's perpetual grin, or the fire-drained airlessness of a winter' s room with too many peo-ple in it. She was about to withdraw her offer, and as tartly as possible, when she was interrupted by the Madman pulling out his sabre right in front of her. He did this with unnecessary vigour and an over-elaborated flourish that brought first his elbow then its brass finger-guard and top section of blade scarcely an inch from her face as he saluted the world with a perfectly studied invitation in prime.

The aloof Monsieur Wodswod was concerned enough on her behalf to knock the blade in one direction and draw her away in another. His touch didn't loiter, but it did much to soothe her temper. She cherished the memory of his hand on her upper arm for long moments after. It had been hurried but unrough, firm yet not grasping; and although she couldn't remember whether it had been warm or cool, it stayed with her as an otherness she wished could happen again. However transiently placed the Englishman's fingers had been, they spoke in ways better than talking. Or she pretended to herself they did. Or pretended she pretended.

Monsieur Wodswod's animal energies – she believed that was the term becoming fashionable in novels – his animal energies must have been powerful, because they entirely blunted what the madman did next. He retreated from the uncomfortable contortion of prime, and instead thrust his sword point directly towards heaven, as if inviting God and his angels, or some imaginary army upstairs, to join him in his next campaign.

'*Idiots!*' he shouted again. Annette wondered what had drawn him back to it. 'Idiot' was an extremely mild word in French, and as such almost totally unsuitable for use by a Frenchman. Perhaps that was why Monsieur Gellet-Duvivier screamed it with such fervour: he wanted to get the best out of it. And here he was doing it again and again. Unusual too to find it flourished as a noun (one of Monsieur Wodswod's naming words – she must make the point to her young Englishman in a moment or two, when the Madman was silent, if he ever was). It was generally a motherly description of a childlike action, a word for a young wife to use chidingly of an infant's error, such as spilling a cup or blowing too many bubbles into its food; a word for a sister to use of a brother's tricks, perhaps, such as offering her services as a language tutor. But it was a *describing* word, that was it – not one of Wodswod's nouns or names.

Monsieur Gellet-Duvivier certainly extracted the most from

it. 'It was an idiot deed,' he shouted, 'an idiot deed perpetrated by idiots, and by idiot idiots.'

This again would be a wonderful demonstration of the word in all its variability. She must find Mr Wodswod or at least catch his eye.

'Yes idiot idiots!'

'What have they done this time, patron?' her brother Paul asked. 'I thought you had already boxed that Besserve's ears once this evening.'

'They have tossed a stone against my glass. No, not tossed – *hurled*.'

'That was ages ago, man.'

'It's thick glass,' Paul offered. 'And a tiny stone. Perhaps it has taken a while to sink in.'

'Why do you think I am dressed in the King's uniform? Do you suppose I put it on lightly, my young lords and gentry – this sacramental cloth?'

'I wouldn't be seen dead in the thing. Give the King back his uniform, patron, and let's have some more wine.'

'The cards are going cold. Send us someone to mend the fire.'

'I propose to lead you against them all *now*!'

The Madman seemed to have wiped his face before donning the sacrificial – or had he called it the sacramental? – cloth, and this led Annette to see all the more clearly from the dark knots of vein in his temples and the tiny flecks of blood in the whites of his eyeballs that he was almost apoplectic. And if his head didn't explode he was likely to bring the ceiling down on the rest of them with the tip of his sword. Even Paul was alarmed.

'Lads and young lords,' the Madman frothed and pleaded, 'There's a mob down there. There's fish women. Let us go and cut their throats for them. Will no one come down?'

'No, patron. Far better to wait till they bring us some prisoners in, some more customers for young Vallon at the gaol here.' It was again the tall captain of hussars who spoke, the one who had offered Annette a glass of wine at the beginning of the evening. He came and put his arm around Gellet-Duvivier and persuaded him to lower his sword. 'Let us wait until Friday when the prisoners are brought in. That will be worth something, patron. They're our own kind those rogues are locking up, our own kith and our own kin. It might even be us.'

'It might even be me,' Gellet-Duvivier agreed.

'You can lead us when the time is ripe. Take up your sword on Friday, and we'll set our kinsmen free.'

The Madman appeared mollified by this speech. 'Till Friday,' he repeated. He shook himself free of the restraining arms that encircled him and set about sheathing his sword. It didn't return easily to its scabbard, let alone elegantly. 'That's it, my young nobility and gentlemen. Let's wait till Friday when there's fresh prisoners coming in. I'll lead you to free them all on Friday.'

'Till Friday, patron.'

'Yes, till Friday. We shall cut throats on Friday!'

Wine is a powerful argument, especially when it is red and drunk in vast quantities in a hot room. Friday had its advantages too in being three clear days off. Annette amused herself by wondering just how many of these others would assault the prison buildings with Gellet-Duvivier. The Madman's own courage was as evident as his folly. Unfortunately he stood alone.

She had been told to spy out these matters and report them as she saw fit. She had friends in Blois who were eager for even the tiniest uprising, and would be pleased to support it. Her messages so far had been full of disappointment. As for this evening, it had revealed nothing worth the ink and sealing wax of a letter, let alone the effort of writing it.

These officers were the essence of her problem. If the army daren't stand up for its king, then the mob would swallow everything. It must be obvious even to a foreigner like Monsieur Wodswod that these fellows lacked stomach. They had no appetite for France. They were cavalrymen too. The cavalry were well born. In many cases, even the private ranks were gentlemen. They were supposed to be the élite, the backbone of tradition, yet half of them were known to be waiting in Orléans to journey to the frontier and join the émigré army at Coblentz. Or so Paul insisted, and she could believe it. Some of these officers of the King cared so little for what was happening to France that they were willing to become the King's enemies. Becoming

France's enemies troubled them even less, providing they could oppose the Revolution, oppose the Constitution, oppose the self-declared National Assembly, and oppose the Third Estate.

She could sympathize with some of this, but in the end agreed with none of it. She was like her brother Paul, and like the rest of her family. She was a royalist because she saw nothing better to be; she was a member of the Third Estate because that was what she was born to; and she was French because that was what she was. These were matters to share with Monsieur Wodswod indeed. Perhaps she could talk politics with him as a way of teaching him French.

She gazed about her, seeking out the Englishman while trying not to be searching for him.

There was no sign of him anywhere. Monsieur Wodswod had disappeared, and his bags had vanished with him. He must have found the Madman's house too much for him, and gone in search of other lodgings, or fled from Orléans altogether.

Or at least gone to The Three Emperors where a man could drink in solitude and wait at his ease to take the diligence back to Paris.

Paul murmured something in her ear. She could scarcely hear him above the din. His dark wig was awry, and showed a lock of black hair. She touched her finger to his forehead to straighten it.

He mouthed at her again, and this time she caught what he said. 'If you're seeking your pupil, sister, the poor man's gone to his bed.'

A tightening in her chest made her feel quite breathless. She didn't know whether it was relief or disappointment. The symptoms are very similar, and she was too dispirited to wonder.

ORLEANS.
FRIDAY, THE NINTH DAY OF
DECEMBER 1791

He woke early. There was no sleeping late at the Coin Maugas, and very little sleeping at all. The Rue Royale passed beneath his window, and at the end of it was the town's new bridge across the river Loire.

The bridge attracted wheels. He would turn in his bed and feel them wince their way downhill to the accompanying rattle of their spoke brakes. Soon there would be a swelling metallic agony, louder than orchestral music, as the carters and coachmen dismounted to tighten or loosen or otherwise adjust the vice that slowed the axle. A cart coming down an incline could be heard a great way off when the night was not quite morning, perhaps as far distant as the little hamlet of Fleurie-les-Aubrais or the forest beyond, whose thickets he'd already walked in.

He would rise to unbolt his shutter, the dawn would be full of noise, yet nothing would be stirring in the street, no sign of coach or cart, only cats and beggars. His window was above the arcade, well out of reach of the lantern. Overhead were a few discordant stars, clearly in need of oiling. This fancy and an unavoidable lungful of fresh air would jolt him fully awake. He would change his night-shirt for a day shirt and trousers, put on his countryman's shoes, then sit himself down to work at his notebooks and wait for breakfast.

He took this alone in his apartment. He ate lunch in a tiny family room downstairs and in theory with the family, but in practice also alone because the Madman spared himself food at midday. He ate supper next door with his fellow lodgers – if the cavalrymen were taking supper. If not he ate with the family in its upstairs dining room. This was an interesting meal, punctuated by the Madman's excitable politics. His host would have drunk himself to life by now, but the table was in need of a woman. Two of the girls from downstairs would wait upon them, and these were cheery enough when left to their own devices, but his host's bereavement lay over everything. He needed wine to cope with it, and he couldn't cope with the wine.

Breakfast was served by the Demoiselle Gellet-Duvivier. She was young, much too young, but undoubtedly nubile. She was also too hauntingly beautiful for a man to contemplate long with patience. She wasn't allowed to bring food to the officers, only to him, and his hunger was as much to see her as the breakfast.

Breakfast in France was usually a fine dull meal, kinder to the digestion than the palate. He and his friend Jones had discovered this on their walking tour last year, when the dowdiness of breakfast had been a topic to last them all the way to the Swiss border. Bread, biscuit or rusk was its backbone, with nothing much to put flesh on it – a little liver paste, perhaps, a stiff jam much more likely. On a good day there would be warm milk to drink. On a very good day the milk would be fresh from goat or cow.

Food was good at the Maison Gellet-Duvivier, better than other lodgings he had encountered, and his life had been all lodgings since he was a child. Even breakfast had its moments of richness. The first morning there had been a magnificent savoury sausage, yesterday a cheese and some cutlets of river fish. These would be brought by the madman himself, nodding in later to check up on things. He was a father with a daughter. He did his best.

First the daughter. Here she was hurrying upstairs with a jug of hot milk and a loaf. He pushed aside his notebook, and was just in time to assemble her image from cloth footwear, bare elbows and a mob cap; then she was gone again.

'Good morning,' he called after her, testing his throat. The loaf was quite recent. France was short of bread, lacked corn, but not Orléans, or not at the level of society that sold stockings and boarded young noblemen from the cavalry. There was bread on the Rue Royale.

She was back again, carrying cake and jam. There was no butter. Her skin was the colour of butter, or it was by the candleflame she carried for the stairs. His own lamp changed everything to pastel.

'Thank you very much, mademoiselle,' he said. In Paris he had been careful to call everyone citizen, especially the women, but at the Madman's house certainly not. Especially the women.

Her shyness hurt him, her grief even more. He felt a kinship with young people who lacked a mother. He still did not know her name, and she would not give it to him, any more than she would find him a word for the first morning's sausage, or the cheese and fish. He tried to ask her name once more, but first he had to offer his own: William by itself was impolite, and Wordsworth was impossible for a French person to say. It stopped speech. The lisping spit-laden improbability of it provoked laughter. The Demoiselle Gellet-Duvivier did not laugh. She could hear her father on the stairs. She had been alone with Wodswod for all of several seconds. She made ready to be gone.

Monsieur Gellet-Duvivier brought him a fine oval plate. On it was the tail of a fish, possibly yesterday's. It was a long tail. It had been a longer fish. Monsieur chewed a little of it to demonstrate that it continued to be good, that the spices still held. 'Today is Friday, I remind you, Monsieur Wodswod.'

'Friday, monsieur?' This was clearly where the conversation was. It was a pity he could not understand it.

'Yes, Friday.' He cut his lodger several inches of fish. 'You came here to study the times, Monsieur Wodswod. I expect you to be there in consequence.' He turned to follow his daughter.

There was a marked absence of nouns and naming words in this exchange, or of ones suitable for a foreigner to hold on to. Friday, for example: what was the meaning of the word? Did it convey a particular sense of mystery, a fish day symbolized by the end of a fish the family had already begun yesterday? Today was indeed Friday, as his host insisted; but William could have no confidence that Friday was the actual word said or that today had been spoken of. He remembered yesterday evening: there had been a lengthy conversation about a trout. Monsieur Gellet-Duvivier had consumed several large measures of wine from what would normally be considered his water glass, so it was not absolutely surprising when he mentioned in passing that the female trout was, weight for weight, the biggest mammalian producer of milk in all of France, if not in the entire universe. 'How else can she suckle eight or ten young?' he had asked his jug of wine and then Wordsworth and his daughter. 'Have you ever seen a cow suckle eight, or even three? Or a sheep or a goat?'

Wordsworth was eager to pursue the topic, although the subject would have been too raw to discuss in front of an Englishwoman. He was deeply studied in the science of field and stream. He ventured to remind his host – with apologies to his daughter – that a trout was a river fish, that river fish and fish in general do not suckle their young, and in consequence a female trout could scarcely outsuckle a sheep. This taxed his French quite considerably. He was not entirely surprised to find the Demoiselle Gellet-Duvivier – even she of the sad eye – reduced to something approaching hysterical mirth at the end of what he'd hoped had been a very pretty speech. Apparently they weren't talking about trout at all: they were discussing sows. French is like that. It confuses pigs with the denizens of the finny flood. So how could he be confident that his host attached so much importance to what might or might not be Friday? He could just as well be speaking of a coat hook or a pretty woman.

William was reminded very forcibly of his need for a tutor. He still hoped to find a cheap one. Not that Miss Vallon, he thought. Her brother was altogether too noisy; he guided her by the hand and seemed to have hold of her tongue. They were a dark-eyed pair of lookalikes, save she was slim and had an agreeable radiance of skin. Then her brows were black and she had a temper.

The Gellet-Duvivier girl returned, bringing him some more milk and a bowl of dried fruit. She would be ideal, of course. She was English-coloured, like his sister.

★

The street was still dark beyond the shutter. Rain fell steadily outside, and storm clouds were holding back the daylight.

He opened the window and examined the weather. This was flatland rain, river rain. He couldn't read its moods. It might stop in a few minutes. It might continue all week.

He intended to spend the day walking, and walk he would. He was totally unused to being defeated by the elements. Unfortunately, he hoped to call upon some people while he was out, and nobody takes kindly to wet shoes.

There were two letters of introduction tucked away among his books. They had been written for him by Mrs Charlotte Smith, a poet he'd visited in Brighton just before crossing to France. What an agreeable lady! One was to a Mr Foxlowe, a Lancashire clothmaker now living in Orléans. The other . . . well, the other was a much more enchanting prospect. He'd think about her during his walk, and lay some extremely careful plans for his first meeting with her. He slipped both letters into an inner pocket of his jacket.

Dawn began to show above the rooftops opposite. The weather must be thinning upriver, if not here. Here the rain beat down harder.

He'd brought an umbrella to France, but it had proved to be a dangerous thing in Paris, almost as dangerous as a wig, which – thank God! – he never wore. He'd only seen two corpses during his time there, each of them strung up to a lantern and then cut down. Both had been wearing wigs. Doctors, noblemen, lawyers, anyone in a wig was at risk among the crowds. The same crowds had jeered at his umbrella. Being English had saved him.

When he finished at Cambridge earlier in the year, he'd come down with the only umbrella to be seen in Cumberland. Children had laughed at him. He had no idea how an umbrella would strike the good people of Orléans, or the woman he carried his second letter towards. She had revolutionary sympathies and, much more than Mrs Charlotte Smith, a voluptuous imagination. Fatal to miss his chance with her. If he turned up on her doorstep with an umbrella he might not be allowed to take a step further. She too was a poet and he intended to present himself as one. He would have to make do with a top coat and wet hair.

Mindful that the letters might crumple he took them out again and laid them flat between a little volume of Charlotte Smith's sonnets and Helen Maria Williams' – there, he'd admitted to himself he was at last going to meet her! – Helen Maria Williams' own precious collection of 1786.

On second thoughts, he discarded Mrs Smith's *Elegaic Sonnets* from the depth of his pocket and interleaved both letters among the pages of Miss Williams' book. He would produce them with a flourish from inside it, and when he came to place her own letter in her hand, he would bring it forth with a copy of his only published poem, cut from the *European Magazine* and addressed explicitly to her: *On Seeing Miss Helen Maria Williams Weep At A Tale of Distress.*

Then he thought again and removed his own poem. It might prove to be as dangerous as an umbrella.

He buttoned up his topcoat, waited only to watch the Demoiselle Gellet-Duvivier clear away his breakfast, this time with covered elbows, then followed her downstairs. He passed by an interior window that showed him the young women in their workshop. They started early. Not all were huddled over needles. Some drew threads around stocking frames, some glued strangely shaped pieces of felt into geometries that might one day be fit for steaming into a hat. He smiled and waved at them encouragingly. He waved in English. None of them waved back. He stepped towards the rain and turned right.

It was a bold move this turning right. On the previous two mornings he had walked left into the City of Orléans, exploring its cathedral, its medieval courtyards, its associations with the Capets and Joan of Arc. He was interested but not enthusiastic. There was history everywhere, he supposed, but he found it as unexciting as a pack of playing cards. It was dulled for him by the mood in the streets. Orléans was not like Paris. Orléans was calm. But its people knew things were changing. If not, its people were going to change them. The hungry knew this. So did the rich and the sleek of the Third Estate. Only the Gellet-Duviviers disputed the matter, and were prepared to fight to keep life as it was. Somehow they seemed as insubstantial as these ghosts of the past. Frosty midwinter sunlight is unkind to ghosts. On Wednesday and Thursday he had left them behind him and tramped the frozen leaves of the forests north of the town.

This morning it was raining. He was going across the river to the South.

The arcade of the Rue Royale provided him with cover almost to the bridge. This was an elegant frontage, and it led him past imposing doors and beguiling windows; but there was a Revolutionary untidiness about the place. It was littered with all manner of persons and objects that would not ordinarily be allowed here. Or he guessed they wouldn't.

Pairs of legs, male and female, sprawled across the flat paving of the footway, interrupting his step. So did several single limbs accompanied by a stilt or a stump. Vagrants congregated here, and in swelling numbers. God alone knew where they had been driven from or where they were aiming towards. In more ordered times they would have pitched themselves into an obscure corner and tried to avoid the watch and the ever present military. Now they lay, and were permitted to lie, where they could keep themselves free of the elements. He picked his way among the sprawl of their limbs and decided it must be an improvement, this equality.

His path was barred by a great stack of firewood, the horse that had brought it, and the man who had brought the horse. They were wet, down to the last inelegant leg and log, but horse and rider had spread themselves out in the arcade and were steaming off beneath the ornamental roof.

For a moment he felt as if he were back home on a market day in Penrith or Cockermouth. At the nearest point to the bridge he found country children selling live rabbits in a basket, cockerels for roasting and hens for broiling (or perhaps for continued laying?), the rabbits timorous and watchful, the poultry immobilized by a hobble of string between their spur and their claws.

Then, and for the first time, he was on the bridge and getting his hair wet. He hadn't been this way before, and there were few people to share his view of the rain-flattened waters of the Loire.

The King's new bridge spanned two small islands, which shrank then expanded in the mist.

The murky weather made it seem impossibly long, though it couldn't have been more than three hundred and fifty paces. Once he was striding out, head down, to cover it, he realized there were only three other figures between himself and the south bank of the river, two of them wearing hats, and one in a capacious cloak.

These three figures, men by the size of them, stood remarkably still, as if waiting for him. A few steps further on, he gazed towards them through wet eyelashes and saw that his way was being barred by two men only – in hats. The man in a cloak was some kind of sentry box. So much for rain-filled eyes.

At this exact moment the rain stopped.

'Stand your ground, citizen.'

He knew that word 'citizen' from Paris. 'Good day, citizen,' he answered, and kept boldly on.

He had not recognized the command or recognized it as a command. Its meaning was reinforced by the lock of a musket being thumbed back.

He stood where he was, and saw two officials of the People's Guard, or whatever they now called themselves, facing him over a levelled gun barrel. He doubted if it would fire, because the powder would not only be damp but washed clean off the pan, but there was no mistaking the authority of the villainous bayonet at its end, a blade so long that it promised to reach almost as far as a bullet.

This pair didn't wear much in the way of uniforms. Even if they had done, their tunics and their trousers would have been made as formless by the rain as a washerwoman's blankets when she beats them between log and stone.

They were chiefly remarkable for their hats. Neither wore the tricorne of the National Guard, or anything remotely resembling the cheapest assemblage from Monsieur Gellet-Duvivier's. One had a bicorne with the oval seam at the top – a fashion that was becoming popular, perhaps because it was so ugly. The other wore a round hat with an enormous brim. This was pinned up at the front to make it resemble a battered coal shovel.

'Your business, citizen?'

'I am going for a walk.' This did not sound well, especially in his version of French, which was always less perfect than the occasion needed.

'Have you no work to go to?'

'He sounds like a Hollander.'

'But dresses like a king. Save for him wearing his own hair!'

'He looks like a wet king!'

'He's one of those émigrés running away from the People's Court back there.'

'I'm an Englishman.' He hoped this explanation would suffice – it often did.

The man with the overlong gun began to massage its pan with the ball of his thumb. When this was dry and to his liking, he grunted something to his comrade, the man with the shovel hat. This fellow unslung his powder horn from his shoulder for him, the gun needing both his friend's hands, and began to cover the pan with a delicate patina of priming as if sprinkling pepper.

William should have run. He could have run. He could have run past them or away from them, but he was a walker and a talker, not a runner. Besides, he saw no need for them to shoot him. It was the lump that rose and continued to rise in his throat that convinced him they *intended* to shoot him, beyond logic though it was. He loved these men – or, if not *them* exactly, he loved what they stood for. He had come to France in order to study the miracle of them at first hand. Only now, in a sickness of breakfast, did he discover that there was absolutely no justice in their miracle at all. He spat out a mouthful of the morning's fish and watched the gun aim itself very steadily at a point lower than his eyeline but well above his waist.

He looked into the depth of the musket and saw how the world's perception of him could be altered by a single shot. At this moment he was a man, not merely that, but a *citizen*, with rights exactly equal in this country and this country alone to the King's, whatever those were. In a second's time he could be just another body lying in the street. People did not argue about them. They were a fact beyond argument. And even if his own corpse were to rise up at them it would have neither the name of its predicament nor the verb. His French remained short of both.

'I am an Englishman, citizens,' he cried, still through his breakfast, the opulence of which continued to set him apart. 'I am your friend, and a *Friend of the People*. Look! – I come from the Jacobins in Paris.' He felt his pockets, searching for papers, glimpsing as he did so philosophies left untaught at Cambridge – that a bullet flies faster than a word, whether it is discharged with a will or a whim, and invariably sets its stop upon a sentence. 'I am a Friend of the Constitution.' This was a lie, he was by choice a nothing; but there were only two lies to tell, and he hoped he had chosen the right one.

He pulled out his English travel accreditation, a French document of cognisance and entry issued at Dieppe and franked at Rouen, and – yes, at last – a letter from the great man Brissot himself, the denouncer of all the Kings in Europe, who had taken him to the Jacobins in Paris and led the debate. Or did he mean the Assembly? The fish continued to rise, and sometimes to fall.

Better to have offered them a bribe. The one with free hands, the shovel hat and the powder horn pocketed the first two documents as if they *were* a bribe. He showed the letter from Brissot to his friend with the two-cornered hat and the musket, and his friend spat upon it, either from respect or contempt, William could not tell. Brissot's letter, thank God, was handed back to him.

'Where do you lodge, citizen?'

The hairs on his nape had scarcely settled. His breakfast lay between them on the bridge. If calling himself a Friend of the Constitution had been the correct lie, then to answer that he dwelled at the Coin Maugas with Monsieur Gellet-Duvivier and a pack of royalist cavalry officers was likely to prove a most dangerous truth. 'I have friends here,' he blurted. 'Monsieur Foxlowe and Mademoiselle Helen Maria Williams.' He did not show these letters, in case they too disappeared. 'Both of them well known in town. Both of them friends of the People.'

'This is true, citizen.' Shovel Hat spoke without knowledge or certainty, but this probably made his agreement the more binding.

'They are, of course, English,' Floppy Hat said, twitching both corners of his headgear much as a fish ruffles its tail to keep its nose against the stream. 'English, even though known to us.'

'One of them is a woman, too. And today not necessarily the worse for it.'

His friend with the musket grounded his weapon on the wet paving. William did not know whether this was a sign of clemency or fatigue.

'I wish you both well, citizens,' he ventured. 'And, citizens, perhaps I may have my letters of passage returned to me?'

'Of course, citizen. In good time.'

'We shall look for you at tonight's meeting of the Friends, citizen.'

'I am determined to be there.' Indeed, he was everlastingly curious. 'My papers, please, citizen.' He narrowed his appeal to the one who had them in his pocket.

'In good time, as I say. That time is not now.'

The sun struck at them all, finding a space between a cloud to his left and the distant southward curve of the river. From the bridge he could see everything. He had almost glimpsed heaven. The two men squinted as if dazzled by it. He felt giddy enough himself, and stumbled quickly beyond them, walking towards the remains of the medieval Fort-des-Tourelles with its English ghosts misting upwards from the stonework. By the time he reached the hamlet of St Jean le Blanc he was steaming and wraithlike himself. Never had he felt his flesh to be of so little consequence.

After five hundred paces – his brain was made of numbers – he found trees and a pathway among the trees, then the peace of the forest. Men had trimmed branches here. It was laundered by rain. The cavalry officers were hunters and had spoken to him of wolves and bears. Never mind wolves and bears. Muskets were his fear. He had never met a wolf or a bear that carried a musket.

ORLEANS.
LATER THAT SAD DAMP FRIDAY

'Marie Anne!'

She paid no attention to him. When Paul called her by her given name instead of using her pet name Annette she knew he was teasing her.

'Marie Anne, today is Friday. Therefore it follows that this afternoon, long and sad though it may be, will presently give rise to Friday night.'

She was repairing her outdoor bonnet. Orléans was a draughty town, and the mob caps she had brought with her were all cotton and lace, and much too airy, more like mops than mobs.

'Marie Anne!'

She gathered the brim back to its former jaunty curl by stitching in some small cleats of thread, rather as she might close a salmon for the oven. Like most men, her brother found it impossible to interrupt this sort of activity: he could only look on with mounting impatience. She spent a few more moments of silent concentration on the progress of her needle, then laid her work aside and said, 'Is Friday evening such a wonderful occasion in Orléans, then?'

'Normally no, my sister. But if your memory is half as long as your cotton, you will remember that this Friday belongs most particularly to Monsieur Gellet-Duvivier. The Madman bids the whole world to attend him at the prison, if you remember.'

'I've had enough of Monsieur the Madman already.'

'But not, perhaps, of the bowlegged cavalry officer who brought you wine and syrup? And certainly not of your pupil the horseshoe'd Englishman, Milor Wodswod? As far as I can tell, little sister, you've not even had the beginnings of that one.'

She picked up her stitching again. It was better than biting her lip. Paul meant to tease her, not hurt her; but any mention of Wodswod hurt more than she chose to think about. Mr Wodswod was a thankless idiot. He should at least have been in touch. It was true she had not left him the address of her brother's lodging, but Monsieur Gellet-Duvivier knew where she was staying. So did his daughter. She had taken care to mention the fact several times. Besides, Paul had returned to the Coin Maugas on each of the intervening afternoons, so great was his appetite for losing at cards. She could only suppose that this Wodswod had not bothered to ask him her whereabouts. He had not even gone to the comparative impoliteness of excusing himself from his lessons with her. Ridiculous of her to be intrigued by such a lout. Then the human heart was like that. It did not beat in time with common sense. It was like the clock on the wall. It could stop at a change of weather. It could start at a blow from a moth.

She finished her work, and sighed as if from satisfaction at a job well done. If her pupil would not come looking for her, then she must go looking for him. 'Very well then, brother, I shall go. I shall accept Monsieur Gellet-Duvivier's invitation. What do you suggest I wear from among my Orléans wardrobe?'

'Something warm, my sweet. We're not parading at the Rue Royale. He commands us to the prison direct.'

Even now fate was against her. So she was to lose even this chance of greeting her Englishman with a suitable rebuke. She nearly didn't go. Yet what else was there to do? She thought of old Vergez, her stepfather. He was a stupid man, by all accounts not so clever a surgeon as her father. Vergez used to say, 'I'm often asked by mothers about their greensick daughters at such times. I tell them the young women have two choices. They can starve or they can eat pie. It is absolutely fatal for them to do nothing.'

Fools are full of received wisdom. She refused to do nothing. She put on her brisk bonnet. She would step out into Orléans and eat the air.

Mr Wodswod was an item Paul intended to stretch a little further. As she left her brother's room she saw him snatch up his overcoat and prepare to follow her. Determined to be alone she hurried downstairs. She could hear him move one of the household children from his path as she opened the street door. 'Walk, sister?' he called after her. 'You? This English disease must be infectious. Your Englishman does nothing but walk, do you know that?' Then he was beside her.

She refused to be drawn. She walked.

Her brother's legs were of a length with hers, but a man's clothing is infinitely more suited to walking. His mockery kept pace with her easily. 'Whoever heard of a gentleman who walks?'

'He can hardly ride a horse in the Arcade. Any more than you can now.' She was growing breathless.

'Stonework does not interest him, Marie Anne. He prefers the woods.'

She turned towards him and gasped, 'Is this another of your jokes, *little* brother?'

'I thought you'd be interested. After all, you came here to spy.'

'I came here to look – is that what you mean?'

'You were *sent* here with a letter.'

'I was asked—'

'A letter from Montlivault. Carrying those letters could cause a person to be locked up.' He tried to encourage her to walk on a little, but his words enraged her.

'"Locked up"? Is that the worst punishment you can devise for me? Locked up! What do you think my life is at home, or our sisters' lives? Aren't we locked up enough already?' She went away from him on her own account now, and very hard she was to follow. 'Vergez is an old swine,' she spat back at him, 'and our lady mother—'

'Maman is the chatelaine and Vergez plays the doorkeeper,' he agreed. 'But prison is another matter altogether, Annette, believe me.'

She saw people watching them, or thought they were being

watched. They were quarrelling like husband and wife, herself the scold and her brother the wheedling husband. She amused herself at the idea and almost fell to laughing again, laughing at Paul anyhow. Then she thought of Wodswod. There were armed bands roaming the woods to the south of the river. They were *supposed* to be there, *rumoured* to be there. There were even hopes that she could pass a message to them. These groups were fearful of discovery, and a stranger would be at risk among them. A foreigner certainly would be. Pray God her leafy Englishman stayed north of the river.

What was her brother saying? He wanted her to return to his lodgings. His friend's wife, his landlady, kept open house in the afternoons, and he hoped for biscuits and hot chocolate before going to play cards. But he confessed none of these less worthy ambitions, or not in so many words. She knew them and acknowledged them by letting him tug her elbow and urge her to return. What he said was, again wheedling like any husband, 'I joke. I only joke, little sister. I know you are here on graver business than love, my Annette. That is why I say the Englishman is a distraction. It is not his war.'

Then why does he pry about the woods, she wondered? Nobody can find amusement in a wilderness, nobody of adult intelligence and sound mind who has enjoyed civilized society in a town.

Aloud she said, 'Is that why you pointed me towards him? It was you who suggested I play the schoolteacher.'

'Only so you could keep your eye on him. You spies should be aware of one another.'

South of the river, the forest made its own warmth. William was surprised to find it not quite dead yet. Even in the depth of winter, leaves hung meaty on the lower boughs and were fleshy underfoot. He seemed to be walking on toadstools or the palms of hands. Often he couldn't see, it was so dark down here. When he came to a clearing the brightness was all high up, and spoke of unusual birds, some of them too brisk to be seen.

He refused to be numbed by the dripping melancholy of the landscape. Woodland is full of dreams. The poetic fancy haunts trees and rivers. So here he was walking in a great forest by a great river, a forest full of wet. How Spenser would have loved this place. Somewhere in *The Faerie Queene,* the old poet had probably invented it. Here there would be no ordinary wolves and bears, and quite certainly no muskets, just a swarm of satyrs, and virgins tied in distressful nakedness to every tree, each of them with the woebegone face of the Demoiselle Gellet-Duvivier.

He strode into a larger clearing. The mature timber had been cut, and the logs shifted. Copse poles sprouted from the stumps and had been pollarded in turn.

Some of the stumps were dead, or so shocked by what had happened to them that they refused to make any growth this year. He sat on one – it was quite dry – and took out Helen Maria Williams' book and Mrs Smith's letter to her. The poems were good; three years ago he thought they were perfection. They teemed with tearful women and wild imaginings, a bit Spenserian in their way, even if not quite able to stand the comparison. The letter recommended him to her as a young enthusiast well able to appreciate such exalted flights. She was reputed to be beautiful and full of revolutionary ardour.

He imagined showing her his own work, but not as a supplicant – that wasn't his way. He would probably fall in love with her. He felt like falling in love with someone. She wasn't too many years older than he was, and thought very similarly. It would be ennobling to have a creative friendship with a mature woman, and abroad too – almost ideal! His instinct stopped short of passion but strayed boldly towards the poetic and the voluptuous. Most certainly the voluptuous. He could attend her soirées and linger in her boudoir. This would allow the Demoiselle Gellet-Duvivier time to grow up a little. His French-speaking Englishwoman, his dream poetess, could teach him enough French to uncover a young woman's name and dally with her in matters more seductive than the milk yield of trout.

The tree bole he sat on struck cold. The sky had lifted and the coppice seemed decidedly chilly after the sweaty tangles of the forest. The grass was frosted round his feet, diamonded with frozen raindrops from this morning's storm, and itself becoming solid. The stump was dry – so recently after being rained on – simply because it was already glazed with ice. The warmth of his feelings for the poetess had melted it. Ice water was a suitable corrective to fantasy. A man cannot maintain his animal intelligence with a damp seat.

He stood up and set off for home, or for Miss Helen Maria Williams at the least. He'd missed his lunch. He'd lost most of a day. On the way back he noticed that more trees had been felled, huge stands of timber tumbled then straitened with the adze. He met no one in the clearings. You never catch foresters at work, very rarely see them. You hear them sometimes, generally in the fog. They are like the pixies, only about when your back is turned. He went quickly now, trying to recover the afternoon. He was walking no longer. He was moving at a lope that went more briskly than a run.

Was he hurrying towards his imagined visit, or away from noises in the wood? He heard his own footsteps pattering after him. He heard owls hoot – surely too many owls? He heard the same birds give a hunting shriek. By daytime? So many of them, too! The barn owls in France must flock thicker than crows!

It was only one owl. It echoed from tree to tree, and round him and behind him like his own footsteps. There was only one pair of feet hurrying after him, and that was his own.

Yes, it was altogether brisker than a trot, his hill shepherd's lope. It was the prance of those huntsmen who followed their hounds on foot across the high fells. He'd known it since boyhood, when he'd scrambled above Grassmere with his friends.

William was extremely sure-footed when he ran. He was running at full stride now. His imagination had convinced him he was being followed. He *fancied* he was being followed, though his brain told him otherwise. Stones, roots, fissures, he avoided them all, just as if he were flying.

He heard another sound, sharper than an owl's, sharper and shorter. He thought of feral dogs. It was the baying of dogs.

He thought of wild dogs, and was brought crashing down, tripped and caught firm by the left foot.

He tugged. He must have snagged his ankle in a bine root, or an unseen tumble of creeper.

He had been brought down by a cord – no, a snare. The cord had a noose in it.

A darkness fell over him. There was no sun for shadow, but he was engulfed by several men, trodden down, then lifted so a blade could be held between his chin and his Adam's apple. A gun muzzle stroked his ear.

'It's one of those villains from over there, I tell you. Cut its throat.'

'Cullions first, and then the throat.'

'Take its balls off first, if you want to cook it.'

William had heard this amazing piece of French folklore. He'd caught it at the Gellet-Duviviers', but not he thought from the Demoiselle. Thinking of her and his ridiculous folly with the trout made him translate his captors' first greeting aright. Villain, indeed! Villain was villein was serf. How dare they!

'No, sir. I am not a stag.' Confounded language. Fancy calling a male deer by a similar sounding word to the English for peasant slave! He shook himself free of their insolence. 'I am not a stag. I'm an Englishman.'

They weren't relaxed enough to laugh, but his accent brought about a change in their silence.

'I'm an Englishman, and as such a stranger. And as a stranger—'

'It is most improper of you to walk in our woods.'

'If it's *your* wood, sir, I am sorry.'

He had to apologize. There were too many of them to bluster at. They were armed, and they were better dressed than the ruffians on the bridge. Or dressed better for the rain. They wore leather or animal skins, and their calves were bound. They were properly shod.

'You have a king in England, I believe? And a church?'

Yes, he did. He was unfond of kings and it was the wrong church, but he had one of each.

'So you know enough French to answer me, sir?'

The familiar catechism. Or the old question couched in a new way, with 'sir' instead of 'citizen' providing the only clue to how he should answer it.

'Sir, I have a church, and I'm in danger of becoming a priest in it.' He had to confess his dilemma to someone, even if they shot him for it. The thought of becoming a priest filled him with such terrible loathing, it was one of the few pieces of information about himself he was prepared to offer to strangers. 'Yes,' he said. 'We have a king, and the king has a church.'

Their leader embraced him. They all embraced him. 'He's a loyalist,' the leader said between kisses. 'A loyalist and a royalist, and he believes in Almighty God. He doesn't give a fig for constitutions. If he didn't smell so foreign he could be one of us!'

William thanked him for the compliment. He thanked them all – ten, twenty, perhaps thirty men surrounding him in increasing numbers. Several stood at the back from the rest, holding horses with their harness muffled in rag. The horses were silent in other ways also. Had their vocal cords been cut? They might not have been horses at all, but men in mumming hoods, the light beneath the trees made objects so uncertain. Everything in France was so uncertain, except for the passion, which was various. Everyone save Monsieur Gellet-Duvivier's cavalry officers were united in having passion, a passion that divided them all.

Meanwhile, they melted away. They left him midway through a thought and took to the trees again. Or to the vapours behind the trees. They did not propose a rendezvous. They were not constitutionalists. They did not spend their evenings in a club.

He wondered if he'd dreamed them. They had left his throat uncut. He had not dreamed that. Nor the cord that gashed his ankle. Nor the pain that dripped from it, till the cold bound it up in a scab.

By the time he left the forest it was halfway to dusk. He wondered why he'd loitered so long before running home to be ambushed. Perhaps he was more fearful of those two cronies on the bridge than he'd cared to acknowledge to himself. There was only one bridge and an endless river. He had to cross one by the other.

A young man does not like to dwell upon those moments in his life when death stands closer. This morning it had stood very close, much closer than just now. This morning it was only a musket shot away.

He brushed these thoughts aside and hurried among the

buildings of St Jean le Blanc, then past the fortifications at Les Tourelles and began the long crossing of the bridge.

His eyes were blurred from the forest, and more still from rushing, but they couldn't hide the fact that his inquisitors were waiting for him.

It was the same pair, drier this time, but red-eyed with wine. They were blinking at him like miners or toilers in the shadows. As he approached them he had a fancy that they were the ones who had felled trees behind him and crept about him in the shade. But they weren't woodsmen. They were ruffians from the town. Their closest sniff at tree bark would be pulling an oaken cork with their teeth.

They seemed to have been cork-pulling all afternoon. As they lurched — no, swaggered — to stop him he noticed they kept a puncheon at the entrance of their box. Revolutions are commonly short of food, but there is always wine, especially here on the Loire which is a river of grapes. They caught him with their thumbs against the muscles of his arms. This hurt.

He shrugged himself free of their hands and hugged them both against him. 'Citizens!' he cried, as joyously as he could.

They regarded him suspiciously with the slow cunning of drink. They did this from under their eyelids as it were, until he released them, when they gave him a glaring examination direct.

'Until tonight, citizens,' he said.

'It's the Dutchman from Paris.'

He glanced towards the grounded musket. Its vent was innocent of powder. If he had the least suspicion otherwise, the slightest fear of a bullet in the back, he'd have tossed the gun into the river, and their ludicrous hats to follow. They'd be nothing without their hats. He walked purposefully away from them. He was a young man with a letter in his pocket, a letter to a lady who lived at the end of the bridge. It did not seem so difficult to cross it this time.

'Tonight, citizen,' one called after him.

The other said something repulsive, as only a townsman can. William knew it was vile from the tone of his voice.

EVENING.
THE SAME DAMP NINTH OF
DECEMBER

She was out. Helen Maria Williams was not at home. He understood the old woman only slowly; she appeared from behind him
as soon as he knocked at the poetess's door, and she needed to be
listened to. There is always an old woman in France, and she
always knows where people are. Unlike old women in England,
she knows because she is paid to know. Knowing where people
are is her job. Unfortunately she knows it, and a great deal else,
in French. Helen Maria Williams was not merely out, she said,
she was gone away. She would return, yes, certainly, perhaps. She
had travelled all the way to Paris with no immediate plans to
return. Who knows what can happen when people go to Paris?
Yesterday Paris was another world. Today it is another time.
Everyone who goes to Paris has her throat cut sooner or later.

Goodbye voluptuous dreams. Farewell dreams in general. He
had hurried from the dangers of the forest and across the guarded
bridge to reach here, and here was a house with shuttered rooms.
Its one uncovered window showed him an alcove with an empty
shelf. He did not know whether this emptiness, without book or
vase, was Miss Williams' own or whether it belonged to the old
woman. It would be rude to ask.

He walked slowly towards the Coin Maugas, wondering what
to do with a day that was already dead for him. He could stay out
a while, find somewhere to drink warm milk and eat, then
attend if he dare the threatened meeting with the Friends of the

Constitution. He took this to be a Jacobin Society. He had been to the Jacobins in Paris, but there he had sponsors. Here he only had his friends from the bridge.

The alternative was to return at once to the bosom of the family Gellet-Duvivier, to his rooms at least, where most things, including warmth, were free.

He was in one of the streets at the back of the Quai du Châtelet and trying to avoid spending money on himself when he noticed the Demoiselle – what was her name? Vallon – who had offered to teach him French. She was on the opposite side of the street, walking just ahead of him, so he could meet her or not, as he chose. *If* he chose. She was not Helen Maria Williams. He was surprised to see her walking alone, and with darkness falling.

She slowed her walk a little, or perhaps he hurried his. Perhaps she knew he was there.

If she did, she seemed unduly surprised to see him. 'Where are you going?' she called across the street. She was quite unabashed at holding a conversation with him in front of then behind a young woman who pushed a handcart on the cobbles between them and moved at exactly the same pace as they did. The cart was laden with squirrel skins and stoat pelts that were not quite ermine. 'Why are you out?' She spoke to him as if he were a child or an imbecile. He supposed he must seem like both. He was a foreigner. And very foreign he felt. He was unused to holding a conversation at a distance like this, yet to cross over would commit himself to more than politeness. Besides, there were horses behind and almost up with them, the clamour of wagon wheels at his back. So he hesitated.

'I've a letter,' he called, so as not to seem rude. It was a simple sentence in French. They stood waiting for the hoofs to pass, then the iron hoops that seemed to be taking an eternity to roll near. They were facing one another across a road that penned them in with noise, a road that led nowhere, not even to the water. It was a muddled town. Not for the first time he wished he'd stayed in Paris. The clatter was intense, but he couldn't look away from her to see what was coming. She was mouthing something at him, as if she could communicate without voice.

He was surprised she felt unembarrassed at this, and even more surprised to see a pretty woman able to pull faces without losing her attractiveness.

The horses came past them at last. They were heavyweights, all of them salty with sweat even on a cold day. First there were eight of them, in two files, leaden-footed to start with and heavier still for the sluggishness of their riders. These were big men, and sat without energy or spring, each of them burdened with a cuirass of steel. They wore the bedraggled uniforms of the Ancien Régime, their drenched cloth in stark contrast to the dazzling display of colour that William saw daily at the Rue Royale.

As if to emphasize the ghostly nature of the occasion, the last two files led a riderless horse, a grey stallion, and it was proving difficult to lead because of the interest it took in the mare to its right. The splendour of its saddle could not be obscured by the fact that its leather was frosty wet. Nonetheless, it was empty.

Behind them came four dray horses. These were badly tended beasts with ill-trimmed coats, the sort of brutes that draw timber or conduct felons to execution. They laboured to pull then to stay ahead of a black carriage, as large as any diligence but lacking windows. It looked like a box on wheels.

After this rode six files more. These were even more woebegone than the leading horseman. They seemed to have been riding all day if not all year in the spatter of that dreadful carriage, whose wheels threw the road over them, the road and everything on it, in a finely considered spray.

They passed by, and their noise receded. William hastened to cross over to Miss Vallon. His haste was not quick enough. She had already crossed over to him.

'I am walking with my brother,' she said surprisingly, 'but Paul has gone on ahead.' She did not wait for him to react to this strange statement, but said simply, ' You were brought outside by a letter, you said?' She spoke as if the delivering of letters was a very pressing matter, as if even the bearing of them weighed upon her greatly.

'In a sense, yes. I had to deliver a letter of introduction.' He showed it to her. She seemed to expect the truth from him, and anticipated his truth would be weighty. 'It was one of several written for me by an acquaintance in England.'

She took it from him and examined it. 'Maria Williams,' she read aloud. 'Helen' was beyond her. 'That's a woman.'

'An English lady.'

'Ah!' She thought about this. 'And who is writing to her? Is this a letter from an English lord or your English King?'

'Hardly.'

'Is it from a member of your country's government?'

'Sorry to disappoint you. It's from a lady.'

'Another lady! So women write to women, and you play the messenger, Monsieur?'

'What kind of letters do you carry, Mademoiselle Annette?'

She grew very still at this. Then she spoke too quickly. 'I? Why, no kind of letters.'

Her vehemence perplexed him. First the overbearing curiosity then the obvious deceit. Why? Perhaps he was reading too much into everything she said.

This could be because she was French. English women weren't at all like that, unless he'd completely misunderstood them.

He smiled at her. He hadn't smiled at her before, though she smiled often and laughed even when she said the most unamusing things.

She smiled now, and he decided one smile was enough. She was so lively, so *womanly,* she inspired fleshy thoughts, even in the street. So, to be truthful, did the Demoiselle. So, too, did Miss Williams whom he hadn't even met.

The thoughts that Annette inspired were particularly fleshy, fleshly even. She gazed at him curiously, he hoped not to read his mind. 'This Maria Williams,' she said, 'this English lady. I suppose she's very pretty.'

'I don't know. She isn't there.'

'Where is she, then?'

'She's in Paris. She's a poet. She thinks Paris is the place to be.'

'France has too many poets.' She spoke severely, as if the matter was beyond argument. 'And England too, I daresay.'

'Not while I'm in France,' he said.

She studied him a moment, as if surprised by his arrogance. 'How old are you?'

'Too old to answer questions like that.' He felt embarrassed at his own ill-manners. Then, as so often when speaking in a strange tongue, he ran out of things to say as well as words to say them in.

'I am twenty-five,' she said simply. 'I was born on the twenty-second of June, seventeen hundred and sixty-six. I am the youngest of six. You have met my brother Paul. I have two other brothers, and two sisters.'

She spoke so directly, and with so little affectation, that he felt shamed even further. Yet he couldn't let her know he was only twenty-one, with his studies hardly completed. It struck him that her frank statement about her family might be more arch than it seemed. It might be his first French lesson, designed to invite an easy response. This helped him to say, 'When I've studied with you, I may perhaps learn some high enough numbers in French to tell you how old I am.' There, he had agreed to study with her. He had delayed his decision for three days, but she could take it or leave it. He allowed a silence to develop. If she took his silence for shyness, so be it.

She didn't notice it. 'I'm an orphan,' she said. 'Well, almost an orphan. My father is dead and my mother has lost patience with us all.'

'I'm an orphan too,' he said simply. His other complexities of family were beyond his French. He couldn't explain to anyone how his father stood closest to him in time yet still seemed distant, nor that when he tried to remember his mother, he found himself stranded among thoughts that lay too deep for tears.

Meanwhile, there were so many questions he wanted to ask her, but couldn't. Why had this young woman left home to stay with her brother? Was the exile merely due to her mother's impatience with her, or had she been guilty of something the rest of her family found intolerable? Was her banishment permanent?

These thoughts were best dealt with by walking. Indeed the two of them did walk, perhaps for some time, though the walk was not comfortable between them. He tried to take her arm, being

English. Being French, she did not seem to expect this. Or being Annette Vallon, she rejected the claims of convention. He did not know how to walk with a woman without taking her arm.

He was unwilling to mention his discomfort, still less to dispute it with her. She was an orphan. Or at least, she was a child who had lost her father. He felt nothing but pity for orphans, self pity at least. Walking uncomfortably, and perhaps even waving his hands to help his French, he knew there was a warmth between them. This was in every way good for his verbs and nouns, but he sensed it could not last. Experiences at Cambridge and in Cumberland had taught him that when a warmth develops between a young man and a young woman, society will be prompt to direct a draught on to it.

So it was now. No sooner did he begin to feel at ease with her than he saw Paul Vallon hurrying back to reclaim her. 'There you are!' her brother called from half a street away. 'And about time too!' He gave a cheery wave towards William as soon as he recognized him. Or perhaps he waved without recognizing him at all.

Annette hurried them to meet him.

The bewigged little notary was much too small to amount to much in the street – he would be better off in a drawing room standing on a chair – but there he was, chuckling to himself then shouting loud enough for a dozen men before they had halfway reached one another. 'I've just seen a pretty sight!' His voice was much too big for the cut of his coat. 'A very pretty sight!' He bounded from the shadowy street they found facing them across the Rue Royale, and placed himself beneath the brightest lantern in the arcade, and waited for them to come up with him as if all of Orléans was his theatre. 'First we have arrive here the only cavalrymen in France who make the least pretence of being loyal to the Constitution rather than King Louis.'

'We saw them,' William said.

Paul seemed to think this was a fact that deserved congratulation. He encircled first William and then his sister in his arms, and jigged them round until everyone felt slightly drunk. 'Then you will have noticed the more noble horse,' he laughed, 'the one with the empty saddle.'

'I noticed an empty saddle.'

'It was raining, don't you see? And here's the joke of it all.' He winked an eye at his sister as if daring her not to laugh with him. 'The horse belongs to one Captain Guy, Count of Lefebvre-Desnoëttes, a name admirably suited to its saddle, don't you think?'

William thought he understood what was being said, and allowed himself to smile at it. Annette meantime squeezed his wrist, or the cuff of his sleeve, ever so slightly, but otherwise said nothing.

'It is not the name for bad weather. This De Lefebvre-Desnoëttes, Captain of Cuirassiers, found his breastplate getting rusty and his knees becoming stiff with wet, so took an increasing dislike to this rain. Moreover he was jealous of his no less noble friends the Hussars, each of them snug in your very own lodging, Wodswod, and enjoying what you'd left of the serving wenches and the wine' – this with another of Paul's winks, directed largely at Annette, – 'so he decided he'd be much better off riding inside the box with his prisoners.' He laughed again at this. He laughed enough for all three of them before adding, 'After all, they were much like himself – sprigs of the blood and suchlike scions of the landed gentry – with I daresay some of their womenfolk thrown into the box to add to its amenities!'

This talk was on the loose side for William, but Annette's touch on his sleeve was reassuring.

'He's so deep in gossip of the kind he can't get among his troopers – costing the family estates, spearing wild pigs, the price of wig-powder – that he doesn't notice they've pulled into the yard at Notre Dame des Miracles. To you and me that's a church, Wodswod, *and* for my sister who prays' – the young woman's grip on his sleeve was intense now: her brother was shooting his eyes about, confident that he'd reached the best bit. 'For those pigs of the Constitution it's a prison, like any other place with a stout door and a good lock. Well, the wheels were blocked up, the box was opened, and out were kicked Baron This and my Lady That, followed by their chamber pots. And then of course Milor Guy de Lefebvre-Desnoëttes stepped forth, thinking to regain his saddle.' Paul Vallon enjoyed the memory of it all. 'We do things very smartly in Orléans, Wodswod, very briskly indeed. The turnkey was waiting for him with the smith, and the smith had leg irons on him as fast a peasant's wife can truss a chicken.

'Naturally the Captain Count de Lefebvre-Desnoëttes protested, but the turnkey was used to that. The gentry do protest. There was his uniform to explain away, but there are dozens of officers in prison, Wodswod, particularly officers of cavalry.

'He called for his cuirassiers in what should have been a very loud and authoritarian voice, but his word-of-command was weakened by chitchat, and wouldn't really happen for him.

'His soldiery came to look for him at last, but their uniforms didn't match, don't you see? – him in his finery, them in their mud and manure – when did you ever see an officer use the same tailor as his men? They had quite a debate as to whether they should vouch for him, leave him to rot in gaol, or hang him on the nearest lantern.'

It was a revealing story, and William liked stories, but he could no longer concentrate on this one. He was aware only of the woman beside him pressing his sleeve, and of wondering what she meant by it.

Paul noticed this too, so his last words were directed at her: 'I tell you, this Revolution is nearly a mutiny, sister. It would become extremely serious for us all if it weren't so very funny.'

Annette ignored him, and turned to William to say, 'I have kept quiet for so long simply because I have been wondering whether to include you, Williams.'

William was amazed at how authoritative she could become in the space of a sentence.

'As my brother has implied, it is not necessarily the case that the wrong people are being locked up.' She gave Wordsworth time to digest this idea, but he was no lover of the aristocracy anyway. 'It is certainly the fact, however, that the wrong people are locking them up. Tonight, there will be an attempt made to set some of them free.'

This was wild talk but she was a pretty woman who had been

clutching at his sleeve, and he had every intention of staying close to her for as much of the evening as she would allow.

'It would be a great thing to see one or two of them released,' she went on. 'It would teach those ruffians from the Club a proper lesson.'

'You mean the Friends of the Constitution?'

'Yes.'

William thought of the musket ball he had been threatened with this morning and found himself agreeing with her. He had been looking to agree with her for several minutes now.

'Monsieur Gellet–Duvivier proposed the idea,' she said. 'My brother thinks it will be amusing to watch him make a fool of himself. I think it will prove to be a matter of rather more significance than that.'

'Do you think the attempt will be successful?'

'No, but I daresay I'll find it instructive.'

The idea that she might be studying such matters intrigued William enormously. Then he noticed her hand was on his sleeve again. He was delighted to have it there, even if it did distract him from everything she was saying.

'Which way to the prison?' he asked, before he found himself dreaming too far.

Paul Vallon gazed at him sadly. 'This city is all a prison. A prison is a place where men are locked up. There are a lot of people locked up in Orléans.'

'Why here especially?'

'We have been declared a regional centre for dealing with Enemies of the Constitution.' He urged them both onward, holding each of them by the hand. 'A Court has been convened here, Monsieur Wodswod. It does not yet function. When it functions, it will sentence these runaways to all manner of deaths it presently lacks the means to carry out. The locals have an aversion to the rope, yet the city is short of a headsman. That is where I shall come in.'

'As axeman – as *bourreau*?' William hesitated to speak the word. It could also mean writing desk and donkey, he believed. He was desperate not to plunge back into the mire of the breasted trout, especially within the hearing of Mademoiselle Vallon.

'No, Wodswod.' Paul was perfectly serious for once. 'As an advocate.' If he pulled a face at William's words, it was because he was outraged by the suggestion itself, not the young Englishman's language. 'I object to Courts that have already made their minds up. They always *have*, of course, or else their minds *never would* be made up. But I object to them on principle. It's a good principle.'

'A noble principle.'

Marie Anne Vallon, Mademoiselle Annette, was impatient of principles. She was in a hurry to see the fact itself demonstrated.

A large number of townspeople were thronging towards the church that Paul had just returned from. William wondered if they approved of having their holy buildings taken over like this or were simply indifferent. As he hastened beside Annette, then increasingly behind and never ahead of her, he was struck as in Paris by the French people's need to be present at these great moments of history. He followed in some trepidation. He'd learnt enough there to understand that history isn't always sympathetic towards its bystanders.

Notre Dame des Miracles turned out to be a cliff of a building standing where a bend in the road made junction with two more. There was a small courtyard to its right, and beyond this a walled garden full of trees. Or that was William's impression. What he saw was neither by star nor lantern, for there were few of either, but by the flame of some hundred torches. These were being waved about and rather blurred his view of things by making steam of the weather. His guess was that there were some thousand persons present or passing by. There were as many women as men, and more children than either. Everyone was very jolly, as if they were at a fair or a market. Quite a number of the men carried woodaxes or long-handled hammers in case they came across anything that needed cutting or beating. Some of their women, the coarser kind, carried covered baskets, presumably to gather what was cut.

These made a cheerful crowd, and a restless one, quite happy to allow William and the Vallons to press among them and force their way to the front. One or two of the basket-women muttered, some of them at William's suit and topcoat, most of them at Annette's bonnet. But they were let through in spite of this. William detected no cause for alarm, though to be fair he couldn't understand a word that was shouted at him. His instinct was to be at the back of a crowd, if he had to be where crowds were at all, but Annette wanted to be at the front, and while he was with her he felt careless of danger.

At the front of the church, and beside it in the churchyard, there were two bodies of armed men. There were the foot soldiers of the National Guard, which William now understood to be a militia for gentlemen. These were spread out by the building's main door. Then there were the cavalrymen he had seen earlier, the Cuirassiers. These were already mounted and formed up in the churchyard. Their horses were becoming restive and they were trying to leave.

The National Guard and the Cuirassiers were what the town had come to see. Some of them were urging the National Guard to attack the Cuirassiers. Some of them were shouting for the Cuirassiers to ride out against the National Guard. William felt unable to unravel the political niceties of all this, so he chose to treat it as some of the crowd did, as a joke. These were the ones with clubs and hammers and baskets. It took him some time to realize that these people had not come here to see a fight, but to have one. They intended to break into the church and chop the prisoners into pieces. Until a moment or two earlier, he had supposed they were merely thieving wood.

The crowd also contained quite a number of decently dressed people, men and women looking much like himself and the Vallons. These people were not carrying tools or baskets, and it was difficult to know whether they would protest at any violence or merely bear silent witness to it.

'Either the cavalry must do something,' Paul said, 'or the Guard must do it for them. If not there'll be bloody murder.' He sounded unusually nervous all of a sudden. Then he caught sight of a big brown-faced fellow pressing forward with a stonemason's maul, and added, 'It's the lack of an executioner, d'you see? When a town lacks a neck-cutter, the amateurs take over.'

This brown-faced lout made as if to beat in the door of Notre Dame des Miracles. His mallet was short in the handle for this, so doubtless his hope was to strike a blow that would encourage others to join him. To do so he had to push between the standing ranks of the National Guard. The first rank parted to allow him through. Two gentlemen in the rear rank took exception to his manners and refused to separate. He attempted to lever his way between them, so one of them banged him in the teeth with a musket butt.

This was one of the kinder reproofs that can be offered by a musket with its bayonet fixed, as William could well testify, but it happened without warning, and some of the crowd did not like it. These were the ones with axes and hammers. They struck a few reproving bystanders on the head, the ones without axes and hammers, and having cleared a way for themselves began to press forward.

They were stopped by the clatter of galloping hoofs. The charge threatened them from their left, so it wasn't the Cuirassiers, but it came on furiously, and – for a second – it stopped them. If they had continued on their way they would have stopped the charge, because no horse likes to trample into a crowd. But they didn't carry on, since only a fool places himself in the way of being trodden on by a horse.

It was only one horse too, but a horse putting his four feet down so quickly that there might have been forty of him. William had a brief glimpse of his rider. He was clad in the uniform of a common footman of the guard, not an officer, and as such he shouldn't have been on horseback. But the uniform was splendid, and its wearer's face was as red as the best Burgundian wine, so splendid and so red that it seemed inconceivable that it should be asked to walk or march anywhere, especially at a time of crisis. Monsieur Gellet-Duvivier was here at last, and as promised. Soon there would be others behind him, his quartet of boarders the Hussars accompanied by their friends the Lancers and the officers of several other regiments of horse. Monsieur Gellet-Duvivier had foreseen the entire occasion, he had quite possibly invented it, and he was here. 'A siege,' he cried as he swept by. 'A siege and a rescue.' Then he reined in his horse to a sparking halt, in spite of the damp stones, exactly in the midst of the cuirassiers in their courtyard. These had been looking frightened, the way the military can be when deprived of a purpose, but seeing their enemy before them and in such a number they got ready to cut him down.

'A siege,' he continued to cry. 'A siege, my young gentlemen – a siege and a rescue!'

The National Guard was not generally popular among townspeople who carried hammers, as William was learning. Nor was Monsieur Gellet-Duvivier himself a favourite with those of the townsmen who could not afford stockings, which was most of them. However, his cry was 'a siege' and a siege was what they were after. A siege followed by a storm, or preferably a storming without the siege, leading up to a massacre or some other kind of popular sport with the imprisoned runaways as soon as possible afterwards. Still, 'a siege!' he cried, and a man who could articulate that while falling from his horse clearly had his heart in the right place. 'A siege!' echoed all the axemen and basket-women, and – as so often when a crowd finds a natural leader – they let him get on with it.

This pressing forward of the crowd made the Cuirassiers reluctant to proceed with their duty, which was to dismantle the intruder as soon as possible. They were further impeded by him drawing his sword. It was a big one, a sabre sharp enough to shave a cat, and the curve of its blade would have astounded an astronomer. In the twinkling of an eye – he drew it clean – he had it glistening under the stars, or what lantern and torch-light there was, and Annette kept herself under Williams' arm because she knew it was a dangerous edge to stand close to.

'A siege!' his shout was. 'A siege and set him free!'

This too found general favour with the crowd. It was a cry that meant all things to all men, and the group of women who most hungered for blood had a very exact idea of what could be extracted from it.

Monsieur Gellet-Duvivier – now Grenadier Gellet-Duvivier of the National Guard – was flourishing his sabre as only he could, sometimes bringing it down from the heavens above the lamplight in a straightforward no-nonsense skull-splitting overhead cut, more generally rotating the blade full circle in front of his own bloodshot eyes and wine-bolstered body like one of those great windmills that confused the road north of Paris. He combined this series of passes very rapidly, moving so swiftly from one to the other that his edge rendered a great deal of the courtyard and a sizeable expanse of the night sky totally uninhabitable.

Even with his sword arm moderately still, the Madman was dangerous to approach, as William and Annette had seen three evenings ago.

The Cuirassiers were bold men. The wearing of a cuirass, with its stout back and breast plate, meant they could only take damage to the limbs and the head; and a blow in those places rarely worries a soldier. They began to spar about him on horseback, looking to cut him down or slice him up, while a couple of the boldest darted from their saddles to come at him on foot, as if they were something lowly like dragoons or some such mounted infantrymen.

'Set him free!' the Madman roared. Once more his message was inexplicable, though much more modest than it had been three evenings ago. 'Lay siege and set him free.'

'Kill him!' The rough elements of the crowd cried, followed by a blood-curdling 'ça ira!' (which William took to mean 'That's how it goes!') 'Ça ira! Kill him and kill the lot of them!'

'Set him free!'

'Kill the lot of them!'

'Let the experts do it,' the moderates advised them. 'Leave it to the soldiers.'

'Set him free!'

'Set who free?' The young Captain of Cuirassiers had already experienced one fright that evening. He had nearly been locked up with his prisoners, and – if Annette was to believe her brother – had come even closer to being hanged by his own guard. 'Set who free?' he demanded of the Madman. He intended to regain his authority over his men by advancing boldly in the direction of prudence.

Gellet-Duvivier was quick to recognize an aristocratic tone of voice. He backed himself into a safe-looking corner between a wall of the church and its buttress, and said from behind his sabre, 'The Count of Lefebvre-Desnoëttes. I can learn no name but his. It has been on everyone's lips for an hour or more!' Glancing towards the serried ranks of gaolers, and seeing them unmoved by his ridiculous request the Madman added, 'I have a whole gallant body of nobility from the Hussars not ten steps behind me and due here on the instant. There never was such a falsely accused man within and without the Constitution. We demand his release immediately.'

'Hussars you say?'

'Yes, Hussars.' Gellet-Duvivier gazed longingly about him for the promised reinforcements. 'We demand an instant reinstatement of the aforesaid nobleman.'

'I am Guy de Lefebvre-Desnoëttes. I never was locked up. And if I had been, I'll tell you plainly, you silly fool of a bourgeois, I'd let myself stay incarcerated rather than allow myself to be set at liberty by a pack of Hussars.'

'Well, praise God for that, sir, and His Mother the Holy Virgin!' Grenadier Gellet-Duvivier sank to one knee. 'Thank God you are already made safe by the entreaties of honourable men!'

A dismounted cuirassier stepped rapidly towards him. So did some of the town gaolers who held the side door of the church.

Nowadays prayer was bought at the price of eternal vigilance. The Madman was a suppliant who could pray with one eye cocked and his blade at the ready. He leapt upright, passed his sabre once about him like a reaper beginning a fresh field of corn, and moved close to the Captain's stirrup.

The stallion was unhappy to have him there, and the rider cried in a loud voice, 'Arrest this man! Take hold of the fool and shut him up where he belongs. Arrest him, I say!'

It was as hard a crowd to arrest anyone in front of as release him into, especially when that someone was already kissing Lefebvre-Desnoëttes' hand and drawing him down in his saddle the better to kiss his cheek. So Grenadier Gellet-Duvivier continued much as before. 'Praise be!' he cried. 'The news of my intention came galloping ahead of me, and look, you are already safe!'

Somehow the Madman retained his horse and remounted, but not before he had treated Guy de Lefebvre-Desnoëttes to a space-clearing salute with his still unsheathed sabre. He would have been safe enough among his colleagues of the Guard, no doubt, but his horse would have been riderless and untended, and there were those among the crowd who would have eaten it. He found it best to gallop away.

Paul had become too breathless with anxiety to laugh at all this. Just the same, Annette was beginning to nurse a suspicion that in general her brother's amusement was justified. Terrible events were taking place in their world, but always without dignity and often at the level of farce. She wondered if it was the young Englishman's presence that made her think like this. Show your town to a stranger, and you see it with his eyes. Fortunately Orléans wasn't her town.

Even so, it could easily be the death of her. And of Paul and Williams. The Madman had been a distraction, and crowds love a distraction. Now the distraction had gone away, and things were turning ugly. The scuffling became general. Nor was it helped by Lefebvre-Desnoëttes ordering his cuirassiers to depart. French crowds weren't fond of soldiers, nor of people on horseback, nor of shouted commands. So it was now.

In order to depart, the cavalry had to ride through them. Or over them. A horse took fright and reared up, then bellied down hard on those who were nearest, all of them thrust forward and underneath by the pressure from behind.

No one was badly hurt. Children were knocked over and bruised. A woman's face was dented by an upflying hoof. Mortal injuries would have been the ideal, serious injuries preferable. They command a respectful silence from their victims. Trivial injuries make people scream. The injured scream from pain, the bystanders from outrage. So it was this time. People screamed. Their screaming upset more horses, so more of them bucked and plunged.

Annette found herself being walked into by a lame-footed gelding as big as an elephant, while Williams tugged her one way and Paul tried to pull her another, each of them unseen on either side of the horse, neither knowing the other had her by the arm. By trying to snatch her from danger they were holding her directly in its path.

Williams it was who saved her. Just as the brute was about to rear up, he sensed her predicament and pushed rather than pulled. He passed her round the breast and shoulder of the horse and followed swiftly after.

The crowd continued to surge forward.

Captain Lefebvre-Desnoëttes gazed down from his saddle and noticed Annette's bonnet for perhaps the dozenth time in the evening. She saw him looking at it and wondered what it was about it that took his attention. She assumed he saw it as some kind of landmark. When he ordered his troopers to draw their saddle pistols, she guessed he'd deduced from it that his troop was making no progress.

Perhaps it was the elegance of her bonnet that caused him to realize that there were people of substance in front of him. In any event, he commanded his men to discharge their firearms into the air rather than directly into the people of substance. This was a stupid manoeuvre, as everyone except those at the front thought they had been fired on anyway. More screaming followed, largely from a flock of gulls that had been ground-roosting in the walled garden beyond the churchyard. They whirled about, hating the darkness, and confining their panic to the tiny band of air between the torchlight and the town lanterns. This sent them flying into tall men's faces. Nothing sets people's gums on edge so much as having gulls shrieking in their ear and colliding with their heads.

Williams said something to Annette. He had been trying to say something for some time, but her brother was laughing and chatting away too, and Williams' French wasn't as easy to listen to as her brother's, though the man himself was far more attractive. What Williams was reminding her of was that he had been to Paris. Only a few months earlier a crowd had been shot down in Paris in similar circumstances. Williams told her he had visited the Field of Mars to inspect the scene of the massacre. So much blood had been spilt and soaked into and under the pavings there that the stench of death persisted, and the city authorities ordered the site to be sprinkled with vinegar at dawn every day following to disguise the smell.

Paul reminded her other ear that the stench – or wind of it – had certainly reached Orléans.

Her brother was right. People in the crowd were mindful of the pickled blood. They decided to pull the Cuirassiers from their horses and set to work on them with their hammers and woodaxes. They had been foiled in their attempts to rid the world of aristos, so why not kill some soldiers instead?

Annette saw one of these unfortunates slam his knees on his horse, only to find it had gone romping ahead of him, having had its girth cut. So he forfeited his steed and fell between two young women with not much on their chests, as the revolutionary fashion then was, and very sinewy forearms. Working women were encouraged to grow sinews, and there is nothing like freezing rain on a bare chest to increase a young woman's bad temper. One of these beauties dragged his cuirass from his body, and the other tugged his body from his cuirass. They pulled him apart so successfully that they both lost their balances to sprawl in the very same puddle that was reminding him he was alive. Their tumble saved him. A comrade drew him half naked on to the back of his horse, over which he draped himself, Williams said, as bemused as a worm that has been quarrelled over by a pair of starlings. The language, if not the observation, was advanced for Williams, so it must have been Paul who whispered it in her other ear.

A busy three-cornered skirmish now developed. Annette and her two men were still trapped at the front of it. The Cuirassiers were fighting to escape the crowd. The crowd itself was divided between those who thought the Cuirassiers should be punished and those who thought they should be encouraged to ride free. Those with hammers and axes and meat-baskets thought they should be punished. So did those at the back of the crowd who thought that the crowd itself had been shot at, as in a sense it had.

Annette heard Williams say something else, something so hard to follow she wished her brother would say it for him. The people at the back of the crowd not only thought the crowd was being shot at, they *knew* that they themselves *were* being shot at. It is a truth overlooked by all but the most mathematical of minds (and Williams explained he had studied at a town called Cambridge where Newton was held to be at the very centre of culture), it is a truth that a pistol ball fired high into the air above the front of a crowd is likely to fall to the ground several seconds later at its back. It will come to earth as inevitably as the frequently cited apple, and much more dangerously.

It struck her that poor Williams must be drunk. He told her she was wrong in this supposition. She was wrong enough to be very nearly right.

Williams did not take wine nowdays, he said – he had once sipped too much of it at Cambridge – but the whole evening seemed to be composing itself for him exactly as it did on that previous occasion of riot. He described it to himself in a series of elegant phrases which the cat-side of his brain told him to be inappropriate to a landscape of waving axes and thrashing hammers. The air was full of more than flying birds. Paving stones and cobbles flew greyly among the white breasted gulls. There was a rain of Loire sediment all about them. They saw faces split, limbs broken, children hurried out of the way. The crowd was making a space for itself at its centre. It was becoming its own arena of unsavoury battle. Williams didn't care. William couldn't care. He *was* drunk, drunk without drinking. He was drunk from hunger, drunk from the exhilaration of fear, made drunk most of all by this beautiful half of a girl who led him along by the arm while the other half of her dragged her brother.

Meanwhile the Cuirassiers were unable to move forwards or backwards. Those who stand still in front of an angry crowd are not likely to remain standing for long, as all sorts of skirmishes in and out of saddles began to testify.

They were saved by Count Lefebvre-Desnoëttes' stallion. It was a proud beast and almost as stupid as its rider, but it had enough intelligence to take fright. It reared up, mercifully without dislodging the Captain and Count, then brought its hoofs crashing down on everything else. No horse likes treading on people, but Lefebvre-Desnoëttes' stallion was perfectly happy to kick the rabble in front of it as often as it could manage. Its aim was to clear a pathway for itself by smashing a few skulls.

The skulls were further away than it thought. It was surrounded by men with hammers instead of heads, and by women who walked behind enormous baskets. It brought its right forehoof down not on a hammer or a head but inside a basket. Its leg smashed through the wickerwork as far as the knee.

This made the beast kick out behind it in shock, catching a mare to its rear and starting her kicking too. Then it began to curvet and plunge.

A horse with its leg in a basket is a very witty sight. The crowd loved it. The crowd laughed at it. Even Williams chuckled a little, though he explained his family was suspicious of horses. Annette didn't quite hear what he said, because the crowd continued to be mirthful at the stallion's expense. They intended to kill its rider and perhaps cook his horse, but if both were prepared to dance for them they were happy to let them continue a little longer.

'Suspicious of horses, why?' Annette was suspicious herself. 'Why don't you love horses?' Surely Williams wasn't going to reveal himself as some sort of ungentleman after so long an acquaintance?

'My father was misled by a horse.' This did not sound well in French, though this was undoubtedly what she heard. Fortunately one of the more enterprising of the fishwomen offered another basket the next time the stallion reared up.

The Captain nearly undid this by spanking her with his sword, but whereas he missed she didn't. The stallion now had a basket jammed on each foreleg. This threw it into an invincible irritation. So did their uncouth laughter, the shouts, the renewed guffaws, the shrillness of the female humans, their quips about gutting and scaling it, topping and tailing it, then the one-eyed jester who reactivated the crowd by calling out during an unwonted spasm of silence, 'It's a long fish that needs two baskets!' – a sally that meant there would be no more quiet for a fortnight.

The stallion went mad. Its rider was mad enough to stay in the mad horse's saddle. The beast danced. It danced with all the rage of the bull before it is stuck. It danced stepping high as a fighting cockerel, Paul said. He revealed to his sister as men do at such moments that this was where most of his money had gone, betting on birds that lacked the staying power of the Captain's horse. These confessions were beyond William's French or anyone's ear. The three of them were caught up in the crowd, and the crowd was scattering, being scattered, by a prancing and dancing horse.

When a crowd scatters, it generally does so happily enough. Some people actually managed to raise a cheer when Captain Guy de Lefebvre-Desnoëttes danced through them at the head of his troop, and then pranced his way out of town, or out of danger at least.

Those who stood nearest to Annette were not at all too pleased to see the Cuirassiers escape them. The mood all about them was sullen, and Williams remarked that the National Guard had slipped away from the front of the building as well. This was a pity, because although it would probably not have moved forward to defend them, a person standing nearby, a person of the kindred class, might well have claimed protection from it by hurrying to its rear.

Once more Paul looked for a way to depart, but the hammers were at their back, and the resentment and the baskets.

Their clothes did not help them, they knew that. They looked as if they had escaped from the higher life. This was specially true of Williams, whose suit was not only well cut but stitched in a foreign place. He looked so much like an émigré that he might well have stepped from the temporary prison of Notre Dame des Miracles.

Somebody thought so. 'Who've we got here?' a voice asked. 'I think we ought to look at this prettiness we've got stuck here in front of us.'

Williams very prudently refastened his topcoat.

If he thought it was one of those voices from the crowd that would stay in the crowd, he was mistaken. A man with an urgent forward lean to him, much like Williams' own, was immediately in front of them, a tall man, a wide man with a jaw that jutted discouragingly. This jaw, and the whole thrust of his face, was made terrible by its absence of mouth, or of lip. His teeth seemed to have been drawn or fallen out in youth, so that nothing held him apart. A single incisor remained in the lower jaw. 'We should have that thing off for a start,' the tooth said. Nothing else moved when he spoke. The uplifted hand was huge and callused. It obviously hewed carcasses or cut trees for a living. 'We should knock it right off her head, then get some mud on the rest of her.'

Williams did an incredible thing. He'd appeared timid when he thought he was the one being spoken to, but once he realized the man was threatening Annette, he punched him smartly on the nose. The blow smashed right through the fellow's expectations and sent him flat on his back in a puddle.

This unusually direct behaviour caused Annette to be overcome with dread. Goodness knows what Williams thought, but it was common sense that brutes of that sort don't lie around in puddles for long.

The man leapt up and shook himself free of wet. While he was doing so, Williams, who was clearly a prudent person, stepped out and punched him to the face again.

This blow was less successful. The man did not have a large amount of face to hit, and although Williams punched him even harder, as hard as you would hit a tree with an axe, his fist landed somewhere on the headbone, sending the fellow reeling but causing terrible pain to his hand.

All three of them were surrounded. The man got ready to kill Williams and was given room. The crowd muttered to itself, and made ready to kill the other two, or at least hold them under a puddle for an improving interval.

There was a bright flash, lightning perhaps, as the brute rushed forward. Williams met him squarely with his good hand and he went backwards once more, but only a step. Then he took hold of Williams around the small of the back, and the crowd sighed with so much appreciation Annette knew it was going to be terrible for him.

Another bright flash, this time followed a clock tick later by orange flame and a round bang immediately after that. The sky shook.

Someone had discharged an enormous piece of ordnance. 'Stand back!' a voice cried. It was an ordinary voice, a town voice, a loud voice.

The lout let go of poor Williams and stood back. He was wise to do so. Such a voice only speaks with authority when it is certain it has it. The authority in this case resided in a field piece or some more substantial cannon that sounded worse than a keg of quarry powder exploding inside the head.

Paul helped Williams stay upright. Annette would have clung to her young Englishman in admiration if closeness between the sexes were seemly. She held his elbow even so. Her ears were still ringing. She felt rather than heard the marching of many feet, and smelled the Town Guard before she saw their uniforms.

This was never a pleasant odour, either in Summer or during the wet, so she was grateful for the reek of exploded saltpetre, sulphur and carbon that accompanied them. Clearly the Town Guard were wheeling their great cannon along with them in order to impress the crowd.

The Guard marched into view. She saw no cannon, no kind of field piece on wheels or sled. She saw swords curved and straight, all of them sheathed, and not a few of those shorter blades that foot soldiers wore and which were not much longer than bread knives or daggers. She believed they were called *sabres briquets*. She also saw a fair procession of pikes, some of them sloped against the shoulder, quite a few of them dangled or towed at the short or long trail, as if their owners were already weary. She noticed several muskets. There might have been more, but those she counted were of a standard size, sensible enough in length to keep their muzzles dry beneath a tall man's armpit. Presumably the men who walked uncomfortably, as if with a splint or a crutch, must be carrying them like this and damaging the city's butt plates accordingly. So much for the Town Guard, or Citizen's Guard. They had such a thing back home in Blois. It was full of revolutionaries who had awarded themselves guns, and a great nuisance it was.

Not that this one was to be regarded as a nuisance, though, coming when it did, vesting its authority in a cannon and discharging it with an entirely suitable effect. She still had not seen this piece. Presumably its carriage was too wide for the street.

What she saw, because it stood itself in front of Williams, was a musket. It was being carried by the man with the weather-stained bicorne hat. It was a long musket, almost as long as her stepfather's fowling-piece, and it was made longer by having its bayonet attached. The bayonet too was long, as long as a sword, which she believed bayonets were in the beginning.

This musket smoked from the touch hole, and its barrel

steamed from being heated by firing. Could this be the miraculous cannon? If so, it must have been stuffed end to end with
black powder to achieve such a thunderclap.

This Town Guard was commanded by the Apothecary
Besserve. Paul identified him for them. Besserve was another
self-important shopkeeper, not unlike the Madman to look at,
even if he did sell philtres rather than felt hats. He commanded
his men from the safety of his own two feet, however, and
ranged them in double rank about the front of Saint Marie des
Miracles, almost exactly where the National Guard had been
deployed earlier that evening.

All except the man with the musket, and a friend who wore
a great cartwheel of a hat, with its rim bent up above his forehead. This pair continued to stand in front of her – no: in front
of Williams. They fixed him with a searching stare.

'That's a strange English trick you played there, citizen,' the
man with the musket said.

'A strange English trick, knocking an impoverished man into
a puddle.'

Williams did not seem to understand any of this.

'As for that other fellow on the horse—'

Did they mean Gellet-Duvivier or Lefebvre-Desnoëttes?
They were long names both; they needed the support of a horse.

'You were slow to restrain him, citizen.'

'I'm a stranger to your town and ignorant of its customs. I lack
your authority.'

'We have been observing you closely, citizen. You are not
afraid to be at the forefront. Nor is your woman.'

Williams seemed worried by this. He tried to bring matters to
a close by saying briskly, 'Till tonight then, citizens.'

'Tonight is cancelled,' the one with the musket said. 'I am left
with but one word more. Where do you live, citizen?'

Only a fool would acknowledge the Rue Royale at such a
moment, let alone a headgear and stockings emporium belonging to Monsieur Gellet-Duvivier.

'He lodges with me,' Annette said quickly.

'In the Rue Poirier,' Paul put in. 'At the house of Augustin
Dufour. She in her turn lodges with me.'

'At the notary's house? This one with you, and you yourself with the other one! Well, these are Revolutionary times, citizens.' Shovel Hat it was who spoke. He flung his arms about Williams then kissed him in total approval while winking at Annette and Paul over the Englishman's shoulder. 'Revolutionary times indeed.' Having tasted the Englishman's flavour, so to speak, he pushed him away and said, 'We must all disperse to our beds, eh, citizens? This meeting is breaking up.'

Clearly Williams could walk safe for at least a fortnight, now he wore this man's kiss, and had been awarded it in front of so many people.

They hurried home, or at least into the Rue Royale which was directly on their way and nearer.

If Williams thought she would object to his allies he was mistaken. She didn't. When people are miraculously snatched ashore from among the waves of a great storm, they don't much mind whether they have been rescued by a shrimp net or a dolphin.

She hugged Paul joyously in her arms, and allowed herself to kiss Williams briefly on the lips. He tasted of fish, and perhaps of something worse, but gratitude does not notice such trifles, nor does love. If she detected any odour at all she supposed it was because he'd been squeezed by that pair of louche men – not to mention the other brute. His smell was something to do with those men, she knew, and here she was correct.

Now they had regained the brighter street, Paul felt he could say, 'My God, Monsieur Wodswod, you pick yourself some pretty friends.'

'Praise be!' Annette said.

'When you swim in the oceans, you must learn to be sociable with sea monsters!'

Hearing her Williams speak like that, she knew for certain he was a poet. Doubtless his thoughts would sound even better in his own tongue, and that was probably where they belonged, but he was a man who could always find the word for a fine phrase, even in French. It was only the triter matters that eluded him.

The Coin Maugas was just a pace or two beyond her own turning. Paul proposed they go there and drink a glass of wine at the Madman's house. When Williams repeated that he himself scarcely ever drank, the idea seemed even better.

The upstairs salons were empty. Or rather they were full of the Madman, who was hurrying from room to room and leaving them to ache with the vacancy of his enormous sadness.

It seemed the cavalrymen had gone, some to run away beyond the borders as they'd always threatened, others to quarter themselves within their own regimental lines in preparation for a concerted move towards a battle which might never happen, perhaps against their former friends. Such moves take an eternity, weeks perhaps months on the roads between France and the Austro-Hungarian Empire. Meanwhile the night was full of cavalry bugles and drum taps, sounding from which ever way the wind was blowing.

Monsieur Gellet-Duvivier was crying disconsolately, for the treachery of friends who had let him ride to the prison church alone, and even more for their betrayal of class and country.

When Williams said that most of them were probably with their regiments, he replied that he knew exactly where they were, and they were all traitors. He wasn't crying for them, he said. He was crying for himself and for his dead wife. Only last Sunday he had lit a candle for her soul in Notre Dame des Miracles, and now the church was full of runaways and the louts who were their guards. Candles weren't cheap either. They cost twenty times as much as they did when those ruffians had used one to set fire to the Bastille just two years ago.

He caught Paul by the arm and began to lead him away. He wanted to make a new will. He must remember to leave less to his dead wife and more to his living daughter. There was no one else. Where should his business go?

Paul agreed that these were grave matters and followed him out and up another flight of stairs into his own quarters. Of the Demoiselle there was no sign.

This left Annette alone with Williams. Williams had wiped his chin with clean linen and rinsed his mouth quickly with wine, which of course he spat out. If there had been music they would have danced. If food had been placed near they might have eaten it. As it was they kissed.

'I love you,' he offered.

'You say that easily, Williams.' Then, in case she hurt his feelings she added, 'You say it very quickly, anyway. I like you too.'

She hadn't hurt him. He was concentrating on his hands.

She moved them away.

'I nearly died today. They were going to kill me.'

'We all came close to death this evening, my Williams.'

'On the bridge. They were going to kill me with that musket, the one that made a great noise just now, and I suppose saved us.'

Only a fool crosses a river guarded by busybodies with muskets. She didn't allow herself to think that. He mustn't be a fool, this man who lied that he loved her. What was he – a poet? Poems were full of lies, but a man cannot be a fool to make them. Or not entirely. She hugged him against her. She squeezed him immoderately, still being careful with his hands. He wasn't a fool – she wouldn't allow it. He was hers, not totally perhaps, but hers.

She let her mind wander too long. His impatience was making her restless.

'Not here, Williams. We must find a proper place.'

'Not—?' He drew back from her, uncertain of what he was being offered and when he was being invited to it. In the interval, she let fall and smoothed down her garment.

'If you are to improve your speaking, yes. We must find a proper place.' She kissed him once more on the mouth. She kissed him tenderly but firmly, and this time she kissed him once only. 'You will come to my brother's lodgings in the Rue Poirier,' she said. 'Yes, come to my brother's lodgings tomorrow morning at Maître Dufour's – you say you know where it is?'

He nodded so intently that she considered another kiss. She could hear her brother calling goodbye to Monsieur Gellet-Duvivier. Why should she trifle any more tonight? The balance between herself and her world was perfect now. This Englishman, her Williams, had disturbed her equilibrium for nearly three days, just by placing his hand on her arm and guiding her away from a sword. Now, thanks to his impetuosity, her heart was quite whole again.

Nor was he done with giving her the advantage over him. He gave a cry of excitement and rushed away to his room.

He was back in an instant and holding something out to her. 'A love gift,' he said. 'The most valuable object in my possession. Now it is yours.'

Yes, her heart was quite whole again.

The present was irregular in shape and folded in a white linen handkerchief. She received it as gracefully as she could.

The thing was heavy, lumpy to handle, and the moment she squeezed it in her fingers it soiled her glove, in spite of the linen. The linen was quickly dirty as well.

'It's a brick,' she cried in exasperation. 'You've given me a piece of brick!'

'Stone. A fragment from the Bastille. Notice the soot.'

She threw it down. 'Orléans and Blois have finer stones than this, Williams. And bricks and tiles. Blois especially.' Seeing how bemused he looked, then how quickly he masked his surprise in a gaze of inquiring condescension, she lost her temper completely. 'That is not the kind of token a man should offer a woman. Especially when he says he loves her.'

'Are women so different then?' He dismissed her snort of rage as if it were the outcry of a spoilt child. 'It's the only gift of any significance that France can offer you. The country's shaking at the roots.'

'It's my country, Monsieur Wodswod. I'll tell you when it shakes.' She said the briefest of goodnights and followed her brother down the main stairs.

'Do you find the Englishman attractive, sister?'

She did not answer. She had no intention of being overheard.

'You cannot marry the Englishman, Marie Anne. I'll give you three reasons. Firstly there's his Englishness. Secondly and thirdly there's his right and left boot.'

Outside, beneath the lanterns, they began to giggle together, growing sillier and sillier. She did as her brother told her. She thought of Monsieur Williams' boots, and laughed out loud.

'If you ever think you love the Englishman, remember his boots!'

ORLEANS.
SATURDAY THE TENTH OF
DECEMBER 1791

The bell woke her. It beat unexpectedly from the Cathedral of the Holy Cross and continued to sound.

Annette lay listening to it in some bewilderment, then rose from her bed. She threw open the shutters and gazed across the half a dozen roofs that separated her from the bell tower. The sky was still dark, though she felt sure it was past daybreak.

She heard voices downstairs, then silence. Nobody stirred. The bell beat on, but it brought no indication of the time. Goodness knows who was pulling its string, or with what in mind. It might be a call to arms for the Town Guard, or an early morning council of war for the local Jacobins, who were mainly the same gang. The bells were available to them all. This was a city where even the sacred places were turned into barracks or debating chambers. Half of the townspeople thought there was no God anyway.

She was amazed at their stupidity. If there was no God, who was sending this rain? Who, in His wrath, kept the morning dark?

She bolted her shutters and lit a proper candle from the night tallow, being careful not to drown its tiny flame.

Now her room was properly aglow, she knelt at her prie-Dieu to be blessed by the baby Jesus and His mother. She crossed herself before the wooden crucifix that belonged to the room. It looked as if it had been fastened to the wall for centuries, since the calendar began. The Christ was carved separately from a pale local wood. His cross was dark brown. The shadowy play of candlelight made Him seem quite naked. He smiled at her.

She smiled too, and rose from her knees. She honoured her God in order to keep Him a happy one. He was going to send Williams to her this morning. He must teach her to hurry. Even if Williams were still half a night away, she would need time to prepare herself and tidy the room.

She went to her washstand, poured water, and bathed what the world could see of her. Her mirror told her that this wasn't much. The water stung – she was lucky it wasn't frozen. Even so, she didn't want to disturb the household by asking one of Madame Dufour's serving girls for warm – supposing one was up.

She dressed herself in clean linen. Yesterday's gown was damp about the hem, but it would dry while she straightened the room. She hurried.

The judas in the shutter was still dark, but this did not reassure her. Williams said he would be here for his lessons as soon as might be. He was an Englishman. She sensed he would rise early. Then again, he could rise late. There was no knowing with people of another kind. Her mother's only advice about guests was to ensure that they were on time. Vergez, her stepfather, was a stickler for time. 'Babies may be late,' he always said. 'People never.'

She heard someone singing. Not singing exactly, but learning a song for the weekend. Monsieur Dufour, Paul's landlord, was tuning a reluctant throat. So he must be up. He didn't have a very good singing voice, but it was confident and cheerful. Cheerful tunes were not very much in fashion nowadays. This was because they were so agreeable to listen to, and royalists and loyalists preferred to stay sullen.

She found herself singing too. The other voice stopped in surprise. She heard Paul laughing from his bed. Paul wasn't sullen. Nor was he up yet.

Downstairs, she found the household awake, just. Fires had been lit, and because nobody fussed with them they did not smoke.

The kitchen stove would take time to boil a pot, but one of the girls said she was almost certain the Master preferred to shave in lukewarm water. She carried it up towards his room where the singing had started again. André Augustin Dufour's voice remained cheerful. It stayed cheerful even when it came, as it obviously did, from a mouth distorted by the nearness of cold lather. The girl returned without showing the least sign of being scolded or worrying that she might be. She took some silver forks from a drawer and began to polish them. Her friend was spreading jam on a plateful of soda bread, while a young woman sitting in the corner of the kitchen unknotted the fetch of her blouse and began to nurse a child of some eighteen or twenty months. Peasant women nurse for as long as they have milk. Annette did not know whether the infant was the woman's own or whether it belonged to Madame Dufour. All she knew was that her own sister-in-law Angélique had trouble with her feeding and could never find a wet nurse. She thought a doctor's wife could always find a nurse, but seemingly not. The infant being fed in front of her was too big to cradle. It sat straddling the woman's knee, and drank noisily. The woman seemed content to have it there, whatever their relationship.

Madame Dufour came into the kitchen. Marie-Victorie-Adelaïde Dufour was unlaced, but the tiny baby she nursed against her had pulled away from her nipple and nuzzled the top of her day gown so that it covered her breast. Marie-Adelaïde gazed inquiringly at the young woman who was already nursing. The child that straddled her had gorged itself and was asleep. She spread her shawl on the kitchen floor, laid the infant upon it, took the baby from Marie-Adelaïde to cradle it against the same breast. 'Plenty,' she said. 'I should have had kittens – no, piglets even.'

Everyone laughed. People did laugh in the Rue Poirier, Master, Mistress and servants sharing the same joke. Upstairs, Dufour stopped singing, as if in a hurry to join in the merriment, and Paul came yawning in, pretending to stretch. Everyone laughed again, this time at Paul. Annette could see that the serving girls adored her brother almost as much as he adored himself. Meanwhile, the pot boiled, filling the room with steam and the smell of mutton; an iron kettle began to spout, and a pan of milk, unnoticed till now on the back shelf, rose alarmingly.

Such a profusion of unsupervised events would never have been allowed in her mother's kitchen. Françoise Yvon Vallon, now Madame Vergez, would have been very loud if she caught sight of even the beginnings of an uprise of milk. Marie-Adelaïde simply smiled and picked up the sleeping child from her nurse's shawl, then swept it towards some other room. In the doorway she collided with her freshly shaven husband, who kissed her good morning and soothed the infant beneath the chin. Annette still did not know whether it was theirs, or whether the Dufours would naturally expect to repay a servant girl's care with courtesies of their own. This wasn't a doctor's house, of course, but a lawyer's. It ran on different cogs than her home in Blois, though she had a feeling the Dufours would bring oil of their own to any occasion. For so many people to be so cheerful at a midwinter breakfast was unknown to her. Every morning here was like Christmas.

Yes, a lawyer's house. Dufour kissed her cheek. This was a salute that Vergez tended to spare himself. He next greeted the serving girls with a bantering reference to Saturday morning that they understood, but she wasn't privy to – poor, poor Williams: now she really sympathized with him: if Orléans was so different from Blois in its talking, how far from London must it seem? – then he went to Paul to shake hands.

Paul was already standing with fingers extended, and had been standing so for some time, as if this greeting between men was the paramount civility in the house. Or was it that a night without courtesy was too long an interval for lawyers to contemplate?

They shook hands with their gloves on, then with gloves off, and the girls tittered. Goodness knows why men should bring their gloves to a kitchen, especially at breakfast time. Presumably this was one of their ongoing jokes with which Dufour oiled the cogs of law, and with which Paul kept himself amused. Paul was flush-faced. He seemed almost drunk as he began to recount last night's events. She wondered if he'd been sipping at the laudanum again, either for the headache or the diarrhoea. Vergez was against it, and she believed that her father had been equally positive that it did no good. She never took it herself. She did not allow herself to have either complaint so could not confess to them by taking laudanum.

Who do you ask when you want to entertain a young Englishman for French lessons? These were Paul's lodgings, but he appeared to have said nothing about Williams to anyone in the house. And now he was gone to his office round the corner in the Rue de Bourgogne.

André Augustin loitered for as long as it took him to under-cut half a dozen new quills and pour himself some ink in a closed inkhorn. Then he too was gone, taking neither. Annette didn't know whether he went to work at the Court – a great number of his papers were kept at home – or whether he simply chose to be out of the house. The place was substantial, but it was full of lodgers and other dependants. She decided to approach Madame with her problem.

Marie-Adelaïde was amused. 'You must use the parlour,' she said. 'Paul has already told me about your Englishman. As for your teaching him here, he asked Dufour last night. Of course, André Augustin agreed. He believes that all men should improve their French. He holds it to be the only pure language. Everything grows from it, he says, including Latin and Greek.' She laughed. 'He tells me Paul is very dismissive of your Englishman's suit.'

'Williams – Monsieur Wodswod – dresses himself in a very elegant suit.'

'Exactly,' Marie-Adelaïde laughed. 'Your brother says it matches neither his feet nor his nose, and as such is totally out of sorts with his personality.'

Annette chose to smile. Marie-Adelaïde's middle name was Victorie, after all.

'Paul says he wears a cow's ankles and a sheep's nose.'

Paul had never quite dared to say as much to her. She laughed just the same. She knew that in these circumstances a woman must laugh or be forever vulnerable.

It was while Marie-Victorie-Adelaïde Dufour was chuckling over her sixth or seventh repetition of 'a cow's ankles and a sheep's nose' that Williams chose to arrive.

One of the maids had let him in, and allowed him to come up unannounced, either because Madame expected him or because the girl was overawed by his foreignness.

Marie-Adelaïde clapped her hands in delight. 'Ah, yes,' she cried. 'I recognize this Monsieur Wodswod. He said he wanted to lodge here, told me he couldn't afford us, then finished up with an apartment on the Rue Royale. You have no need of lessons, Monsieur Wodswod. You drive a hard bargain in any language.'

He waited as if looking for something. 'Well, Madame,' he said. He bowed fractionally towards Annette, not so much saying nothing as saying next to nothing. Possibly he wished them good day or spoke about the weather. Possibly not. Annette was in such a fever of embarrassment for him she could not tell. He was neither shy, nor reserved, nor downright rude. His mind was somewhere else.

During the long interval that followed, Annette noticed that the sun was up. Was his introspection down to his lack of French? Hardly that, he certainly spoke some. Had she chosen to interest herself in someone who didn't care whether she was interested in him or not? In spite of telling her last night that he loved her?

Marie-Adelaïde Dufour chose to be delighted in him. She clapped her hands again, but with quite a different note, and called one of the girls to bring coffee. There hadn't been coffee before. Coffee was in short supply and expensive. It was what made coffee houses rich and, just recently, on fire.

The maid brought cups. Wodswod downed his with such haste that Madame thought it best to indicate the way to the parlour and leave them. She smiled at Williams as she did so. On the way to the door she glanced back towards Annette over Williams' shoulder, and pulled a face of amused approval.

Annette was used to this sort of grimace from her sisters, but had not seen it outside the family. Then everyone was family to André Augustin and Marie-Victorie-Adelaïde.

The lobes of Annette's ears felt amazingly warm as she led Williams to the parlour. So, unfortunately, did her cheek bones. She could hear Madame Dufour laughing downstairs. She could hear the maids – she could hear the *children* – all of them laughing.

Once inside the parlour, she left the doors open as was prudent and sat down.

Williams closed the doors and stayed standing. 'So many servants here,' he said, as if making a painful moral point.

His French sounded particularly formless. This wasn't the voice that had whispered against her neck last night. 'France is full of people who work in exchange for food,' she snapped. She knew how to put this rubbish in its place.

'How much work for how little food? How much bondage and for how long?'

Was England so very different, she wondered. 'Monsieur Williams,' she began. She did not know where to begin, his examination of her was so direct. 'Monsieur Williams, you've come here to learn French.' That's not what Vergez would say. He insisted that all the young males in the world came to France to study Revolution. 'Let me say that if lawyers like Maître Dufour and my brother cannot provide employment and therefore food – or surgeons such as my stepfather – then who can?'

He wasn't watching her eyes any more. He was gazing at the ribbon binding her bodice as if fearful of confusing his words. The ribbon wasn't really a binding. It was worn loose and was threaded about her house gown as a kind of adornment. She felt it tighten against her chest just the same. She should have done as the world was doing and dressed loose from the neck, or full from the throat and then with her gown caught once around the waist, as if a woman were a figure eight, which she wasn't, but which would have made her entirely fashionable. She smiled and wrinkled her nose.

'Yes,' he said, as all men do when they're uneasy with a language. 'I've come here to learn French.' He glanced upwards at last. 'Let me say at once that common sense bids me include the peasants in your list of the privileged. The peasants too should be able to provide food and work because they live on the land that makes it. But—'

'The peasants are starving!' She found herself saying it as he did, and wondered which of them was surrendering to the other's argument. Her cheeks were becoming hot again.

He didn't seem to notice. The talk was finished. He had other matters in mind. He'd looked preoccupied ever since he'd arrived. He reached in his pocket and took out a notebook.

She was amazed by his dedication to the task of learning French. She tried to indicate that he should show her what he'd written, sit by her, sit close to her, sit down at least. He refused to understand her French, or her gestures. Having felt his pockets in vain for a pencil, he seized upon one of André Augustin's newly cut quills which had been distributed all about the house, or wherever Madame would allow them to be.

A pen is an intimate possession, entirely personal to whoever cuts it. Annette was outraged that he should make himself so free here. She rose quickly, took the quill from him and hurried to her room to fetch a feather of her own.

He seized it impatiently. 'I thought you were getting me an iron pen,' he said. 'A pencil even. You'd think there'd be some metal nibs in a place like this.' He pulled out his pocket knife and trimmed the feather as he spoke, cutting it so short in his hurry that it would be impossible to make use of it afterwards.

Then he sat for the first time. He sat at a small writing table a long way away from her, opened one of Marie-Victorie-Adelaïde's all too feminine slide boxes and dipped the point of Annette's quill into the family's ink. 'Too much gum,' he complained. 'Not enough soot.' France was clearly a very backward country, and Orléans its least satisfactory place. 'I'd just as well write with Madame Dufour's coffee,' he said. 'It is dark enough to stain the paper, and it flows.' He laughed and encouraged her to do likewise.

After a minute or so, she supposed for politeness' sake, he indicated his notebook and said, 'My new poem. I was keeping some verses in my mind.'

'Indeed.'

'My memory is usually very good, but even so—' he smiled in her direction without really noticing her— 'compared with Madame's ink it lacks gum.'

She watched him write for one, two, three minutes. She

watched him while she counted silently to five hundred as her mother had taught her. She watched him while a log took flame in the fireplace and another settled. A thousand. He really was quite handsome, in spite of that sheep's nose which apparently her brother had noticed and she hadn't. She should have counted in dozens. Yes, even his nose was pretty. Walking and writing were what he did best. Oh, and fighting. He must have a bruised chest.

'My poem is about France.'

Beneath that suit was his shirt. Under his shirt would be his bruised skin. 'France is very big,' she offered. She was the one who needed lessons – in conversation, at least.

'I know. I've walked across it.'

'I mean it's a big subject.'

'Mine's a big poem.'

It needed some more of the Dufours' ink.

He sipped the nib, almost as intently as he'd kissed her last night. He was writing again.

The Dufours' oldest child came upstairs and loitered by the door – thank goodness she'd thought to leave it open again when she'd gone to her room for the pen – then Madame arrived in person to reclaim her. Adelaïde nodded in at them approvingly, as if sitting alone at tables was what lessons were all about. Then, having done her best for propriety, she too departed.

The fire grew silent. The quill point whistled gently on the paper. Each time it dried it scratched like fingers on skin.

She realized that this notebook, this bundle of words he kept in his pocket, was what he was used to making paramount in his life. He didn't share her faith, nor her politics, but he didn't want for an altar this Englishman. He carried one around with him and expected everyone to bow down to it, or at least wait endlessly while he made his own obeisances.

He crushed her quill between his fingers. She watched him do this in a kind of disbelief. She saw him regret what he had done, but only because he needed to write another word with what was left of it. 'I shouldn't have been so bad-tempered,' he said. 'About feathers and pens. After all, in every European language both feather and pen derive from the same word of Sanskrit.'

Before she could say 'indeed' again, he had left his desk and was kissing her on the mouth. And before she could demur at that, he drew away from her and said, 'Last night was a sorry affair, wasn't it?'

The remark was even more brutal than his kissing. He walked back across Marie-Adelaïde's carpet to retrieve his notebook. He too was flushed, hot-faced at least, if not exactly blushing. He turned towards her again, then halted, as if stopped by a draught from the door at his back. 'I didn't mean what we—' he stammered for a moment, he lacked words. 'I wasn't talking of what passed between us at Monsieur Gellet-Duvivier's.' The door jarred against the latch. A breeze had opened it, or a breeze had closed it. A breeze or a child. He shut it firmly. There was nothing secretive about his securing of that door, nothing furtive anyway. 'I was thinking of the politics, the soldiers, the mob. In Paris everything is so very different. You must let me show Paris to you.'

The arrogance of this Englishman, his impossible ordering of even the most simple words, added starkly to the impropriety of his suggestion.

'We must go to Paris,' he insisted, crossing the room to her.

'So you can be near your lady poet? You want to deliver your letter to this Ellen Maria Williams?'

She had no idea why she said this, nor why she spoke so petulantly. It must be the English name Helen which annoyed her, simply because she could not fit it to her mouth. Watching him write had been another irritation, such an eternity of ill manners for so few words on paper. He had shown her none of them, presumably because they rhymed in his own tongue. Then he had crushed her quill as idly as a housemaid tidying a spent taper or a parchment scorched from the curling irons. She felt so angry with him that she was quite unprepared for the inevitable, which was that he should kiss her again. He did so kiss her. He kissed her several times. Then, because beginning a kiss is difficult, lost himself in one that seemed never to end.

She protested, but the words could not get beyond his mouth, even if they left her own. His lips tasted of goose quill, then of soot and gum, which she supposed was the flavour of Marie-Adelaïde Dufour's ink. 'No!' she said. She thought she said 'No!' She heard nothing. Nor could she breathe.

Last evening had been fleshly enough. This morning she wasn't sure whether he sought her body or some preprandial fantasy his imagination allowed to inhabit it. He seemed to be after something not quite herself, in fact quite a long way from herself. Then, fancying he had found it, he fell upon it with a greed like an infant's hunger. Hunger is either contagious or repellent, when we can breathe and move and act upon our instincts. Fortunately, nothing about this man could ever seem repellent to her; ridiculous, yes, but never repellent. Not even now, when it was almost impossible to bear his facial pasturings. This breathless smothering of her lips, undertaken with so little tact and absolutely no finesse, even this did not repel her – a fact she recognized with some alarm, for not to be disgusted by the obscene came close to matching her sister Angélique's definition of falling in love. She tried, in considerable desperation, to push him away from her. She wanted the use of her lips and to prise him free of several other points of her consciousness. She was unsuccessful. Unless she could speak to him, she saw no way of making him budge.

Since she could not command him outright, he was not to be deflected, for all her muttering. If she detected anything in his kissing, and she was soon to know its language, then she understood his need not to be alone. She might have been his mother, his sister, his nurse: he clung to her as a child would cling, as her tiny niece often did – save he wasn't a child, and these boyish emotions were dressed much too evidently in the body of a man.

Then there was the question of hands, one hand at least, though it might have been several, behaving as no child's fingers would be permitted, and nor should these. This hand or these hands were pushed away, restrained at the wrist and then best ignored, save they could not be ignored till she had control of her voice again.

She felt about his person until she found the pocket she was looking for. He was so surprised at her daring that he uncovered her mouth with his own and gazed at her in bewilderment.

'What's this?' she managed to say. 'I don't think you quite—'
She had hold of his notebook, she felt the shape of it inside the
cloth of his coat. This compelled him to move both his face and
his hand and find it for her.

'Thank you.'

The notebook fell on her lap, striking her leg just above the
knee. Once more pushing his hand away she took up the book,
decided to ignore the hand which at once went elsewhere, and
repeated, 'What's this?' pretending to hold a conversation the
way people do when they try not to notice they are making love.
In truth, she knew she was talking neither to him nor to herself,
but to imaginary listeners in heaven and beyond the door.

'A poem. I already told you.'

'What is it about?'

'France.'

'France has too many poems.' Yesterday she said France had
too many poets, but only because her mother told her men
delight in being contradicted.

'It touches on Switzerland too. Switzerland needs poems,
believe me. It's far too grand for anything else.'

Grand, in French, was a very imprecise word for an
Englishman to use. For the moment, she lacked the voice to
remind him of this. Instead she asked, 'Why are you writing this
one?'

'So I shall publish it and become famous.'

'I do not think I can continue to kiss a man who expects to
make himself famous with a poem.'

'If I remember correctly, you have already told me to stop
kissing you.'

Indeed she had, and he now confessed to being aware of the
fact during all those moments he had spent half smothering her
to death.

What he was doing now was neither kissing nor not kissing.
He was kneeling with his breath close to her ear, his breath and
his voice when he could be bothered with it. His hands continued to behave in a manner she would shortly have to give her
attention to.

'Your kissing is like your poetry,' she said.

He put his face in front of hers and wrinkled his nose in inquiry, though he was altogether too proud to ask the question outright.

Conceited was the word that came to mind. 'Foreign,' she said.

She lay against what she thought was his arm then realized was the padded end of the settle. She again became aware of his breathing, which was perhaps her breathing. His touch was clumsy, his fingers hesitant or perhaps over-reverent; but her mind could interpret them, imagine them *passionate*. They became passionate. They *were* passionate. Passionate made clumsy acceptable.

They had stopped talking now, and in this age of reason she knew that to be speechless even for a moment was highly dangerous. Even for a moment. Yet there were certain adjustments to be made, allowances for differences of clime, divergences of custom, and for the greatest chasm that lay between them, which she knew to be ignorance and hoped was common to them both.

The more adventurous his touch became the less he would find she was wearing, where perhaps an English woman, this one whose name was already Williams, might wear most. And yet he did not seem surprised. She wondered if this was something he knew from experience or something he merely guessed at.

Could she accept the pleasure of what he was doing, his hand inside her clothes between her legs where for most times the flesh was bare? Could she allow it to go on until what she knew would be the end of it, here in Marie-Adelaïde's drawing room just along the corridor from her brother's lodgings, even though she hoped both of them were out and taking the air? Could she?

'If you must go on talking, Williams – of such things as books, I mean – perhaps we should go to my room.'

'And what books have you there?' Her poor fool was no kind of opportunist, her Williams, and certainly no strategist. He was a literalist.

'My prayerbook,' she answered, knowing the truth was always best. She began to giggle, and he chose to laugh as well.

Couples always laugh together when they climb the stairs,

laugh and find sentences full of charm and wit. That is how they demonstrate their innocence to the world. The world is too old to be deceived by them, but is always glad to recognize they are at peace with it.

Once more she was reminded of a child. When a nurse takes the babe from her breast because she has something else to attend to, it will return to the nipple the moment she has time for it again and fasten itself on to her as if nothing has intervened.

So it was with Williams. Her room had a bed and a chair, but he walked with her in a way that made it clear that the chair was an unthinkable resting place for either of them, even for a moment's excursion into speech. He indicated a position for her on her own narrow bed, then treated the bed much as he had the settle. That is he behaved exactly as downstairs, by kneeling briskly beside her and lifting her clothes.

She looked at the ceiling, then at her white-limbed Christ on the dark flesh of His Cross. She congratulated herself, as if to settle her mind, on the orderliness of her room. She remembered the minutes, no – quarters and halves of an hour – she had spent tidying it by candlelight before the shutters had been lined by dawn.

She remembered her sisters telling how exquisite pleasures were to be had from young men's sighings and breathings. If you kept them at a suitable distance, her sisters had assured her, and were careful with them, and *firm*, then they could and would with considerable coaxing do things to you which were far too enjoyable to treat with absolute honesty in confession.

Similarly, and again if you were *firm*, you could generally without coaxing in their case do such things to young men as would go a long way towards satisfying your curiosity concerning certain matters. These things would leave them grateful to you, moderately grateful at least, an emotion, her sister Françoise Anne insisted, that was by far the safest and most comfortable kind of gratitude to arouse in men.

These transports were best not described to a priest, for the clergy could grow disturbed by the notion of young people obtaining disproportionate pleasures from modest transgressions.

A big sin was always best for the confessional. It could be covered in a single word, whereas the simplicities which stop short of the biggest sin are far from easy to express in any kind of language. A big sin was comfortably clothed in its name, while the smaller sins led to a prying agitation of the figleaf, if not its total removal. Sometimes, her sisters insisted, in drawing them out of you word by word and grope by gasp, the clergy seemed to enjoy them too much.

Oh yes, she thought, as her eyes returned once again to the Crucifix, a young woman must be firm, firm with herself, firm with the young man she dallies with. She must remember that to advance this pleasure just a tiny step more towards imprudence could cause lasting trouble. A woman has to think a long way ahead, because a man never will.

He was enraptured by this body, this new body other than his own. He recalled dancing on Cumberland farms, whirling to the fiddle, snatching at kisses, clinging to hands and forearms, dancing sometimes until dawn, but never with this freedom, or anything more than a dizzying sense of the limbs beneath. No, never *this* freedom. Farmers do not leave their daughters unattended, any more than they neglect the rest of their stock. Then there had been heady moments among whores at Cambridge – *heady*, yes, because his pockets were too shallow for anything else. He couldn't afford women as well as an umbrella and new suits. His instinct was for suits. Old Ann Tyson had told him at Hawkshead long before he went up to university: 'A man with a suit and a horse shall want for nothing; a man with a suit very little.' Well, he had his suit and a woman molten under his hand, so old Ann was right.

Whenever he performed an act so full of wonder as this then his mind stole away from the ordering of the event itself and lost itself in imaginings. Love, being in love, was brighter than the Song of Songs, more miraculous than Milton, and this making of carnal love became a perpetual, almost a Homeric, simile. So now, as he lifted first the hem of her everlasting gown, and ravelled up underskirt after underskirt, or imagined that he did so, losing his way in the folds of her outer and perhaps only cloth; and as his hand felt its way ever so gently and not a little furtively beneath the pressure of that strange double loop of binding that squashed all her layers or crushed her garment's only layer into a tightness just above her knees, and as he reached higher than beyond her innumerable warmth-enclosing underthings towards her uncovered flesh, he was reminded of creeping as a child into a charcoal burner's hut, an inviting cone of saplings, tapering upwards like this and lined with peat or moss, which his intelligence began to pick at with its blinded fingers.

No wonder his sister found his imaginings over wild . . . not that he wanted to think of his sister at a moment like this. Much more convenient was this subjection of the actual to the imaginary, this metamorphosing of event until it was fit for the inward eye.

And if the actual resisted a trifle, began to set up a tittle-tattle of demands, even to struggle? Subjection was an interesting word, well suited to the mind. Subjugation belonged to the body.

Annette could hear, she had heard, a sound on the stair beneath her. Here it was outside the door. It might be Adelaïde. It could be a child, a serving girl, or even a dog. The family kept dogs.

Whatever it was, she would have to move. So she moved. 'I have only brought the one book,' she said loudly, 'apart from my devotional papers, that is.' She nudged him to a proper alertness. '*The Confessions*. It belonged to my father. No, that one's my prayerbook.'

Williams was too bemused for books. Consequently he did not answer.

'Borrow it if you like.'

There were some problems that even an English tailor cannot camouflage for a man. She straightened her dress, and not just her gown, as quietly as she could, while she gave herself over to self-examination in the mirror.

The room smelled very heated for such a cold mid-morning.

A cat pushed in at the door. Only a cat? It must have been battering a ball of paper, or following a particularly heavy-footed mouse!

Williams sighed.

He seemed minded to resume matters. She stopped this, and not before time, by murmuring, 'My lodgings are not quite the ideal place I thought they were.'

As it had done hours earlier, Augustin's voice began to rise through the floorboards. For a man who has gone out to be back again suggests a huge advance of time. She began to move Williams towards Marie-Adelaïde's drawing room, hoping to find nobody there, still less interrupt the singer, but knowing it was the proper place to take her leave of him.

'I have a whole apartment to myself,' he said as they went down. 'A whole nest of rooms. And, as you know, the house is empty. Till this afternoon, then?' He was speaking much too loudly.

'Perhaps.' His trousers were an interesting sight. Thank goodness his tailor had at last managed to reaffirm the purity of his original intention. She smiled, she hoped not roguishly.

The drawing room was empty. She handed him her father's copy of Rousseau's *Confessions*, still loud in her comment about it.

He tried to reject it. 'I've read it in England,' he said. 'Everybody has.'

'Read it in France,' she said. 'And in French. Everybody does.' It was as much of a future promise as she was prepared to let him have of her. He had spoken to her about being an angler. Now he was going to experience what it was like to be a fish.

ORLEANS.
SUNDAY 11TH DECEMBER AND
SEVERAL DAYS LATER IN 1791

So she began to visit his room. More exactly, she visited his rooms. Annette Vallon could find any number of excuses for not going to his bedroom as such. She told him she saw no reason, since he did not keep his books there, only his notebooks; and faced with such an overwhelming piece of logic he felt it would be inappropriate to move them after they had been noticed in another place. Also his bed, on first inspection, remained unmade. She knew nothing of English customs, nothing of what this Madame Helen Maria Williams might expect from him in Paris for example, but a French woman from a good family simply could not allow herself to be seen near an unmade bed.

Instead they sipped dessert wines with Monsieur Gellet–Duvivier, or tea and sugared tarts served to them by the daughter of the house. The girl never spoke, but she sometimes scoffed encouragingly at Williams' French and his reluctance to take wine. How old was she? Thirteen? Fourteen? Fifteen? She was very beautiful in a bloodless Norman fashion, and much too aware of herself for Annette's liking. Clearly she was head over heels in love with Williams, though she was too silly to realize the fact and Williams was too conceited to notice.

Once Monsieur Gellet–Duvivier left them unattended in the salon, or the Demoiselle Gellet–Duvivier parted with her varied pastries and her assorted silences from the family room above or below, and once Annette and Williams were seated alone in any such place, or even in Williams' own sitting room, then he would fall upon her. That is he fell upon her once. He did so at the very first opportunity. He crossed the considerable space between them at a stride, sank down half kneeling beside her and half crouching above her to place his lips very passionately to her ear, and use whichever hand was not holding her or supporting himself to fondle the back of her right knee.

She enjoyed the touch of his hand, but knew it could get them nowhere save into trouble. She removed it, and another hand replaced it. This too she pushed aside. 'No, my Williams,' she said. She spoke gravely. She tried to speak bravely, but for a moment the mathematics of it defeated her. She had noticed the fact before – and it was a truth more astonishing than the tumble of an apple from a tree in a Cambridge philosopher's garden – she had noticed that, whereas she as a young woman only had two hands, every man of her acquaintance could produce an infinity of them and any number of stray fingers at will. A man might boast a mere two sleeves to his jacket, but once he was allowed close he could grab at her more ways than an octopus. Like a lizard, he was forever growing tails, though that was a subject even further from speculation at the minute. 'No, my Williams,' she insisted. 'Not until we have had a little talk, you and I.' She disengaged herself from his every hand and its grappling fingers entirely, but finding his lips withdrawn from her ear she held him her cheek to be kissed in recompense. Thank the Good God he had not blocked her breathing with his mouthings of passion. Thank the Good God also that he was a poet as well as an Englishman, and on both accounts unwilling to squander words.

'"A little talk"?' he repeated, clearly not realizing that in French a little talk means a disputed negotiation of considerable and possibly extravagant length. 'Very well, Annette. We shall have it now.'

'Several little talks,' she said as firmly as possible. 'Little talks of substance. Any number of long little talks. As many as seem necessary and both of us have a mind for.' Hearing him gasp, and glimpsing while appearing not to notice it yet another alteration to his anatomy, as geometrically incredible in its way as the production of extra fingers and hands, she relented a little. 'We can begin the first talk now, if you so wish.'

'"Begin" it?'

'Indeed, my Williams. I do not anticipate that it can reach towards an end, do you?'

Poor Williams was looking increasingly hangdog of late. He seemed to think – she believed his view of the matter was not uncommon among young men – he seemed to think the female body, her body, was like one of his country paths, to be strayed over at will and revisited whenever it suited him. Poor poor Williams. It was more entertaining to watch him suffer than to tell him the truth that pained her. And what was this truth? Simply that much as she wanted him all about her, the Good God would not let her have him. Nor would the rest of Christian society, nor above all would Françoise Vergez her mother the former Madame Jean Léonard Vallon.

Nor, between Sunday the eighteenth and Saturday the twenty-fourth of December would her own body. Between those dates in the Third Year of Freedom she would be reduced to chewing on the tarts brought to her by the consumptive Gellet-Duvivier girl and envying her for being too young to experience the tribulations of maturity.

Vergez had a theory, and her brothers the surgeons Jean Jacques and Charles Henry Vallon shared it, that childless women were to be oppressed by this awful malaise earlier and earlier in their lives as history unfolded. If Vergez's graphs were believed there would be a time when even girls as young as the Gellet-Duvivier thing would suffer a recurring blot in their calendar. Indeed, come the millennium, females would be menstruating as young as eleven. Human females, not savages from islands beyond the sea.

Men were full of such theories. Annette had hoped to deflect her stepfather Vergez from his customary ridiculousness by observing that, if her understanding of chronology and mathematics was correct, then Mother Eve must have lain fallow until she was at least a hundred years old. 'Very likely,' the old fool agreed, tapping his nose, which was never fallow in winter. 'We have Abraham's good wife Sarah as evidence of it!'

She could not discuss her impending predicament – or Eve's – with Williams. She must fret alone. He was, to be fair, very knowledgeable concerning the parental habits of waterbirds and sheep, and lately – and much more daringly – had begun to tell her an absolutely incomprehensible English joke about trout. When it came to the workings of the human female he was as prudish as he was inquisitive. His own body was an item he never spoke of, and, quite clearly, rarely thought about. If he did, then he would have reached some alternative conclusion regarding the footwear he punished it with. For her own part, she knew a great deal about Williams' physical attributes. Chief among these was the certainty that before winter was far advanced she would prevail upon him to enhance them with some town shoes suitable for Marie-Adelaïde Dufour's drawing room. Thus does a young woman dream of perfecting her love, or of improving him at the least. So, too, does a young man fret at her preoccupations.

'This little talk we must have,' he said. 'We never begin it.' He was thinking of his bed again.

'Not yet,' she said. 'Not now, at least. I believe the words should steal upon us, and doubtless they will when they're ready.'

This bewildered him. He was unused to waiting for a conversation that might hover about his ears for an eternity like an unmade poem before deciding to settle.

'The sky is bright,' she said. 'Perhaps we should look at the Cathedral together? Or spend some time with my brother.'

'I'd rather walk.'

Annette hated walking. Gentlewomen of the town do not dress for it; they are in general much too fortunate to own anything as practical as Williams' ridiculous shoes. On the other hand, a woman determined to keep herself away from bedrooms has to do something with her lover – if she has any interest in him at all, that is.

She followed him downstairs past a window of giggling girls. They should have been stitching stockings or steaming hats, but they were growing too insolent to work any more. In Paris, they would be thronging the streets. Here they could find nothing better to do than scoff at Williams.

She might as well scoff at him herself. Lover was a word without a future unless you were already married. Married women might have lovers, though not in her mother's case. Marriage was Françoise Yvon's profession, and she had bound her daughters in a long apprenticeship to it.

Once Williams was outside he seemed determined to rush. This meant that she was drawn after him as briskly and as breathlessly as her costume would allow. She wondered if he was demonstrating his freedom from her or insisting on her own subjugation to his wilder impulses. There was little time for thinking, and none for speaking. He dragged her by the wrist, the forearm, or simply guided her by the pressure of his will; and their progress was so violent that she forced herself to laugh aloud at it. Laughter was all their haste made possible, and the sound of her pretended mirth made him slow down in astonishment. She realized he had become unaware of her presence. He had swept her along with him only to forget her entirely. He was in a hurry. He had come to France to witness the dawning of a new age. If he did not dash to overtake it, it might never occur.

All that was certain between them was that he was leading her towards the bridge – to the river's edge at least. This was a chilly way to be walking in mid December. She had rather he led her almost anywhere else, except towards his bed. How she regretted not allowing him the beginnings of that 'little talk' she had demanded and then refused.

He knew she did not like approaching the bridge. And nor should he. It was guarded by imbeciles. Imbeciles, as Williams must know by now, were eternally dangerous. Safer to fall among thieves than meet with an idiot determined to advance his cause. Especially if his cause made him a present of a gun.

She tried to blurt out her fears. He would have none of them.

'You object to the ordinary people carrying weapons, and meeting together to discuss all matters of public safety?' he asked at last. He wasn't the least bit breathless himself.

'Yes,' she said.

She had no choice but to let him lead her by the arm now, as they apparently did in England. She felt like one of those serving girls she'd seen being dragged about by their young men at the Easter Fair. 'Yes, I do. Absolutely.'

'In England, many of us are excited by such an idea. All thinking men approve of it.'

'And what about your King, for instance? Does he approve of it? Or his chief minister milor Fox?'

'Fox is not a minister.'

'Do they approve of it?'

'I said thinking men.'

Thinking women was not a possibility.

Her sudden eloquence, many syllabled though still largely unspoken, was the result of their halting close to the bridge and high above the water. She did not have her breath back, but her legs were still and calmness began to catch up with her.

Not that there was a great deal of calm to be found in the situation Williams saw fit to place her in. Orléans was a flat town and a level one compared to her native Blois, so she was surprised to find what an airy perch he had found for them.

The road divided at the bottom of the Rue Royale. The part they now trod on passed along a quay that seemed to have been built on the back of the East wind. It was backed by menial wharfage and fronted by a precarious ledge, firstly of slippery cobbles then of timber, where the town fell away into the river.

Williams loved it. A brief stretch of parapet lined the beginnings of the way from the bridge. He led her slowly to the very end of this, as if he didn't want her view of the Loire to be interrupted. He stood with her, but where there was no parapet, and told her he liked to bestride the top of things.

She began to say she was glad she hadn't taken him to the cathedral of Saint Cross, but once more he wasn't listening. He was exulting at the wind in his hair as if he were a lunatic from the asylum. She noticed the parapet beside her was coated in ice. What an extraordinary man her Englishman was. Drawing rooms were no use to him. If he couldn't persuade her to his bed, he seemed perfectly content to share his mind with her in a wilderness.

She ignored the mouthings of her personal madman, and consoled herself with the river.

The Loire flowed quickly. At first she did not realize how quickly, since nothing floated on it, not a log, not a wherry and certainly no waterbird, and it seemed to lie at different levels as if frozen. Then she saw it moved with so much force that the lips of its surges were held stiffly in place by the pressure of the current. It was as if the entire river was set in gelatine or aspic. Upstream from her, its dark races were folded over and over in serpentine tangles across reed bed and shingle, then they compressed themselves round the piers of the bridge or the stone prows of its two little islands before disappearing from sight beyond long spans of masonry. Pretentious bridge – unnatural waters! She felt queasy just to look at them. A leaky sun hovered above them and drowned in its own wormy reflections like a Medusa. Her head buzzed, and she felt sickened as if by the damps of a feverish dream.

It was being dragged here that had done this to her – being dragged here, urged ahead, hurried to where she didn't want to be.

To be dragged about is demeaning. She got ready to be angry with him, and she would be angry the moment she was in possession of herself; she knew her anger to be certain and capable. Yet even in her sickness she felt a deeper emotion, and it stifled her protest. To be demeaned is scarcely to be tolerated, especially to be demeaned by one's love. But to be demeaned by love suggests love lost. And to lose love, even a love one does not entirely want, is rarely acceptable.

Her breast ached and she leant against Williams' arm. He leant against nothing. The ache receded. It had not been physical.

He smiled at her, and his smile should have given her back to herself. It didn't. 'We could talk now,' it said. 'You know – have our little talk.' The wind draughted about them, or perhaps there was no wind, just a coldness eddying on the water. His smile was not entirely kind. It accepted that a hurrying woman might be breathless, but proclaimed that itself was never out of breath. She could not answer it. Breathless and slightly sickened, she saw nothing in his smile except an unmade bed.

She could not blame him for this. She too wanted his bed, or her body did, and she knew her body tormented his body quite as much as his did hers. But a body is a long-lasting object, unless it falls into the hands of surgeons; and a woman has to go on living inside her body with whatever time provides for her.

Meanwhile she took comfort from Williams' arm and let the waters race away with her mind.

And the Loire did rob her of her mind. As she gazed into the depths of it she had a vision of her own nakedness reflected there. She was lying in indifferent sunlight without a shred of clothing, her limbs uncovered by sheet or counterpane, she supposed on Williams' bed. She saw herself, face bruised by kissing, being dandled to and fro. Her teeth were clenched beyond joy as if in a lover's dream. She could not see Williams, though his reflection hung above hers in the water. She had no need of him. It was her own predicament she examined, lying face upwards in her nakedness, her body hair soaking wet.

This unexpected clarity of detail brought Annette to her senses. The face did not belong to Annette Vallon or anyone she knew. She was looking down at a woman's corpse that just a moment or two earlier had been cast from the main stream into the narrow margin of shallow water beneath the quay.

'Poor thing,' she found herself saying. 'To have drowned in that.' She shuddered to think of such a death, but even as she spoke she knew her description of it was inadequate. People do not take their clothes off before drowning themselves.

'She's been murdered,' Williams said in that matter-of-fact way of his which enabled him to ignore everything he didn't wish to see, including the disturbing facts of the woman's nakedness, which were several. 'She was killed for her gem stones – those among other things.'

The woman's earlobes were torn, something Annette hadn't noticed at first, because she lay with one arm thrown back against the side of her head. Now she floated in still waters it was possible to see the blood. There was blood all about the corpse now, but a woman is entitled to produce a little of that.

'She was dead when she was thrown into the river,' Williams went on. 'Otherwise she would have sunk straight away.' Annette was appalled at the sort of things he knew, and by how little she understood of him otherwise.

'I think her throat was squeezed,' he said. 'Then she was plundered and perhaps stabbed from behind. That is why there is so much blood.'

Blood was to remain an issue between them, she could sense that. The body meantime was fascination enough. Once she separated it from her own preoccupations it became less of a moral tale and more of a medical history, floating face up as it was, and with all of it, even its knees and its feet, clearly visible. Williams had seen sailors' corpses fished from the Irish Sea, he said, and other ones drowned in the Seine scarcely a fortnight ago. They always drifted face down and leg heavy at first. Then their lungs filled and they sank, she supposed according to mathematical truths he had learned at his English university. Then a day or two later, even though they were bone heavy with their flesh lightened by fishes, gases inflated their viscera and they came back to the surface.

Vergez spoke like this, so she chose to ignore it. She might have made a joke with her brother, but not with Williams, not about gases. Besides, the dead woman was too serious a concern to trivialize with detail. She was too beautiful. Her hair had been fair, though it was soaked dark and leaked river tar and the caulkage of boats. Her eyelids were half open. Her eyes appeared to be blue, though their blueness might be no more than the wintry sky reflected in the starkness of their whites.

Annette was certain the woman was well-born. She felt certain that poor women did not have bodies like this one, as slim-breasted, as pale-skinned, as delicate about the arms and thighs.

'She looks like an angel in a prayer,' she said. 'Though I expect you will tell me she reminds you of an angel in a poem, Williams.'

'She puts me in mind of a poem, yes. Not an angel in a poem.'

'A poem by your Madame Ellen Maria, I daresay. Well, she's lucky, whoever she is.'

'Lucky?'

'Yes, she's floating down to Blois. I shall be going that way myself soon.' She knew how to make a man uncertain of her, though even as she spoke she felt her words were somewhat diminished by the fact that the corpse continued to bob slowly past them along the river wall instead of being snatched away again in the current. It was delayed by a backflow from the inner pier of the bridge, and might soon be trapped under the quay for ever. 'I suppose she came from a good family,' she said wistfully. 'If her clothes were to be stolen, and her earrings.'

'We don't know whether her clothes were taken because they seemed valuable, or because she was about to be violated.' Williams might be ponderous of speech but he found the appropriate word without the least appearance of difficulty. He squeezed her arm as he reached it, whether from pride or to comfort her against the idea she had no way of telling.

Nor had she any more stomach to discuss the matter. She was returning to her dream again. Lovers always think and behave as if they have the whole world to themselves, and on an icy day at the coldest edge of town the world is never in a hurry to dispel their illusion. They stood above a busy river, not twenty paces from its main bridge and at the end of the Rue Royale: it seemed impossible to suppose they were the only ones to notice the dead woman. Yet Annette did so suppose. She wanted the dead woman for herself. Her starkness, her beauty, the proof her body seemed to offer of God's peace and grace being visited upon womankind, even after the worst indignity, all this was an instance of Christian revelation aimed directly at herself. Williams followed a religion outlawed in France by Church and State, or she thought he did. Williams was a heathen. Failing that, he was a man, which was almost the same thing. This floating serenity might not be herself, principally because it had fair hair and its eyes were blue, but it belonged to her.

Annette reached this conclusion by an emotional process she chose not to be logical about. As she came to it, a single gull swooped at the corpse – stooped might be a truer word – and gashed the poor woman's abdomen with blood. A second gull, also solitary, landed on the blood and stood there for a second, head alert and inspecting the river and then the blustery sky as if it were the tillerman on a barge. Before it could enlarge the blood it was displaced by a crow. This began to feed itself with remarkable accuracy.

Williams made noises, not of disgust. He seemed to understand birds, even to approve of them. They had an interest for
him beyond death and naked women.

A stone struck the crow on the head. She did not know
Williams could throw with such accuracy, but the man was like
daylight itself – eternally full of surprises.

The stone was followed by grappling hooks, a set of claws on
a chained rope that dabbled all over the dead woman, bruising
and breaking her and in general threatening to do as much
damage to her as the birds' beaks.

Annette continued to feel shocked by what she saw, but was
happy to dismiss the idea that Williams was in any sense responsible for what happened. Such brutishness belonged to a separate
world. This world existed a long way beneath her, and the
corpse, now less than elegant, had been appropriately diminished
and transmuted. Praise God that neither the bird-killing sling nor
that slippery grapple came from among the surprises in Williams'
jacket pocket. They belonged to someone else. That someone
was standing on the foreshore beneath them, sheltered from their
view by the overhang of the quay.

His grappling iron did nothing. A boat hook – or some such
pole – reached from under her parapet, and attempted to entan-
gle the corpse in its turn. It wasn't successful. It darted at neck,
armpit and thigh in disgusting progress, prodding then snatching,
slipping and drooping as if it were the neck of some large heron
or, worse, a snake-sized worm.

Somebody chuckled. A voice spoke while the chuckle continued. So there were at least two men beneath her feet! The
corpse, previously so still, began to jerk obscenely. Williams
whispered something in his own tongue. Annette did not ask
him to translate. She was beginning to understand a whole number of things on her own account, and fear even more.
Meanwhile the dead woman continued to stir and twitch, not in
some final death spasm, though – alas! and after all this! – it
might have been, but with more of a jointless motion, in the
manner of an adult glove being flapped by a child or one of those
Italian marionettes that perform on streetcorners in summertime.

Certainly this one had its string, if not its strings. What

Annette now saw, and what Williams had perhaps always seen, was that the corpse wore a ligature round its neck, and the free end of its noose was a long piece of cord that was concealed in the water but ran shoreward. Someone's hand jerked it clear of the Loire even as she noticed it, and the corpse again suffered an ugly but disturbing spasm. Again she heard laughter.

How foolish she had been in nearly all of her deductions. Williams had spoken of strangulation, so was perhaps more clear-sighted than she. Yet his greater keenness of eye did not prevent him from being equally stupid.

The plain fact was that their corpse could not float away from them in the current because its neck was attached to a line that ran ashore immediately beneath them. It was in all probability the very noose that had caused the poor woman's death, and if this was so then there was a good chance that it led to the hands of her murderers.

These people either wished to retrieve the body or had never intended it to fall into the water in the first place. She had been dragged down on to the undershore, subdued, and then perhaps struggled away into the water before being arrested by the cord. Or perhaps she had been assaulted in one of the wharfing sheds behind them, staggered injured across the road and quite simply fallen in?

Whatever the circumstances, Annette and Williams were very likely in a situation of considerable peril. The river edge was a long way beneath them, easily the height of three or four men, but there must be ways up. Where the wall ended in front of Williams, for example, there was a sloping buttress of stone that would certainly offer a path in less slippery weather. And there could well be steps set into the quayside beneath the ledge they stood on.

She tried to draw Williams aside and urge him quickly towards the Rue Royale.

He refused to budge. He was eternally curious.

What he could see, what they both had in view now, was their enemy from a few nights ago. The string led to the hand of the animal who had reviled her and tried to kill Williams. Now he stood on the riverbank, it was disconcerting to find that his

mouthless and toothless face was not only turned towards them
in arrogant recognition, it was a whole lot closer underfoot than
she had first calculated.

His companion in corpse fishing, and probably in murder, was
none other than one of their rescuers of the same evening. It was
that bicorne-hatted lout from the Town's Guard. He, too, scowled
at Williams. Whatever they had been doing in their little niche
beside the river was not meant to be overseen. They had been as
private as lovers. Murder was an intimate affair.

Single Tooth made up his mind to involve them in these inti-
macies as soon as possible. He glanced about him for a way to
come up at them, and obviously decided the buttress offered him
the best footing. He grinned wolfishly and reached out a hand
towards Williams as if asking for an accommodation.

He was naked to the waist, and smeared with blood. Unless
the blood were his own, he had handled the dead woman before
she fell into the water.

Incomplete face, ruinous torso. His breast muscles looked as
hard as pump handles. He could cause them terrible harm if they
allowed him close to them. So what was Williams doing?

Williams was behaving as if the whole matter could be discussed together, disputed, argued through. While the brute tried
to find a way up the icy buttress, Williams reached out a hand to
him, oblivious of what the consequence might be. The fellow
grinned and grabbed at it.

He missed – Annette had, quite simply, dragged Williams'
arm out of reach by seizing his sleeve – so he missed and grabbed
again, wildly this time because he was already tumbling down
the icy stonework.

His legs shot from under him and went skidding into the Loire
as he reached the foundation of the buttress. The side of his head
struck this same jut of stone, and carried the breath and quite
probably the life out of him. He went under the water – it was
shallow for less than a pace inshore – and lay motionless just
beneath the skim of the flood as it carried him away from them,
out and under the first arch of the bridge at the speed of a trotting horse or perhaps faster. There was no cord to hold him back,
nor the woman's corpse any longer. She too had disappeared.

Williams appeared deeply shocked by what he had seen. If Annette expected gratitude she was disappointed. He had come here to discuss the nature and consequences of the new order, and she had robbed him of an encounter with an expert at its very point of evolution. He could scarcely manage a word except to mutter 'you' in the plural and respectful form – hardly the expression of an intimate. She had heard better speeches in her time.

'I saved you, Williams. I saved both of us. There are no detachments of the militia to help us this time.'

Williams pointed towards his friend with the floppy hat as if he still held the clue to all things.

'And what would they have done to me! Do you want to see me throttled and naked like that other poor thing?'

It was a disordered image, and far too confusing to dwell upon. Floppy Hat, who still held William's letters of credit, was gazing towards them as if happy to oblige her expectation, but he seemed to be alone. She was glad to be able to think so clearly, even as she felt about the top of the parapet with her free hand – the hand that had been clutching Williams. Yes, the villain was entirely alone.

'That citizen saw what happened. He will—'

'Citizen is a word from Paris. He's a murderer.'

'You've made a murderer of me,' Williams mouthed. 'You've—'

She nudged him to silence and studied Floppy Hat.

Floppy Hat was counting them. He counted Williams and Annette as carefully as he could. He saw a man and a woman – a man *with* a woman. In a fight a man with a woman is worth half a man. A man in a rich suit and a woman in the clothing of the bourgeoisie clearly amounted to even less – especially a woman in such a silly bonnet.

He had seen his friend's mistake on the ice and saw no need to repeat it. He had climbed this way before. He had scaled worse places often. He took the buttress at a run, reached the top, halted in mid stride then toppled back, his face creased with a black groove that flooded with blood even as he fell.

Annette had disdained the hallowed fragment of the Bastille

Williams had offered her, but she was quite content to smash in a man's cheekbone with a piece of coping stone from the parapet. She dusted her glove as if murder was the most natural thing in the world.

It was certainly easy. In a moment, there was no sign of their assailant or his hat. His fall was more absolute than his friend's. It reversed a climb of greater energy and he was unconscious at a far higher point in it. He went into the stream further out, plunging immediately into one of those dark bands of current, rather than the littered water of the shore ledge. There wasn't even a splash. The current had no time for splashing.

All this caused by a woman who rejected the Revolution, a woman of more wit than passion who spoke of having 'little talks'! She had certainly killed a man. Directly or indirectly she had killed two, and women do not do such things, not women of *her* class. She began to lead Williams away. They are not even supposed to do that!

'You speak of political beliefs, Williams. You speak altogether too much of them. Ridding France of matters like that is one of mine.'

'"Matters"? They were men.'

'Murderers, Williams. We discussed it at length. Such people are all murderers.'

He began to talk of her religion. She could see how difficult it was for him. Not for the first time, a young man was finding a woman's sincerely held beliefs would allow the greatest sin while preventing her from committing any of the lesser ones.

Love is an abstraction. Loss is always a great deal nearer. She did not think she would lose this man. She feared she might forfeit him, and that she could never allow. 'Hurry, Williams. I feel cold.' Indeed, her teeth were chattering. The dead woman had looked so cold. 'You must comfort me a little.'

'Comfort?'

'You have, perhaps, such a thing as a blanket I could borrow? A rug by your fire, or a counterpane?'

There are moments when lovers know very clearly what they will do, no matter what words have passed between them.

Luckily, Williams' intentions seemed uncomplicated by any experience of these occasions. He led Annette slowly towards his lodgings, then upstairs to his apartment. No dogs slid away from her as they passed, perhaps because dogs were edible and therefore becoming rarities. The Gellet-Duvivier seamstresses kept themselves quiet. It is hard to scoff at a resolute woman.

She sat in his room and shivered. His little fire was unlit, but through an open door she could see that his bed was made. He brought her the counterpane from it, and settled it about her. The stitching was neat, but in a strange coarse thread. She wondered whether it was the Demoiselle's work, or her dead mother's. The cloth was too bright to be old.

Williams found some wine in the large salon. She thought of the fire there and continued to tremble. He poured two glasses, and actually drank one himself, downing it at a gulp. He persuaded her to have several.

She did not want the wine, nor even like the taste of it. But she needed some. She also needed more in the way of comfort than to hear him say, 'You were very brave, so very brave.' He spoke to her as huntsmen talk to their horses. In all the circumstances he was showing himself to have fewer words than a cavalry officer, though of course with more of an excuse.

She refused a fourth glass of wine, fearful that something, or everything, was slipping away from her.

He had been holding an empty glass. Now he set it back on the tray, took her own and placed it beside it. The stopper going back into the carafe, glass chiming on glass, seemed to signal the end of love. Worse was his speedy unwrapping of the counterpane from her knees. In the novels she shared with her sisters, young women were cast aside with equally dismissive gestures.

He caught her right hand in his left and persuaded her from the chair with an invitation that was only slightly short of a tug. Then he led her towards the bed she thought they might have reached sooner or not at all.

Waiting for comfort had considerably lessened her need for it. She certainly could not put up with another siege of loving, let alone tolerate its accompanying barrage of entreaties – the mouth smothering her own, the voice against her ear, the everlasting pressing and prying.

Perhaps she would not have to. She found herself sitting among opened bed linen, with her left shoe already unbuckled. The buckle scarcely needed this attention. It was an ornamental device, a point that escaped Williams. If he saw a buckle he unbuckled it. Her grasp of events was confused by her need to unfasten her bonnet and separate it from her hair, an act she performed slowly because it was heavy with significance and ought to be accompanied by a considerable amount of thought. Meanwhile he was unbuttoning her neck fastenings. She did not know whether he was being considerate about her gown or merely foreign. The material was soft and could be lifted. Equally it would crush. She removed his fingers from her buttons, raised her bottom then pulled the garment clear of her shoulders. She could as easily have stepped out of it – after all, she had stepped into it earlier so she could preserve the intimate relationship between her hair and her bonnet – but she was reluctant to stand. To stand at this moment, with Williams looking on, would suggest a wildness of abandon that would be quite inappropriate. Besides, she was in no mood to stand.

Williams had been considerate of her gown, and not entirely, or not merely, foreign. He placed it at large upon a chair, then threw the hem of her undergown and as much as he could grab of her petticoats on to her chest in a great heap. This left her naked from her thighs to well above the waist, though she sought to recompose a layer or so as quickly as possible.

She was hardly dressed for seduction this afternoon – was she ever? Every young woman in the land (from those on high to a low that would certainly have included Monsieur Gellet-Duvivier's seamstresses) wore knee stockings. These were kept above the calf with a bow. Naughty girls – and every woman is naughty as far as her knees – made the bows as saucy as they could afford, even if their own eyes were the only ones to see them.

Annette was wearing bows of most expensive ribbon. Williams would notice they matched the sash that made such an eye-catching figure-of-eight across the breast and back of her gown. Unfortunately her stockings did not stop here. They reached an accommodation between common sense and the icy weather by climbing at least a handspan higher up her thighs. In the nature of stockings that lack support, these last few inches were probably wrinkled and in consequence worn. Bows and delicacy of cloth aside, she was dressed as her mother would wish. She was dressed like an older woman. What would Williams think?

Williams thought nothing. He was a man confronted by a miracle, and men are beyond thought at such moments. Besides, he was pulling off his clothes, though he showed a proper respect for Winter by retaining his shirt. What she could see of the rest of him, which was most things of interest, was as bone white and shy as a newly peeled stick. There were to be no poems in her ear. He threw himself upon her.

There was a great deal of gentleness in his rushing at her, just the same – perhaps because their bodies were cushioned by her piled-up petticoats and his own rapidly rising shirt. Everything that passed between them happened very quickly, except for the one thing that should happen slowly, and that was slow enough. Young men are supposed to find these matters difficult, but Williams seemed to experience no trouble with them at all, perhaps because he had been thinking about them so often.

And so she lay in Williams' arms, feeling first a terrible joy, then a great confusion. She had been comforted, exactly as she wished and demanded; she was comforted, but it takes only a tiny comfort to satisfy love.

So tiny a comfort that it was immediately swept aside by a sense of her own foolishness. She could not explain it to herself, think about it or even talk, because Williams kept darting about her, never crushing her or minutely creasing her piled undergarments, but pouring out a torrent of words that were both more and less than speech, for they consisted of all manner of loving sounds and exclamations of joy in that language of his she was unable to understand. A few moments earlier, they had swept each other into a world beyond semantics, and he at least was still rejoicing.

Annette had other matters to cope with. All day, all week she had been marooned in her lumpish season. Now Vergez and her own body came rushing upon her on the crest of a dark tide. She had searched for other explanations and found them: Williams had done this to her, Williams had left her like this because of the dangers he had loosed from what her sister Angélique wickedly called his 'Cupid's quiver'. This was what she had told herself. Now she knew she was wrong, and only the moon could be relied on. It was her own blood that flowed between her legs, and she had no napkin to stifle it.

Williams was better able to cope, though – in common with most men's – his remedies were destructive. He tore a towel into strips, while his mind stayed on higher matters. 'I want us,' he said, 'I need us to be together.' To make love is never easy in any language.

'Yes, my Williams.' As declarations went, it said everything but promised nothing. For the moment she had larger worries. She had loved as a beast loves, just as the heat comes. A woman is not supposed to do this, her mother insisted. But if she does, she will certainly not conceive, her sister Françoise had assured her.

But the beasts conceive. The cat conceives, and the dog, and the domestic pig. When they are in blood they conceive.

She tried to talk to Williams. He was beyond talk. His love for her, and his delight in her body, had lent him a most wonderful pride. As if he needed that. Still, he was her lover now so she would forgive him anything, forgive if not allow.

As she busied herself to stem her flow and make herself decent for a speedy return to the Dufours, she realized he did not understand what was happening to her. He thought he had captured the most rare of maidenheads – as indeed he had – and that this was the natural consequence of his act. It wasn't.

His pride was so great, his contentment so exquisite, that even as he sat with his love in their half nakedness he felt beneath the pillow and began to busy himself with his notebook. After a few minutes of contented introspection, he muttered something – not, she thought, an excuse – and carried it to his table, which was spread with books and papers. He was writing his poem, his same poem. He had begun it before he met her – who

knew where they would be at its end? Still, she gained an interval in which to find her clothes and dress herself, and there were
some matters best attended to without his eyes upon her.

Her own eyes never left him. She noticed in particular the
strange way he crouched over his writing, nuzzling at it like a cat
with a dead bird. His shirt was crumpled, and his legs – she
wished she could share his legs and feet with Paul and Marie-
Adelaïde Dufour, but she wouldn't; they were hers now and
priceless beyond the winning of silly arguments. They were
exquisitely formed, long and tapering and graceful, their skin
whiter than white, purer than the most costly altar candles. Then
she saw the blemish, the thin bruise of shadow that marred the
nearest one.

'You've been cut,' she gasped. She crouched and caught his
left ankle. 'You've a scar,' she wondered, 'a scab at least.'
Something had encircled his calf just above the ankle bone, tearing it at back, and cutting deeply into the shin. She soothed it
with her hand, would have kissed it, but she felt that even now
he would find the gesture excessive.

'I know.' He spoke idly. 'I was brought down by a trip cord
the other day. That afternoon I met you in the street. Or it
might have been a whip, something like that. It was certainly
deliberate.' He told her offhandedly about his encounter in the
forest. Then – with a laugh – he balanced it against his more
serious adventure on the bridge. This led him to think about the
murderer she had tipped into the river a brief while earlier, and
stilled further comment.

She wasn't interested in ruffians with muskets. She had heard
that story several times. The gentlemen in the forest, and the
gentry who sided with them, they were another matter. She
was in haste now, a very great haste indeed. She already needed
to deal properly with her bodily tribulation. Now there was this.
Those few words about the scar on his foot had transformed
everything. She had letters to write, and people to talk to.

She was fully dressed again, completely remade. Williams was
back to his writing.

'Why go?' he asked.

'I have to.'

He indicated the notebook, the lines that came into his head and left his hand almost without erasure. 'Give me a few moments and I'll walk with you.'

'Williams, I must go now.'

'Then permit me to call on you this evening.'

She didn't answer. She was in too much of a hurry for words. It was irritating to notice the look he gave her, as if someone had just told her the moon was on fire, and she was in haste to see it burn.

Embarrassing also to find the large salon had grown populous during their brief time together in Williams' rooms. Monsieur Gellet-Duvivier must be boarding officers again, albeit from another regiment – a factor which would make her visits here much more of a problem.

The doors were open. Again she saw colour and glitter, and smelled cavalrymen, much as she had when she'd made Williams' acquaintance just a few days earlier. They clamoured at her as she passed.

Even more embarrassing she met two of the Gellet-Duvivier servants on the stairs. The girls were carrying coach-boxes. A gentleman followed behind them, flourishing an ornamental stick and still wearing a hat. He was at least as well dressed as Williams, though in the fashion of Paris.

Monsieur Gellet-Duvivier came last of all. They all stood back for her, but only the women noticed her. Monsieur Gellet-Duvivier did not expect to see an unaccompanied woman on his stair.

Outside, Orléans was much the same. It held three fewer people than it had started the morning with, but its skies were still cold and cloudy with snow or rain.

He thought – how could he stop thinking? – of the dark-eyed, bright-skinned woman whose beauty had just burned him. He sat with his notebook open and wrote her into his poem:

> *Those steadfast eyes, that beating breasts inspire*
> *To throw the 'sultry ray' of young desire,*
> *Those lips . . .*

He did not usually work like this, but his love for Annette was

worth the crafting. Normally he liked to compose while walking. He preferred to walk for a long time in solitude until the
poem strode along with him and at last entered his mind. Sitting
with an unmade poem like this, among couplets unformed by
footfall, he could only go slowly:

> *Those lips, whose tides of fragrance . . .*

Dreaming of kisses was one thing, to taste them, to feel them
now like an everlasting perfume—

> *Those lips, whose tides of fragrance come and go,*
> *Accordant . . .*

Thank God for his steel pen! 'Accordant' was Milton's word,
but none the worse for that. You wouldn't write a word like that
with a quill pen, not in the year seventeen hundred and ninety-
two—

> *Accordant to the cheek's unquiet glow . . .*
> *Those shadowy breasts . . .*

Dare he? Dare he?

He dare, and as he achieved it so would he read it to her:

> *Those shadowy breasts in love's soft light array'd*
> *And rising by the moon of passion swayed.*

He liked that 'moon'. Annette had spoken much about her
moon. Very breathless her moon had been on her lips with their
tides of fragrance when she'd hurried from his room.

A clock struck. It began before his mind took notice of it and
began to count. He thought it said eight. If it did, she had been
gone four hours. The world outside was dark, had been dark for
most of the intervening period. His bed was dark. What a pity
he could not, with propriety, ask her back to brighten it tonight.

On the other hand, four hours was an appropriate time to
have left her to herself. He jumped up and realized he was freezing cold, still only half dressed. He hurried to pull his clothes on
and warm himself in his greatcoat. Pausing only to smooth his
hair, he hurried to meet her.

He beat for some time on the door in the Rue Poirier. The
serving maid who answered his knock was too polite to giggle,
but she scarcely avoided giggling just the same.

He asked for Annette.

The girl beckoned him inside and found him a seat – someone trained by Madame Dufour would hardly do less – but he sensed that his request for Mademoiselle Vallon was receiving a very strange response indeed. He had come from his poem, so perhaps had lost his way in the French? Scarcely. His request had consisted of little more than her name.

Marie-Adelaïde Dufour came to greet him, holding out her hand and quite a bit of her arm as the fashion was. She spoke of the cold, the book she had just left, the impending solstice. She asked – he thought she asked – if he would like some spiced wine.

He refused. Love was not going to be an excuse for drowning his imagination in liquor again, spiced or otherwise.

'Annette – Mademoiselle Vallon – has left,' she said. She spoke the bad news suddenly. Apparently there had been the chance of a fast run home on the flood, there had been a *bateau* – was she really saying what she seemed to be saying, in this cipher of a language of theirs, or was a lover's mind, besotten with poetry and passion, mistaking the boat for an offer of a cake to go with the mull?

His mouth did not drop open. It wanted to. He forced its lips more tightly together, and the shuttered mouth, the weather-numbed nose, the eagle's cheeks, the bewilderment that blurred his eyes – he felt himself unmaking his mask particle by particle even as he tried to clench it shut – all this was too much for Madame Dufour. She excused herself and hurried away to fetch Paul Vallon.

A maid brought him a biscuit on a plate, as if he were a beggar or a dog. She came hurrying with it from the downstairs kitchen. Young women do not often have the chance to gaze upon a love-stricken man. When they do, it must be seized and shared.

The other girls stood at the head of the scullery staircase, seizing and sharing.

Paul came down from above. He descended slowly, straightening his brown notary's wig as he did so. He trod deliberately, a busy man disturbed in his hour, but willing nonetheless to oblige.

'Ah, *maître*.' The sinking vessel saves its best salvos to the last.

'Not yet, Wodswod. You flatter me. I must strive to deserve your expectations of me.' No need to understand him word for word. He sang the whole tune behind his hand, like a courtier taking snuff. 'Augustin Dufour – my host whom you have met – Augustin heard of a vessel imminent to depart downstream. He heard of it in his official capacity, you understand. My young sister' – his eye mocked his own advancing years and measured William's age as best it could – 'my young sister, your friend, was taking tea when she discovered in herself a sudden need to be on that boat.'

'Bound where, monsieur?'

'For Blois, Wodswod. She will be there by now, the river is in such flood. Unless the vessel could not stop – in which case she'll be adrift in the American Ocean, or even beyond.'

'Blois. I see.'

He did not see. There was clearly no note of hand from her, no further message. He had far too much pride to ask for one.

He thanked Paul Vallon as best he might, and went slowly back to his lodging. Walking in the gale made the words come easily –

> *Soon flies the little joy to man allowed*
> *And tears before him travel like a cloud*

He did not write them down straight away. He threw himself on his pillow in total misery. His bed had been full. Now it was empty.

ORLEANS.
TOWARDS THE FOURTH YEAR OF
FREEDOM AND YEAR ONE OF THE
REPUBLIC

William was now a deserted lover as well as a failed mathematician. He refused to wallow in self-pity. He told himself he was practised in pain. Equally, he took little interest in the calendar. First he ignored the midwinter solstice, then Christmas: each as dull as a water biscuit.

He woke early on Christmas morning, determined to beat the bells out of town. He left the city to the East, with the dawn late and to the south of him. He could not bear to travel in the opposite direction, towards Blois and Annette.

He walked briskly along the Loiret, the 'little Loire', tracing its frozen springs, its ornamental sources. It was a sad pathway of icy fountains, artificial falls – a miniature lakeland tidied up. He did as people said he should. He enjoyed it.

Full daylight was slow to come, and when it did it brought a sleet which dusted his coat like soda crystals. Once the weather had emptied itself, he saw the sun. It was sharp edged, like the full moon, and as cheerless as a snowball.

His greatcoat had again kept him sound. He kept it tucked about him like an old wagon–flap and strode among orchards and tiny fields until he was soaked in sweat. He didn't mind this. As old Ann Tyson had said when towelling him, 'You'll never take a chill from your own juice. A man isn't built like a horse.'

He turned after perhaps ten miles and began to retrace his footsteps towards the City. If he wished to be festive this

Christmas morning, he had an invitation to the Foxlowes, where he could meet 'the best people in town'. He didn't wish. The 'best people' are always middle-aged: he needed the distraction of pretty faces.

He went briefly to the Dufours. He hoped there might be a letter from Annette, a message, some form of greeting. Nobody offered him any such thing. He was much too cautious to ask. André Augustin and Madame Marie-Adelaïde volunteered any amount of cheer, but no letter. Paul did not even present himself. The black-haired little notary's clerk could be heard in the kitchen, helping the children tease the maids, then teasing them on his own account.

William returned to the Coin Maugas. Monsieur Gellet-Duvivier's salon was again crowded with cavalrymen. Some three or four of them were lodgers – an impermanent population – the rest came searching for wine, free hospitality, the imaginary availability of the emporium's needlewomen. The women were kept away from them. The Madman was many people – a divided person if ever there was – but in none of his manifestations was he a pimp. What they found was a fool and his playing cards. Since they paid nothing, both were cheap at the price.

William scarcely nodded in. His way was blocked by a dandy from Paris, his nextdoor neighbour on the landing, a man who smelled of scented wig-powder and snuff. The man made a fullness of his own, especially when he shook his head or cleared his nostrils, and was loud enough for two or three aristos. He was clearly a spy for someone – the problem was to discover who. He too cheered William's arrival, and offered to include him at a table playing cards for extravagant sums of money. William had no time for cards, and no money to gamble with aristocrats. One of their kind owed his family in England its livelihood. He had nothing to say to such people, and a great desire to box their ears.

He crept away to be alone with his notebook. Walk with it or sit at it, his poem was becoming irretrievably sad.

Christmas evening was even sadder than his poem. December the twenty-fifth was his young sister's birthday. She would be twenty today, and he hadn't seen her for an eternity. He thought of her, then of Annette, who had put herself at a distance as well. Her parting was an even worse betrayal of his love than his young mother's had been when she'd surrendered to pneumonia all those years ago. Save Annette's had been crueller, more abrupt. She had done as she had promised and gone floating off downstream like the dead woman. Still, he was used to loss, and did not intend to let hers incapacitate him. He would write and read his way into the New Year. He refused to drink away his frustrations with a pack of cavalrymen.

After an hour's distracted scribbling, he sought his bed. Unfortunately his bed was small and its memories ached. He did not think he could sleep among so many reminders of betrayal and aloneness. Then he thought: it is only when a young man has company that he cannot sleep. Lonely he sleeps. Annette was not here. He slept.

Even for a deserted lover, morning was still the best part of the day. His fellow lodgers weren't up, or if they were they were out, and riding slippery horses under grey skies. Only officers from regiments of cavalry were accommodated at the Coin Maugas. Being cavalrymen, they either paraded or they hunted. That is they rode their horses in noisy groups over the bridge and away into the dripping woods of the Salogne. The only sounds from the big room would be of maids muttering and mopping, the comforting rasp and rustle of the fire being raked clean and kindling being spread.

Monsieur Gellet-Duvivier brought breakfast. He was losing control of his household. The maids refused to come upstairs on solitary errands, presumably because of the cavalry officers, who had country manners with women.

The Demoiselle was not allowed to wait on Wodswod any longer, or not at times when he might still be in his nightshirt or somewhat less. Not now he had revealed himself, or allowed the young woman to reveal him, as a man who entertained a person of a certain age and sex in his rooms including possibly his bedroom without the protection of her brother. William did not know of this embargo, but he could guess at what the man guessed at, and his conclusions made him bad-tempered.

His host and landlord irritated him in the morning, partly because he wasn't his daughter, mostly because there is nothing so disturbing as a fool being disagreeable. Early mornings after late night drinking – and these mornings were frequent – made Monsieur Gellet-Duvivier highly disagreeable indeed.

On the morning of Tuesday the third of January in the year of Our Lord seventeen hundred and ninety-three, as the Madman continued to call it in the teeth of mounting odds, he still had not licensed the wistful Demoiselle to bring breakfast. William's landlord and now host produced smoked venison in her place, and felt he should serve it with a smile.

The smile was not an improvement. Nor was it necessary. Fresh bread, hot jam and smoked venison made this the best breakfast of all, better than spiced sausage, better than pike still dripping from the souse, especially when the milk jug was still warm from a clean cow, and with not too much water added.

'There will be a romp today,' Monsieur Gellet-Duvivier said, prancing about the room. 'Yes, Wodswod, you can believe me before God when I say we shall make a romp of it. Just you wait and see!'

'A romp, sir?' Did the fool mean a kiss-dance, a disruption or a chestnut? He saw no need to ask. The smoked venison melting in the mouth transcended every linguistic consideration.

'That apothecary, Besserve—'

'Ah! The great revolutionary!'

'The very man, young sir.'

'He of the dubious philtres and formidable imprecations?'

'Monsieur is very exact. He is this day about to smoke a swarm of the indolent poor from their steaming hives and lure them to Paris.'

'How will they go, and how will they afford to get there?'

'They'll go on their own two feet, monsieur. And since none of them can afford shoes the journey will cost them nothing.'

'And why should they go to Paris?' He envied them both their journey and their distraction. 'To petition the National Assembly, I suppose? Such a right of access to the very seat of government represents a notable constitutional advance.' Seeing his host's face darken further – a year's grief-stricken drinking had already taken it almost as far as it could go – he added quickly, 'Come, sir. Frenchmen should be proud of their representation in this Assembly. You have won rights which are the envy and admiration of the world.'

'Words, Wodswod. Words and wind.' He was full of both of them today. 'Your so-called National Assembly was known as the Constituent Assembly until some few weeks ago.'

'I beg its pardon!'

'It now calls itself the Legislative Assembly. It's not even a talking shop. It's a shouting shop, and in any event subsidiary to the Commune of Paris.' The Madman sat himself down at Wordworth's table and sliced himself some venison, a gesture of political complicity the poet could do without. 'Listen, young sir. I have lived some several summers in advance of you, and more than a dozen winters!' The sum of so many sorrows threatened to make him cry, but he gulped and said, 'Names, sir, names and nonsense. Believe me, you do not bring about progress simply by seizing the babe called Yesterday and rechristening her Tomorrow. No, Monsieur Wodswod, you do *not*!'

This was an unanswerable piece of wisdom, and they chewed on it in silence. William placed his nose closer to the venison and breathed defensively. If there was to be a petition he must go along with it. That much was clear. It was in accord with his curiosity and very possibly with his political ideals. Besides, Paris was full of all sorts of distractions that Orléans demonstrably lacked. Helen Maria Williams was one of them, and Mrs Charlotte Smith's letter to her was already growing limp with handling.

He must have let slip something of his intention. The Madman picked up the plate of sliced deer and left with a sniff and in something very close to a huff. William had scarcely found himself a shirt and tucked it about his waist before his host's place was taken by Paul Vallon, who until now had been conspicuously absent during these painful days.

'You do not intend to join such a rabble, Wodswod? You cannot! Williams, my dearest friend, my sister will be deeply disappointed in you.'

'I am somewhat disappointed in your sister, Vallon.'

'As a language teacher? Listen to you!' The little man clapped his hands and laughed, just as if he were teasing a kitchen maid. 'You are making progress, Williams, I'll grant you that much. Believe me you make progress. I myself—' he laid an ornate hand upon his heart as if to launch a great truth upon the world— 'I, myself, I know *nothing* of language teaching, nothing. But be assured on one point – I speak without condescension – my sister Marie Anne still has a more precise pronunciation than you.'

Wordsworth began to feel for his boots, like any Cumberland farmer surprised at his breakfast by a tinker. Give him his boots and he could stride away from such rubbish.

'She still has things to teach you, Wodswod. If only you had called upon me at my lodgings to pick up her tablet of explanation.'

'I called on you at—'

'And *expiation*, Wodswod. You do not think she left such a friend as you *willingly*, do you, my Williams?' He began to pluck sleeves, William's and his own, as if upset at the bitterness and misunderstanding he began to detect in his friend, while finding himself innocent of causing them. 'I at least thought you would call since, if not at once, to see if poor little Annette had written. You will disappoint her.'

'So give me my letter.'

'Letters, Williams. Did you not detect my plural? The plural is hidden in French, but never completely invisible. You see how you still have need of her!' He touched Wordsworth's hand, then tapped it away, giving him nothing. 'Yes, *letters*. She has written almost daily. I'm afraid I forgot in my excitement to tell you. Such a *bundle* of *billets-doux*! Really there was no way I could bring them from my lodgings all at once and by myself. And which one to bring as an *apéritif*? You must go there and ask for them!'

And demean himself again in front of Madame Dufour or a giggling parlour maid? Williams decided this improbably bulky correspondence would have to wait until later. If it existed. The fascination of the young woman they spoke of made him stay with the subject, just the same. 'So your sister keeps at home in Blois?'

'One could say that.'

'She is not back in Orléans, at any rate?'

'Not precisely, no. But the minute she gets wind of your intention – and I shall let her know at once – believe me, my friend, she will hurry here on the instant.'

Too many untrustworthy expressions of friendship, Williams thought. And at least one untrustworthy friend. He gazed at Paul. 'My mind is made up, Maître Vallon.'

'"Maître"? Dearest man – again you flatter me!' He watched Williams stoop and fasten those shoes that were so nearly boots. 'If you must go, my Wodswod, I insist you march bare-footed – bare-legged also if your knees can draw breath in the cold. Bare buttocks would ensure your safety entire. That march will be made up of two sorts of men, my friend. There will be those who will kill you in order to possess your footwear, and those who will kill you for wearing it in the first place.'

'Nonsense, Vallon. I walk abroad constantly in these things.'

'You do, my dear, and a great pity it is.'

'I travel quite safely in them. Your sister tells me that no self-respecting Frenchman would give them a second glance.'

'My little sister is a gentlewoman, Wodswod. Naturally she is very exact in matters of taste, but exact according to the standards of her own class. There will be another class of women among those marchers, believe me there will. French women who walk in processions will kill a man for any reason they can think of, and often for no reason at all. I hear they throttled an old fellow in Angers yesterday on no better grounds than that he smelled of soap and clean linen.'

'Angers is a long way from here, Monsieur Vallon.'

'So is Paris, my dear sir. And I do not think a gentleman will be allowed to reach it by walking. Not if he marches in a crowd. The crowd won't let him.'

'As you keep on telling me.'

'It's my very best advice, my dear.'

Having given his best advice, Annette's brother Paul nodded brightly and left him. Unfortunately the conceited little rascal left him with thoughts of Annette, hints of letters indolently concealed, and all manner of unsettling images of her else. A brave man would march to Paris. A man would march to Paris. A lover could not. Not today. Not on this march. The only march would be towards those letters, and the only bravery, the only manliness would be seen in how long he could resist doing so.

These thoughts were interrupted by a scuffle on the stairs halfway below him, a raised voice as between man and woman, the man speaking softly, the woman protesting. The sound was unusual only because it was so early in the morning, and the woman's voice – surely the voice belonged to the voiceless Demoiselle?

The idea that one of the cavalrymen was treating her as if she were grown up, and a serving girl he could practise his tricks upon . . . William snatched his coat, as if to announce he was stepping outside anyway, and hurried below.

The new lodger, the dandy, stood on the main staircase. The young woman, dishevelled and still sobbing, was vanishing through the street door. William pushed past the man and rushed downwards. Beyond the door he could hear a crowd, the crowd bound for Paris, or a rabble bound for that crowd. The young woman disappeared among them.

He bumped into Monsieur Gellet-Duvivier, emerging from among his needlewomen to inquire into the disturbance.

William's French was not hasty enough. He still did not know her name. He pushed the girl's father aside and called him to follow. As he did so, he saw the young woman, he saw the weeping girl, and realized that it wasn't the Demoiselle. So his rush downstairs had been a mistake.

Then he noticed that this girl wasn't weeping. He gazed wildly about. As so often with faces in a crowd, he couldn't be certain whether the Gellet-Duvivier girl was here or not. Worse, his pursuit of her had led him to attract the attention of people it would be safer to steal among unnoticed.

His quest took him a good many running steps forward, going this way and that, darting wild-eyed and anxious. A man shouldn't try to run in a crowd, stumble about or gasp his annoyance. He knew this too late. He barged against shoulders which refused to give way, men and women who parted briefly but only to contain him, not to let him through.

They closed their mouths sharply, or opened them from habit and by reflex, but no sound came – not in words, anyway. He heard the expulsion of breath, and – worse – its sucking in through the lips and teeth. They eyed his coat with suspicion and his boots with the contempt of pure envy.

'He's a spy,' one said, starting at the other end of him. 'Look at his hairs.'

'A spy from abroad, or just *one of them*? His hairs are his give-away.'

He wore his hair short rather than long, though longer than very short because of the interval of pain that had elapsed since he had fallen in love. There was danger in wearing it long and very little safety in wearing it short. It was of a length or a shortness – and crowds have varied opinions on these matters – at which a man might set an ornamental wig upon it. A man could wear an ornamental wig for any number of reasons, but all of those reasons would make him an enemy of impoverished people.

'If he's a spy he must be searched!'

'Stripped and then searched.'

'Closely examined – now and at once!'

Some began to lay claim to his clothes, which were unique in having holes only where the tailor had cut them. Others wanted him strangled now rather than afterwards, since a naked man is an even greater affront to public decency than a naked woman, and fewer questions will be asked if it is plain that he was dead before he was stripped bare rather than stripped bare before he was dead.

William began to have a fairer idea of what was being planned for him, just as somebody objected, 'That kind of reasoning might satisfy a farmer and his sons. They can wring a stranger's neck as soon as they meet him – or save it till later. It's all right if you live at the end of a wood with a dunghill to bury what the sow won't eat for you.'

'True – very true.'

'We are townsmen, citizens of a great city. If we are to take revolutionary action in order to uphold the constitution—'

'Exactly. That's our argument.'

'Then we must proceed in a way that will satisfy the watch committee. We must search him first.'

'That's right. Croak him and search him.'

'Search him then croak him.'

William found he could understand every syllable except 'croak', and whatever this word was in its semantic origins its meaning was even clearer than the ones he understood.

Just then a voice called, 'You will find no papers on the Englishman!' The voice came from the back, but it was familiar.

'An English, is he? Then he's one of those plotters who swindled us with cheap goods, then refused us any salt.'

'Their salt was a scandal.'

'Never mind their salt. What about the green corn they sold us?'

'And the hailstones! Those things weren't natural.'

'That was last year, citizen. In fact, for the last day or so, it's been the year before last.' Shovel Hat it was who had been speaking, and he pushed himself to the front as if he belonged there. 'The Englishman has a proper set of papers, believe me – papers from his King, papers granting entry, cachets of acceptance from Rouen and Paris—'

'Rouen and—'

'Unfortunately those papers are missing.'

'They were impounded by a comrade of yours, citizen,' William put in.

'Impounded, and properly so. On the bridge. Correct. And now that comrade is missing also. And a comrade of that comrade as well.'

The mystery lay heavily between them.

'So let us consider just what we have here, citizens. What we have is an Englishman who offers his papers to a citizen who has since gone missing, and whose friend is also missing. If the Englishman can be shown to have reacquired his papers, then that would be very suggestive indeed.'

'Most suggestive.'

'If we search him—'

'Let that wait until we stand before the Tribunal.'

As far as William knew, there was no Tribunal, or not a proper one, but its absence, or its lack of propriety if it existed, made the threat of appearing before it seem infinitely menacing. A proper committee could not harm a proper man, he reasoned. An improper one might do him all kinds of mischief, with no need to move him further than the nearest lantern bracket. He was in great peril, and he knew it.

'You tried to give us some letters, I seem to remember. One was to Citizen Foxlowe, also an Englishman. Show it to me, please.'

'I can't. I have delivered it to Mr Foxlowe in the interval.'

'So the letter for the Englishman is missing. You had another letter as well.'

'Yes – and, if you remember, I was to deliver it that very afternoon.' He intended to preserve that letter at any cost, beyond life itself if need be. 'The lady has now travelled to Paris.'

'So the lady is missing as well! You have been delivering a great many letters, citizen, and with some very peculiar consequences.'

'There were only two letters,' William said. 'The rest were my documents of accreditation, which were impounded by your friend.'

'All of them missing.'

The fellow had the tenacity of his kind, together with several of the incidental gifts of a great advocate. William wondered if Paul Vallon could ever be half as effective, at least before jurors such as these. He appeared to see evil in everything that was said to him, and he knew how to scorn the devil by laughing. He went off in another direction. 'You were with a young woman when I last had occasion to speak to you.'

'Yes – you saved my life.'

'To what purpose, I wonder. To what purpose.'

'You did the town a bad turn then, my friend.' That was a voice from behind them.

'And where is the young woman – missing, I suppose?'

'She *is* – mark my word! Look at his face.'

'The citizenness is in Blois.'

'Blois? Blois of all places. You're sure she's in Blois, citizen?'

'Yes, I'm certain of it.'

'You sent her away with one of your letters, perhaps?'

'No.'

'Well, he'll have given her something to shift her, I'm sure of it! I don't like the sound of Blois. None of us here like Blois, do we? There are some very strange people in Blois, I can tell you that. Aristocrats, returned *émigrés*, *ci-devants*, *soi-disants*, enemies of the constitution. People like—'

'Monsieur is speaking a trifle fast for me.'

'"Mon*sieur*"? "Monsieur" is a dangerous word, *mon*sieur. People like you, I was about to say: you're the sort of devils who live at Blois. Before God, I was right – wasn't I, *mon*sieur? You're not drinking tea at the Coin Maugas now!'

Hadn't Brissot told him in Paris never to say 'sir' to a citizen? Well, he'd done it now, hadn't he? He'd let his English tongue run away with him, albeit in French.

William was in the middle of a crowd that threatened to digest him. It is possible to run away from a crowd, but only if you're on the edge of it. Once you're inside it, you can no more escape than a worm can wriggle out of a rooster's belly. Keen in these matters as he was, William knew that worms only travel in one direction. He was moving downwards.

He still glanced about him for the Demoiselle. She was young. She was without deceit. She spoke colloquial French, when she spoke at all. If he could find her, if she saw his plight, she would carry enough conviction to save him. Or she would if she weren't a rich man's daughter.

He was spared by the arrival of the procession's leader. The Apothecary Besserve descended from the meeting rooms of the Friends of the Constitution and planted himself astride a grey horse that had been fetched out of an alley an instant before his arrival.

It was a stallion some twenty-two hands high, a grey with plaited mane and a modesty curb on its tail. It was more than a gentleman's horse. It was an aristocrat's horse, fitting for a Colonel of Cuirassiers. Those who stood nearest to it remarked aloud on most of it, the prevalence of its whitebreads most of all. These looked uncomfortably large for a fast gallop, but Besserve's friends pointed out that, properly dried, these organs were recognized to be a potent ingredient in the apothecary's art, whether tinctured in oil or swallowed from a knife blade as a powder. A dram that can cure everything from baldness to the thrush is not to be sneezed at, save by hungry men and women lacking warmth and imagination.

William tried to concentrate on Besserve and his horse, since this is what most other people were doing. It was difficult to overlook such a lofty beast. It towered so far above the sea of wild faces that even its testicles hung higher than a tall man's ears. He was unable to give it his total attention because he heard Floppy Hat say, 'Never mind the Tribunal, friends – not now we're moving. Paris calls. It's marching time! The further we go from here, the nearer we'll be to the tall trees. Let's get ourselves a step or two down the road; there'll be dungpiles out there, and pigs—'

'*And* wild boar!'

'Yes, it'll be peasant justice out there. No need for the Watch Committee once we've got him among the bushes.'

William was slow to understand their excited grunting. He tried to edge towards the margins of the crowd, but there were hands to halt him and guide him, and women's voices to call, 'No, no, citizen! This way, *citizen.*' Not since old Ann brushed his coat had female fingers caressed his clothing in such an ecstasy of caring. They held him, then pressed him backwards as Besserve moved among them on his horse. The beast had awkward feet. They were shod in thick iron for a long march, and were best avoided.

His mind grew numb, numb from people's breath, their butting and probing. When he walked he thought usually of poems, but this wasn't walking. He thought, just the same. His mind, being strangled, filled with the objects of his loathing. He thought of Parnell. He plodded with Dyer.

William went slowly. It was a slow crowd to walk among. After a half mile had taken an hour of his time, and he'd seen no further glimpse of the Demoiselle, he saw a chance to break away. He left Besserve's stirrup and pushed towards an alley that ran behind the last houses in town.

Hardly surprising he was caught almost as soon as he started.

Before he had taken ten steps to his left he felt an old woman's fingers on his neck. She snatched at him and hung on behind him, a frailty almost without weight yet full of force, something with a claw like a skeleton's but as irresistible as Father Time or Death itself. He was tripped flat on his face, kicked, lifted up, laughed over, and set upon his feet again. The old woman's fingers still clung to him.

'He's trying to run away, citizen.'

'No, not run away, citizen. *Disappear!*'

'He's just handed himself a letter!'

Laughter. Discordant and jeering laughter. He was to become a victim of the great and universal passions of men and all manner of other verbal formulations that rushed from his mind almost as soon as they rushed in, largely because he was being brutalized by women and spat upon by their children.

'Stay with us, citizen, and you'll live longer!'

'Not much longer, but longer!'

What a merry time they were having with him, at and beyond the town's edge.

To give their wits a better hold on him they fastened his neck to a rope.

ORLEANS.
JANUARY 1792. THE ROAD TO
MURDER

It seemed to have been dark all day, but it was dark in earnest when Annette arrived at the Rue Poirier. She was in a hurry, too much so for good manners. She could scarcely contain her anxiety during her exchange of greetings with Marie-Victorie-Adelaïde. Even when they had blurted out their pieces of news and shortened their names for one another – Madame was married, and older, and their former intimacy could not be resumed in a mere sentence or two – she had to endure an endless sputtering of kisses from a personal maid, a wetness like the sucking of oysters when such luxuries were available to be sucked. Madame Dufour meant well, and her maid merely followed her example, but Annette was in a fever because Williams had not written to her, not one letter, not a note, not a line for a whole half month. She rushed upstairs as soon as possible, saying she needed to go to her room, but in fact to find her brother Paul. He was the family's post-bag. As officers of the courts, he and André Augustin had the easiest and cheapest access to the mails.

He was not there, of course. Had he been there, someone would have mentioned the fact and sent for him. Nor would he be at work. It was the witching hour, one of many, when noblemen and the indolent among the bourgeoisie deceived themselves with playing cards.

Paul's room was neat, she had to give him that. It always looked as if a doll slept in it. He was the brother she most cared for, and to step inside the tidiness he created was like coming home.

Then she saw the bundle of letters that lay on the corner of his work table. Among so much order where could they hide? Six of them – no: seven, all firmly addressed with one of Vergez's iron pens, and sealed with her own seal.

Not one of her letters to Williams had been delivered, not one. Worse, the last one she came to was on the Dufours' own paper and disfigured with splashes from a badly cut and hastily dipped quill. This was the one explaining her hurried departure. It had not been delivered either.

She ran back downstairs. It wouldn't be easy to leave the house with any appearance of decorum.

Adelaïde was already organizing her kitchen for the evening meal. She was surrounded by nearly all of her womenfolk, babes and wet nurses as well. The place smelled agreeably of soup, hot linen and human milk. It was disorderly but calm.

Annette blurted out that she had an urgent message for Paul from one of his brothers, and everyone smiled at her with much understanding, or was too discreet to meet her eyes at all. As she went towards the house door their amusement followed her.

Her coat was unfastened. She still wore her bonnet. She did what she could to straighten her appearance before braving the upstairs salon at the Coin Maugas. Paul was not there. There was nobody there she knew. Even the uniforms were unfamiliar.

Her request for Monsieur Vallon was met with yawns, and when she asked, albeit hesitantly, if anyone had seen the Englishman Wodswod there was a tut of disapproval.

'He's gone marching,' someone muttered. 'He's gone to Paris to fetch soup.'

'To Paris?'

'Yes, Paris.' The speaker slewed in his chair, smiled, and touched his extended knee, as if showing her a nearer place. 'You'll have heard tell of Paris?'

Her first thought was that he had gone searching for his precious poetess. The moment she'd leapt to such a wild conclusion, she realized how love-sick she was. The knowledge did nothing to increase her sense of safety.

He was not in his room, though his books were still there. So were his valises.

Her copy of *The Confessions*, her dead father's copy, lay crushed in his bed like a giant butterfly a child has rolled on in the grass. It was such an image of careless yet frustrated longing that she nearly burst into tears at the sight of it.

She turned from his room, wondering what to do next.

She was stopped in the passageway by a man of roughly her own age. He stepped from the door next to Williams' as if he had been waiting for her, and barred her way. 'I heard you ask for the Englishman,' he said scornfully. He was in shirtsleeves and wore no shoes on his stockinged feet. She recognized him as the Paris Dandy she had seen arriving with Monsieur Gellet-Duvivier at the very moment she had fled from Williams' room, her brain whirring at her own predicament and her lover's explanation for the scabs upon his leg.

The man caught her upper arm. 'If you have a mind to loiter in gentlemen's rooms,' he smiled, 'I think you'll find mine has the better view.' His hands moved to her shoulders in a very practised way, and began to feel inside the collar of her coat.

Her anger was so violent that he freed her immediately. She was glad of this. His grip was much too strong for her to have broken it otherwise.

'This Englishman Wodswort,' he said, 'he's no sort of man for a woman of your class. He's a constitutionalist and a republican – as well as being some kind of spy, I daresay. He scribbles messages in books all day.'

'Where is he, monsieur?' Better for a woman with a pretty face to question one man direct than try to interrogate a room full of cardplayers who have been drinking all afternoon.

'Paris. He'll be on the road by now. He's joined some riff-raff in a petition to the Assembly, the silly fool. They'll never listen to him, not dressed in a suit and clean stockings. I thought I heard Captain De Grouchy tell you as much?'

She had already broken away to find Gellet-Duvivier on the stairs. The Madman was wild-eyed but sober. He wore, or half wore, his uniform as a grenadier in the National Guard. His sword belt was proving stubborn at the buckle, so he was trying to struggle into it like an old lady into her binder.

She heard her brother Paul shouting behind him, 'Patron! Patron! When we've found where they've hung the Englishman, *patron*, he'll present us with a most unusual sight. I insist we have a painter take a portrait for my sister. I'll bet a hundred livres to anything he's got in his purse, I'll bet that, even though those ruffians have throttled him an hour over a slow coal, I'll bet he dies with his tongue in – he's a fellow with so little in the way of words!'

It takes a little time for a man in his full spate of drunken oratory to recognize there's a woman among the figures ahead of him on the stairs, and a little longer still to identify her as his sister. Paul recognized her, blanched, recoiled, crushed her in his arms and said nothing.

'Well, he'll be dead, however he dies,' Gellet-Duvivier said. 'I've been told he was seen with half the crones in town fingering his neck, and the rest of them cutting cloth from his jacket and trousers.' Seeing Paul's efforts to tut him on to a change of tack, he told Annette, 'I shall hang some of them if he's dead, and that's a fact.' He gave the matter his full attention as a grenadier before adding, 'I took Wodswod to be a royalist and a gentleman. As a businessman I've never had anything against the English – not a single thing! But he refused a second helping of venison this morning to go marching off to Paris! Not marching, either.' And it was here the Madman told them both a confusing story, of himself being disturbed in his workrooms by a jostling on the stairs, then being brushed aside by Wodswod leaping from the house and yelling something about a young woman lost in the crowd bound for Paris. 'I thought he meant you, Mademoiselle Vallon.' Whatever the trouble was, Williams had apparently been fighting over it with the new lodger, hence the sound that had brought the Madman rushing from his work. 'I'll not have women being wrestled over, not in my house,' the Madman added pointedly. 'Nor being pursued out of doors in consequence!'

Annette's brain would have numbed with jealousy, save her other anxieties were more pressing. 'Has he really gone marching to Paris?' she asked. 'Or is he simply swept away in the riot?'

'Yes, to Paris. I saw him with that scoundrel Besserve. Not that Besserve'll do a man any harm, except sell him poison from a dirty bottle.'

'That I can accept,' Paul said, enthusiastic again to the last detail. 'I accept that Besserve is a scoundrel, and I accept that he's an honest one. But he has a following of ruffians who'll do for him and the Englishman too, if my judgement is anything to go by.'

Annette had never known Paul to exercise anything in the way of judgement before, but during the last terrible minutes she had heard nothing to suggest her brother's instincts were wrong.

She watched the Madman hang his sword to his liking, turn on his heels and go stomping off, followed by her brother. She went slowly after them, wondering whether to follow them, or whether there was anything more effective she could do.

A figure stepped from the shadows at the corner of the Rue de Tabour and touched her wrist. She recognized a familiar face from Blois, one of the sons of Lacaille the gunsmith, or one of his apprentices. 'Mademoiselle Vallon?'

'If you like. I know a Lacaille when I see one.'

'I've been watching out for you for over a week now. Guyon de Montlivault is a name that will indicate our business together.'

'How did you come from Blois?'

'I walked. It's a day and most of a night. I have a horse now, if you'll ride with me. I met your friend's friends in the forest, and they have mounts aplenty. They live like gentlemen that lot, believe me, albeit in a draughty hall.'

'My friend is dead.'

'Perhaps. Or perhaps we crossed the river in time to prevent it. And perhaps you'll ride with me and find out.'

His horse was tethered to the corner post of the arcade. It had clearly been there for some time. Seeing her hesitate, he said, 'A woman can do anything now. She can go as she pleases – so long as she does it as by right.'

Impossible to ride pillion or up front on a horse dressed in a Loire saddle, unless the beast was gone in the backbone. This one was wearing a pack saddle, not one shaped for panniers, but a kind of wrap-round leather corset with straps. It looked suitable for carrying firewood – or a bundle of muskets.

She climbed up behind the Lacaille lad, to save him sitting with his arms around her. As she did so, he said, 'There are fifty of us.'

'I hear it whispered there are five thousand on the march.'

'Perhaps. And perhaps the whisper can't count and there's only five hundred.' After a few dozen paces, he added, 'However many there are, they won't be looking for a fight, only for plunder. Whereas we are armed and ready to defend our principles.'

She didn't ask him about those, in case she embarrassed his inability to answer. Instead she told him that the National Guard had been alerted that the march was growing violent.

'Let's hope they can stop it, then. We leave the Guard alone, and they leave us alone. That's our compact along the Loire. They don't like us, but they like what we do.'

'Providing we do it quietly.'

'No, Demoiselle Vallon. Providing we do it quickly.'

'Yes, quickly,' she thought, in a terror again. But could quickly ever be quick enough for Williams, or call back the time they had lost in between? Murder wasn't noted for being slow in France, and even in storybooks once it was done it stayed that way.

William was bruised, though not worse than when he'd been skating as a boy. He was bleeding from his nose and his finger ends. He remembered a winter's morning on Helvellyn when his veins had burst open because of the hardness of the frost. They had not spoiled the climb. Bruises and blood were things a child could bear.

He wished worse things had been done to him a few minutes ago, kicks to the chest, blows on the head, savageries to dizzy his fear and numb him to unconsciousness even. The idea of struggling skywards on a rope's end, kicking and retching like a slit pig, unable even to bring up his own vomit . . .

He had his moment of hope, dragged as he was by the neck like this. Every death has its hope. He blundered at last upon the Demoiselle. He was actually being dragged along now, this instant, by a fellow who walked beside her and led her too. He recognized her walk, her aloofness, her slimness, her ankles and neck.

Then they stopped, he stumbled, and she turned. It wasn't the Demoiselle Gellet-Duvivier at all, merely a young woman who resembled her in every conceivable way.

The noose loosened, tightened again. They were tying him against a tree. He heard Shovel Hat's voice, he lost it. He gazed into the face of the demoiselle who was not the Demoiselle. He realized, fighting for breath as he was, that life is full of young women who resemble the young women that life is full of. This was a constricting idea that refused to leave his brain, because the noose was tightening endlessly round his neck. The string hurt him moderately at the apex of the knot, and immoderately on the inside of his head. Pain, he knew from experience, never made itself felt exactly when he expected it. Like young women, it was always somewhere else.

The pressure slackened. He no longer saw or sought the Demoiselle. He gulped air and gazed upon Shovel Hat.

Shovel Hat gazed upon him.

Shovel Hat had promised him he would die like this. The man had ordered him to be trussed to almost the first tree in the Forest of Orléans so he could discuss his revenge with him.

William had come to France to study men like Shovel Hat, and Shovel Hat was determined to make him suffer for it. William had tried to put things right between them even as they'd pinioned him. 'Citizen!' he'd cried in that voice of his which could burst so strongly out of his silences. 'Citizen, we have met on several occasions, but I do not yet know your name.'

'Your own is Wodswod. I have seen it on your papers!'

'Wordsworth.'

'Not a name to exercise a Frenchman's tongue any longer, Wodswort. I shall see it rots on your own.' He closed his fingers suggestively about William's neck, while everyone and everything, including the trees and the invisible stars, laughed encouragingly at the wit of him. 'My name is Goulu, citizen. Goulu. There's an easy name to choke on.' He allowed William a little air, so he could think, then choked him towards further contemplation.

'Goulu means "fatty",' William protested at last. 'And you, if I may say so, citizen—'

'Say on, citizen—'

The words would not come. He was allowed air but the words simply would not join together. Shovel Hat, Goulu, know him as he would, was now one of a forest of faces, each of them as jaundiced in the lamplight as winter leaves. Even as William tried to communicate to these faces, they seemed to disintegrate and fall. Or perhaps it was that actual leaves fell past them from the winter poles. Only their eyes were steady, their eyes and their implacable knots and hands. He knew what they saw.

They saw not just a bourgeois but a foreign bourgeois in a funny suit, a fellow who had pushed one of their heroes into a puddle, and whom Shovel Hat and his friend had rescued before his back could be broken by means of a decent wrestling man's stratagem, like folding it over a knee or a sharp stone.

And where was that wrestling man now? He had disappeared from the face of the earth without leaving so much as a tooth-mark behind him. There were several women here to testify to the fact.

'Say on, citizen.'

'And you, Citizen Goulu, are, if I may say, extremely slim.'

'I *was* fat,' Goulu roared. 'I used to be lucky enough to have a good belly on me, didn't I, my friends? I was a man who did-n't have to care about my knees, count my toes, or fret myself about what my smallpiece was doing. It could amuse itself as it would, get me as many bastards as it liked. Nothing to do with me. We had a belly between us. We lived across the hill from one another, him and me, and so did my priest at confession.' Shovel Hat's hands circled William's neck joyously. 'Yes, I used to have a belly, but now, as you say, I'm extremely slim.'

William began to feel giddy. His eyes ached.

'I'm not slim. I'm *skinny*! I've been starved away. I've had the goodness eaten out of me by stoats like you. Well, my belly is going to be revenged on your neck, mon*sieur*.'

William was not yet twenty-two years old, and already with a rope round his neck. Once more he saw how easily this French business could be the death of him. If he lived, he told himself, he'd have bad dreams for the rest of his years.

Just then Besserve allowed himself to ride by. He did so with some diffidence. Besserve was a revolutionary. He wasn't the man for mobs. Mobs took no notice of their leaders. Recently in Paris they had fallen in love with the King. He knew what they were doing with William. If they had done it, it would have been done, and there would have been the end of it. Unfortunately, they hadn't quite done it yet. He stopped his horse.

'You can't do that to the Englishman. Strangers are strangers and can be treated as such. Foreigners on the other hand are foreigners, and their ministers complain if you harm them.' He examined William with distaste. William was a mess. 'Besides, many sympathizers come to us from England.'

Shovel Hat searched his mouth for saliva and annoyed Besserve's horse with what he found. 'Sympathizers need feeding,' he said. 'They steal the food from our bellies.'

'Brissot says you should declare war on every country that has a king,' William said helpfully. 'Or a queen.' He was once again surprised at how little progress his acquaintance with Brissot could make for him.

'Hang Brissot,' Shovel Hat said.

'Somebody will,' Besserve agreed. 'My advice to you is — release the Englishman.'

'He's for the lantern.'

'There are no lanterns in a forest.'

'Wait till the moon is up. I know a tree to swing it in!'

The poetry of Wordsworth's situation made them roar with anticipation.

'Think how well that suit will look kicking in the moonlight.'

'That suit is not going to hang,' Shovel Hat said. 'He hangs without his suit. The suit belongs to me.'

A woman giggled and said deeply unpleasant words about the fate of suits whose owners have hanged in them. William tried not to remember them. He couldn't bear to hear the voice of women utter blasphemy.

'You must not, dare not hang the Englishman.'

'I've got an itch to hang someone,' Shovel Hat said. 'If not an Englishman, an apothecary will do.' He caught hold of Besserve's foot as if to pull it from its stirrup. When Besserve kicked out at him, he reversed his pressure and tossed him the other way, clean over and out of his saddle.

Besserve fell among excited hands, and was dropped at William's feet. 'I'm one of you,' he protested. 'I'm a Friend and a Jacobin!'

'You may well be, but your horse clearly isn't,' Shovel Hat said in a reasonable tone of voice. 'A horse can't be a member of the Club.'

'Not a club that meets upstairs,' someone chuckled.

'No – the horse is an intruder and most clearly a spy,' Shovel Hat went on. 'Why else is he here, sneaking on poor folk who never get to ride a horse, and only rarely to eat one? Why else is he here?'

'Why else indeed?'

'And as such must stand condemned. True I've never seen the hanging of a horse before,' Shovel Hat said. 'But the hanging of a horse is a sentence in common law.'

'It's a sentence in common law.'

'A sentence that has been carried out, for the murder of horsemen, treading on babies, witchcraft and such like. Now this is a tall horse. It's also the only horse we have. As such, it will be a fine horse to hang. We'll hang the Englishman on one side of the fire, the horse on the other, and see who gallops the longest.'

'Not my fine horse, lads. Citizens. It's a thoroughbred. Not that one. It's a breeding stallion.'

'Stallions cook better than mares,' a woman said. 'Bulls taste better than cows, and rams than ewes. It's a fact well known.'

'I'll say it again,' Besserve cried, springing to his feet. 'Citizens, I'm one of you. Citizen Goulu, you explain to them.'

He tried to remount but Shovel Hat stopped him. 'Without your horse, you'll be one of us even more.'

'And his horse will be one of us too.'

'Once we've eaten the beast, it most assuredly will.'

'We'll all gallop better with some red meat in our bellies, Citizen Besserve.'

Somebody knocked the apothecary on the head, not a fatal blow, and not a particularly fierce one, but sufficient to remind him that there was one set of laws for the Friends of the Constitution and another set for the Forest, and the Forest made the best ones.

William lost interest for a moment – perhaps the horse kicked at him or trod on his leg – but events soon had his attention again, as he was deeply interested in the language and manners of ordinary men as well as their treatment of domestic animals. He had wrung the necks of Ann Tyson's chickens in his time, but he had never strangled anything as big as a horse. Besides, these were townsfolk and not at all handy with knots. His own were working loose – he had been fingering them for some time – so it was vital he was seen to pay absolutely no attention to himself at all.

First they boiled water in an iron bucket – William had no idea why they needed water so early.

Then they replaced the stallion's harness with a rope and drew its end over a tree branch not much higher than the horse. The tree was an oak with the rough bark of an oak. It took an age to draw the noose tight and lift the beast's neck. When they had done so, the poor thing was still not suspended clear of the ground, merely sitting upright on its haunches or a little less than that. It hung the way a rabbit droops under the huntsman's fist, with its legs bunched up beneath it. It struggled and began to strangle, but much too slowly.

The owner of the steaming pot watched it with interest. She was a middle-aged woman, or coarse-skinned enough to seem middle-aged, even if no more than thirty. She was one of the 'bare-chested ones'. They wore skirts only, without blouse or upper petticoat, then wrapped themselves away under shawls and other cloths or not, according to the weather, coddling their breasts in any old clout to hand, much as a fisherman protects a brace of freshly caught salmon.

She drew a hand from beneath her shawls and other comforts, a hand with a knife in it. She sat with her back to William, so he became aware of this slowly. She leant towards the stallion, which shook the tree and screamed, half-dead though it was. She threw something into her bucket, and those who were nearest applauded.

'The seed spoils the meat,' she said. She spoke as if quoting something. 'Leave the seed hanging and the male tastes brackish.'

The idea of castrating a conscious animal always nauseated William, though he'd seen men do it to lambs every year of his life. He became aware that some of the women who stood nearest were eyeing him with fresh interest.

The one who had operated on the stallion now turned her attention to him. 'It hurts them to cut them,' she observed to William. 'But once you've sliced them off they don't feel a thing.' She winked at him, never an attractive overture from a woman with a knife in her hand. 'Which shows how valueless they are.' She examined William's Adam's apple, then dried her blade on his hair. 'A bit like heads, really.'

'Don't drip on his suit,' Shovel Hat called.

The disobedience of woman was a favourite topic in much of William's early reading, beginning with Genesis; so he shouldn't have been surprised at her reluctance to move away from his clothing. He was by now completely free of his bonds and desperate to conceal the fact from this harpy who stood much too close for comfort, so he was totally unprepared for what happened next. His eyes were stung with salt, his face sprayed with wet, and his Cambridge suit – or Shovel Hat's suit, according to who was looking at it – spattered, no – *splashed* – with blood. Someone had parted her scalp with a sword, though the blade had bounced off her skull.

As his eyes were blinded, so were his senses numbed and his ears abruptly deafened by the pounding of hoofs, the hysterical neighing and windy snorting of horses, followed by the clash of steel not on steel but that uglier butcher's note of cold iron striking and sometimes severing bone.

This was over quickly. Horsemen cannot maintain a charge through a forest, even when its ground foliage is slimmed by winter. Men and their women and children can easily run away through the gaps in the trees, especially when their attackers lack the will to pursue them.

William was still distracted. The injured woman ran in circles round his tree, blade in hand, shaking her head and shrieking, both of these actions squandering her blood. Fortunately her brains still held a lot of it. Meanwhile another female curled and writhed and sobbed all over him in a manner equally unpleasant, though her gestures were more friendly and she was considerably fresher of person, as well as softer about the curves and younger.

She too splashed him, with tears rather than blood, and salt water made a duller mess on his suiting. It was only when he tried to prise her loose and run away through the branches in his turn that he heard her say 'Williams', which was not his name, especially when mispronounced, and recognized who it was. It takes time to relate to objects one has long since given up for lost or severely mislaid, and the brain thinks in elaborate sentences while it adjusts to them. This was Annette, who was supposed to be in Blois but never stayed anywhere for long.

A horseman stood above them. William did not greatly enjoy the company of horses, even as hanging companions. He had been less than fond of the animals since one of them had brought his father home half dead in its saddle. This horse had a familiar figure on its back. It was the man who had cried like a barn owl at him in the forest, tripped him in a wire, and then tried to insist he was a gentleman, a nobleman even.

William helped Annette stand up from him, then climbed to his feet to thank the rider for his life. The injured woman clung to his other stirrup while the man did something brutal to her. As far as William could see he was tying knots in her head. He laughed and said, 'I don't mind sabring a lady's scalp open with my falchion. She has all that hair to bind herself together again.'

Figures came darting back through the trees, and somebody fired a gun at them. The ball passed very close to the rider's teeth – he clapped his hand to his mouth at the tingle of it – but fortunately outside his cheek. He rode off to rally his horsemen, who were clearly outnumbered. They were bold fellows in a charge, and had come dashing in, but there were too few of them to stand and fight.

It was then that William heard a sound even more insistent than Annette's voice, which he'd quietened a little by kissing the lips and nostrils and neck and ears it continued to leak from. It was a fife, or some similar kind of short pipe, and it was backed by the note of a marching side-drum or some similar beat.

A considerable body of men was on the march then at the halt behind them. 'Men of Orléans,' a voice called. 'I can see you all.' This was patently a lie, but an impressive one. 'Gather up your wives and your children and your lunch baskets, and return towards your city in small groups and in good order.'

There was a howl at this, and Shovel Hat shouted something defiant. William thought it was Shovel Hat, though one ruffian sounded very much like another in Annette's language, which was the perfect tongue for villains, because no one could understand them.

The shouts died away completely at the sound of muskets being cocked. It was the National Guard, and the hammers were drawn back by fingers of varied age. It wasn't a prettily executed piece of drill – it was downright slack – but in consequence it gave a very clear indication of just how many pieces there were. William heard dozens so there must have been hundreds. He heard the order given for the half present, and then the Guard began to move forward, with muzzles at the short point, and hammers cocked. Only a very foolish person indeed would continue to stand in front of them, and behind them too in all probability.

Again he was stood over by a tall horse, this one corseted in a strange kind of pack saddle. He had spent the last few minutes telling himself he was strong and unharmed, and very much the hero in his own story. But it was the heroine who, after a final kiss, part lifted part pushed him astride it. He found he was so bruised it was all he could do to swing his leg over.

Annette sat herself behind him. It was agreeable to have her thighs about him, except where he was bruised, and even his bruises felt better for having the soft inner sides of a young woman's legs warming them gently in a kind of heavenly lint.

'Shouldn't you be riding side saddle?' he asked sleepily, or at least found words to convey as much.

'On a barrel like this? I should fall off.'

'And how shall you steer the horse?' His French sounded inadequate and ugly, but what else was his young saint for, save to be forgiving? He nestled against her. He would ride like a child, cradled against his mother, with her arms all about him. He was half fainting already, as well as in ecstasy at the thought of it. And so he sat trembling and bloodied, with his love holding him in place.

He was too weak to see far, but glancing forward then downward – the horse had a busy head – he saw an oily hand grab at the cross strap of its bridle. He supposed one of Shovel Hat's ruffians was trying to unseat him, and did his best to kick him away.

The fellow laughed, so he kicked again.

Annette stopped him. 'Lacaille is the horse's owner,' she explained.

'Lacaille?' He felt dazed, and in desperate need to repeat everything she said, in case his brain was slipping away from him.

'Lacaille, or one of Lacaille's sons who is also a Lacaille, of course. Or one of the Lacaille apprentices, who is known as Lacaille for convenience.'

Doubtless she spoke as her mother spoke. Most women do. 'Isn't that a rather inadequate introduction?'

'It will save you from identifying him on oath, if you're ever called upon to do so.'

The horse did not move very fast or far, if at all. Lacaille or his apprentice were in no great hurry to be elsewhere. They were curious about the here and now.

The National Guard was chasing the marchers through the Forest of Orléans. This was the cause of much shouting, but no shooting. The Forest was huge and black – there was still no moon to hang William by – and seemed to stretch for ever.

Nearer to hand, Besserve was supervising the cutting down of his stallion from its tree. This was being done for him by three members of the Guard, who thought the castration of the apothecary's horse was a wonderful joke. The beast still had not succeeded in throttling itself, though its saliva was flecked with blood. It was keeping up a plaintive noise like a seagull, and continued this unequine complaint even when it sprawled free and lay on the ground with its flanks heaving and its leathers chalk white with sweat.

Monsieur Gellet-Duvivier stood nearby, having very properly marched here like the true Grenadier he was. He seemed to be enjoying himself, if such a melancholy madman can be said to enjoy anything unless he has drunk himself into a frenzy.

Besserve, with a wounded horse to attend to, did his best to ignore his old adversary. The Madman did his best not to be ignored.

Besserve busied himself.

'That rabble have served your horse a pretty turn, Besserve.'

'I'll have reparation from you for disrupting this march of mine, Gellet-Duvivier.'

'Praise God I was here in time to rescue you, my little apothecary – I and my fellows in the Guard. I seem to spend all my days rescuing people,' he added, eyeing Williams as if he personally had unfastened him from his tree. 'And praise God I was in time to rescue your horse – most of him, at least. I see he has one or two bits missing, but hardly the worse for that. They cut you down to your proper size there.'

Monsieur Gellet-Duvivier paused to take a little snuff. He offered a pinch to Besserve, but the apothecary refused to join him, even when assured it was of the highest quality and bought at his very own counter.

'A druggist should never ride an entire horse,' Monsieur Gellet-Duvivier went on conversationally, and offering the friendliest advice possible, 'Not by himself and for himself, he shouldn't! Whole mounts are reserved for the gentry. Male mounts with their whitebreads attached certainly are! Well, my little friend, you've been doctored according to rank. Thank God it's only your horse, I say. It might have been your lapdog.'

Besserve came and stood nose to nose with him, but Monsieur Gellet-Duvivier followed a profession that taught a man to keep on talking, however dissatisfied the customer. 'Sprinkle some salt beneath his parts, walk him gently back home – and pray that he forgives you.'

'To hell with your prayers.'

'Now that is a religious oath, Apothecary Besserve. And I thought your lot had turned their tails against religion.'

The Madman could be magnificent when he wasn't drunk, William thought. He had no time to admire him. Lacaille had seen enough, or Annette had told him to move on. They returned to the high road for Orléans, just north of Fleury-les-Aubrais. Here some of the Guard were reassembling. Lacaille moved past them with the high-stepping delicacy of one who knows he is not invisible, but hopes to be seen to be trying to be so. 'The National Guard will not fire on us owls, Monsieur. We even have friends among them. Equally, they prefer not to be reminded we are here.'

There seemed to be lots of owls hooting tonight, all of them close at hand. William heard both their hoot and their night shriek, and was amazed to think of so many in so small a compass. In Westmorland and Cumberland a breeding barn owl and her mate are reckoned to need a fat wood and a fair moor to feed them. This wood must be fat indeed, and its clearing fair, to hold so many together.

These were difficult thoughts to think, when your head is damaged, and your hands blunted, and you are being held on to a funny saddle on a foreign horse. His bruises were so slippery and her grip so gentle that he nearly fell a dozen times into pot-holes and puddles. At one point, Lacaille began to tread delicately again, and the horse to float. The Guard overtook them at slow march in extended order.

Shortly afterwards Lacaille carried him upstairs, he thought Lacaille, though only Annette was there when he opened his eyes and found himself lying on his bed. She was bathing his face, having long since cleaned off the rest of him. His fine suit had been hung, though not brushed for fear of driving in the dirt.

'I must stay here,' she said. 'For tonight. It is nearly morning, and quite the wrong hour to disturb Marie-Victorie-Adelaïde.'

'Yes, you must stay here.'

'For tonight.'

'Until morning.'

'Yes.'

Gellet-Duvivier could be heard shouting, and playing cards with himself in his mirror, and possibly threatening himself with his enormous sword. He was drunk but happy. Several times he told the entire story to his dead wife.

Annette was dressed and already leaving when William woke. Williams was an injured man, or at least a bruised one. He was bruised all over. He found it extremely difficult to remember what had come to pass in such a narrow bed between her soft body and his damaged skin. She was gazing at him more than fondly as she went through his outer door, so he decided it was probably nothing.

She almost collided with the Demoiselle, who was carrying a large jug of hot milk and a small trout folded in a loaf. The Demoiselle smiled. She smiled timidly at Annette and boldly at Williams. The Demoiselle was all smiles today. Her father was sore from drinking, so after two whole weeks she again brought the Englishman breakfast.

He smiled back. The smile never left her face. She had seen Annette. She now saw the wreckage of his bed. Clearly her idol was made of imperfect clay, but she was still young enough to find him more wonderful and mysterious in consequence.

Or perhaps she thought Annette was his mother?

BOOK TWO:

BIRTHDAYS AND
DEATH DAYS

THURSDAY THE SECOND DAY OF FEBRUARY 1792
(By Some Called The Fourth Year Of Liberty)

'My mother will take you in for a few days.'

'In the circumstances, which are several, she can hardly do less.'

'You don't know my mother. She has a saying—' She stood close to him, she stood almost within him, inside his coat at least, because of the intense cold. 'She says—'

'I think I shall like your mother.'

The icy banks of the Loire went slipping by them. The river was swollen. Sometimes he could see over the flood walls. To the north there were park lands, orchards, fields neat as cushions. To the south it was sombre and wild, forests on low hills, with frozen pools or glassy coppices between; he noticed lonely animal sheds built from wattle and reeds, and once the ornamental roofs and cupolas of a great château emerging from the mists of a snowstorm, its coping picked out in gold, its chimneys crowded with gaudy birds, angels even, before the weather dimmed it again as if in a dream.

'Your mother seems full of saws and proverbs. My own childhood—'

'Words stick to mother. She has very few of her own. Her best, which we rarely hear, out of deference to Vergez, her best ones are my father's.'

He lifted his face from the wildness of her hair – no bonnet was safe on a boat running free on these floodwaters in such a wind – and found the river banks dark with birds. The storm touched them all, blackening the light. He recognized only gulls and crows, the feeders on floating meat. Then his eyelashes blurred with snow.

She had not let him leave his rooms above the Coin Maugas for a whole month. She had nursed him in his bed, careless of what people thought downstairs or along the corridor. She was her own woman.

Being her own woman, she had not been his again, not since the night of his rescue. Her love for him was apparent in everything she did. It was physical and caring. She had bathed the broken places on his skin. She had washed him. But she had not let herself lie in his bed again, though they had completed many a 'little talk' together. And what had come from those 'little talks' of hers? No more than her decision that Orléans was unsafe for him, because of Shovel Hat and his cronies, so she must take him to Blois.

Only Blois was not really where she was taking him. She was taking him to her family.

Somebody shouted. It was the first sound they'd heard for half an hour, other than their own voices and the wind on the braces. Their boat was a yawl, with only its jib and mizzen rigged, and the whole thing balanced in the current with a long tiller. Except for the helmsman and a lookout, the crew were huddled out of the weather. The lookout was leaning forward on the prow, and pointing.

'Blois!' Annette exclaimed. 'There she is.'

Blois stood higher above the river than Orléans, though there was less of it. He saw two splendid châteaux, one of them fortified, towering above the water. The houses had bright blue roofs.

They waited for the yawl to turn across current, then warp into place. This was a difficult manoeuvre, and it took time because of the fierceness of the current.

William remembered where their windswept conversation had started. 'You mentioned your mother had something to say about house guests – some kind of proverb or saw, I think you said.'

'It would take too long to tell you the ideas she has inherited on the subject. The plainest thing to say, Williams, and the shortest, is that she doesn't like them.'

'But she will be expecting me?'

'Possibly. Paul has written a letter of introduction.'

'I thought Paul, being a lawyer, was always tardy with letters?'

'He is. So I've asked him for another, which I am carrying with me!'

Françoise Yvon Vergez smiled fixedly at Williams, who stood uneasily in her 'polite-parlour', then closed the door on him.

'I've been teaching him French, mother.'

'Make sure he doesn't teach you any English, Marie Anne — English manners at least.'

'Morals is what your mother means. The only honest Englishmen are Scotsmen, like yourselves, and they've sent all those to America.'

Annette glanced gratefully towards her stepfather. It was rare enough for him to pay compliments to the Vallon bloodline, perhaps because her mother was not part of it. She realized he had another reason for speaking. He wanted to cover his move to the door. If there was to be family tension, he preferred to be on the far side of the river with a fowling-piece.

He pulled the door open and said, quite careless of the fact that Williams was now within earshot, 'You know what's troubling her? She hates to have strangers here to stay.' He noticed Williams, as if for the first time. 'She quotes Old Pardessus on the subject, something about why should she give beggars house-room, when the Good God Himself could spare his own Son no more than a bundle of straw in a stable.'

He shut the door, and could be heard chatting to Williams about a number of his favourite subjects, such as wild ducks, puerperal fever and soldiers' women having babies. He chuckled a great deal, whereas Williams hardly spoke.

Her mother did. 'Well, you have let this extremely young Englishman carry your bonnets as far as the boat, and now you encourage him to bring himself onwards to me.'

The silence between them grew delicate. Delicacy, for

Françoise Vergez, was like disorder. She refused to tolerate it. 'Fortunately you bring me a letter from Paul Léonard. He never writes to me – if he weren't a notary, I should suppose him to be an illiterate – yet you bring me a letter from him instead of telling me his news yourself.' Her mother began to saw the packet open. 'I do hope there is no connection between this letter and the totally unforeseen presence of this youthful Englishman, who I must say appears younger each time I glimpse him.' She seemed to be able to produce a packet knife in every room, as if her life consisted entirely of letters. 'He's a kind, sweet boy is Paul, as well as a completely careless one. Let us see what sort of trouble he is in that he couldn't trust you to tell me about it!'

The letter was gummed, and waxed with the court seal. Annette could only suppose that this was to prevent her from learning in advance the strength – or weakness – of his advocacy of Williams' cause. Whatever was its message, it took some time in the opening.

Madame Vergez peeled back the gum at last. She snorted. 'He tells me nothing of himself. Instead he speaks excessively of this Englishman Wodswod as if he is an old friend. He commends him to me as a house guest if I will, a lodger if need be, and a suitor and husband for yourself unless you can quickly do better.'

Annette was blushing at her brother's directness, and enraged with him as well, but her explanations were interrupted by her mother adding, 'He asks me not to be misled by Wodswod's footwear but base my entire opinion upon his suit – which I must try to touch often – and his umbrella, if he remembers to bring it.'

Annette giggled. Her mother snorted her to silence. 'Who is this Gellet-Duvivier he speaks of?'

'He is Williams', that is Wodswod's, landlord in Orléans.'

'A hatter and a stocking-maker? I suppose there *is* such a person in Blois!'

'Mother, Williams – Monsieur Wodswodth' – she felt she owed it to him to take particular trouble with his name on this occasion – 'Monsieur Wodswodth is being kept waiting. What am I to do with him?'

'In the longer term, nothing. In the shorter, we'd better have someone make up a bed for him. *You* can see to that. I shall invite him to supper. He can stay for a day or two if he has no disagreeable habits or unacceptable ideas.'

'Meanwhile, mother, where shall I teach him French?'

'I am sure it will be less disruptive for us all if he confines himself to his own tongue during his stay here.'

'Maman, he is already—'

'What I have in mind is that after a day or three, we shall board him out. Your sister-in-law Angélique may perhaps be glad of a lodger—'

'Excellent. I shall teach him in a room in my brother's house.'

'That will not be proper. One must not teach in a room, and certainly not in a room in one's brother's house. No, we shall board him out but let him eat his evening meal at our own table.'

'And his lessons, mother?'

'He will learn here, from as many of us as possible.'

The surgeon Vergez was the senior doctor in Blois, and his position was important enough to allow him a great deal of leisure, as it had done this afternoon. He always used the time constructively. On this occasion, as soon as he had taken leave of his wife and stepdaughter and their Englishman, he went straight across the river to the damp woodland beyond. There, armed with no more than a long-barrelled gun and a double ox-horn of black powder, he made in the space of two and a quarter hours a prodigious slaughter of water birds. Some of these had migrated, and were weak from returning too early. Others had not left their breeding ground at all, but died because it was less than three half moons from the solstice and they were surprised during a period of contemplation when they were totally unused to being shot at.

Vergez bound their bloody corpses to his gun-barrel, which he carried horizontally on his shoulder, and hooked a few more to the fingers of his left hand, having slotted their legs.

He gave these birds away on his laboured return across the bridge. The town was hungry by and large, and none of its teeming urchins would be the worse for a little duck soup, even duck soup with no duck in it, but a greasy broth of crested grebe, and on one occasion, seagull.

The shooting, the slotting, the carrying and distribution stained his hands with a good deal of blood and a certain amount of other tissue as well, including fluff. But a surgeon is never the worse for a little blood on his cuff, nor even his boot, especially when going home. It lends a certain validity to the day. Nor was the fluff a give-away. It was soft and winter white. Anyone glimpsing it in conjunction with the blood – anyone who knew his calling, that is – would assume he had just been peeling the face off a very old man in an attempt to uncover his toothache.

The house stood just along from the bridge, so William watched quite a lot of his progress from his upstairs window, and then from the salon.

Vergez stood with him, clean-handed, within a few minutes of entering the house, but someone had clearly had a word with him in the interim. He handed William a glass of sweet, brown wine in a manner that brooked no argument, and said, 'You must tell me at once what you do with your life, sir. Do you run a family estate or are you a professional man?'

'My father was a professional man, sir, and he ran a family estate. But the estate was not ours. It belonged to the Lowthers, who owe my family a substantial sum of money in consequence.'

'Enough to buy a town, sir, or enough to buy a street?'

'Enough to buy each of us a house, I dare say. But that's a sad story.'

Every time William looked away from the fire and stole a direct glance at Vergez's face the doctor seemed to smile at him. It was neither a warm smile nor a cold smile, and it certainly had nothing to do with his calling. It was a fixed habit of the muscles, a permanent but probably accidental expression of joy that hung from his ears like a sheet from a line of washing.

'So you can't cut a corpse in half or draw me a deed of conveyance?'

'I followed the studies usual at my university, sir. Principally I read Mathematics and Classics.'

'Ah, so you could compute for me the flight of a cannonball?'

'Sir, I am exhausted with examinations, and yet it appears you would set me another.'

'Only in usefulness, sir. I have been instructed to examine you in that.'

'I think I shall fail at usefulness. Let us find another topic. Sir, I am a poet. Ask me about mountains, rather. Or rainbows.'

'Rainbows, sir?' Vergez was in urgent need of wine. He did not offer any to William, since William's glass remained full. 'Rainbows were invented by an Englishman.'

'An Englishman from my university.'

'Here in Blois we have little use for them, our females especially. Let us take Annette as an example.' He drank reflectively, as if allowing William time to catch up with his thinking. 'Annette has no need of rainbows. She needs the friendship of a man like her father. A man who can cut a corpse in half.' He laughed, and his laugh was genuine enough. 'Still, why are we talking like this? I live in a house of women, don't you see – they'll be waiting for us at table even now – and women are unnatural company for any man with the least spark of imagination about him.' Vergez used too many words, as doctors often do to hide their feelings from their patients and protect their patients from their own.

He took William by the arm, still talking volubly; but then William too was his patient in a way. All his family were his patients in that all must suffer him. He led him first to the magnificent dining room next door, with its table glowing, its principal silver set and a quartet of fine ornamental tureens in waiting. This was a ghost of a room, preparing itself for a banquet that Madame Vallon Vergez might or might not give. Still talking, he began to walk William further upstairs. They were going to take supper in the family parlour, he explained, a place reserved for themselves and their friends, where the atmosphere would be more intimate and convivial.

Four women were already waiting at table for them – Annette and presumably the two sisters she had spoken of, and their mother, all of them in their finery. There were also two serving girls in unbelievably clean linen, as pretty a half dozen faces as William had encountered in a very long time, including the Demoiselle's.

He thought of Horace's often misconstrued line about mothers and daughters. It had been misquoted in Latin, misapplied in English. Françoise Yvon Vallon Vergez had certainly been a most handsome woman in her time. If her time was not quite now, it was also not long or too far gone. She gave off an unmistakable air of womanliness. Like her youngest daughter, she could be honey sweet, she could be hard as iron. She could never be sour.

Annette's likeness was to her brother Paul – William had not needed to come to Blois to find that out. What he could see now was how different she was from her sisters, in colouring at least. If the Vallons had settled here from Scotland a century and a half ago, as Annette had told him, if their real patronymic was indeed Leonar or Leonard, then the darkness of Vallon the Celt had fused with the grapelike Loire-born darkness of Françoise Yvon to produce Paul Léonard and Annette. The other two daughters were lighter-coloured and more brittle in temper, but in no way less fair. It was a stimulating table for a young man to find himself at, even though Angélique Adelaïde was a year older than Annette, and Françoise Anne must be all of thirty, and consequently past civilized marriage and childbearing.

During their progress past the banqueting table and then upstairs, Vergez had continued to talk. He had even spoken through and round the introductions, his subject continuing to be women – either because his life and domestic circumstances had taught him a lot about them, or because he thought that, since the two men were outnumbered, it would make for a fine jangly evening to set on edge as many female nerves as possible.

'Now these young daughters of mine are beautiful examples of their kind or species, young Wodswod. I mean the same beautiful kind as their mother, though they're not quite their mother's kind yet. They had another father before me, and their mother another husband.'

'God rest him,' said Mrs Vergez, who loved his memory dearly but saw no need to resurrect him while they were serving the soup.

'Now he and I were, I daresay, one another's equals as doctors, Wodswod.'

'Call him Williams, father. No one can say his name otherwise,' Annette said. 'Even I can scarcely pronounce it.'

'There's no way to put the matter to the test here and now,
but as surgeons we were probably the equal of each other, I
with him, and himself certainly with me.' He pointed a finger
at the table then lifted it respectfully towards Heaven. 'But
where he was pre-eminent, Williams, was in ordinary intelligence – the sort they don't teach you at Cambridge, I dare say.
And how do I know he was more intelligent than me, sir?
Because he contemplated his family with its preponderance of
women – preponderance, that is, if you count their mother –
and sons who though splendid men would be liable to marry
women, and beget women, and do you know what he did? He
died.'

Vergez himself was the only one who laughed, yet his remarks
caused no kind of shock. It was clear his wife and daughters had
heard the joke before.

'You see, old Vallon, my dear old friend Jean Léonard Vallon
had specialized in women's ailments. As a doctor he discovered
that women have only one kind of ailment, and that ailment is
themselves, and principally that portion of themselves that was
set there to distract mankind in general and irk themselves and
their families in particular.'

Madame Vergez had no intention of allowing such a mono-
logue to continue. It was unseemly that a guest should hear the
women of her family being forced to listen to such talk. 'Paul has
today written us a letter, Vergez,' she said.

'I shall read it later.'

'It is important I tell you now that he commends Monsieur
Wodswod to us—'

'Mr Wodswod is self-evidently a gentleman, and has no need
of your son's commendation.'

'He commends Monsieur Wodswod to us as a storyteller and
wit.'

Annette began to giggle. She nudged Angélique Adelaïde
who looked at Françoise Anne.

'In particular, Monsieur Wodswod tells a very agreeable story
about a trout.'

'Not about a trout,' William protested. 'The point of the story is that the trout is—'

'The trout is a fish,' Vergez said. 'No one can deny that the trout is a fish. Now fish and the catching of fish, my dear young man, are topics appropriate to fishermen. I despise fishermen. All along the banks of the Loire I shoot waterfowl. I hunt them with considerable success, ducks especially. I shoot birds who pull out fish. A fine fool it would make me to compete with something I kill, or to indulge in a sport wherein my customary prey so evidently excels those who already practise it!'

'Finish your soup,' Madame Vergez said. 'I want to serve the trout. We are eating trout out of respect to Monsieur Wodswod's story.'

'No trout for me,' Vergez said. 'I shall enjoy my soup and wait for whatever may follow.'

'You have never said no to trout before.'

'I do not intend to compete with a duck. I leave you women to do that. If the truth were known, you cannot even emulate the duck, let alone surpass her.'

'Say on, stepfather,' Françoise said, smiling flirtatiously at William.

'The mammalian female has a great deal to learn from the duck. If only all of you could be as straightforward in your workings. And – what is even more attractive to a scientist – as simple.'

'We don't want to go into details,' his wife said firmly.

'When the duck decides to increase and multiply her kind, all she does is sit down on her bottom and make a nice nest of eggs. Can you do that, Françoise Anne? Can you, Angélique Adelaïde? What an agreeable habit that is, of all the habits of nature. It causes the duck no pain, and it has the great merit of keeping her quiet for as many weeks as it takes her.' He took a little wine to congratulate himself on the beauty of it. 'When they crack out of the eggshell, the eggshell has no need of a doctor. If only the Good God, who taught the world everything it knows, if only He could have learned just a little from His very own duck when it came to the making of woman. But there, he made her in too much haste. He probably had entirely different designs for her until she was unmade by the Devil. He probably

intended our Mother Eve to be like a duck until she grew greedy
with that apple. Ducks can't even eat apples. She was intended to
reproduce like a duck or, more comfortably still, a serpent, and
of course in all the subsequent circumstances that was out of the
question. Instead He made the completely unsatisfactory female
parts I've drunk two bowls of soup discussing.'

'What parts are we talking of, father?'

'I'd prefer not to express myself more nearly, Annette, even in
medical terminology.'

'Shame on you.'

'I'm thinking of Monsieur Wodswod here, quite as much as
yourself. God knows you young women hear all manner of delicate things, living in a doctor's house as you do, and
eavesdropping at table. Your speech is coarse enough!' He managed another wink, possibly at William, but his uncontrolled
smile made it difficult to judge who it was intended for. 'It is not
proper for an unmarried man to know anything precise about
the anatomy of the female of his own species, save to take general cognisance of the fact that it is, in certain specifics, different
from his own.' He moved his unaltered and unalterable smile
back towards Annette, and added, 'I am speaking of her *physical*
person, you understand, the superficial geography of her fleshly
integument.'

'I never supposed otherwise, father.'

'In *essence*, of course, she differs totally – but Heaven forbid I
should talk philosophy to you.'

'Heaven forbid.'

'A young man must accept the latter and expect to remain
ignorant of the former. As for the young woman, or the woman
of any age, she need know nothing of herself.'

'What are we speaking of, father? Her body or her essence?'

'Both. All talk of essence is beyond her, and her body is a
matter for experts.'

William did not know when the meal ended or how long it
lasted. It became a blur his memory found it impossible to
reassemble. It was like rain falling on a water-colour painting,
forever enlarging the brush strokes but confusing their impression, and increasingly difficult to identify or explain. For a start,

there was the brightness of the colour box, the undoubted beauty of the women. Dining with them was an even more ecstatic experience than his dreams of an endless breakfast served by the Demoiselle Gellet-Duvivier. Yes, for a start, there was the beauty of the women.

For a finish, and for a long time after that, there were the everlasting monologues of Annette's stepfather. They began in a dribble, progressed through a drizzle and finished up as a storm. They obliterated everything, but in the jolliest manner possible. Subjected to this prolonged bullying by the ear – and the mother's acerbic asides – William wondered why the children should grow up to be such conformists. There must be a revolutionary somewhere in the daughters' immediate ancestry for themselves to be so staunch for Church and Crown. Perhaps their politics were all the fault of their natural father: the oldest son, his landlord-to-be, was seemingly called Jean-Jacques, and Annette herself treasured her father's copy of *The Confessions*, whatever she thought of the book's content. Yes, old man Vallon must have been the rebel: his were the politics the younger generation resisted.

Not that this brief moment of revelation did William any good. He fell asleep as soon as he reached his bed, and slept without dream or nightmare. He should have slumbered among visions of bright eyes, blushing cheeks, the pale flesh of shoulder and neck, bosoms threatening to emerge from the gathered looseness of gowns appropriate only to home and to evening. Above all his imagination should be at work upon the intoxicating perfume of all that scarcely or scantily covered female skin.

No such luck. Vergez's monologues acted on him like spiked toddy followed by spiced wine. Without so much as a parting word from Annette he collapsed into the blankest of sleeps.

BLOIS.
FRIDAY THE THIRD DAY OF
FEBRUARY 1792

'The English,' said Madame Vallon Vergez, 'are notorious for lying a-bed. Not their women so much. Their women have a hard time of it, by all accounts. The menfolk, being idle themselves, have a great need to keep the women of their household busy.'

Annette felt deeply embarrassed for Williams. Where was he? Why was he late this morning of all mornings?

Before the family had retired last night, her mother had proposed, and in the clearest of terms, her firm intention to take Williams and her daughters for a walk immediately after breakfast. She would show him forth, she would exhibit him to the best people in Blois and introduce him to the world at large. And Françoise Vergez knew the very best people – there could be no doubt of that.

'I do believe he is having trouble with those boots of his,' Françoise Anne said. 'Is it our brother Paul who is most acquainted with him, Annette? When you next see him, you must ask him about the Englishman's feet. I declare they must be malformed.'

'They are English walking boots,' Annette hurried to explain.

'A gentleman should never propose to his footwear that it be fashioned primarily for walking,' Madame Vergez said. 'Such a philosophy would give his snob a very unfair advantage.'

'Then just what *are* shoes for, mother?' Angélique had been waiting as long as anyone, but she felt sorry for Annette, and hoped a little disputation with her mother might disguise the delay.

'Shoes are principally for sitting in,' Madame Vergez said. 'It is true a gentleman stands quite as often as he sits, so he should select a shoe that is, above all, kind to carpets. Now where is that lad? Chocolate at Berruet's is not an inexhaustible commodity, and I shall faint if I don't have a cup of it in a very few minutes' time.' The air was cold, but she used a fan on it. No one used a fan as sternly as Françoise Vallon Vergez.

Annette had been to his room to seek him out. She had been there early – not something she was about to profess – but Williams had gone. He had vanished without trace.

'I don't know why Berruet should call his place The *Three Merchants*,' Angélique said. 'He doesn't have enough coffee for one, let alone three! And his chocolate is always in short supply.'

'It's those ruffians from the backstreets,' their mother said firmly. 'Those and the Constitutionalists. They're trying to rule the king. They're certainly running the Church. And what is the result? I can't find a proper cup of chocolate after eleven o'clock in the morning.'

'Worse things are happening, mother.' Françoise Anne was becoming bored with small talk.

'Not in Blois, they're not. Nor should you pretend otherwise. Not having coffee or chocolate is terrible enough.'

'You don't leave the house at night,' Annette said. 'You don't walk alone in the streets at all.'

'Nor do you.'

'In Orléans I do.'

'Orléans was yesterday. If that boy isn't up yet, we must do without him.'

Williams was growing younger in her mother's estimation by the minute. Annette felt he might be sinking there in other ways also. Madame Vergez hadn't regarded him too highly to begin with: he was foreign, which was one disadvantage, and English, which was another. Then there was the archness of Paul's letter. It implied that Williams was some kind of suitor, as indeed he was; but as far as her mother was concerned, candidates for her daughters' hands need arrive on horseback or not at all, and be accompanied by at least one manservant to hold the horse for the duration of their visit.

'Well,' Madame Vergez muttered. It is a chilly word in most tongues, and always means the exact reverse of what it seems to say. 'Well, well, well.' She examined Annette as if this morning without hot chocolate was her youngest daughter's fault. 'When women walk abroad they need to be accompanied.'

The thunderous clamour at the front door came as a terrible shock to them. Someone was hammering the knocker, then drawing at the bell cord at the same time. The bell, with its brass draw-knob, was a recent innovation of Françoise Vergez's very own, and she hated to hear such a delicate invention abused.

Madame despatched a maid to answer the summons. Her expression suggested that she wished she had a quartet of footmen to send after her, preferably with pikes or muskets.

The renewed ringing of the bell made it clear that they were not to be invaded by the Friends of the Constitution, or the even rowdier friends of the Friends. Bell-pulls were beyond the understanding of people like that.

The maid returned with Monsieur Williams, who came bounding towards them. He saluted Annette's mother. 'I am sorry to be so late, Madame. I miscalculated the time.'

'It's those boots, monsieur. They cost you one pace in four.'

'Not quite, Madame. But very nearly. I have been to Cheverny.'

'To Cheverny?'

'Yes, Madame. I thought I should inspect your friends. I saw some dreary houses in the half light, and then after another half an hour, an enormous château – was I in the right place?'

'I know of no dreary houses,' Madame sniffed.

'Perhaps my eyes were misled by the twilight.'

'The great Court of Cheverny is halfway across the Salogne Forest,' Annette chided. 'Nobody goes there on foot.'

'It is eight English miles by my calculation. I go everywhere on foot, and your countryside is magnificently flat.' He bowed again towards their mother. 'Nowhere in England is there a forest to compare with the one I have walked through this morning.'

'If it is eight English miles there, it is eight English miles back again,' Annette said, still not believing he had been so far.

'It was less coming back. Going away from Madame I could only walk. Coming back I ran, for fear of keeping her waiting.'

Madame sniffed. Annette hoped this was not meant to suggest Williams smelled like a person who had walked eight English miles and then run another eight. She thought not. He was a young man, and clean. He smelled of the countryside, which even in deepest winter made him seem to her like the pollen of spring.

Perhaps to her mother also. As her mother sniffed again, Williams merely smiled at her, and Madame Vergez gave over sniffing, and instead took to breathing deeply.

Annette wondered what words would result from this transformation. She did not have to wait for long.

'Well, young man, you did keep me waiting. And now I shall have to do without my chocolate. It's almost time for the Montlivaults to call. If I'd known you were going to Cheverny I could have sent a message by you.'

'Dawn was scarcely breaking, Madame. I'd have hated to disturb the Count while he was still in his night-shirt and winkie.'

Williams didn't have a word for 'winkie', and it wasn't one Annette had ever heard or could translate, so she had to leave it where it was, poking out from among the wreckage of his French.

Madame Vergez turned away, but with a smile. She could be heard saying as she retired, '"Vinkie"? What is "vinkie"?' Annette had the feeling that for some indefinable reason Williams had won her mother round to him. She couldn't tell why. What was certain was that he had set out to defeat Madame Vergez, and possibly the rest of them as well.

'It was a good walk,' he explained to her. 'I like to walk.'

'Your body needs it?'

'No – my brain.'

How quickly they moved to the front door now Williams was with them and their mother had gone elsewhere. How quickly too they separated once they were outside, Françoise Anne and Angélique Adelaïde to coax belated chocolate from old Berruet at The Three Merchants, Annette and Williams to anywhere within reason it pleased them to be. Annette had planned a divergence of routes as soon as her sisters could contrive one. Williams returning late had made everything happen sooner than she had dared to hope.

Annette did not congratulate Williams on his conquest of her mother, nor speculate about that lady's amazing defeat at his hands. He might become overbold towards her family, saucy even, and the social norms in the Rue du Pont kept within boundaries which were difficult for a stranger to identify, and which Madame Vergez was constantly redefining.

Instead she showed him as much of the town as could be encompassed without walking too far − this was most of it − before taking him towards one of the several infirmaries where her stepfather worked.

They found lots of nuns but no Vergez. 'He is probably hunting,' she explained. 'He shoots duck, he shoots deer, he shoots pig.'

'I thought pig were best hunted on horseback.'

'If he saw a horse, he would probably shoot that as well.'

'But this is quite the wrong season to hunt such creatures. They are waiting to breed.'

'He thinks Nature is able to overcome a little disappointment in that direction. He has no children of his own, and doesn't see why a tusker should expect more.'

This was a strange conversation to have in an infirmary run by sisters of mercy. Williams whispered that nuns always seemed like beetles: they were black and they lived inside stones. He could understand why the Revolution felt a need to abolish them.

The cloisters were full of draught. In spite of the shifting air the place smelled strangely of leaf mould.

There was another odour too, which always reminded her of toothache. Williams said that so much blood had been spilt here, it felt like a clearing in a forest where hunters gather their kill. She could not answer this. She saw little purpose in forests, or not until recently when she had discovered that they were suitable for hiding large bodies of armed men.

'I'll show you where Vergez plies the knife,' Annette told him cheerfully. 'Though he says the knife is little use to a surgeon, and the bold man cuts quickest with a bone-saw.'

'Indeed.'

The relative silence, or at least the absence of screams of protest, seemed to confirm Vergez's absence. What they could hear was a much more homely sound – the rhythmic slap and thump of a razor being stropped.

Turning a corner they saw that the blade was too narrow to shave with, though certainly sharp enough. It was being honed by a nun.

She was watching a man in shirtsleeves use a similar blade to dig into a small boy's neck. The boy had ginger hair, and his blood was an amazing contrast to the whiteness of his skin. Some of it trickled down inside his collar, most of it splashed out on to the man's apron.

The blade was evidently very keen and the surgeon skilful, for the boy made no sound.

'Splendid,' the man said. 'Splendid, splendid, splendid. You've lost a great deal of bright red muck, tell your mother, but not much blood.'

The boy began to breathe very loudly.

'Oh, and tell her I've left your brains intact.'

His intensified breathing seemed to disturb the surgeon no end. He threw down his knife and seized the fresh blade. 'That's better,' he explained. 'Keenest cuts kindest. Didn't feel a thing, did you, young Carrot?'

The ginger-haired boy rubbed his neck with a bloody hand and said nothing.

'That wasn't a carbuncle you've got on your head. It was a string-mine. You didn't know string came from mines, did you? Well, nor did I till I sectioned that wen of yours. It's got a core you could use to catch a salmon. There, I make you a present of it. I thought I was pulling out your *vena cava* for a moment, your neckbone even.'

'So did I,' the boy said. He seized his trophy, produce of his own flesh as it was, and made off with it.

'Your nephew's a brave lad,' the surgeon said to the nun. Then, turning to Annette, he added, 'Well, little sister, we're very well met. This is infinitely better than chipping away at elbows and knees, isn't it? Our brother is performing an amputation at Saint-Saturnin this very moment. Neither of us takes any pleasure in the thought.'

He was shaking William's hand even before the introduction was made. 'Monsieur Wodswod, I am Vallon. Maman has already spoken about you. It seems we are to add your name to Angel's list of boarders. You are very welcome, but stay with Maman as long as you can. The food will be better at our place – Angel presides over an excellent kitchen – the trouble is our rooms are full of soldiers just now.'

'I am used to soldiers, monsieur. I have just come from a lodging house full of them.'

'In Orléans? I thought so! There are soldiers posted to every city on the Loire. Our government detects the stench of insurrection all about us. It knows how to sniff. Governments always have good nostrils, by whatever name they call themselves.'

William was glad to meet at least one Vallon who was politically ambivalent. Jean-Jacques – this was clearly he – seemed as independently minded as his name suggested.

As brother and sister fell to chatting together, the poet realized why the man had introduced himself so proudly as 'Vallon'. It wasn't a lack of manners. The patronymic was his by right. He was the first brother, as well as the oldest surviving male. He was the Vallon of the Vallons, and wore the title as proudly as the head of any Scots clan. Annette was clearly fond of her brother, and treated him with a respect he had not noticed her afford to Paul. They were celebrating their kinship in a way that Vergez would not necessarily understand nor Madame agree with.

As they walked back into the cold winter sunlight, he remarked on her brother's assumption of the family name and explained that the tradition in England seemed more in use among women. His sister, for example, as the only and oldest, could call herself Miss Wordsworth, without forename or initial.

Annette wasn't listening. She had something on her mind. 'I had no idea mother went out early this morning. She went to see Jean-Jacques and Angel almost before the family was up. She wants you to move to my brother's house as soon as may be.'

'She couldn't throw me straight out into the street, I suppose. I had no idea I had made such a bad impression on her.'

'You haven't, Williams. Not for yourself.' She saw no need to mention religion. She said, 'There is a tradition of dislike for the English in my family. We are Scots in origin, and see the English as our oppressors.'

'Ah!' he said. 'The Old Enemy.'

'It's all the fault of my brother Paul. His letter introduced you *as my suitor*, Williams. Better if he had left that to me, and allowed you time to make your way with my family.'

'Then we must be married, and have done with the matter.' He spoke the words lightly. They seemed to come as easily to him as his brief words of love on their second meeting.

It had taken her a long time to bring him to this point. How long had it been – two months? Now she must remind him of what he doubtless already knew – that nothing could be that simple.

They were in the cloisters next to the infirmary, the cloisters of the nunnery where she and her sisters had their schooling. There was nobody in sight, and Williams was holding on to her impetuously.

She let him have a kiss to acknowledge the ridiculousness of his proposal, but the fact was he was a man, and not one of her schoolfriends playing Queens and Kings. He was not only reckless but much too rough with her hair and her clothing.

'We know this must never be,' she said. 'Not again.'

'As I say, we must get married.'

'How?' She pushed him away from her. She was playing for advantage, and there was always power in that. But she was playing for truth as well, and in her experience truth always brings pain. 'How, Williams? Two people can be in love and trouble no one.' Except themselves, except the woman, she thought bitterly. 'Try to get married and we trouble everyone.'

'We can do it.'

'A marriage is a matter between families, Williams. Surely, even in England, it is families who get married? The man and the woman, they are by far the least important people.'

She led him slowly from the convent and then down to the

river. The river at Blois held no threats for her. The waterfront on the north shore was well-kept, like the rest of the old city. What was wild and insurgent and new daren't show its face here, not by daylight.

The lack of danger did not make the walk any more pleasant for her. She was happy that her Englishman had proposed to her at last – if such a simple statement of cause and effect could be counted as a proposal. It wouldn't have been adequate for the heroines in any of the novels she read.

Real life had little to do with books. She knew those few words were likely to be the only proposal from Williams she would get. She wanted to be his wife, she intended to be his wife, but her parents were likely to place many obstacles in her path. She had brought him to Blois so he would act decisively to clear them away.

Instead he seemed to accept the situation almost with gratitude. He had done what was necessary. He had proposed. His proposal had been rejected. Excellent. Now he could admire the waterbirds and the grey mass of woodland across the river.

'Frankly,' he said, touching her arm, 'your difficulties are as nothing compared with mine.' He squeezed her elbow affectionately, but without the least hint of encouragement. 'In truth, I'm not allowed to marry anyone. I'm not allowed to do *anything*. Quite simply, by reason of my family situation, I am not my own person.'

'No,' she said. 'Neither of us is. We are both God's people. We are both children of God.'

'I am supposed to be a priest,' he said. 'I have a parish waiting for me.'

'I thought your priests—'

'Oh yes. We can marry. I would have a house, and a few pennies to live upon. But to what purpose?' He caught hold of her, roughly. It wasn't a gesture of affection, though he could only behave this way with an intimate. 'A papist wife, speaking no English—' He thumbed her shoulder, as if to share the agony of his mind.

'This is a public place,' she said. 'I do not glue hats. I am not a serving girl.'

He glanced at her as if she would be preferable to him if she were, but he let go of her just the same.

'I should, of course, learn English.' She was moving from rejecting him towards proposing to him, and all with no intervening discussion. 'It can't be too difficult a tongue,' she joked. 'You can speak it.' Someone had to be decisive.

'I've no intention of being a priest. Why do you suppose I'm in France?'

'To write poetry, study fools like Besserve, and carry letters to poets.' She didn't stress the last point further. He was fluent enough to recognize a feminine noun when he heard one.

'I am here to learn French,' he said simply, as if that explained everything. It explained nothing.

'And when you have learned this language of ours, what will you do with it?'

'I shall find a young gentleman to accompany about Europe and teach it to.'

'For money?'

'Yes, for money. As a way of life.'

She saw no place for herself in this way of life, not with a Williams who accompanied gentlemen. 'Do you think that's a fitting occupation?'

'You seem to find it so.'

'I do it for love, Williams – not for money. Besides, I stopped teaching you as soon as we met.'

She was being foolish. Her sisters would tell her she was foolish. Angel, her oldest brother's wife who spoke to her about such things, would say she was being extremely unwise. Her mother would heap scorn upon her. She had uncovered her deepest feelings and gained nothing of substance in return. She paused in a fury at herself. She had not intended to conduct the morning like this. In her anger she could find no more words to say.

A bell struck. It was the great clock above the street by the bridge. It was going to strike noon.

He turned away, as if the signal was for him. He was the man ruled by clocks, by footsteps, by miles and by time and by destiny. He led her, she thought towards her home but perhaps only towards his notebooks, with a fury comparable to her own.

Within a few steps they were in the shelter of a building that was half wharf, half dwelling. A building that leant into the sun and offered a tiny corner of shadow. Here, he caught her, but not this time to hurt her shoulders. 'I love you,' he said. 'I shall never set this love aside, Annette. Not this love, nor you. Not ever.'

A Frenchman could not have made a finer declaration, though he would doubtless have said it more neatly.

Annette didn't know what to say in reply. What came to mind, a long kiss later, was, 'The house will be empty. Well, not quite that, perhaps. Mother has guests!'

She knew she was surprising Williams. Never before had she shown such an appetite for walking. But the family home overlooked the main street, so she would need to reach it by another route.

After a five-minute scamper up and down sloping alleyways and paved steps that left her breathless, she entered her mother's house by the scullery door. This, unfortunately, led into the kitchen, but there was virtue in this. She entered it noisily, talking to Williams about the château not a stone's throw away. When she had his attention, and she sensed the whole house was listening, she told him how the gigantic Duke of Guise had been assassinated there on the King's orders by eight noblemen with poignards, twelve gentlemen with rapiers, and any number of loose women.

Shouting jokes about loose women made her feel slightly more comfortable with herself, and a lot more adult. She might be twenty-five years old, approaching twenty-six, but no woman who still lives in her mother's house can ever be fully grown up, whatever her age.

There were more kitchen maids than there were when she'd last left for Orléans, and this talk of loose women made them laugh and grow boisterous in other ways, especially since Williams was here and manifestly understood little of what they were shouting.

Their laughter encouraged Annette to explain how the King had plotted to weaken Henri de Guise's sword arm by subjecting him to a night-long battery of the Queen's ladies-in-waiting. As each one left his bed, she refreshed him with a loving cup in which a thimbleful of cognac disguised a liberal squeezing of prunes. In the morning he was ambushed on his way to the commode. The giant de Guise was so debilitated by the excesses of the night that he succumbed to his wounds almost immediately, and only managed to slaughter five or six of the assassins.

'Five or six noblemen or five or six ladies-in-waiting?' William asked.

This caused immoderate laughter. Annette had already noted the extra maids in the kitchen. In times of famine, even comparatively modest establishments like her mother's and the Dufours' acquired innumerable servants. People were pleased to place their daughters where they would be fed; and a house where there was only a Vergez, a house run by Madame Françoise, moreover, presented very little risk that the girls would be meddled with or otherwise abused. Williams, and an unintended joke in awkward French, were as close to mortal sin as they were ever likely to get.

There was also a cook. She too was a sign of the times. Now that so many people were prepared to work in bourgeois kitchens for next to nothing, Françoise Vergez had allowed her own formidable skills to be supplemented.

Annette tasted the woman's sauce. A junior daughter does not taste the sauce often – she wondered when she had ever tasted it – but she was loud about the sauce, then loud about their laughter.

Having made her mark down here, and feeling certain she would be heard if her mother's ears were listening, she went briskly upstairs. She did not enter her mother's drawing room, where the laughter was more subdued, but led Williams quickly towards his bedroom. She had matters to supervise.

She was a determined woman. In her case, determination was not so much an attitude as an emotion. She felt her resolve as clearly as her other tempers, whether of rage, or love, or – as in this case – ecstasy. A woman of the bourgeoisie, a woman of the Third Estate, only had herself to offer in any bargain that might be struck. And for herself there was only one bargain to make. It was between her wits and any resource of human nature or urbane society that might provide her with a husband. God had sent her the man, and a great love to go with him. If the Good Lord had done so much, He would surely help with the rest.

So she stood in Williams' little bedroom – a room that had been hers until her brother's marriage – and helped him off with his jacket, a deed that spoke more loudly than words – and when it came to words, she found that even a determination as fierce as this could find her none.

Save that, having removed Williams' jacket, she thought it useful to say, 'We must be careful in case we are disturbed. And we must be quick.'

William was a man of preternatural animal sensibilities: his studies in the zoological kingdom, as well as his observation of his body's response to the body of this young woman, made the matter abundantly clear to him. Was this the second time or the third time? Or the third time for her, only the second time for him, because of consciousness lost through weakness and wounds? Already his biography was coming to lack some of its most intimate chapters. Second time, third time – these were no more than cardinal mathematics, and he had crossed over to France in order to set Cambridge squarely behind him. In its place his bed and Annette were no less squarely in front of him, though in a post-Euclidean theorem of dissolving lines and pulsating rectangles. Quite simply – and it was in such ordinary phrases he was coming to believe that Poetry and her Muse must reside – quite simply, he could not believe his luck.

Nor could Annette come to terms with the splendour of her own inspiration. The whole matter was so direct, so beautiful, so breathlessly beyond language, so far above trout and sows and suchlike unseemly mishaps of translation that, clouded in the skirts of her own uplifted dress, she was not entirely sure whether or not Williams retained his boots for the loving act, or what if anything else he had abandoned other than his composure and his jacket.

His stockings were there: somewhere on his legs a man wears stockings to rub such a miracle of sparks against her own calves

and insteps that she nearly forgot what she had come here to say,
then almost got it said, with his answers unheard, till she realized
she had said it.

What she must have said were enough words to prise from
him his intention to marry her, God and guardians willing. She
found herself arguing for a *fait accompli*. 'We must get a priest to
bless us,' she said.

'How so?'

'Here,' she said, 'a priest can do anything. A priest can do
everything.'

'A constitutional priest? A *legal* priest?'

'No, Williams. A *priest*.'

'How can I have a piece of paper binding enough to take back
to my guardians?'

'What this priest will give you, Williams, will be binding
before God. With it, I shall see you as God sees you. I shall see
you as my husband, in every way my husband. With it we can do
this, and face the consequence of this.'

Given such assurances, they seemed to be about to do it, then
already to have done it, at least once more.

William felt himself bound to her beauty and her love for
ever. He felt himself bound as any man would be, and saw no
harm in savouring the binding. As to what would follow after, he
had no way of knowing. Nor, for the moment, did he care.
What he knew was he was committed.

The person he was committed to, Annette, love's self, his
perpetual and recurring miracle – she was no longer with him.
She was up, and soothing her clothes, and talking noisily, to him
if need be, if not to herself and to whatever ears were listening.
She had an appearance to maintain. She was on her way downstairs to greet her mother's visitors.

The people in the drawing room were huddled in a conspirato-
rial circle. They sat with their chairs pulled forward and their
noses together. There were six of them, and Annette's mother
was the only woman among them.

For the first time in France, William felt himself to be a
stranger. Their manner seemed completely alien to him, as they

nibbled at some secret or other like rats round a potato. And like rats, they sprang apart the moment they were disturbed.

Neither Annette nor her mother made any attempt to introduce him.

Jean-Jacques Vallon was there, this time wearing a jacket and with no blood on his hands. So was another young man, similarly dressed and with the same confident air of being a member of the family. Presumably he was Doctor Charles Henry, the other surgeon brother. Both men sat back calmly in their seats, as if whatever secret the group had been discussing was really no concern of theirs. They wore the detached expression that William associated with their calling, midway between butchers and saints. He supposed executioners must look much the same, though he'd never met one. It didn't seem a good observation to make to Annette, as they found chairs and sat towards but not quite among the rest of the circle.

'I shall take the oath,' a middle-aged man said abruptly. 'Grégoire is a good bishop, and he requires it of me, so I shall swear.' He wasn't robed, but presumably he was one of the priests in the family. He had Paul's laugh, and showed something of his deviousness too, for he was clearly changing the subject.

The fat man next to him wore a black cope that was too tight to accommodate the bulge of his belly, at least while he was sitting down. 'I have already signified my allegiance,' he said with a chuckle. He was built for chuckles, but they made him sound sly. 'Grégoire is more than good. He is devout.'

'I never thought to see a member of my family—' Madame saw no reason to finish her sentence. The priests never were her family, not her blood, but it was clear she had no intention of relinquishing her hold on the Vallons just because she was married to a Vergez.

'The clergy go with the bishop,' the fat one said. 'Here we have a bishop who gives a proper lead.'

'Nonsense. He's a Constitutionalist.'

'But devout,' the other priest put in, with a sideways look at Annette. 'Many of the old order you so much admire, cousin Françoise, many of those bishops and archbishops are corrupt. They were not appointed by God from Rome, but in France as a favour. Ask your daughter. She prays at all of our churches, all the time. She knows where the good priests are.'

Madame Vergez was already trying to move people towards the meal table. Annette stood too and said, 'It would be impolite of me to express an opinion, uncle. What does the Seigneur of Montlivault think?'

The tall, raw-cheeked man was already standing in deference to the soup, which was being served in the next room. He smiled, held out his hand to William, and said, 'Guyon de Montlivault,' as if his name explained everything in the world that needed to be explained. He had a quick, unsurprisable eye, looked like a mountain shepherd but smelled of horse leather. He examined William for a moment, then turned quickly towards the priests without waiting for his answer. 'I admire you both as honest men – there must be some in your profession – but I'll decline to discuss my business in front of you.' He laughed, slapped the middle of William's back as if they were intimates, and caught hold of Annette's elbow. William knew Annette ran errands for him – indeed, she'd left his couch in Orléans to seek out Montlivault with a message. He wondered if he should be jealous. He ached with the realization of one of life's sadder facts. To go to bed with a woman does not cure a young man of jealousy. It makes him want to be in bed with her again.

They chuckled their way through the double doors into the next room and towards the dining table. Madame walked with the Seigneur of Montlivault, so that worthy had to do without Annette's elbow. Annette seemed determined to place herself by William whatever happened. They stood while the thin priest, the one in ordinary clothes, said a grace. He spoke it in French. This surprised William. Listening to their talk, he was beginning to feel, and for the first time, the *foreignness* of Annette's religion steal about him like an extra conspiracy. The French grace was an additional surprise. France had always seemed unutterably worldly to him, but its brief moments of holiness had always occurred in Latin. He would have felt at home with a Latin grace, after his time at grammar school and at Cambridge.

The fat priest was not going to let Montlivault's taunts pass without challenge. He tasted the soup, then said, 'Amen. Anything said to me at this table shall enjoy the same rights as in the confessional.'

'Ah, but how secure is a confession made before one of your cloth?'

'We're discussing the matter, Montlivault. Believe me we are. Think what the Secret Police could do if only they were privy to the confessional!' His smile was even slyer than his chuckle. 'For the moment, I hold to my old habits. Whatever you confess before me belongs exclusively to God.'

The fat one dried his hands upon his cape and looked towards the thin one, who said, 'Perhaps you should use me for what I am, Count. The Jacobins – if I may call them that – have appropriated my church for their meetings. They even stand in my pulpit to harangue one another, and – for whatever good it may do them – to denounce *you*.'

Montlivault sat very still at this piece of unwelcome news.

'I have an ear to all their business, Count. And *that* certainly does not belong to God.'

Madame Vergez glanced sharply towards him. William guessed he was straying too close to matters she preferred to keep secret. He was surprised at Annette's abrupt change of subject, just the same. 'Williams could be a priest, if he wished.'

'A priest?' the fat one asked. 'In the alternative tradition?'

'An *English* priest, yes,' William said. He noticed the tightening of Madame Vergez's mouth. Other mouths could tighten as they would.

'But he doesn't want.'

'But how can a *boy* become a priest?' the thin one allowed himself to ask.

'My uncle arranged the matter for me.'

'It sounds almost as corrupt as the disposal of our bishoprics under the Ancien Régime.'

'I follow neither your God, nor the English God. I have an alternative religion.'

This piece of apostasy was more than Madame Vergez would allow him. Before he could whisper the one word 'Poetry' which would set him free of uncles, guardians and papists alike, she turned towards the fat priest and said, 'Cousin Charles Olivier, Father Charles, you talk of devout Constitutionalists. Surely there are fathers among those who refuse to swear who are equally holy?'

'There are some good men among them,' the thin one put in. 'Good enough to mislead their whole flock.'

'As my brother Claude says, these good men mislead their congregations to a damaging degree. Then the bishop turns their congregations out of church, so their congregations insist on hearing Mass somewhere else – in a barn, shall we say?'

'You can't celebrate Mass in a barn,' Claude snapped.

'With a non-juring priest you can.'

'A non-juring priest is no more legal in a barn than in a church.'

Madame Vergez knew when a subject needed to be changed. 'I am not too certain about the duck,' she said firmly. 'I've recently taken on Berthe Lacaille as my cook – you know, old man Lacaille's sister – so there'll be no accounting for the sauce.'

'Her sauce is very good,' Annette said no less firmly. She beamed at her uncle Charles Olivier as if he had just told her everything she wanted to know. 'I've tasted the sauce, and you can believe me when I say it is excellent.'

Was the daughter trying to put her mother in her place, or merely insisting she had at last found a place of her own?

BLOIS.
FRIDAY A FEW HOURS LATER

The February dusk closed about them, and the cobbles glazed with frost.

Annette walked quickly. Her quickly was slow for Williams, but he seemed surprised at her willingness to walk at all.

'St Saturnin's is over the bridge,' she said. 'It's my uncle Charles Olivier's church.'

'The sly one.'

'The fat one.' She missed a word of Williams' French, but presumably he saw Charles Olivier as the fat one.

'I thought you don't approve of his sort?'

'It's a church. Its doors are open. He allows another priest to be there. A Christian priest who could marry us and make everything right.'

'A non-juring priest?'

'A Christian one.'

St Saturnin was just visible across the river, in a tiny cluster of buildings already becoming indistinct against the dark trees of St Gervais le Forêt, and beyond them the marshy wilderness of the Salogne. If the inhabitants of Blois spoke of what was out there, and they rarely did, they called it 'Forest'. They had their own wood on their own side of the river. This too was vast, but it was well kept, with carriageways and clearings. They built their furniture from its logs, and used its twigs and branches for firewood and kindling. This was known as *The* Forest, The Forest of Blois.

She was explaining this to Williams as they crossed the bridge.

He wasn't listening. This deafness of men to everything important had been remarked upon by her sisters. He caught her in his arms and began to kiss her, crushingly.

She allowed him freedoms, but not many. She intended to make it clear to him that today's noontide in bed was not so much a consummation as the end of a conversation she had insisted on beginning several weeks ago. Annette had at last had 'her little talk'. She was now reminding him of its consequences. She tried to hurry him across the bridge.

She could see he was as uneasy as if she were taking him to a blood sacrifice or a meeting of witches.

'I thought a Mass can only be said at certain times,' he asked, 'and never during the hours of darkness?'

She had so much to teach him, even about the crossing of bridges. She wished he wouldn't loiter. It was one thing to go across boldly in the forenoon as Vergez did, with a gun on your shoulder, quite another to steal towards a secret ceremony at dusk. He quickened his pace.

'This will not be a full Mass,' she said in order to say something aloud. 'Not a High Mass.' Conspirators are never loud. 'There will be no chanting and – I daresay – not enough lights. It will be some kind of votive Mass, I suppose.'

'Votive?'

'Mass is Mass,' she said fiercely. 'High Mass, Low Mass – every Mass is a requiem nowadays, whether it's on a saint's day or a Sunday.'

'A requiem? Whose requiem?'

'A requiem for the Death of France.'

They were on the South side of the bridge by now. She led him into a side street.

'I see the church is guarded,' Williams said.

She was annoyed to see a line of men armed with staves barring their way to the porch. There were some women, too. Even in Blois, events seemed to be encouraging the poorer members of her own sex to believe they could behave as badly as men, and join in the roughness in the streets.

'They're not in such good order as either of the Guards in Orléans!'

She had to disabuse him. 'These people are trying to stop us from going in,' she said. 'They don't like non-juring priests. And, as Father Claude says, they use the church for their own meetings. They say it belongs to them.'

'It does, doesn't it?'

'It belongs to God.'

William eyed the crowd, hesitated, and said, 'I don't know what we are doing here.'

'Then ask the Good God for guidance!'

Annette spoke these words so vehemently that they opened a way for them. This was in part because several groups of worshippers, mainly women, arrived immediately in front of them and were jostled on their way to the door. The protesters were distracted by the fury of their own efforts. Their victims were ageing ladies with a few old men concealed in their midst, not a young couple striding boldly forward.

Inside the church there were men in considerable numbers, a few men by themselves, most of them brought by their wives. They had obviously been prudent enough to arrive early, before the crowd had gathered.

William and Annette were the last arrivals, or the latest to succeed in getting in. Once the congregation was assembled, the men and women outside the door set up a shout, and then began a regular chant punctuated by frequent howls, presumably to drown the act of worship. They were making other sounds as well, groans, and scrapings and curses that William couldn't quite distinguish.

This faceless scuffling and muttering outside made the unseen crowd sound like a giant animal breathing against the door, and it had a dismal effect on the service.

William had twice looked into the cathedral at Orléans, more from curiosity than any religious impulse – though a lover who fancies himself to be spurned will haunt all manner of places. In Orléans, Mass had been a glittering affair, even though people complained they couldn't afford candles. He'd been struck by the large number of priests, almost an army of them, so that the celebrants in their robes seemed to outnumber the congregation.

Here there was one priest only. He hung a cloth round his neck, but otherwise kept himself as plain as a Quaker. His voice scarcely rose above a whisper, so his people huddled conspiratorially towards him, some of them from deafness, most no doubt from devotion.

From time to time an old man would cough, and his wife choke with anxiety. The priest would interrupt his prayers and offer words of comfort to them both in a voice louder than he seemed to be able to manage for the Mass itself. He was terrified, but bristled with defiance. He chanted his Latin so quietly that it sometimes seemed no more than another version of silence, yet everything he uttered was slow. He refused to let his God be hurried, perhaps because he was frightened to end. He had even more reason than the rest of them to fear the crowd at the door. He couldn't be brave with composure, not 'bravely brave' as William whispered to Annette, but just to be brave at all was braveness enough. To celebrate Mass against the noise in the doorway was an act of considerable courage. The door had now been thrown open, and people stared in so they could identify the priest and show him they knew who he was.

William said as much to Annette. He was surprised to catch himself whispering to her so often – he had no wish to offend her religion – but in fact everyone about them was muttering. They chatted to keep their courage up.

At the latest growl behind them, she said, 'You must believe me when I tell you our Mass is a beautiful thing – Latin is God's own language.'

'I know Latin.' Such a statement was never quite true, of course. 'It was a language spoken by men who believed in gods other than God.'

She was frightened. They were all frightened. She needed to hear herself speak, not listen to what anyone said to her. 'Pope Gregory ordered it to be said nine times,' she said. 'Pope Gelasius ordained the Epistle, and Pope Damascus the *Credo*. Pope Sextus—'

He felt too anxious to pay attention to her. It didn't matter what girls and young women were talking about – it might be of popes, it could be of girdle-cakes – they invariably had all manner of trivial information at their fingertips which he always regretted not having himself.

'Pope Alexander—'

He felt a surge of warmth for her, and a spasm of alarm for himself. Her involvement with her faith was so passionate, so intricate, so *political*, and his own religious convictions were no more than lukewarm.

'Will you take the cup with me?' she asked, drawing him forward as she did so.

'Just this once,' he said, with no certainty that he would live to see another time.

Only a few dared go up for the sacrament, and Annette and Williams were the last of the few.

The wine was sour as ancient blood.

Annette waited until the old priest had finished, then said, 'We want you to marry us, Papa Rock.'

'Pray God I don't have to bury you first. Do you have your parents' permission?'

'Yes,' she lied.

'Well, I'm sure you have your poor father's blessing, Marie Anne.'

'My father is dead.'

'As I say. Well, there will be no weddings here. Or not ones made in Heaven. You must come to the barn at St Gervais le Forêt. I can't tell you when, if there's to be a when for any of us again. But when the time comes – *if* it comes – I'll send you word in secret, and marry you before a whole congregation of Christians. Will your mother be coming?'

'Mother has other matters on her mind.'

'Mothers often do, my child. And other priests in their family, whatever their politics.'

So I'm to be married in a barn, she thought bitterly, just as Uncle Charles Olivier said. She watched Williams press the old priest's hand. Then she followed him towards the door. The night outside was surprisingly still.

★

The French tended to pave their towns. This made their streets a great deal more solid than most English ones. It also gave malcontents something to pick up and throw at people they did not like.

The road beyond the bridge was not paved. Some of it was loose stones. Most of it was a mixture of frosted ruts and softening mud. But the church of St Saturnin stood at the back of its own tiny square, which formed an unfenced 'yard'. This yard had been paved at the start of the service. While the devout had been worshipping, and the raucous deafened the angels with their howls and imprecations, the diligent had been quietly prising up ammunition. They now had a huge arsenal of cobbles. This had been built into an encircling wall, behind which the whites of eyes and – just occasionally – teeth glimmered. The churchyard was now a pitfall backed by a barricade.

The worshippers hung back on either side of the door. Those at the back were naturally bolder and more inquisitive than those at the front. The watchers behind the barricade gave them time to pack themselves tightly together, then they set up a shout to send them back on their heels.

They lifted the top layer of cobbles from their barricade and threw them into their tightly massed target. Most fell short. Those that did not arrived with a great snapping of bone.

French cobblestones were bigger than English cobblestones, William had learned. English cobbles were split flints or pebbles dug from gravel. French cobbles were dressed stone, cut from the living rock. They were bigger than housebricks, so they couldn't be made to carry far. This meant they gave people scant time to avoid them, and did terrible injury to those who didn't.

As far as Annette could see, several people lay felled to the ground and were possibly dead. Children shouted, a number of the injured cried aloud as they were struck, then moaned, mumbled or were silent. Few people screamed. When there is horror it generally happens without noise. She had learned that fact in the Forest of Orléans. So it was here. The congregation retreated into the church, drawing as many of the fallen after them as they could. Annette picked up a trampled child, Williams dragged its mother inside by her coat. When he turned to go outside for others, Annette stopped him.

There was still no noise, save from an old man with a broken elbow trying to be sick. His retching jarred on and on, beyond alteration or comfort.

The priest closed the door. It had no bolt or bar, and he carried no key. As it swung into place, the besiegers stepped over their barricade and turned to pick up another layer of stone. These slammed against the door with an appalling clatter.

The priest said, 'This is a church, remember. If they break in upon us, you must claim sanctuary. Do so in a loud voice. But let me go forward to talk to them first.' He was trembling with fear. It was a truth outside story-books that the brave do tremble with fear.

William looked for a weapon. He found a staff with a candle bracket on its end. He did no more than place his hand upon it and wait, fearful of offending people by claiming it prematurely. Several other men had found similar weapons for themselves.

The door burst open.

For a moment, the congregation hung back, then one or two of the younger men strode forward. William joined them. He heard Annette shout after him in alarm, but he tried to compose himself nonetheless. He stood among the others, brandishing his candle-staff, and feeling foolish to do so.

It was snatched away from him. The old priest had it and now advanced with it to the door. He placed it carefully in a bracket there, dusted his hands, then faced the people outside.

'Why don't you come in?' he asked. 'You are always welcome here – you know that. Our prayers are finished. We know you conduct your business here – Mass with Father Charles, and all manner of other such secular meetings. Welcome, in the name of the Father and of the Son.'

The silence was heavy. People muttered together, squabbled. No stones were flung. Men respected the old priest. Some of them were reluctant to defile God's House; others had no wish to damage a floor and furnishings they considered to be their own.

'I beg you to come in – all of you or your representatives – step inside the door and receive a blessing, in Christ's name.'

A woman giggled, then shouted something offensive.

Someone tried to throw – or merely let slip – a cobblestone which crashed down in the porch. A few of those outside pressed forward, and the giggling woman – several women – began to blaspheme, then joined their voices in a crescendo of shrillness. They knew their men were susceptible to argument. The best way with argument was to drown it out.

The old priest stepped closer to them, so close that William feared he would be snatched into the crowd. He began to speak directly to the women. He spoke, William thought, of Mary who was a mother, because 'mother' and 'Mary' and 'Virgin' were the only words he could hear.

The women grew calmer. They lifted themselves towards him. They eyed him agog with that awful blank expression that poor wives can summon when they don't know whether to scold you or mock you or cut your throat. William felt sure the old priest was winning the argument, or winning it for now, winning it for a pace outside the door, or until the congregation began to disperse and become individuals, and those individuals' backs were turned.

One woman in particular – she was scarcely more than a girl – stood with her face right against the old priest. Like the poor women of Orléans she wore shawls instead of any proper top to her dress, and somewhere inside the shawl there was a child.

The child burst open and the woman's breast exploded in a great gout of blood. Her head shattered also. The crowd at the door fell apart, and bullets whirred and skidded about the pillars of the nave. The sound of discharging muskets followed after.

By this time the old priest was kneeling by the dead woman and her extinguished child. Other people lay bleeding about him on either side of the door. Some of them moaned. Some of them were dead.

The interval was not long, about as lengthy as it takes an untrained but eager hand to reload a musket, say half a minute. It was filled with screams and curses from beyond the door, the sound of hurrying rather than running feet.

The second volley was not directed towards the church but explored the world at large. There were echoes, distant cries, the sigh of wasted shot brushing among the branches like a flight of birds.

There was another face at the door, beckoning those inside to escape while they could. It was that Lacaille who had led William through the Forest of Orléans on a horse. He smiled in recognition, then said to Annette, 'We're gunsmiths. We make them. We repair them. We sell them. You'd expect us to use them to protect our friends.'

William was appalled by the woman's death, and by the meaty doll at her breast. The dead child's face was no longer covered by its mother's shawl. Impossible merely to view it as bundled blood and hair. It was a babe no less than any he'd seen nursed at Marie-Adelaïde Dufour's.

The priest looked up from ministering them and said, 'You didn't have to shoot, Raymond Lacaille. I was starting to talk to them.'

'You stick to your business, father. And I'll stick to mine.'

'Yours leaves me with too much to do,' the old man said, 'and God gives me more than enough already.'

William thought the priest was crying. Annette urged him through the porch and away, treading among a dozen or so bodies brought low by muskets and three felled by stones.

'I think we should run,' Annette told him.

Young women do not run, not beyond early girlhood. They cannot. They have neither the clothing nor the joints for it. They are made for walking with brisk steps over a short distance, then sitting still in an upright chair. Annette ran.

William knew running was a dangerous exercise, even for limbs that were hardy. If they ran they would attract attention to themselves. They had a long bridge to cross. The swirling darkness seemed to magnify its length. Running was one way to cross it just the same. So he ran with her, holding her hand.

As it happened, Annette ran well, so William let go of her hand to let her arm swing free. It was a newly discovered activity and it liberated her. It was wonderful, so breath-stealingly exciting that just a few steps of it were more than enough.

She wasn't allowed to stop. At their back they heard a howl of rage. It flowed behind them in a patter of footsteps, some of them bare, some in rag bindings. A group of protesters was on the bridge not thirty paces behind them, and the women among them weren't impeded by the restraints of clothing that hampered ladies of degree. It was lucky that Annette and William had a flying start, since there was nobody close to aid them. Lacaille and his companions had gone, and their fellow worshippers had dispersed into doorways and alleys.

Annette turned and saw flashing blades, heard the epicene baying of the crowd.

'We must outrun them or jump in the river,' she heard Williams say.

The river was impossible for her. She ran. She ran faster than the men behind, but more slowly than some of the women. Unlike Williams and Annette, these wore little on their feet. So they gained. The end of the bridge drew nearer, but with its end the couple lost their last chance to escape into the river.

Annette turned, and felt Williams catch her against him, hurrying her backwards then swinging her round to run properly again. This time she found herself running freely, more freely even than Williams. She had gazed much too closely on her pursuers.

These women had long since outstripped their men. They had no need of them. They did not belong to the same kind as her mother and sister. They were like men in skirts – when they wore skirts, or anything much like clothing at all. Dark-faced, dirty, with foodstained chins and mouths, they rushed bare-breasted, bare-chested, and showing strangely masculine knees under uplifted petticoats.

It was clear to Annette, and doubtless to Williams also, that they would be caught at the very beginning of the town. She felt, or imagined she felt, their blades pecking at her back, as she ran like a sick chicken being chased by the other hens in the farmyard. She was going to be killed, badly used at least, not a hundred steps from her house.

At this precise moment, and to her terror, she ran into a leg. Hanged men were a rarity in Blois – the citizens had hardly ever allowed themselves to grow sufficiently angry – but the idea that she had collided with such an emblem of hell planted itself very firmly in her mind.

In fact the leg was booted and hanging from a horse. It was limp enough, as its owner was drunk though not so entirely that he couldn't sit astride his mount. His horse was one of several, and their riders were all in much the same condition.

French crowds were no respecters of horses, even when they had soldiers astride them. These soldiers were officers, and Annette was content to shelter among their hoofs for an instant, while the women and then their men closed around.

The drunken officers were members of the Bassigny Regiment, frequently entertained in her home, and billeted widely about among her family and her family's friends. They weren't liked for this very reason. Fortunately they weren't alone. The drunken officers – a major, two ensigns and a captain – were accompanied by upwards of a dozen more officers of the same regiment who were on foot. They had been drinking together in the town's hostelries.

It was one of these who stepped towards the women. 'You know me, citizens.'

They knew him. The would have preferred to stick their blades into Williams and Annette and perhaps drag an aristocrat from his horse, but they had to confess they knew him and that he was unpretentious enough to stand eye to eye with them.

Even so, their grievances were many. 'We have been slaughtered with muskets,' they pleaded. 'This woman caused us to be fired upon by muskets.'

'What – the Citizeness Vallon? I see no musket.'

How Annette hated the word citizeness, especially on the lips of a gentleman. It wasn't seemly to utter such an obscenity let alone apply it to her.

'I know her well. I know her as an honourable lady of spirit who keeps company with foolish men.'

Annette was surprised at how well the chase had cleared her head and how swiftly she could recover her breath. Her anger came back with every gulp she took.

'Her brothers the surgeons are well known to you, as was her father. They do good works among you, I believe.'

'They work at the Hôtel de Dieu, yes, if that is good work.'

'Believe me, it is, citizeness – although I hope you never have need of it.' He produced a tiny wallet full of coins, and examined it suggestively.

The officer who had obliged Annette with his leg thought it was time he asserted himself. 'I say, Beaupuy,' he said, 'there's no need of that. I've got a pistol here that will blow off a face or two.'

'It depends how much you like your horse, major,' the captain said quietly. 'You can fire off your guns if you will, but you'll have no more use for saddle leather.' He handed the nearest woman some money. 'This is from the Citizeness Vallon. She bids you go bathe your hurts, citizeness. And you, citizen.'

'I can pay my own reparations, Captain Beaupuy,' Annette hissed at his back.

'Doubtless you can, citizeness. And doubtless I shall seek repayment from your stepfather.'

'Come home, Williams.' She tugged her Englishman by the arm. 'That Beaupuy is an aristocrat, would you believe! An aristocrat and an officer in a noble regiment. The man owns estates, and yet he demeans himself with riff raff such as that.'

'A good job for us that he does.'

'He even attends meetings of the Friends. I hate him.'

'He seems less than popular with his fellow officers also.'

'He's a traitor to his rank and to his station in life. He deserves to be killed.'

William was in no mood to argue with her. He had seen terrible deeds done by ordinary men and women to ordinary women and men. People he had come to France to befriend were eager to kill him because he kept dangerous company. It was disturbing to realize that the woman he loved so passionately appeared to many to be the most dangerous company of all.

These thoughts lasted the few steps to Annette's door. He already thought of it as the dragon's lair.

'Where have you been, Annette? There's soot upon your cheek.'

Madame Vergez was before him now, or he before her. In her own way and in her own house Annette's mother was every bit as threatening as anything in the street outside. She stood with her other two daughters and her husband, as if she had formed up her family to wait for them.

'We've been to church, to St Saturnin.'

'Not, I hope, to hear Cousin Claude Olivier?'

'Mass was celebrated by the old priest, mother.'

'Nothing on that side of the river is suitable for a daughter of mine. Or for a guest in my house.'

'I found the Mass extremely interesting, madame. The evening was intensely lively.'

'And you bring back my daughter covered in soot. From *Mass*, monsieur?'

'Madame best knows what kinds of Mass are celebrated in Blois. I am only a visitor.'

'Indeed. And as such you are welcome, monsieur. I insist you shall be comfortable during your time here. It is to this end I have arranged for you to lodge with my son Jean-Jacques.'

'So he tells me, madame.'

'His wife, my daughter-in-law, is expecting you tomorrow.'

'Thank you, citizeness.' This was a horrible mistake, not entirely to be attributed to foreignness or ignorance.

Vergez had been grinning at his wife's elbow, and surveying the world with that surgical smile of his. William had already decided it was not so such an expression of amusement as an act of God.

To his surprise it altered. Vergez's face registered pain, consternation, alarm, even while the smile persisted.

Annette's stepfather beckoned him towards the fire. 'Religious disturbances?' he asked. 'Republican congregations against the traditionalists?'

Williams nodded, and Vergez poured him a glass of apple brandy.

'It's a bad day when priests start fighting one another,' Vergez said, drinking for both of them. He toasted Williams solemnly. 'So long as we doctors don't start cutting one another up, eh? When doctor anatomizes doctor, the poets will really come into their own.'

BLOIS.
THE FOURTH DAY OF FEBRUARY,
1792

'So, monsieur.'

'It has been most incredibly kind of you, madame. Remember me to your husband. I feel honoured to have met him, and shall continue to think of him especially fondly.'

He had risen early, but Madame Vergez had risen before him, urgent to see him on his way. Her gaze as she stood by the door said it all. Mr Wodswod was a man who returned a woman's daughters with soot on their cheeks. He encouraged them to stray across the river and loiter in his bedroom – don't think she hadn't noticed – when soup was already on the table and her guests were waiting. They looked each other in the eye, and – no – he didn't suppose she hadn't noticed.

'I shall show him the way to Jean-Jacques, mother.'

'I have already arranged for someone to carry his bags, Annette.'

'Impossible I should allow them to leave my own hand, madame. I *do* assure you.' Two nights at the house in the Rue du Pont had burnished his French in ice.

'I see no need, Annette.'

'Mother, I see every need and am quite resolved.'

'As I say, madame, my *fondest* regards to your husband.'

'He is at the hospital, monsieur. At the Hôtel de Dieu.'

'Yes, madame. He crossed the bridge early.' William had seen him go, with a hunting wallet on his arm and an arsenal as formidable as the Lacailles'. He was probably a favoured customer of the gunsmiths, at least for pellets and powder. And, like William, he needed to escape from Madame Vergez.

As she led her Englishman up the hill, Annette said, 'I am sorry about mother, Williams. It is me she is quarrelling with – you understand that?'

'No,' he answered. 'But I understand Cumberland tinkers well enough.'

This reference was cryptic, and since it was being applied to a member of her family she decided not to ask for an explanation. But after a few paces, he added, 'When a tinker sells a foal at Cockermouth fair, he always insults the buyer and pretends there is no way the poor fellow can possibly afford such a splendid beast.'

'Maman is like the tinker?'

'If you say so.'

'And you think she is trying to sell me to you?'

'There's no way I could possibly afford such a beast.' He moved towards her, but his valises prevented him from clasping her to him. This was fortunate, for her mother's cook was coming downhill towards them.

When she had passed, Annette said, 'So my Englishman feels obliged to marry his horse?'

'Your Englishman does.'

'I thought you didn't like horses, Williams.'

'Only in poetry.'

She indicated her brother's house, just a few steps ahead of them.

Williams put his bags on the floor and said, 'Surely a young woman is not her own property, not to the extent that she can dispose of herself in matrimony?'

'According to the Constitution a woman enjoys every freedom.'

'You love this Revolution well enough when it is convenient to you.'

'The law is there to be *used*, Williams. Promise me you will marry me when the old priest calls us.'

'If you insist.' She let him know this was not quite the answer she hoped for, so he smiled and added quickly, 'It's Leap Year.'

The expression meant nothing to her. He was as foreign as his own Cumberland tinker. Presumably he was saying yes.

Her sister-in-law Angel had left a note and directions. She had gone to the market. Her note was for Williams, but it seemed simplest for Annette to read it and follow what it said.

The note led them both to a room much bigger than the one in the Rue du Pont. The room held a bed. The house seemed agreeably empty, and he tried to take her in his arms.

Annette shook her head and gave Williams a single kiss. 'Not till after our appointment with the old curé.'

He seemed distracted rather than disappointed. She wanted him to accompany her on a walk, but he preferred to remain with his notebooks.

William wanted to be alone because he was becoming stifled by other people's arrangements for him.

He had come to France in order to make something of himself, not to be marooned in Blois. Englishmen were speaking in the political debates in Paris. So were men from the Americas. And where was William Wordsworth? He was elsewhere. He had entered the little world of Madame Vergez, and even that had been snatched away from him.

His notebook was open, but he was in no mood to work. The room was wrong. The town was wrong. He had vacated perfectly good lodgings in Orléans so he could come to Blois as a guest. The hospitality had lasted less than two days. He was back in lodgings again, but no longer his own man.

He willed himself to go on with his poem. He read it diligently. It was growing. It was good. It was almost very good. It was good enough to be an acute disappointment to him. His couplets were beginning to irk him. They always ended worse than they began. The only good ones were the unfinished ones. They were like the ecstatic and only recently experienced act of love, better a moment before their end than at the end itself.

The room smelled strange. Perhaps his nostrils were suffering from love's fever. His poem certainly was. Love was a cramp that afflicted everything.

He heard a woman's voice. The house was no longer empty. The voice spoke again and was answered by a girl talking the local *patois*. Both of these adult voices came to him above and around the shrillness of a child, singing to itself and chattering to the world in general.

So Jean-Jacques Vallon's Angel was back from the market or wherever she had been. William decided to go downstairs.

Here he found two extremely plump young women. One of them was dressed in a coarse linen dress and a knitted coat. She was swinging a two-year-old child by the arms and was presumably the serving girl. The other was about the same age as Annette, and she was in the later stages of pregnancy.

He stepped forward to introduce himself, and collided with the swinging child, who was a baby girl. The three females laughed or were otherwise amused, and William failed to find suitable words of apology.

Still smiling, Angel said, 'I am Madame Vallon.' She held out her hand with the palm turned inwards, as if she were a man. 'And you are Annette's friend, Monsieur Williams.'

He took her hand and shook it. He didn't correct her. He wondered what Madame Vergez would make of such a greeting.

'Angélique,' she added. She indicated the child. 'This is Anne Angélique. This' – here she touched her stomach – 'this mountain is Anne Zoé.'

'Perhaps Madame is hoping for a boy?'

'It will be a girl, Monsieur Williams. My husband for once agrees with me on the subject. Look how high under the heart she sits, and believe me when I speak of indigestion. She will be a girl.'

'Will Madame be disappointed otherwise?'

'Surprised, but not disappointed. Mothers want babies, Monsieur Williams. Only men want sons or daughters.'

Angel was a pretty woman. She had the same colouring as Annette, and spoke in a rush, just as she did. He could see why Annette was fond of her.

Her morning at the market had clearly been a scrambled one. She and the maid stood in the entrance to the house with their purchases dropped about them on the floor. There were two heavy baskets. One of them was covered with a bloodied cloth, the other full of vegetables – a strange assortment of roots he couldn't recognize and funguses he was reluctant to know about. Also on the floor there was one of those endless sausages that curled up on themselves to occupy a space no bigger than a soup plate but which would stretch across the street if unrolled, and four piteous hens who lay with hobbled feet and gazed one-eyed about them while waiting for the axe. With a child to manage, and one of them pregnant, this had been as far as the two women could bring such a load. They had flung everything down just inside the door. Goodness knows how the chickens had been carried.

The child was the first to be got rid of. The maid picked her up again, grunted, and carried her up a flight of steps into the kitchen, presumably to find her some jam on a crust. The house was built on a hill, like every other dwelling he had seen in Blois. Some, like Annette's, were conveniently lower at the back. This one was higher.

William did not see what became of the food and livestock. The house shook. Feet, a great number of them, pounded on the floorboards overhead. He heard groans, moans, laughter, an insistent dominant cry, every voice masculine and loud. It was as if a besieging army had entered an upstairs window by a ladder and was now walking downstairs.

He and Angel Vallon, and presumably the chickens, were thrust to one side by a rabble of yawning and largely unbuttoned men. They wore, fastened or otherwise, the uniform of an Ancien Régime regiment of the line. The elegance of their cloth and the splendour of their epaulettes marked them as officers, though their ranks escaped him, and they left behind them an overall aroma of oils, colognes, and an aftermath of soap. Otherwise they were in very bad order indeed. They had drunk late and risen late, and then exited untidily. It was as if the Greeks had overslept inside the Trojan horse.

'The maids set breakfast for you hours ago,' Angel Vallon called after them.

'And the Good God set his sun in the sky,' one of them grumbled. 'But no one thought to tell us about it.'

'I've already eaten it,' another one groaned. William watched the man totter on the doorstep, clutch his hand to his forehead and howl in pain. One by one they disappeared down the street.

'They're the gentry of the Bassigny Regiment,' Angel explained. 'The Thirty-Second Regiment of the Line, if numbers are at all interesting to you, Monsieur Williams. They're better when sober, but not entirely disgusting when drunk.'

'I met some of them last night.'

'So maman told me when I called on her just now. You must not let Annette keep you out late, monsieur. It affects maman very badly. Annette doesn't care. She treats her as she pleases. It's the rest of us who suffer.'

William worked on his poem. Somewhat to his annoyance, his melancholy evaporated.

The midday meal at Angel's table looked exactly as her husband had promised him. It was elaborate and excellent.

He sat while she fed her infant some vegetables mashed in broth. Then the girl took the baby away, and he joined Angel Vallon at the feast.

He sat with her alone, and they began to eat a double rack of lamb that stood upon the table like a boat's hull.

'I thought my little sister-in-law would be here to look after you,' she said. Angel was taller than Annette, as well as being indescribably large in other directions.

'I sent her away.' The explanation did not sound well, and would not have done even if he could have offered it up in English. 'I had things to do.'

'"Things"?'

He must try not to flirt.

Angel seemed very happy to flirt.

He was spared the embarrassment of explaining himself by the return of several of the officers. They entered boisterously from a long way off. They threw themselves at the food and ate loudly and loutishly. William thought all Frenchmen ate badly, but refused to moralize on the matter. The Demoiselle Gellet-Duvivier had presented him with an entire paragraph on the subject, some six or seven sentences spoken in sequence while her father spread mustard on a flake of batter then dipped it in wine. 'The Dutch are the worst eaters,' she had told him, 'and would carry the prize for gluttony above all nations were it not for the English.' As far as he knew, he was the only Englishman she had encountered, so he stopped eating in front of her at once. He always left the drinking to Monsieur Gellet-Duvivier, because the man had both a need and a talent for it.

These pleasing memories of the Demoiselle were interrupted by one of the officers asking him a question. He always found a new accent hard to follow, especially with food in its mouth. He was shaping some words that might serve as an answer when Jean-Jacques arrived in the room and at table in what seemed a single continuous movement. The surgeon was as neat of collar and clean of cuff as on the two previous occasions; but when he reached to carve himself some meat there were droplets of arterial blood on his right sleeve, clustered about the buttons like holly berries and as bright as death on a rabbit's nose.

The officer broke off questioning Williams and asked him, 'What have you got for us between now and supper, patron?'

'I am to saw off a woman's leg. It will be a melancholy occasion, believe you me.'

'But one that will pass the afternoon for us.'

'Alas, no. Common decency forbids. You can watch a man lose his leg, and I'll willingly give you a demonstration of every vein and sinew. A woman's leg I cannot possibly allow, not while the poor creature is still at the end of it.' He brushed aside their objections and carved himself another cutlet from the rack.

'How high will you trim this leg, Vallon?'

'About a hand's span above the knee.' The surgeon chewed reflectively. 'By rights it should be taken at the hip. Its disease insists that I take it at the hip. Such an operation has been done, of course. Even so, it remains a surgical impossibility.'

'Below the hip or above the knee – won't the poor woman die in either event?'

'Almost certainly, yes. But she will definitely perish if I do nothing. This way I give the Almighty a sporting chance with her.'

'So she will suffer?'

'But not in front of you gentlemen. It will be, as I said, a melancholy occasion, noisy and full of fuss. Think on it the next time you cause a cannonball to be discharged, or even the issue of a musket.'

This caused a rowdy debate, during which the surgeon managed to eat the remainder of the lamb. It became clear within a very few sentences that these officers of the line were very much like the cavalrymen at Orléans. They had no stomach for the Revolution, were keen to join one of the armies beyond France's borders, and believed their next targets were likely to be Frenchmen. The meal had begun without a grace and seemed likely to break up in good-natured confusion. William thought it would be a suitable time to leave.

He managed a half-bow to Madame Angel, who looked as if she might appreciate such a gesture, then made towards the door.

'I say, Englishman! That's an exquisite shoe you have nailed to you. You appear to have discovered the perfect footwear for a soldier of the line – midway between a grape-treader's sabot and Old Noah's Ark!'

'If you like I'll send to my cobbler and have him make you a pair.'

'I was thinking of the men, not for myself. Even in a regiment of infantry an officer wears only one shoe.'

'He wears it on his backside, Englishman. It's called his horse.'

William had already started to go. Now, without further comment, he went. He looked for the street door and the road that led to the river.

He wasn't allowed to walk alone. A voice called, 'Stop a minute! Two of us can make the way seem shorter.'

William glanced behind him but kept on walking. The man who had shouted after him followed the poet out of doors, and had no difficulty overtaking his deliberately brisk pace. 'You don't seem to care overmuch for your fellow lodgers, sir?'

'I don't enjoy the company of army officers or aristocrats – you could say I've had my fill of both of them.'

'So have I. So have I.' He adjusted his stride to William's. 'Why do you lodge among us, then?'

'The place was found for me. And I doubt I could find otherwise. The town is full of regiments.'

'And if a gentleman wishes to live as he is accustomed, he must lodge among his own kind – which breed is largely made up of aristocrats and officers.'

William began by being angered by the fellow, but he always felt the better for walking quickly. After a pace or two more, he laughed and said, 'I've just come from Orléans. The officers lived rather well there, too. So well, they were a clear incentive to revolution.'

'We live well everywhere. But here in Blois our men don't do badly either. Our warrant ranks and non-commissioned ranks are in lodgings much like ourselves. Some of the soldiery are billeted among families as well. The rest are either in the town's remarkably spacious barracks or out there in tentlines across the river. That's where I'd like to be. It's nothing but ancient forest, virgin except for a few woodsmen.'

'And armed bands of rascals you call owls, I believe. Barn owls, *chouans*, isn't that the word?'

The officer stopped abruptly. He was a captain, William noticed, and agreeably full in the face, but his face was no longer smiling. 'Never, as an Englishman and stranger, *never* never mention that word again. It is not safe *in any company*, do you understand me?'

He turned and walked ahead, but slowly. When William stepped alongside him he added, 'In the Vendée, I am told such people hide in the woods. In Brittany too, so I hear.' He sank his voice to a growl. 'In Blois, and further up river they live in the finest houses, believe you me. Never talk of them, monsieur. Either they themselves will cut your throat for noticing them, or the Secret Police will have you knocked on the head for claiming they exist.'

William thanked the officer for his information, and thought it best to change the subject. 'We have spoken of my own prejudices. Now tell me of yours. Why don't *you* like aristocrats and officers? They're your own kind.'

'None of them, by and large, like *me*, my dear sir. Is that a good enough reason? My family is ancient, and my pedigree on my mother's side is longer than the tail of an ox. You could make a fine soup of my lineage, sir, and still have some meat left for breakfast – but the fact is I *like* what is happening in France, *like* and have hopes of it. The corps of officers doesn't. It's a backward-looking trade is soldiering, Monsieur Wordsworth – I believe that is your name?' He was the first person in France to pronounce it correctly.

'Yes.' He found himself half-halting his walk to take a hand, taking it, shaking it and still walking on.

'My name is Beaupuy. Michel Beaupuy.'

This stopped William entire. 'Then we are met, sir. We met last night. I owe you thanks for my safety, and very possibly my life.'

'I thought you didn't recognize me.' They chuckled and walked on again. 'Danger is like wine, Wordsworth. It colours the midnight and leaves nothing for the morning after. You, for instance, are taller than I remember, even though you had a little parrot on your shoulder.'

'That's—' William was still slow to translate emotion into language, or he would have terminated his walk with Captain Beaupuy immediately. 'You are speaking of your host's sister, sir.'

'Don't think I disapprove of your choice, my dear Wordsworth. I adore the Vallons, and love them all equally. I have enjoyed hospitality at their tables for months, and not merely Madame Angel's. You may run across bridges with them, and welcome, as far as I am concerned. But be careful, my friend. *Be prudent.*' They were on the bridge now. It was much less daunting by daylight. 'Be particularly cautious of any talk of owls, even though the stepfather shoots them. Keep your ideas on all such topics to yourself, especially when you stand among the women. The old surgeon seems all right, except for his musket, and there are priests among their relatives who've actually jured for the Constitution; but the women are a separate matter – their mother sees to that.'

They walked the remainder of the way across the bridge without further speech. There was an East wind blowing, a river wind, and it was too numb on the cheekbone to encourage argument.

Beaupuy was like most men who enjoy walking in company,

perfectly happy to allow himself to be punctuated by the weather. At the far side of the bridge, the officer went on as if there had been no interruption. 'What else would you expect of a woman who lives in a street with a royal château at one end and the River Loire at the other? She draws up privilege with her drinking water, and expects her friends to think likewise.'

Outside St Saturnin, a sad group of priests stood supervising the replacement of paving stones. William recognized none of them.

He explained last night's confrontation to Beaupuy, who seemed deeply moved by the account.

'There are good priests and bad priests on both sides of this argument, Wordsworth. It's a pity the Church couldn't have been left out of the matter. Save that, in France, the Church *is* the matter.'

They seemed to be making towards St Gervais le Forêt, retracing William's walk of yesterday in the general direction of Cheverny and the Salogne wilderness. Beaupuy said abruptly, 'Speaking of nocturnal birds with silent wing feathers, and all such creatures I've forbidden you to mention, why don't we walk up river to Montlivault? The trees will protect us from the wind, and we can steal a glance at the marauder's nesting place.'

'How long will it take us?'

'There and back – well, the paths are wet – say three hours.'

He should think of Annette. But he was no longer a guest in her house, and his banishment still rankled.

'Yes,' he said. 'Let us walk to Montlivault, Captain Beaupuy.' So many little villages, and so many arrogant friends of Madame Vergez to take their names from them.

The matter might be beyond Annette's control, but he still thought she should have managed her mother better.

Annette was glad for the distraction provided by little Anne Angélique and her chattering nursemaid; but one was shrill and the other maddeningly stupid. Between them and Angel's kindly small talk she was slowly being driven out of her wits.

'My poor, dear Annette.'

Angel's words failed to reach her. They were sharing a tisane of herbs that Angel claimed were good for the miseries of pregnancy, and the fume in the cup did nothing for Annette's vapours.

'Poor, dear Marie Anne.'

She hadn't been mistaken. She was laying herself open to the pity of her sister-in-law and friend. That was unthinkable. It was bad enough that Williams should be excluded from her family's dwelling. She felt overcome by guilt just to contemplate the magnitude of her mother's disapproval of him. But for him to compound her anxieties by deserting her—

'It has been easier for me, much much easier since I had the baby. I mean for entirely *practical* reasons we married women—'

It was *miserable* of Williams not to understand how *difficult* it was for her to love him in the midst of so much family prejudice. But for him to *blame* her, for him to *sulk* and run away like this—

'You have my *entire* sympathy. The tisane will help. My poor dear!'

'I merely have a megrim, Angel. I am *not*—' That was two lies, both of them unnecessary. 'I must have taken a chill from our little adventure on the bridge last night.'

By walking away like this he had removed himself from her control. He had placed himself outside the influence of love. She felt her eyes moisten again even to think in such terms. She dabbed at her nose and wished she could be alone. There was nowhere for her to go. Once she left her brother's and sister's house there could he no coming back, not today. She could not be seen to dart about in so absolute a dependence on the wretched man.

He might even have gone away from her entire. She knew he was a prodigious walker. Last year he claimed to have walked from Calais to Switzerland or somewhere equally ridiculous. There was no knowing where a man of such monstrous energy might take himself now he was in a sulk with her, and he clearly was.

'He's walking with Captain Beaupuy,' Angel said, speaking out of nowhere and as if reading her mind. 'That Beaupuy goes everywhere on his own two legs. You wouldn't think he was an officer with estates and an aristocratic quartering.'

There was no comfort in the idea that Williams was walking with such a man, none at all. Beaupuy was a Jacobin. He was a traitor. How could Williams allow himself to be beguiled by a renegade like that?

Now what was Angel saying, and the wretched nursemaid, both in a gabble, with the child too?

'He isn't lost,' Angel said at last, finding a space to talk in by herself. 'I do declare I can see your Englishman on the hill. There's something about his walk, Annette. I'd recognize it even with a megrim myself, and in a fog!'

There was a crashing at the door, and after due interval Williams came bounding in, caught Annette's hand, bowed to Angel, then went back to the front door to knock his shoes against the stones to clear them of mud, just as if he were a toiler in a farmyard.

'I've been to Montlivault!' he shouted. 'Charming village, invigorating walk!' He came back, took the baby from the maid and gave it a spin. 'My poem is making progress,' he said. 'Come and look.'

The smile stiffened on Angel's face somewhat, then relaxed when he handed her the baby. Annette gazed apologetically at her sister-in-law as if excusing Williams' bad manners, but in reality she was making Angel into an accomplice – they both knew that.

Williams was no more interested in showing her his poem than she was to see it.

The time was not in the least suitable, not according to her sisters' gossip and that book of her father's. She saw no need to lie to Williams. Nor was there time to lie, with his hands all about her.

'No,' she said. 'I can't. It will be as awful as that time in Orléans.'

'You will be safe,' he said. All times with her were an enchantment for him.

'The beasts are not safe.'

'You are not a beast.'

'No? Then what am I?'

'You're an angel,' he said.

This was very inexact theology. 'One Angel is enough in this house,' she protested. By then he had succeeded in getting her completely undressed. Or if not completely, at least more extravagantly bare than on the other occasions that were so precious to her.

DOG DAYS IN FEBRUARY 1792, SPRING DAYS IN MARCH

Now Williams was safely inside her brother's house and away from her mother's, Annette had asserted her rights in him. Or as far as Angel went, she had. She intended to go on doing so. She doubted if Angel would tell her brother, because this was clearly a matter between women, and if it wasn't it was probably too shameful to be spoken of. Either Angel must confess she allowed a lodger, who was also a family guest, to take a young woman upstairs, or she must tell her husband quite frankly that his sister had accompanied a lodger to his bedroom. It was the sort of topic that loses a woman sleep, especially if her husband is talkative, and Angel needed her sleep now she was in the later stages of pregnancy.

Meanwhile, to be alone with her love was what every woman wanted, and in Angel's house she could insist on this freedom. William was a good man, a *passive* man even. His love for her was so strong that he was prepared to be led in all manner of ways, principally towards prudence. It was good to hold him, to cling, to shift such clothing as was crushable, and explore whatever it was difficult or imprudent to remove, but cautiously, remembering St Paul and her confessor and Jesus her Lord, as well as every busy midwife in town. Williams and she *were not wed yet*. Never, as her sisters said, give a man too much. Or if too much make sure it isn't often. Better marry than burn, but if this was burning he might come to prefer it to being married.

Meanwhile his hands on her body were pleasurable. He did no more than she allowed, and a little pleasure, though intense, is only a little sin.

One way to stay calm was to be curious in her turn, and she did need to know this man who was hers, this poet whose poems were in another language, who spoke always of himself as a poet, but only mentioned his poem when he wanted her to come to his room, this man who was hardness and softness, and muscle and bone. She would let her hand search his body through his clothing as his searched hers underneath. She learned his limbs and their sinews, as if she were a bird hovering in the cosmography of space, and then she would feel for a button and slide into a nest, sometimes above his heartbeat, sometimes in the heat of his belly.

'You've made a pretty mess of your trousers,' she breathed.

'It will clean.'

'Just like a stallion when he misses the mare.'

'A stallion doesn't wear trousers.'

His jokes were so ponderous, and because of that funny.

'I had better—'

Sometimes she wondered if he were joking at all, or merely instructing her in another natural truth he feared she'd overlooked. 'Take them off. I'll clean them.'

'I'll—'

'I'd better do them for you now.' She admired him without his trousers, his boyishness, his red-facedness, his peculiar bone-white legs. 'Lie down,' she said. 'You'll feel less foolish.'

She looked for a cloth and some water at his wash-table, and thought it was just like a stallion's stuff, or a ram's she supposed, or a rabbit's. Stuff to be very careful of. She wiped her hands and said, 'Your trousers will have to dry.'

'They'll dry best on.'

'They'll dry best off. They'll stay neatest if you let them dry off.' She hung them on a chair near his fire. 'Now let me have a look at you.'

His body needed cleaning as well.

He was shy and then not shy. It was pleasant to have a man to look at, to hold. She no longer thought of the passions that had burned her just now, whichever fires of St Paul they were or however he meant them. She moved her hands about him, moved his clothing quite away, and held him.

Williams didn't protest, not any more. He was proud of himself. This was much better than stealing glimpses of her brothers with Françoise Anne and Angélique Adelaïde, peeping and hiding, and giggling at what they had seen.

He had more of the stuff in him too – not as much, but still lots, just like a stallion. 'Do you still think you're here to write poems,' she scoffed gently, 'poems about France?'

He tried to take hold of her, but she needed nothing from him, nothing more, not now. It was comforting to be in charge of him. 'You can give me a kiss,' she said. 'My little revolution-ary. They call themselves "the trouserless ones", you know – and that's what you are!'

'You don't have to tell me that. I've been to Paris!'

Nor did he have to lecture her about Paris. He had mentioned the place far too many times already.

'This one's quite the little aristocrat,' she said, 'and much to be preferred to Citizen Williams. Look how he kneels at the block. There – he's quite lost his head.'

'Be careful of yours, Annette! From everything everyone tells me, yours is the head that's at risk.' He kissed as much of it as she would let him, principally her nose and ears.

When she led Williams downstairs he looked extraordinarily neat, even to his hair, and she made sure that she was likewise. 'Tell me how I look,' she laughed. 'Tell me in English.' It was important for lovers to be noisy and self-assured, and therefore seem innocent. '*In English*, Williams.'

'You look spike-and-span new,' he told her. 'As bright as a newly made carpenter's nail,' he translated.

She did not altogether approve of the expression, but it gave them something else to laugh at, though there was very little comfort to be had from the way the English thought about anything.

Captain Beaupuy was sitting downstairs, with his legs spread across most of Angel's parlour. He was helping her ball some wool, and he sat perfectly still with the skein round his out-stretched hands until Angel had finished rolling it round her fingers. The child watched the thread unwind from him line by line as if he and her mother were performing a miracle, or at least a conjuring trick. The maid watched all three of them in turn as if embarrassed to do anything else with her eyes.

As soon as they had finished, Beaupuy leapt to his feet with a cry of greeting. Annette didn't think the greeting was for her, or genuinely given to anyone, for the officer merely nodded in her direction and pulled a quizzical face at Williams.

His standing up acted as some kind of signal, for the maid snatched little Anne Angélique away, and Beaupuy persuaded Williams outside for one of their never-ending walks.

Angel was breathing rapidly, and her face was flushed.

'Dear Angel.' Annette caught the wool from her hand, squeezed her fingers, and kissed her. 'I am not being truly wicked, believe me.'

Angel seemed tired. Tiredness often masks disapproval.

'You wouldn't have me offer Williams less encouragement than I could in my own home?'

'What will *maman* say?'

'She will never know, Angel, because if you tell her she'll not speak to you again.'

There was more than a measure of truth in this, and Annette felt wicked to say it. Certainly its effect on Angel was profound. She shuddered. This was such an unusually physical reaction that Annette glanced at her, wondering if she was ill as well as tired.

Angel was hard to examine, being vast. Her body was like a globe set with swellings and mountainous valleys much like Williams' description of the Alps or his native Cumberland, or Beaupuy's tales of the Auvergne. As Annette watched it, and she did so with awed fascination, it experienced an earthquake, a ripple of flesh and of forces beneath the flesh that convulsed it underneath her chin and ran visibly down to her thighs and left the rest of her determinedly a-tremble.

There was a moment of stillness, then the tremor repeated itself. Angel spoke with great clarity. 'I'm—' she said.

'You're?'

'Yes. Send a maid.'

Annette sent several maids, some about the house and some for whoever seemed appropriate.

Jean-Jacques arrived first, with his brother Dr Charles Henry Vallon, only a moment behind. Madame Legroux, Angel's own mother, was there, followed by Vergez. His knowledge of women and babies was famous throughout Blois, and his curiosity concerning the subject even more widely acknowledged.

These came close to being an embarrassing superabundance of doctors, but the situation was saved by medical etiquette, which on this case turned upon precedence and ties of blood or matrimony.

Vergez won easily on both counts, though Charles Henry advanced a claim, and seemed to have his brother's approval. By this time, Angel had been helped to bed, and Vergez had taken off his jacket, rolled up his sleeves and spoken comfortingly to her of ducks and the convenience of their sky-coloured eggs as a prelude to examining her.

Madame Vergez, who let nothing happen without being present herself, decided to intervene. She seized him by the elbow, handed him his jacket and led him downstairs. 'You have married me,' she reminded him, 'and I am as far as your intimate inventory of the female Vallons need go.' She released him towards his waterbirds, and herself rejoined the excitement in the upstairs room. Annette had no idea her mother was such a watchful woman.

Jean-Jacques solved everything by installing a midwife relative of the Lacailles under his own general direction. This allowed his brother to return to the severing of limbs and securing of arteries. 'Women are best at women,' he told everyone who would listen.

Anne Zoé's birth didn't take very long, though everyone except Angel made a great deal of noise while it was happening. Once the baby was crying clearly enough for the household to hear, the officers of the Bassigny Regiment burst into polite applause, some of them sitting with wine below stairs, some lounging above, some even standing up and down the staircase. Beaupuy wasn't there. Nor, of course, was Williams.

Annette felt tired, at least as exhausted as Angel had looked while she was rolling wool. It struck her, not for the first time, that a birth was a great precipitator of arguments, and brought all family matters rapidly to a head.

Michel Beaupuy led ahead quickly enough but, once across the bridge, not in the directest of lines. They began by promising themselves whole days at Chambord, Amboise and Vendôme. They did so idly, each of them speaking as if he had other matters in mind.

Then William said, 'Your comrades disappoint me. Not one of them will stand by me at a conventional wedding in front of a non-juring priest.' He slowed where the road south changed into a woodland track, before saying ruefully, 'I couldn't ask you, of course, because—'

'No, William. You couldn't ask me, because I believe in the wrong kind of priests, and the subordination of Church to State, is that it?' He laughed, and added, 'Who knows – I might have said "no", my ideas of friendship being constitutional and shallow.'

'I believe you're a man of – of *wholeness*, Michel. I wouldn't ask such a man to betray his opinions, friendship or not.'

'Friendship carries its own kind of duty, William, a duty that transcends mere opinions. Duty is a daughter of God, and the sternest. Friendship speaks with that daughter's voice. As for the officers of the Thirty-Second Regiment of the Line, you were a fool to ask them, my friend. They're not going to form up behind you in such a church, still less beside you, because that would be to stand up for something, and they never do. Never.'

The track had become a path. It lost itself in a porridge of marshland. Beaupuy planted the next words as carefully as his footsteps. 'It's not that my comrades-in-arms—' he stomped on ahead, feeling for tufts of dryness— 'It's not that my so-called comrades believe in the wrong ideas. They're not like the daughters Vallon. They don't believe in any ideas at all. Ideas bore them. To formulate a complete sentence on any subject that actually matters is regarded by them as being in very bad taste.'

Had Captain Beaupuy spoken of the voice of God or the sternest daughter of God, or both? William wanted to retrace the idea. He was interrupted. A musket had discharged itself close at hand and towards them, so close it seemed to burst inside his head. Or that was the rational explanation of spray being struck from the wet about their feet, spray that stung their calves and ankles like a fistful of stones, and made the pair of them skip.

'A huntsman,' William grunted. France was full of huntsmen. 'He came close to killing us.'

'Ball or birdshot, I wonder? Pray God nothing in our lives ever comes closer.'

They walked a few seconds in silence. They couldn't see their huntsman, and there was no point in listening for him. The air was full of startled birds. The trees dripped. Their branches were noticeably greener and more secretive every day now. The forest was full of private sounds, as if getting on with its growing.

'We shall kill some of them, William.' Did he mean careless huntsmen or fools like his brother officers? 'I don't know how many of them or when, but we will.' He was speaking of the enemy in general. 'We may need to kill a few hundred, we may need to kill a few thousand. It won't be more. I'll promise you one thing. We won't need to kill as many of them as are killed in any battle. There'll be many more Frenchmen dying on our frontiers than by any act of revolution.'

The next shot was less exact, but nearly lethal. It struck a tree bole or stone a dozen paces to their front and ricocheted between their heads with the shrillness of a pea vibrating in a whistle.

Beaupuy began to laugh, not the most natural reaction. 'I thought I was being killed by the Chouannerie, and in a sense I am. It's the baby Chouanne's stepfather.'

His lingering on the feminine of Chouan was not lost on William, but he didn't need the commentary. He saw the bush move, then the branch. He recognized the smile and the fowling-piece. It was Vergez, husband of his belovèd's mother.

'Good God, sirs, did I hit you? I'm very glad I missed. I thought you were a flock of waders. I shot by ear, sirs. I have a wicked ear.'

'You thought you heard deer. Tell me you fancied eating deer,' Beaupuy said.

'I'm not strong enough to lug venison. No, Captain Beaupuy

and Monsieur Wodswod, I was convinced I shot at waders, and I apologize for my self-deception. My brain is full of waders at the minute. And just why is that? Because my wits are turned by women. I've spent this last half hour wondering how to extract the feminine principle on a scalpel and plant it inside an egg, so that every breeding woman and the ones who are merely brooding could come out here to the forest and sit on it till hatched.'

'I've heard you on this subject before,' William said.

'So you will again. So you will again. I think of it every time I come out here to study the simplicities and shoot myself some of them for breakfast.' The grin did not falter, but the eyes were bright with a great sadness. 'Dine with me soon, Wodswod, and you even sooner, Captain Beaupuy. Young Monsieur Wodswod is merely mortal, whereas you, sir, are an antidote to much that is merely nonsense and to all that I find abhorrent in this ego-centric generation.' He stuck his thumb in the muzzle of his fowling-piece to protect it against tree-drippings and dragged it away and himself away in a manner that could at best by described as disconsolate. As he went he called, 'Praise God I missed you, gentlemen, and praise His good name even more that it wasn't a flock of waders I missed.'

Meeting him like this brought on a change of mood. Their walking accelerated. Beaupuy grunted and said, 'I'm older than you, William, at least by a dozen years, and all my seasons have been spent among Frenchwomen. So I'll tell you what to do with your young Chouanne, my friend. Run. Run as fast as you're running now, but in a prudent direction.'

It was the sort of remark that puts a man in a fury, even when made by a friend. Neither of them quite ran. They walked, but at least one of them panted.

'You've lost your head, William. She's certainly going to lose hers – or have her heart stopped by a musket ball.'

This brought Wordsworth to a dead stop.

'I've told you I admire your choice. I'd marry any of the Vallon sisters if I were available and if they'd have me. But they're dangerous, and you're young. If you must marry her, then do it soon and take her away. I mean away from France.'

They were on the hard trackway now. Where there were

holes they had been filled with stones, and in between the holes
the earth was packing down and waiting for Summer. Just before
they reached the paved road and the houses about St Saturnin
they met two figures coming towards them, an orphan girl and
an emaciated cow she part led, part clung to. She was perhaps ten
years old.

Captain Beaupuy stopped her and gave her a coin from his
pocket. She seemed worried by his uniform, as if it represented an
unforeseeable menace. The cow nibbled at it, then lost interest.

'Is it your cow?' he asked.

'No,' she said. 'Not my cow. She's my sister and friend.'

She continued to lead the animal towards the forest and its
lusher clearings. It was dying. It was clearly all she had in the
world.

'*That's* what we're struggling to change,' Beaupuy cried out.
'That's what we're minded to put an end to. But not your rich
folk of Blois and their friends. They want the world to stay just
as it is.'

'Not Annette. I've seen her give beggars coins.'

'Coins, William, yes. They all give coins. But there are too
many beggars and there's not enough change in the great ladies'
purses.' He caught his friend by the shoulders, a gesture much
too effusive for William ever to grow used to. 'I tell you what,
my friend. I shall stand beside you in church, if you can't find a
better man. I'll even stand beside you in a cowshed, for that's
where such matters are likely to be. I'll do it out of friendship. I'll
do it out of duty. And my respect for a young woman who gives
coins from her purse.'

He turned to point after the girl and her cow, as they dwin-
dled into the forest. 'Let's hope she sings every step of the way,'
he said. 'She must go very noisily or in total silence. I'd hate her
to impinge upon your father-in-law's ear. Or the Vallons will be
eating soup tomorrow, girl soup or cow.'

'There's not much flesh on either of them.'

'These last three years have taught our cooks to be very clever
with bones.'

BLOIS.
NOT MUCH LATER IN MARCH 1792

'I see no reason to go to St Cyr-du-Gault on a weekday. Especially not in a closed carriage. Are my daughters prisoners in their own countryside?'

'A proper priest is to celebrate Mass there, mother. So it will be a proper Mass he celebrates.'

This was her sister Angélique Adelaïde speaking up for her, her middle sister. Why leave it to her sisters? Annette had arranged it all. She had caused it all. She was the guilty, triumphant, totally confused purpose of it all. Or she would be when the time came. She stood hot-faced in her best dress and said nothing. She could not speak.

'Look to your hair, Annette! I simply cannot let you leave my house like that.'

Her hair had grown very troublesome, as if unused to the temperature of her head. She stood meekly while her mother smoothed it back into its forehead roll as so many times before. She nearly burst into tears, she felt so guilty. Yet what else could she do? Her parents had rejected Williams as her suitor before she had time to declare him as such or he to announce himself. So much for filial duty. She was what she was. Annette was impatient.

'I mean how far *is* St Cyr-du-Gault?'

'Not very far, maman. Not in English miles.'

Her sisters were flushed as well. They had been sipping their

stepfather's *eau de vie de Mesland*, a local brandy he took to prepare himself for the hunt. They had been sipping for several
hours to keep their courage up, and now it was making them
cheeky.

'We must ask that Wodswod when he next comes here.'
Françoise was letting the grape run away with her. 'He won't
answer far. He only counts on his fingers.'

Madame Vergez shifted her foot rapidly forward beneath the
hem of her gown. She was beyond irritation and close to bad
temper. There it was again, that in and out quiver of the toe.
They must watch their tongues and pray the carriage would
arrive soon.

Angélique Adelaïde still wanted to be cheeky. 'It will be an
inordinate distance for us to go, mother, I do so agree. And
without protection too.'

'We shall have Captain Beaupuy,' Annette said, 'and Monsieur
Williams among others.'

'And just who will pay for this coach? Not Vergez, I'll be
bound. I *trust* not Vergez?'

'Captain Beaupuy,' Françoise said brightly. 'And Monsieur
Wodswod among others.'

'Among others,' Angélique Adelaïde agreed, smiling at
Annette.

'As a pair,' Madame Vergez said, 'as a *pair* – and nowadays they
hang together like grapes on the vine – as a pair they are my least
favourite people in Blois.'

'We agree, mother.'

If only it weren't so far to St Cyr, Annette thought. If it were
at St Gervais-le-Forêt as originally planned, there would be none
of this worry and far less trouble. She had to trust her sisters with
the deception – she had to trust someone – but they were
becoming much too silly for comfort.

'When gentlemen call on ladies in a closed carriage the ladies
must be very sure of themselves,' Madame Vergez said firmly. 'Very
very certain. And when a man who can't afford a carriage of his
own actually goes so far as to *hire* a closed carriage, then any young
woman with an ounce of prudence must be thinking—'

'We agree, mother. We're very prudent. We'll be thinking.'

'Beaupuy and Williams will not be in the carriage,' Annette said, with rising bad temper herself.

'We agree, mother. Men are such *peculiar* animals.'

'And *such* a pair, as you say, mother.' Françoise again. 'Your daughters will be most unsafe among such men. So why don't you accompany us?'

Annette was in a fever at this point.

'In a closed carriage! In March? To hear Mass in a barn?'

'They'll have swept the shed, mother. The devout parishioners of St Cyr will have swept it quite free of—'

'I refuse to have country talk in my house.'

'Quite free of cattle, mother. It will be strewn with flower petals and in every way fit for a bride.'

Annette was saved from her sisters' foolhardiness by a loud knocking at the door. The bell was not being pulled, nor the knocker rapped. Their coachman must have sent his boy downhill ahead of him to ensure they were ready. The lout was beating on the door panel with his staff.

Madame Vergez refused to tolerate this insult to her eardrums and her paintwork. She asked Annette to tell a suitable woman to open the door. She needed some men. She hated them, but she needed them to box such people's ears.

It wasn't a dream, though like most events that are totally strange it was dreamlike. He was trotting a borrowed horse beside Michel Beaupuy. The Captain was supposedly riding his own, though he seemed as ill at ease with his mount as William was.

William could manage a horse, but his life had not given him many opportunities to practise the skill. Now here he was with his head twice as far above the ground as it was used to, and his brain quite witless. Finding himself here of all places, in the town's well-kept Western Forest, on high as it were and prancing, was almost too much to register.

They had passed this way before, but on foot. As they walked, so had they talked. The miles went uncounted, the landscape unnoticed save by the inward eye.

Michel urged him to ride faster. 'We shall be late for the Mass, William.'

'We're never late. Besides, it's my Mass.'

'It is not your Mass. It is never anyone's Mass. You are only the excuse.'

'If I'm no more than an excuse, it can start without me.'

The Mass would be a lie. So would the wedding. His problem was to know what truth could ever come out of it. His reason told him none. Was that why he had consented to it so easily?

Everything was a sham. What a pity the wedding was this way, and not on the tangled margins of the Salogne as originally promised. The Forest, now he looked at it, was as disconcerting as fairyland. He could see neither coppice nor natural stand of timber. There were no wild coverts nor random clearings. The whole area had been quartered and cut into by lanes. It was like riding across a chessboard or a maze without a puzzle. As if the woodsmen had not barbered it enough, they had pollarded the mature trees all the way up their principle branches, so they resembled the tentacles in his schoolmaster's book of sea creatures.

He glimpsed a hut among the warty trees, and felt a terrible chill descend on him.

Beaupuy caught at his rein. 'Come on, William. This place is not for us.' They set off briskly, and began to gallop in earnest, but their horses soon slowed. The way had become slippy, and perhaps even thick underfoot. There was rising green all around them. They were moving among this year's shoots across last year's rot.

'Evil,' Beaupuy whispered.

'Here?'

'No, that hovel back there. I didn't know whether we were going to be set upon by Chouans or pixies.'

'The Chouannerie have no quarrel with you soldiers, Michel.'

'Not until the Army sends us to hunt them down.'

'Well, you've gained a reprieve at their hands, even so. You're helping at the wedding of one of their fairest daughters.'

'I'm helping to join her to a poet and an Englishman. Disembowelling offences both in natural law.'

They laughed. It was William's first laugh of the day, and very likely his only one. He said, 'I agree with you, Michel. That place smelled bad. It smelled of unspilt blood.'

'"Unspilt"? Glance ahead of you, my friend, and let's hope we can keep it that way.'

A band of men barred their path. William didn't count them. There were at least a dozen of them, perhaps a score. Three of them were mounted.

'Chouannerie?'

'I doubt it. Ruffians certainly. Robbers perhaps – or the Village Guard – it takes a wise man to tell them apart.'

'Shall we pass them at the gallop?'

'Never run from a man on horseback, William. It's the first rule of war.' Beaupuy rode briskly forward, as if confronting an armed group in the backwoods were the most easy matter in the world. 'Good day, citizens. It's a very fine day, indeed.'

South of Paris 'citizen' had become a partisan word. William wondered he used it so boldly.

'For us, yes, citizen. For you, who can tell?'

'My name is Beaupuy, citizen.' He spoke directly to the horseman who'd answered him. 'Michel Beaupuy. I'm for the Country and the Constitution, and I'll tell you very frankly it takes a bold man to question the right of an officer of the Thirty-Second of the Line to go anywhere.' He drew his flimsy half sword and moved a man away from his stirrup by pushing the flat of the blade against the side of the fellow's nose. 'Country manners, gentlemen. The mare kicks. She dislikes impudence.' He tossed the half sword to the horseman who had thought to interrogate him. 'Only my dress-sword, citizens.' He smiled. 'My pistols, of course, are loaded.' He waited, brightly, until the weapon was handed back to him.

'You haven't told me your business, citizen. Nor this citizen's name.'

'This citizen is an Englishman whose name is unpronounceable and who speaks atrocious French. He is a guest of the Bassigny Regiment. I am escorting him to St Cyr-du-Gault.' Since this didn't seem to be enough, he added forcibly, 'My regiment has extended its protection to him, and takes it as a matter of honour that he will reach there and come profitably home again.'

'Officers of regiments are rarely for the Constitution, citizen.

Nor are foreigners. Those are facts so universal you may even read them in the broadsheets of the day.'

'Indeed, citizen, and such journals are never known to lie. But I, Michel Beaupuy, am for the Constitution — and for much more besides — so is this gentleman, insofar as it concerns him.'

'It excites the world,' William put in, receiving an ironic cheer for his lumpishness of tongue, and advancing his cause not a bit.

'Never mind my fellow officers.' Beaupuy continued to smile, and ease men away from the rumps of his and William's horses. Once he even laid his hand with admirable frankness upon the butt of a pistol, and made not the least pretence of soothing his mare's neck. 'Never mind my fellow officers. I am Michel Beaupuy, and I command a company of grenadiers, and I'll tell you plainly my men will follow me anywhere and perhaps a little further than that. Now if you want them out here growing boisterous among your women and children, then I must congratulate you upon the straightforwardness of your thinking, for you are well on your way to achieving such a visit.' He allowed a little time before adding, 'If I do not return to the Regimental lines tonight, or if this uniform is carried back to them with the least lace of an epaulet ruffled, then you may take it as being as certain as sunrise that my men will be out here tomorrow morning asking for breakfast. Make way, please. I am riding on.'

He rode on, and William tried to follow through whatever gap had opened for them.

'Stay a moment, citizen. You go to St Cyr?'

'As certainly as night will fall.'

'There is to be a wedding at St Cyr.'

'There are weddings everywhere. Weddings are for women.' Beaupuy grinned and rode back among them. 'When did you ever hear of a soldier getting married? The men-at-arms are not allowed to, the officers cannot afford such a luxury.'

This talk of weddings filled William with alarm. No one had spoken of the Western Forest as a dangerous place, not *the* Forest of Blois. He feared for his love. Were the Vallon daughters in their coach ahead of them or behind them? The supposition must be that they were behind, since it was the groom's duty to be ahead.

He and Captain Beaupuy had scarcely hurried themselves, and now there was this delay.

If these men suspected there was a bridal party on the way, God knows what they might do. Worse still if they thought it was to attend a nuptial mass celebrated by an outlawed priest.

The fancy is a powerful instrument. No sooner had he begun to fear than he felt certain he could hear the tingle of iron wheels approaching. His ears did not deceive him. He heard pebbles fly, the relentless crushing of leaves.

'There's a coach coming!' somebody called.

'Then I shall ride back to meet it, and you will grant it safe passage.' Beaupuy spoke with the self-assurance of a man who knew he was bluffing. William wondered if he would get away with it. These were countrymen. As well try to fool Cumberland farmers at a fair. They could tell from your manner which sheep you were trying to pass too quickly, and which you believed in enough to hold back for their better inspection.

A knot of armed men surrounded their horses, and this time caught irrepressibly at their stirrup straps. The three horsemen moved ahead of them. The bluff had not succeeded. They were to go back for the bridal party in a gang. What would the coachman say? And what about the sisters? William knew Annette could keep a cool head, but on her wedding day? And what about the other two?

A man cursed. Several spat. The horsemen turned aside from in front of them. The danger melted away before they had time to appreciate its implications. William and Beaupuy were alone, their ears empty of sounds save for those made by the approaching coach and horseshoes retreating across leafmould and twig.

Then they saw what had frightened the ambush away. Four or five officers of the Thirty-Second Regiment of the Line were riding behind the curtained coach. These worthies were in full dress uniform, and their hats alone were tall enough to scare off a militia much more resolute than the previous band of crows.

'I didn't invite them,' Beaupuy said. 'But I've never been more pleased to see them.'

His fellow officers were already extremely happy with themselves. They were slightly drunk, and had clearly been keeping themselves in good spirits by calling flirtatious sallies to the occupants of the coach. As William and Beaupuy took up position behind them they explained themselves in a series of shouts over their shoulders, sometimes backing or sidling their horses, their joy was so exuberant.

'We were going to the surgeon's sawpit.'

'That's it. We were hoping to glimpse a limb being pruned. Then we heard a young fellow was going to lose his head. Or I take it so, Beaupuy, since for your friend to surrender his freedoms *illicitly* is tantamount to giving up his head!'

'How did you hear tell?' William asked desperately. The wedding could not be kept secret from the family now.

The Bassigny Regiment did not, as a group, talk to foreigners, so Beaupuy had to ask for him.

'The carter's boy – I call him that, since this coach is scarcely more than a cart – the boy knocked on Madame Vallon's door.'

'Madame Vallon's or Madame Vergez's?'

'Vallon's. How can Vallon be Vergez? Nobody heard, save us. And there's really no staying there, what with the Vallon baby, the nurse's baby, the other nurse's child, and the *stink* of swaddling and tit.'

The coach shook a little, possibly with laughter.

'The *bosoms*, Beaupuy. If you weren't out walking every day, you'd know the good doctor's palace holds more bare breasts than a decent brothel has cushions.'

'There's no closing the doors because of them!'

'I never knew that two young women in milk could have so many of the things. You're the farmer, Beaupuy, you've got estates. Did you ever discover such a miracle?'

Beaupuy pulled a serious face. It was probably a disapproving one. Officers of thirty-five and more who have not advanced beyond Captain of Infantry are allowed to be serious, especially among their juniors and in the scarcely disguised presence of ladies. The group became less rowdy, and after a few minutes more William and Beaupuy rode ahead, where a groom's party should be.

Beaupuy's brother officers didn't seem sorry to see them go, the aristocrat who held unfashionable opinions, and his friend with the funny suit and his English way with a horse.

William had an English way with gratitude as well. 'We were lucky, Michel. Praise God you're a soldier.'

'Thank God I'm a countryman, you mean. Those ruffians were up to their tricks from the beginning, running their fingers round our horse-straps and waiting to sit us on their pocket knives.'

'Then praise Him you're a countryman!'

'He's a dangerous animal is your average countryman. He's not so timid as your townsman, and there's the risk in him. He's scant use for preliminaries. He doesn't need to be in a group to slit your throat. He's always got his blade about him. And he's already practised on his pig, so he knows where the veins are, and the big artery.'

The Forest continued to menace them. Here they were, half a dozen horsemen, some of them armed. Two coachmen, furnished with a staff and whip and quite possibly a blunderbuss, yet they rode in fear.

'Not the place you'd choose for a love tryst, William.'

'Nor for anything else.'

William returned to his sense of guilt, his obsession with the lie. Was he comforting Annette with this charade or deceiving her? The ceremony could have no force in law, certainly not in England. He felt a great surge of compassion for her just the same, his fellow orphan, his little half-orphan. He thought *Never mind the lie. Love is always a lie*. Even his parents had lied. They had cheated him by dying.

Captain Beaupuy was his truth, and Captain Beaupuy was clapping his spurs to his horse. Captain Beaupuy was his witness, and with truth as his witness he let himself gallop behind him.

They were free of the Forest now, among ordinary fields and ordinary woods. These helped. So did the sun on his left cheek. It smarted where he had touched a razor to it.

They stopped well short of the village, though its church was clearly visible. The barn was by the side of the track, tucked between his sore left cheek and an imminent sunset.

'This is altogether the wrong time of day for a Mass,' Beaupuy said, as they led their mounts round the back of the building to tether them where they wouldn't be noticed. 'What it is for a wedding I can't possibly say.' He chuckled. 'I agree with those rascals in the wood. Any time is wrong for a wedding.'

'You're supposed to support and comfort me. Or I take it that's your role.'

'Support yourself on your bride, sir. Let her be your comfort. The only reason a man undergoes matrimony is to win himself a bride. Annette Vallon is a bride worth the gaining, William – I'll give you that. You must enjoy the bride, and hope she isn't in too much hurry to turn herself into a wife. As a bride she should last a careful fellow like yourself for a year or two.'

They walked back to the front of the barn.

The old curé was already waiting for them. So were a great many other people William did not know.

This was meant to be a hole-in-a-corner affair, but he wasn't going to be allowed to get away with it, neither in a hole nor in a corner. The villagers of St Cyr – pray God there were no bourgeois from Blois – the villagers and forest dwellers were here in force, and if the barn was a hole they were in no mood to treat it like one. They sensed a fête. They were happy.

As for the priest, the old man appeared to be younger than he had when William had last seen him at St Saturnin. He'd probably felt nearer his death on that occasion. He greeted William warmly and Michel Beaupuy with downright enthusiasm. His eyes positively sparkled when they glimpsed the uniforms of Beaupuy's brother officers wedged tunic to tunic in the doorway.

Beaupuy led William towards the front of the barn, where a table had been set as an altar. Apparently the wedding was not to be yet, but the groom could go forward, if not the bride.

'Yours will be the only nuptial mass I've celebrated in a shed, Wordsworth.'

'The old priest seems triumphant.'

'He triumphs because you represent continuity, my friend. Marriage is a traditional institution that offers imbeciles hope for the future.'

'You're not proposing to do away with it?'

'Not exactly. But we certainly intend to set women free of their matrimonial shackles, and that may well have the same effect.'

'Meanwhile you're here as my witness and friend, so keep me cheerful.'

'I'm your truth, William. There's no comfort in me. Why don't you take whatever your love will offer you, then be on your way, without all this nonsense?'

'She doesn't offer me enough without marriage.'

'Then it's your failure as a lover we're discussing, not society's need for reform.'

'I'm in love with her, Michel, and there's an end.'

'Pray God not. To be in love is to be mortally wounded on the battlefield of life. Who will stop to bathe your hurt, William? Who will bind you up?'

'My friends.'

'Friends leave lovers where they lie, William. We've all gone, galloping by on our chargers.'

If Beaupuy was playing the jester, his darts were tart.

It was clear to Annette that the village of St Cyr had come to her wedding in force. Perhaps it was that people adore a wedding, none more than countryfolk. Perhaps it was the novelty of a Mass in a barn, though these events happened from time to time and were spoken of. More likely it was because it was against the law. Wine, venison, salmon – each of them tastes better when illegally acquired. A wedding in a barn sounded as illicitly improbable as a steak cut from another man's bullock and fried in stolen oil. The Constitution forbad it. The State forbad it. Common sense said it was ridiculous. That was why everyone was here. So there was to be no open war between the Constitutionalists and the King's men, not on her wedding day. She was to be fêted by all men equally, exempt from trouble because of their universal curiosity.

The priesthood was here without rancour too. St Cyr's curé was a juring cleric, but he harboured no ill-will towards the old priest, who was known by him and respected.

And now, amid all this curiosity and bustle, to have soldiers at her wedding, officers *loyal* to the King unlike that Beaupuy, and to see her Williams with his suit brushed and sponged and looking new as freshly cut turf, what a joy it should be.

Yet it wasn't. She wanted her mother, and her poor dead father, and – yes – she even missed Vergez. He was good at weddings. He was in his element at feasts. There were strangers to share his mysteries, and sometimes to listen to him. Even those who knew him accepted him as a famous man, and therefore presentable.

Also there was to be no bridal procession. They weren't yet in a church, they were in a barn. The barn could only be turned into a church, *transfigured* as it were, in the sight of a reverent congregation. She was part of that congregation and a friend of the priest. She could hardly walk outside and process back in again.

Meanwhile the old man had started. He started in a loud voice. He was better in a populous barn than he was in St Saturnin's among timid people with murderers throwing cobbles and howling at the door. *'Terribilis est locus iste: hic domus Dei est, et porta coeli: et vocabitur aula Dei.'*

The local curé, acting as server, offered a couple of *Alleluias* at this point. Annette had no doubt they were in the natural order of service, but she had never heard the cry of exultation offered with such irony.

'Quam dilecta tabernacula tua, Domina virtutum. Concupiscit et deficit anima mea in atria Domini.'

The local curé knew how to conduct his own people through a *Gloria Patri* at this moment, and they obliged him in unusually good voice, grateful to be given something to do.

The old priest gazed at him briefly before saying, *'Locus iste a Deo factus est, incæstimatibile sacramentum, irreprehensibilis est.'* Now each was reproving the other, as if they both thought a mistake was being made, but not by himself.

By then they were into more *Alleluias*, and everybody seized upon the chance of using their voices again, a hundred villagers boiling over with praise and quite unstoppable, just like a field of grasshoppers on a Summer evening.

Adorabo ad templum sanctum tuum: et confitebor Nomine tuo.

The *Alleluias* echoed again, banging about the walls of the barn like shouts in a street at night. The congregation was over-boisterous, and saw little reason to be reverent. Man for man, and not totally exclusive of its women, it was drunk.

Montes in circuitu ejus, et Dominus in circuitu populi sui . . . et usque in sæculum

Annette's mind began to wander. The Mass ran on, or quite simply ebbed away. She had not been to a *Terriblis* before, a dedication, so she had no idea which variants the old priest had been driven to, or whether he simply decided to abandon the preliminaries and plunge straight into the wedding. The locals were noisily restless – cheerful would be a truer word – and the bride was what they had come for. They were making little jokes about cattle fleas – not a subject town dwellers like herself and her sisters felt expert enough to rebut.

The old priest beckoned her forward at last. Was she right to think his name was Papa Pierre, or was Daddy Rock a nickname she had called all the clergy since childhood? She stood trembling beside Williams and his open air suit, and he bowed towards her and her sister Françoise Anne in welcome. Well, she had got him here.

Captain Beaupuy inclined his head. She smiled at him. She smiled at Papa Pierre and the Father from St Cyr-du-Gault, and thought how lucky she was to have Williams in a blue grey suit so splendidly enriched by the presence of a Captain of the Line in his number one tunic of royal indigo with gold epaulettes.

Papa Rock banished these thoughts by eyeing her sternly and saying, 'I am not the Priest of your Parish, Marie Anne. Nor can I be of your Parish, William, for you have no Parish.'

Williams seemed mildly affronted but in the main indifferent to this remark, as he always did whenever she mentioned these matters to him.

'Once the Constitution of Men seeks to deny the Parish of God, then God's Parish reasserts itself. It is everywhere. It has no boundaries. This is a fact you both recognize. You have given me evidence of your faith by attending a Mass celebrated by myself at the church of St Saturnin by the river in Blois.'

He spoke these words quietly. They clearly dealt with matters he thought might divide a congregation that had at last fallen decently silent. Once he had disposed to them, he set about Williams in a loud voice.

'As to your intending marriage, Marie Anne Vallon, I declare it to be sinful. There is an impediment in that you, William Wordsworth, are an unbeliever. It is this impediment that renders it sinful. Insofar as this is only an impediment of the second class, I nonetheless declare the marriage shall be legal before God.'

Williams' mind appeared to be elsewhere, or at least as far away as Captain Beaupuy, who whispered something in his ear.

'Who are the witnesses?'

'I, Michel Beaupuy, Captain of the grenadier company of the Thirty-Second Regiment of Line Infantry.'

This announcement was by far the most imposing event in the entire ceremony so far.

'I, Françoise Anne Vallon, sister of the aforementioned Annette that is Marie Anne Vallon.'

Until now, or at least from a moment or two earlier, the congregation had merely been spellbound. Now it was dumbfounded, though being made up of villagers it found tongues to speak. So this second young woman was not the young woman's very young mother at all. Nor even her aunt, and clearly not her grandmother. How was it possible for a young woman to be married in a barn, and to a man with a funny name and in a funny suit, *without even her mother being present?* It was clear from the outset there was no father. Were they all dead, the seniors of her house? Was she a vagrant? An orphan? Or was this how they did such things in large towns – *cathedral* towns – like Blois?

When Papa Rock spoke further, and in his loudest voice, there was no hearing him, even in the vernacular, which they all more or less spoke, being French.

'William, wilt thou take Marie Anne here present for thy lawful wife, according to the rite of our holy Mother the Church?'

Williams must have answered in the affirmative to this, as did she herself to her own question. They held hands, and she heard

Williams say, 'I, William Wordsworth, take thee, Marie Anne Vallon, for my lawful wedded wife, to have and to hold, from this day forward, for better, for worse, for richer, for poorer, in sickness and in health, until death do us part.'

A silence fell about them, because the congregation were keen to hear how the foreigner would speak, and what sort of voice a bourgeois from Blois could manage without the support of a single senior relative.

Annette did very well. Old men, in general, thought she was splendid. Women of all ages by and large were by and large not so sure. When they asked their young men or their not-so young husbands for an opinion, they were given an opinion. Which was that, by and large, they didn't have an opinion. Moreover—

Ego conjugo vos in matrimonium, in nomine Patris, Filii, et Spiritus Sancti.

—moreover there was an awful amount of Latin to endure before the *vin d'honneur*.

She was aware of these murmurings, but only faintly. She wore no troth ring – her mother would not have allowed it. Now she had to make do with the plain ring from Williams' own finger. She did. It was still warm.

It was then, and at last, that she felt terror at what she had done. After the *Kyrie*, Papa Pierre began to talk of her fecundity, the sobering fact that marriage was about childbearing, in the eyes of the Church at least. She was to be fertile:

Uxor tua sicut vitis abundans in lateribus domus tuæ

The Curé from St Cyr was even more specific:

Filii tui sicut novellae olivarum in circuitu mensæ tui. She not only had to be as a young vine about Williams' house, but bear fruit accordingly, even if they were olives. Had she indeed? Yes, she supposed she had. Unfortunately, Williams had no house. What was she to be about her mother's house? And how many olives could she bring forth there? She clung to Williams' elbow at the thought, and he squeezed her hand. The fact was he didn't listen to what the priests were saying to them. He had learned Latin at school and university, but he could understand it only fitfully when it was spoken in a French accent by someone who pronounced it according to the Roman tradition.

She on the other hand had never learned Latin, but she had been to Church almost every day of her life. She had been winked at by Uncle Charles Olivier at least once a week whenever they came to the saucy bits. She understood what went on in Church. Today the Church was a barn, and – for the first time – the words terrified her.

The most terrifying realization of all was to find herself, at that second, *married*. Married before God, that was. Married according to the Pope and the rituals of the Church.

Never mind the rituals of the Church. Never mind the Pope. How would it appear to Madame Vergez?

William's mind did not so much wander, as shift and focus more clearly. It was as if his brain had become one of Newton's celebrated lenses – or was it prisms – separating colour from brightness until what was left was a chink of purest light.

He was reminded of the earlier Mass at St Saturnin. The Latin was witchlike and unnecessary. Yet he found it unbelievably awesome, as well as deeply pagan. Popery was not for him, but much as he tried to tell himself he hated it, he felt the God in it.

As with his impulse to a poem, he began by feeling overcome and confused. Then he saw. He saw why he had come to France, and he saw it in the clearest light. He knew he had come here to delay taking holy orders. What he also saw was he never could take them. He had learned religious awe here, but he'd felt more reverence on a mountain top. Churches were alien to him, even this church, which was the holier for being a barn, and holier again for being on the edge of a wood.

In England, in church, he had never even felt this much. God, if there was a God, was elsewhere, and so was his career.

If there was a God? There was certainly a Mighty Spirit, and his career was to search it out in poetry. In the meantime he was marrying, had married, this woman. She was *his* Annette. She would expect him to keep her. And his only chance of doing that was to take the living he had been offered, and fit her into an English Parish as his bride. It would be cruel to her and impossible for him. The crux was upon him already.

Meanwhile he had her. Marrying was like poetry. It was a young man's game.

The Nuptial Mass came to an end. Williams should not have taken communion; but he was offered communion, so he took it. This was Papa Pierre's ceremony. Once he had reminded Williams of his apostasy at the beginning of the service, he saw no reason to deny him anything. The old man was here to celebrate tradition, to do everything within his power to bring yesterday a little closer to tomorrow. Tradition is much more persuasive than propriety. Heavens! This wedding itself was improper enough.

Françoise Anne had brought a modest cake, and Angélique Adelaïde as many tiny biscuits as could be baked by idle town girls with Madame Vergez's flour in Madame Vergez's kitchen while her back was turned. Flour was in short supply, and Madame Vergez's back was never turned for long.

The family and the officers of the Bassigny Regiment all ate cake, because it was acknowledged they had travelled far. William ate cake. Annette, of course, ate cake. Everyone in the barn had a crumb of something, so Annette, who was reminded of such things, thought of the wedding at Canaa. She saw to it that Williams, who wasn't otherwise reminded, also thought of it.

Wedding guests do not need particles of cake, still less of biscuit, when there are crumbs of comfort. The officers of the Bassigny Regiment had been urged to bestir themselves by a very sombre Captain Beaupuy, and – true to the traditions of the Thirty-Second Regiment of the Line – prevailed upon a farmer to bring in a large barrel of wine. The best local wines were all white. The contents of this barrel were as red as sow's blood but none the worse for it. A few coins changed hands. Men spoke to their wives, and wives and then children brought cups. When the wives went home, they returned with other sweetmeats as well.

Beaupuy stood with his mouth full of cake and his cheeks red with wine.

He said, 'No, William. There will be no wedding feast. And

yet there is a nuptial banquet.' He too was reminded to the wedding in the gospel, and said so, for miracles of food continued to arrive at the door. 'Even if there is a meal, the woman is your banquet. You must pasture upon her as if you were your horse and your horse were upon his favourite grass.'

William's horse on this occasion was a mare, but his friend as so often was talking poetry, so he did not contradict him. What he said was, 'The wine has already shown itself in you to be strong, Michel Beaupuy.' He hoped he said it in French. If in English, the words were in execrable order. He had, he thought, used the wine sparingly, except to toast his bride.

A little later, or several hours later, he heard himself say, 'What you have done, Michel, is play the best man.'

Beaupuy's brow furrowed in anxiety, as if he were the victim of a monstrous accusation.

'No, no. I do not mean you counterfeit the groom. Or counterfeit anyone. I know you are modesty personified, indeed *deified*. "Best man" is what we in England call the *garçon d'honneur*.' This was a ridiculous expression to apply to Beaupuy. He laughed at it. He found himself in Beaupuy's arms. 'You are the *best* man here, Michel. The only real *man* – by real I mean solid, uncounterfeit, integral – the only *real* man I have met in a lifetime.'

They wept. Or Beaupuy wept and William experienced a moistness of the eye. Weeping together like this was an admirable preparation for dealing with his bride as the Captain had commanded him. What had he been told to do to her? *Treat her as his horse would treat a field of grass.* The words were immortal, yet subject to ceaseless metamorphoses. *Favourite grass*: that was it. He must go and whisper the whole splendid phrase in Annette's ear. Better change it from a field to a Spring meadow. Immortal metamorphoses. Or possibly the singular. He wasn't Ovid.

The most immediate, and best, consequence of acquiring a bride was that he was able to be rid of his horse. He did not like the beast. It was not noticeably fond of him. Tonight he had no further need of it.

He took Annette to the coach, and helped her climb into its

pitch-dark interior. Then he watched Michel Beaupuy hand in his wife's bridesmaids and sisters. Then he placed himself on board, guided by Annette – he supposed Annette – and a great deal of giggling. The coach was no more than a little hutch set against the dark hill of the night, and to perch inside it with three beautiful women was a highly agreeable enterprise. He could not, of course, see them. Nor touch them, save by a happy accident of forearm or knee. But he could breathe them. He breathed. Then a whip cracked. The coach dragged a wheel from a soft rut and across a hard one, and the four of them were thrown together like so many squirrels in a sack.

Men cheered. William did not know whether these were the villagers of St Cyr or the officers of the Thirty-Second Regiment of the Line. These last seemed to have increased in number since the ceremony began, and multiplied even more strikingly once it had ended; though he was in doubt whether there were in truth more than five of them, or whether the whole giddy roundabout of expanding numbers was simply the result of three hours' din between the ears and a large amount of wine being passed through Michel Beaupuy's lips and beneath the amiable portcullis of his friend's teeth then being wafted back into his own capital orifices by every operation of both men's human bellows. In short, William, who was confident he had not touched a drop – well, only a cup or two in answer to some several dozen toasts, rouses, speeches, shouts, prayers, and general exhortations to behave towards his bride as any Frenchman would, began to feel at least *mildly* drunk from breathing the mayor's wine, the potations of the two curés and the pickled breath of any number up to a century of villagers.

That was all in the past, of course, the past tense at least. But it was a hideously imperfect past because the military component of the mirage still rode behind them in loud and increasingly *louche*-mouthed disarray, so that while William bounced into and snuggled against a pleasing jigsaw of feminine curves and angles with scarcely a bone among them, his French was improved by the officers naming, frequently in song, all manner of anatomic parts that are not generally encountered in poetry, and by terms that no Muse, not even Juvenal's or Chaucer's, has ever permitted. The ladies seemed undisturbed by all this, and William's mind had been broadened by these last few months in France, but the darkness blushed.

Then Michel Beaupuy, who had as he said begun the day old for a captain of infantry at thirty-seven, and now felt even older, clapped his hands and persuaded his juniors to sing lullabies instead. These songs made a far more fitting accompaniment to the trotting of hoofs, the feminine murmur and rustle inside their shuttered box of night, not to mention the everlasting grinding of the axle. A young woman giggled. A young woman toyed with a door handle and whispered through her star-white teeth of the enchantments of midnight. A woman slept. He had no way of knowing which one of these prizes was Mrs Wordsworth and which two were his recently acquired sisters because darkness is like that. Inside it, lakes sink, keels make unaccustomed music, and mountains rear their stark heads and continue to rise. Even this mutilated Forest of Blois made a windy noise between stem and leaf which drowned out their escort, for all the pounding of hoofs and the drumming of wine.

Annette, poor poor Annette, what did she think? Poor boldly timorous clinging Annette. She hung against Williams' arm and kept her hands from the comforts of his body not because her sisters were here, nor even as the victim of a new shyness. She was afraid.

Her hope was that Williams might run away with her somewhere. They needed a nest, and she had taken enough wine to believe he might have found one. Where else and why else did he walk with that Beaupuy, unless it was with her in mind? Yes, he had been preparing a nest, as the novels said.

They needn't settle far off, just a step or two beyond the influence of her mother. Just a step and a stare or two beyond.

It would be pleasant, for example, not to see that ruler of her life again until several years had passed. Annette would reappear back home all unannounced one Summer's day in an open coach that would be a large enough announcement in itself. The coach would have footmen. Or did she mean postilions? There would be two postilions, and any number of footmen.

She would arrive in the Rue du Pont and alight from her rugs and her cushions with her children – hers and Williams' children – clinging to her arm. She wasn't sure how many children would be appropriate in three or four years' time, two girls and a boy or two of each according to how closely her vine had twined about Williams' table and the health and fecundity of her olive tree.

She and her mother would greet one another like old friends, which they were entitled to be. They would drink coffee together, Madame Vergez and Madame Wodswod. By now she would be able to pronounce her own name with a strange English flourish, with a lisp even, Wodswoth, just like that. It was a pronunciation to dream about. She and her mother would eat tiny cakes together. They would embrace fondly, and she would invite her mother to – to what? Not to the château. She hated all country places. To her large mansion in Orléans or Angers, or – miraculously – just round the corner in the next street.

Williams wouldn't be with her. He would be undertaking some important errand for the King of England.

That Beaupuy wasn't all bad. The least that could be said of him was that he was blessed with the wisdom of the entirely wicked.

Somewhere between Françay and St Lubin-en-Vergonnois, he had arranged an inn. The distance between Françay and St Lubin was itself a matter of English miles. The lanes all about were as devious as a poacher's trousers – and the bourgeois French were being forced to learn more and more about those, or their contents, by the month as the national disturbances continued. Yet here, somewhere from a block of shadow, Beaupuy had conjured an inn and secured a room for them by prior parley.

Annette was privy to this stratagem. She had spoken to Michel Beaupuy quite boldly on the subject, some would say saucily. But Captain Beaupuy was a nobleman, even if he was only descended from a male line of bailiffs when you analysed his blood as thoughtfully as Madame Vergez had. In any event, he allowed not the least flicker of disapproval or amusement to distort his gaze as he agreed to see what could be done.

Williams looked surprised. He had been clinging to her shoulder for the better part of an hour – she hoped not in the pleasing supposition that she was one of her sisters – and now his ride through the rutty dark was ended he seemed reluctant to bid it farewell. Hadn't Beaupuy told him? planned it with him? consulted him just a little? *warned* him?

It was typical of her man – and very beautiful he looked in the firelight that flooded through an open door – it was typical of her man that he should have left such an obvious stratagem to others. Did he think he was going to confront her parents *now*? Her mother kept to a strict régime in the evenings, and Vergez viewed the world through a glass, brightly.

Her sisters conducted her through the open door and upstairs. The presence of bridesmaids, of attendants at the least, numbed the innkeeper and his wife sufficiently to obtain a proper respect for her situation. It also brought her some hot water, a dish of the local brandy, a fresh application of the warming pan, and an overall sense of decency and order.

Her Williams chatted downstairs for a minute or two while her sisters put her to bed. Then they went back down. She could hear them being kissed by the Bassigny Regiment as they were handed into the coach. All this was below her window, and very amusing it was to nestle against her bolster and listen to it.

This overloud smacking of lips and bottoms was interrupted in all its fervour by a knock at the door.

'Madame Wordsworth!'

Still an impossible title to pronounce, though Beaupuy managed it better than anybody else she had heard. She would try to afford herself time for a little practice with tongue against the lip before she met her mother in the morning. For the moment, the Captain had brought her husband to her. She thanked them both kindly. Beaupuy bowed, poured a little brandy for Williams and herself, slapped Williams on the back, bowed once more and went downstairs. He called over his shoulder that he had arranged for the coach to return a little after ten in the morning.

She knew her husband was a passionate man. Lads of one and twenty summers were widely rumoured to be at their pinnacle of immediacy if not higher. Even so, she was surprised to find herself in his arms without a whip being cracked, with the Bassigny Regiment still at its song, and the coach still bound by its wheel irons in its self-made rut. Then she heard the whip, and it dragged away to a grating of metal on sandy mud. What a tingle there was, what a sliding after, as if the bedposts themselves were being towed into the night and transplanted as trees again.

William enjoyed having his bride's total attention in the sibilant dark. This was either the third or the fourth time during the three months of their knowing that she had set aside her natural caution and allowed him to be absolute. The result was a very exact experience, superior to Mass, comparable to mountains – not least because there was a deal of mist where the ascent grew precipitous.

Four times now – surely four. Mathematics aside, he was able to view her body with experienced eyes. She had been beautiful by candlelight in Monsieur Gellet-Duvivier's salon, beautiful again by diffuse starlight in his own little room next door. Now, on her wedding evening, the flame from their bedroom's tiny hearth left her extravagantly aglow. He did not know whether it was her skin or the hot coals that shed so much radiance in the room. Not even Newton dare deny the moon as a creator of light.

Annette had married her Williams now. As she was a woman, she had needed to be cautious until this very moment. As from tonight, everything would be different.

For tonight at least.

BLOIS.
THE VERY NEXT DAY IN MARCH
1792

Williams was leaning over her when she woke. The morning was bright, the sky noisy with the winds of March. He was in his shirt and his stockings, which is how husbands wake their wives the civilized world over. His trousers were on his legs as well, again as is usual, though trousers she knew were far from being a universal stratagem.

He smiled. His smile had been awaiting her for some time. She smiled back.

'The carriage is here,' he said.

'Is it ten already?'

'No – but it is here and waiting.'

So Beaupuy was waiting. 'And then?'

'I shall accompany you to your stepfather.'

'By which you mean my mother.'

'Let us see what *he* means, shall we?' Williams smiled again, and encouraged her from bed. She did not feel in the least bit encouraged. Bed was very rarely for her, not once the sun was up, but if she could have remained in this one on the edge of the forest at St Lubin-en-Vergonnois she would have done so, at least for a year or two.

He continued to smile. He was probably reflecting that a nearly naked woman – or any woman less than properly dressed – is an object to smile upon, at least by broad daylight.

It was a philosophical point she was not prepared to argue.

She needed to be alone for a while. She explained this pretty briskly, not to say curtly. He didn't seem in the least bit crestfallen by her directness. Everything she said was a delight to him. Everything she did. Everything she didn't do or say. He found his shoes and his jacket and left her.

Before he left her he kissed her. She liked that, even when her thoughts were distracted and elsewhere. There was still a corner of her heart, and possibly her stomach, that could be made to tremble.

Clearly he would have preferred to stay and watch her transformation from nearly naked to almost dressed. Clearly. But he was a sensible man, she knew that. Sensible and not greedy. He couldn't be on every mountain top a minute before dawn, waiting for the sun to strike. She was grateful to be numbered among the mysteries he so often spoke to her about.

The moment he went downstairs she busied herself with her toilet. That is she let her fingers be busy.

What her brain said to the face in her mirror was that she had been married not much more than a dozen hours ago. She had been married by a priest with Almighty God's blessing and the full authority of the Pope. She had eaten no wedding feast, but she had drunk and she had danced. That was last night.

Williams could not keep her. Nor could she keep Williams. A woman has no money. All Williams had was a handkerchief full of crowns. He could send letters to England and demand letters back, but that was all they would buy him. A handkerchief full of crowns.

She had run away to love. Her choice was like any other woman's. She could wander the streets or go and talk to her parents. It was what Williams offered her, and it was no choice at all. She would have to talk to her parents anyway.

The door was not open, nor did it welcome them unasked, though the house was watchful. William performed his first public duty as a husband by beating upon it. He rejected the bell-pull in the wall.

It was drawn back – presumably by a maid – to reveal Paul Vallon. His presence surprised both of them. He caught Annette in his arms.

'So Wodswod got you lost in the woods, little sister. You must give him a ball of your knitting wool to unwind, the next time he's allowed to take you anywhere.' He kissed her, urgently. 'How was it? All right?' He joked round her neck at William, 'Our parent is very angry. If I had not been expected home, she would have summoned me.'

It had happened as she had expected. Either last night or this morning her sisters had been bullied into telling the truth. Now they stood nearest to the door, trying to express sympathy and welcome through faces that were already rendered pathetic by shock.

Vergez was next, his grin as exact as the first phase of the moon. Like the moon, it offered nothing in the way of emotion, only a white toothy light.

Her mother stood last, for this was where the first should stand. This was a matter for the Vallons, and quite possibly for the honour of civilized Blois. Her battle line was drawn up accordingly.

Annette wondered briefly why her brother surgeons and her cousin priests weren't in attendance, and guessed they soon would be. She smiled at her mother in amusement, if not joy.

'Our little sister is home!' Paul cried. 'Wodswod has brought her back to us after a night in the woods!'

'Mother,' she said, and tried to go to her.

Madame Vergez made herself tall and drew away from everybody.

Kissing her was not such a pleasure that Annette felt any need to go on trying for long. She was relieved to hear Williams begin with her father.

'Sir, I think I should speak to you in private.'

'Mademoiselle being madame's daughter, sir, I must insist that madame stays.'

'Then I too shall stay,' Annette said.

'No, Annette. You will go to your room and wait there.'

'My room is no longer suitable to me, mother.'

'Sir, I have to tell you and madame that your daughter and I have gone through a form of wedding together.'

'A form of—' Her mother feigned surprise, as if the whole

story hadn't already been dragged out of Françoise Anne and
Angélique Adelaïde detail by detail many times over between
midnight and daybreak.

'What form of marriage, monsieur?'

'Sir, we were united by a priest of your faith at St Cyr-du-
Gault.'

'A *juring* priest?' Madame Vergez did not require an answer.
She merely sought to establish the enormity of Williams' pre-
sumption before denying him her presence for ever. Almost any
exchange of words would serve for that.

'We were married by the clergy who were available to us
there.'

'Such priests may be available to you, Wodswod. I am afraid
they are available neither to myself, nor to my husband, nor to
the Pope nor to the King.'

Williams seemed unimpressed by several names on the list
that she offered him. He said nothing.

'My Williams is mistaken, mother. We were married by a *non-
juring* priest, by old Daddy Rock who sends you his greetings. So
God is content.'

'God may be content or not – as He pleases. We have no way
of knowing His pleasure in this case: He has not written your
banns in a register, nor furnished Monsieur Wodswod with the
necessary papers.'

The illiteracy or otherwise of God was not a subject that
Annette felt she should comment upon. She was enraged by her
mother's deviousness. According to Madame Vergez her wedding was either blasphemous or illegal. Therefore it had not
taken place.

The lady would have to be softened slowly. Her sisters were
trying to make the occasion more gentle with whispers, and
Paul was doing his best, though his giggle was something he'd
picked up in Orléans and sounded oddly out of place in her
mother's hallway.

For the moment they were not being encouraged to move
further in. She tried to hear how Williams was faring with her
stepfather.

'You kept my daughter out, Wodswod. That's an impious

device to fasten on a parent. And as for the young woman herself, it's a damned pernicious stratagem.'

'I was marrying her, sir.'

'A woman will consent to almost anything on a chilly night. They like to keep the frost out of their tailfeathers. You're a huntsman yourself – you know the way it is with them.'

'I saw no other way, sir.'

'Why didn't you come and ask me?'

'Her mother wouldn't have agreed to it.'

'There you interpret the situation wrongly, young sir – I mean as between Madame Vergez and myself. Matrimony is a very stormy pond, I'll allow you that. So be kind enough to grant me I've learned sufficient watermanship to stay afloat on it.'

Annette thought she'd best divert her mother from this exchange, in case the war became general. 'Mother, I have done no more than worship as you instruct me.'

'Nonsense, child. Marriage is not worship. It is commerce. And you're clearly not old enough for it. You strike a very poor bargain.'

'Williams—'

'—is a heretic, a pauper, and a foreigner.'

'I could forgive him that,' Vergez grumbled, 'and the rest of him too, if only he'd learn to take something a little stronger than water with me after supper.'

It was then that Williams made an error Annette should have warned him against. He allowed himself to become separated from her. She had a moment's picture of him standing with Paul, Françoise Anne and Angélique Adelaïde, then Vergez closed his hand upon her forearm and drew her into the side room that overlooked the street. It was a place designed for watchfulness rather than comfort. It was where strangers were received, Vergez kept his guns there. Certainly there was no comfort to be found in her mother, who was one step ahead of them and waiting for her.

'I am ashamed at your deception of us,' the lady began.

'I don't think I've deceived you, mother. You've not allowed me to speak a word about Williams in all the time I've had him here – indeed, I don't think you let any of us finish a sentence on any subject that's not of your choosing.'

'You've encouraged that young man to mislead you.'

'I am wearing his ring.'

'That ring is a blasphemy, Annette. The young man's beliefs are heretical, and no Christian priest could have married you to them.'

'Williams is going to be a priest, mother.'

'Priests cannot take wives, or in other ways cohabit. Tell her it's against God, Vergez.'

'My study of the Almighty lacks international credentials, my dear. All I would say—'

'God is indivisible. Isn't that the sole truth of the matter?'

'My ideas of God are different from yours, my turtle. I'm like the Sybil of Cumae. I have to consult entrails before I can comment on questions of philosophy, and sometimes I can't put them back or—'

'Monsieur Vergez!'

'—or they've gone mauve or green, which I never find auspicious. So just like the poor old Sybil, I burn them on a brazier.'

'Odious!'

'All I'm saying, Fantail, is that a surgeon's God has a very different smell from yours. Mine certainly has.'

'Your God doesn't stick to the point, Vergez. If He stood in any sort of blood relationship with me, I should box His ears.'

Annette could hear Paul making jokes to Williams, who continued to sound grave. She wished she could be with them, but this was where she had to be, if she wished for a hopeful outcome. Her mother was spending her rage on her husband, and that was a promising development, or it would be if the lady didn't have such a lot to spend and if she weren't always so calculating.

Vergez brought his own sense of outrage to bear on the situation, too. Annette daren't ignore his ability to influence things, nor overlook the great deal of cunning that her parents were capable of when they appeared to be in disarray but were in fact acting in concert.

The old surgeon was genuinely upset by her action, she could see that. He felt outraged by Williams' marrying her. He was like a Turkoman with his quartette of women, even though his relationship with three of them was spiritual and with the fourth more culinary than carnal. Previous remarks had made it clear that any man who meddled with them would offend both his sense of religion and of natural history. Men became more and more villainous the closer his imagination placed them to the feathered not to say frilly or membranous parts of his household of ducklings. For a moment he could only think in blotches, and very black and then bloody those spots became. When a man inherits a family of post-pubescent females ready-made, without the confusion of having to watch them grow up from goslings or even tadpoles, he does tend to view their nubility in the round, so to speak. You only have to sit in a hayloft for half an hour to know the hen is always the victim. If he had his way, he'd shoot only cocks, all the cocks in the world until he was the sole rooster left. It was the only certain road to justice.

'What Vergez is saying,' her mother said, 'what he is telling you very clearly – and I must say he has my complete support – is that you cannot have this man.'

'Mother, I already have.'

Vergez's grin was everywhere, much too pervasive to be natural. His everything else was apoplectic, everything visible at least, from the whites of his eyes to the quicks of his finger nails. He croaked his agreement with madame's agreement, then as Annette proclaimed her defilement in those terrible words, 'Mother, I already have,' he reached towards his gun cupboard for his fowling piece, as if intending to blow Williams to bits, and leave his foreign suiting strewn about the front hall in a litter of feathers and wishbone.

Annette would have laughed at him, save his gesture was so absolute. It stilled even Madame Vergez's tongue. Annette heard her sisters whisper beyond the door. She heard Paul chuckle. His laugh, coming after such a prolonged period of giggle, meant that his calm had been restored.

She could not hear Williams! She rose to her feet. The realization that she had been sitting, all three of them sitting, came as a complete shock to her, and she sat again.

'You have wronged your family,' her mother said sternly. 'I say nothing of the upset to your sisters, and as for myself—' words failed her for a moment or two of self-adjustment— 'it is poor Monsieur Vergez whose situation troubles me. He has to open veins this afternoon.'

Vergez nodded. He completed his move to the gun cupboard.

'I shall forgive you after a due season of expiation, Marie Anne. Your stepfather is a religious man, and I can only pray that he will see fit to do likewise. Whether he will find it in his heart to forgive *me*—'

Vergez was already gone, as on so many occasions before. Gone so swiftly, and with so little of him left behind, it was difficult to imagine he had ever been there.

Annette saw no reason to indulge her mother any further. She said, 'I had hoped he was going to listen to Williams before he left. No matter. Since you are the one who decides matters, mother, I suggest you invite him in here to tell us what he proposes for me.'

'He can afford nothing, child, or by his earlier accounts very little. So he can propose nothing. Consequently I have already decided to send him away.'

She had not been invited into this shut-away room for a discussion, still less a reconciliation. It was a ruse the pair of old devils had planned to separate her from Williams. 'Where—'

'He could not stay here, Marie Anne. He was never right for here. First thing this morning I arranged for Jean-Jacques to come and collect him.'

Meanwhile she had been ushered into the street room, from where she thought she could keep an eye on everything, but where, the moment she sat down, she could watch nothing.

Annette was enraged beyond speech, and completely nonplussed by her mother's cunning. She and her husband intended to behave as if her marriage did not exist. They had not banned Williams, not totally, not quite. They had simply returned him to the *status quo*.

Another man might chafe at this, break out, run wild. Not Williams, she thought. He was strong. He was stubborn. But the *status quo* was his natural habitat. He would be content with the *status quo*. He had things to do there. He had a poem to write.

BLOIS.
THE LAST OF MARCH, 1792, AND
SUNDAY THE FIRST OF APRIL

Williams was forbidden to call at her door, but the monsters could not keep her in.

She would go out with her sisters and come back by herself when she chose. In the interval, she sulked. She could not share Williams' appetite for walking, so a great deal of her sulking was done in his bed. She sulked away the remainder of March and she did not always sulk alone.

Sometime towards the end of March, he leant over her and said, 'If we go on as we are, you will have a child.'

She had been thinking this and related thoughts very actively since the first day of her sulk. 'Shall we stop doing it, then?'

'It will be *our* child, Annette.'

'And God's. It will not be conceived at the town's end.'

He went on doing it, but more thoughtfully. They went on doing it. She went on doing it in a bed in Angel's and her brother Jean-Jacques' house. Angel couldn't tell Jean-Jacques, and she had a story ready for his mother, who would be certain to ask because she already had, twice a day. 'Annette calls on me only sometimes, maman,' she would say – and to be fair, she and her sister-in-law saw very little of one another, since they were both occupied about the house in their different ways – 'and as for Wodswod, he's frequently out with that Captain Beaupuy.' Angel could be very emphatic about this component in the mendacious equation because it was true.

Annette finished being breathless – Williams was never breathless – and said, 'She could not ignore a child – mother, I mean.'

William was not so certain. Madame Vergez was curiously akin to his university's notions of God. When she ignored things, they quite simply ceased to exist.

The two men rested by a ruined chapel, green with lichen and darted through by birds. It was as fairylike as anything in Spenser, and a deal more melancholy than even the best of Helen Maria Williams. The late afternoon sun receded up its south-western angle – the trees were only lightly in leaf – and a single green lizard followed its warmth slowly up the brickwork.

'This Helen Maria Williams you are half in love with—'

'I'm a married man, Beaupuy!'

'That's why I only allow you to be *half* in love! What sort of stories does she write?'

William would have preferred to talk about Spenser. He spoke about Miss Williams instead. He surprised himself with the warmth of his commendation.

Michel interrupted his recital. 'Her fantasies are rubbish, William. There will need to be a revolution in England sooner than you think.'

'She lives in France. She approves of the Constitution.'

'It will abolish her. Did I ever tell you the story of Vaudracour and Julia?'

'I think not.'

Michel Beaupuy spoke of young love, and a conflict between families and cultures, of a girl shut away from her lover, himself driven mad with grief. It was a remarkable story for a soldier to tell, though it was full of Beaupuy's usual antipathies – the abuse of power and privilege, the enslavement of women, the misuse of *lettres de cachet*.

William liked stories, and this was a good one. It lasted them most of the way back to Blois. Difficult not to see himself and Annette in this tragedy of love denied, though *her* parents were the villains who were behaving like Vaudracour's aristocratic father, and *he* was in Julia's position, impoverished and shut away.

Only temporarily impoverished, and certainly not shut away for ever, he told himself.

Beaupuy shattered his optimism by saying that Julia had a child, and was forced to part with it, and then she died and Vaudracour was left to bring up the baby alone.

This was more anguish than the young husband could bear. William hurried to be with Annette, to be in his bed and dream of her at least. The story burned into his being. He knew he would never forget it, whether thinking of France or recalling Beaupuy.

Although the vagaries of its plot couldn't quite be twisted to fit his own situation, somehow they represented his last four months in essence. The tragedy was a prism rather than a mirror. It showed him nothing of himself, yet all he was became diffused through it in a strange mad light.

On Sunday the first of April, William would return from a long trudge through the tedium of politics, love and the disintegration of society to find Annette in his bed. Or that is what she planned for him, if he bothered to come and look for her.

She told Angel that she was going upstairs to arrange some flowers in his room. The wild flowers of Spring are poor limp things and they distressed her terribly, so she decided it would be best for him if she arranged herself instead.

Even in Williams' absence with that peddler Beaupuy, even in her husband and lover's absence, his bed was full of comforts, remembered ecstasies, and even more precious to her because so brief, remembered dreams. There was also the wifely fact that she could inspect Angel's bed linen and assure herself her man was being tended according to standards she would one day be able to insist on.

Unfortunately for Annette, William was still some English miles away as she slipped between his sheets. He was knee-deep in the wilderness of the Salogne and a ceaseless conversation. He passed several roosting bands of Guyon de Montlivault's *Chouannerie* and once, unmasked by Beaupuy's stalwart frame, blundered in front of Vergez's gun barrel as her stepfather knelt at his Sunday devotions among the ducks.

Perhaps none of this was true. Perhaps she dreamt it. She was wakened by the door of her lover husband's room bursting open, and the hard-footed entrance of a huge bunch of forest flowers.

They were not borne by Williams but by Angel, who had been brought them by Jean-Jacques who sometimes, principally on churchdays, found it convenient to kneel among the ducks with his fellow surgeon and stepfather.

Angel stood and looked down at her. She gazed up at Angel. If Angel didn't know, now she knew. Now she knew Angel knew, and Angel knew she knew, nothing in any way embarrassing remained for them to speak about.

Annette smiled at Angel and Angel arranged the flowers. She wasn't better at flowers than Annette, merely different.

Annette went back to sleep, and was wakened by Williams coming in downstairs. Jean-Jacques must have gone out again, because Williams spoke only a sentence or two, and then he was in the room with her.

'We saw your stepfather in the forest,' he cried as he caught her in his arms. 'He had made prodigious slaughter, such a carnage of wildfowl – principally waterbirds – that he'll need an ass to transport them.' He was delighted to find her naked, not merely in her underdress and stockings, but naked. 'Know what he called out to us – as if we were still on speaking terms, I mean?' Williams was unhandy with his own clothes, or simply forgetful of wearing them, so she reached up to help him. 'He said he only had three stepsons. The youngest was never here. The middle one refused to shoot, and the oldest shot only flowers! I see he shot some for me.'

Feeling round his clothes and helping him with his jacket she found something clinging to his back. 'Did you walk among the children?' she asked. 'It's April the First.'

'We call it Fool's Day in England.'

She showed him what was stuck between his shoulders – a paper cut-out of a fish. Lower down, the nap on his fine English cloth had been glued with the actual head and tail of a tidily eaten fish.

'Poisson d'Avril,' she said. 'This one comes from this house – from the maids, perhaps.'

'How do you know that?'

'A poor woman wouldn't have left the head. She would stew it for soup.'

'What does it mean, beyond making me an April Fool?'

She told him. Or she tried to tell him. It was too late for him to listen, or for either of them to care. He was in bed with his bride, who lay with the forest in her arms and felt the Springtime quicken while her fingers played April games on his back.

BLOIS.
EASTER SATURDAY 1792. THE YEAR ACCELERATES

Half of the population were busily disowning God, and the other half were starving. This made Lent a difficult time for Christians of substance. The Vergez household and the several families Vallon solved the matter for themselves by maintaining the appropriate posture of reverence and humility but eating all they could get. As Vergez himself said, 'Jesus didn't invent black powder for me to dine on cobwebs!' At the moment he had an unmanageable mouthful of cake.

Annette began Easter well. She prayed busily and alone on Good Friday, then accompanied her mother and her sisters to church. Every service in the diocese of Bishop Gregory was conducted by a juring priest, and if that caused Madame Vergez to sit with her nose in the air, Annette did not notice. She had Williams and related matters on her mind. Worse, she felt ill. She knew she was due for the usual misery of megrims and vapours, but this was more like a fever, and had been going on for some time.

Prayer kept her away from Williams, prayer and anguished contemplation. This was as God intended. He meant it to be the longest Friday of the year. Annette's Good Friday was a long one indeed.

Madame Vergez had no such perception of the church or the calendar. Her youngest daughter had been for several months afflicted by a folly. She had lived for far too many weeks in error.

Now the Risen Christ and His Holy Mother had kept her away from her silly Englishman for a night and a day and a night. Today, the Saturday of Easter, could be a further unit of abstinence. From these tiny bricks of time Madame could build Eternity.

Unfortunately for her mother, Annette had other plans. It was scarcely a stroke beyond mid-morning, say a quarter chime, and the girl was getting her hat on, a hard outdoor bonnet with pins.

'It is Easter,' Madame raged to Vergez. 'Tell her it is Easter and she is not to step out.'

Vergez managed his cake. 'It is Easter,' he agreed.

'What are you proposing for me, mother – to keep me in a nunnery?'

'Unluckily those villains are doing away with the monastic orders.'

'Do I honestly understand you to be saying—'

'Honestly—' The word dried in her stepfather's mouthful of cake-crumbs. He licked his palate and began again. 'Honestly is the only way your mother can possibly be understood.'

Madame Vergez needed no further testimonial. She decided to be understood absolutely and at once. 'You cannot leave the family at Eastertime. Vergez and I insist on it. Isn't that so, Vergez?'

Annette's stepfather rinsed his speech with a tiny mouthful of Easter wine. 'Your mother insists on it,' he said firmly. He inspected the statement for any flaw it might contain, satisfied himself as to its inherent truthfulness and decided to repeat it. 'Your mother insists on it. Easter is Easter, she says.'

Annette took a large breath. 'Today is Easter Saturday. The Saturday of Easter is far less significant than either the Friday of Our Lord's Crucifixion or the Sunday of His Resurrection.' She was a Frenchwoman, and Vergez had to concede that the daughters of France are notoriously hard to interrupt when they are embarked upon anything they perceive to be the larger truth. They acquire the habit from their mothers. 'Moreover, this Saturday of Easter is April the seventh, the seventh day of April. It is Williams' my husband's birthday.'

'That man is not to be regarded—'

'That *boy*,' Madame Vergez corrected.

'That young man is not to be regarded as your husband! He lacks both the means and the legal entitlement. As such, Madame Vergez and I have forbidden you to see him.'

'See him I have and see him I shall.'

'Indeed. Then—'

'If he is not to be thought of as God thinks of him, as my husband, then perhaps my family would prefer to fly in the face of the legitimate church and know him as my lover!'

Annette did not intend to stop at this point – she was scarcely into her stride – but the effect of her words on her mother was terrible to behold. At the word 'lover', Madame Vergez emitted a gasp of enormous volume but totally without breath – as if her daughter had just plunged the cake knife into her windpipe – and collapsed into Vergez's arms. This was a messy proceeding, damaging to her dress and her dignity, as the surgeon's hands were full of cake and wine and his fingers crumby. And he was sitting down, in order to eat and drink more comfortably.

'If you leave the front door,' her mother said, 'then you need not come back.'

'I'll be back, mother. I fear I shall be here again in an hour or two. You and papa will not want me explaining my situation to the town.'

Vergez helped his wife leave his lap and find a chair. He began to chew cake again, approvingly. He liked that 'papa'. He disliked any mention of controversy. His appointment to the Hôtel de Dieu was a private one, a personal one, and it was, in theory, for life. But life was a fragile commodity in these times of change. It could stop suddenly at a streetcorner, or halfway up an alley. Often, on his way across the bridge to succour female ducks or females in general, he noticed life floating away down the river. But 'papa' now. 'Papa' was better than life. 'Papa' wasn't even real. It came straight from the pages of a novel. Vallon's youngest child might be the dreariest gosling in the clutch, but she had just called him 'papa', and he adored her for it.

Madame Vergez did not adore her daughter. She knew what Vergez had not yet begun to notice: Annette Vallon had already left the house.

★

She could not hurry up the hill to her brother's house. She felt too sick. She prayed she was ill with a Summer cold or a surfeit of duck, and would soon feel better. She knew the more likely cause, and didn't regret it. It was only the illness she wanted to be rid of.

'He's out,' Angel said. Angel looked lovely, in spite of her two babes. She grew slimmer by the day, and prettier for there being less of her. 'He's out on a two-day walk with Beaupuy. They've gone to Chambord.'

'Two days?' Annette was close to tears at the thought.

'It's all right, my sweet. They started yesterday, walking as if in a race. So at least one of them will be back today!' Angel did a flounce. Then another. She had not twirled her body, not all of it and all at once, for over a year. 'I've stopped nursing,' she said. 'Jean-Jacques says I'll be slimmer, and spare him the smell once I cease giving suck.'

'I'm sorry for my brother's manners.'

'He's found me someone. This time we've been lucky, or the nuns have. A lady mustn't nurse, Annette. She must leave that to her woman.'

Annette was in a fret to lie down. She said, 'I thought you already have—' she couldn't think of the girl's name, but it wasn't necessary, since she was already there and could be pointed out. 'Isn't she supposed to—'

'She suckles Anne Angélique, my sweet. She can't manage little Anne Zoé as well. Not and feed her own offspring. She's not a cow.' She patted the girl affectionately, as if guiding her through a hedge. '"Different milks, different goodnesses," your big brother says. He says everyone should feed off several women!'

Annette felt too queasy for all this, and her dizziness must have been obvious, since Angel at once sent to the kitchen for some flowers, and when the girl had brought her a tiny bunch of jonquils handed them on to Annette. 'Could you change the vase in our guest's room?'

Annette was grateful for her discretion. Their complicity was the better for being so well mannered.

Annette was asleep when Williams came in. She woke and said, 'You haven't told Angel it's your birthday?'

'No,' he said. 'She'll say "What birthday?" and I shall have to confess my age.' He slipped into bed with her, smelling of the woods, and warmth, and his strange foreign cloth. 'By which I mean my extreme youth.' He caught her in his arms.

She was in no mood for love. She needed loving. She drew away to gain his full attention. 'I'm expecting our child.'

'You're expecting a – how can you be certain of this?'

'I am certain.'

'As the daughter of Léonard Vallon would be certain?'

'As the animals are certain. I think I suspected it on the First of April when I saw that April Fish on your back.'

'Some child fastened it there.'

'And you had already fastened a child on to me. Well, I'm glad.'

He kissed her, beginning with her hands and finishing with her lips. 'You are quite sure?'

'Yes.'

'Who have you told about this?'

'Only you, my Williams. You must be first.'

'We must tell your family at once.'

'I think I need to be a little more certain before I talk to my mother.'

'How can you be more certain than certain?'

'What I mean is—' what did she mean? 'What I mean is – and any woman will tell you this – is that, although I *am* certain, I need to be certain for longer.' She hadn't grown timid of a sudden, merely the more cautious because her mother kept a surgeon in her bed, and surgeons know apothecaries. She felt wary to the point of terror, the more she thought of her mother, because her mother could take an advantage from almost anything, and Madame Vergez's advantage would almost certainly be her own catastrophe. 'No, Williams.' She saw the pitfalls very clearly. 'We must avoid giving an early warning to my mother. We must tell her when it's altogether much too late.'

Williams sighed and adored her. William sighed. There isn't much else a young man can offer his wife when she's first with child.

BLOIS.
MIDSUMMER 1792. AS A WOMAN
GROWS OLDER

On the mid-morning of June 22nd, Annette sat and took a glass of wine with Angel. Madame Vergez was aware she was at her brother's house, being befriended by her sister-in-law. Madame Vergez trusted that Wodswod was elsewhere. Angel constantly reported him to be elsewhere. Annette said he went walking with that Captain Beaupuy, another person born many English miles away from the true centre of France, which Madame Vergez took to be within a few paces of whichever part of Blois she found herself in.

Williams was here. Beaupuy was here. Beaupuy took wine, and Williams – with extraordinary largesse of mind and an exaggerated smacking of his lips – pretended to. They were toasting Annette's twenty-sixth birthday.

Angel, who was growing slimmer, gazed fondly at her sister-in-law, who was growing plumper. She felt sorry for Annette, though perhaps her sorrow was tinged with envy as well. The slimmer she grew – and she was especially slim now the new wet-nurse spared her the need to keep herself in milk – the slimmer she grew the more attractive she became to her belovèd Jean-Jacques. The resulting sport was flattering but dangerous, and best saved up for the cool months of the year, when the shutters weren't open for Wodswod to hear, and the neighbours, and the officers of the Bassigny Regiment to roar their approval and encouragement.

Angel had to concede that Annette spent an awfully long time in the Englishman's room. But where else could she teach him anything? His speech must be improving out of all recognition in consequence. Catching her friend in Wodswod's bed had been a shock and a worry to Angel, but the man was a long way away and in male company at the time, and a bed, any bed, was a natural place for Annette to rest if a megrim overcame her, as again it seemed to have done just recently. She doubted if her friend had done anything totally wicked, at least since that sham of a wedding. Marriage always makes a woman prudent between the sheets, because carnality is no longer an adventure but a lottery. The reward may be half a lifetime of parental travail. It can lead to an almost immediate sentence of death in the childbed, even with a surgeon as husband. A woman with only a poet for comfort would be wise to devote herself entirely to continence, attractive as Williams was to contemplate for the other thing. No, Annette was entirely safe, and if she was growing plump, it was probably through happiness and the undoubted fact that the Vallons as a family presided over three of the very few tables in Blois that had an adequate supply of food on them.

Besides, Annette wasn't like other women of her age, which was Angel's age too. She had politics on her mind. Violent politics! She had even been known to speak calmly of shootings and swords and the mixing of gunpowder – as if they were proper objects of enquiry for members of her sex. It was impossible a baby could enter a mind with such an interest, still less come out of one, however beautiful its face. What was she saying now?

'The naked ones have forced their way into the Tuileries.' This vocabulary was typical of Annette, and did her no kind of good in civilized society. 'Vergez heard only last evening.'

'The naked women?' Beaupuy asked. He seemed to relish such talk.

'Yes, the fishwives. They forced their way in front of their Blessed Majesties and the royal children as they sat upon their thrones. One of them asked for His majesty's cap, and He gave it to her.'

'The King's cap!' Beaupuy laughed. 'Then was her shame covered.'

'No,' said Annette indignantly. 'She marched out with the royal cap on her head. Not in hand and upon her stomach.'

The Englishman sighed. Whether he shared his wife's sense of outrage or his friend's amusement it was difficult to tell. Angel was glad not to see him sucking a pencil end for a change.

'At least he's got himself some children now she's been dressing up as a shepherdess,' Beaupuy observed. He winked at Annette, whose fury was enflamed even further by this latest turn in what was meant to be a serious discussion about affairs of state. 'Not that shepherdesses and cow-milkers wear very much where I come from, either! In the Summer they go much like the fish-women – bare above, and breezy below.'

'The Queen is unpopular,' Annette said, still determined to steer her birthday celebrations towards a higher level of discourse.

'She's certainly unpopular with her husband's family,' the Captain said judiciously. 'She falls in love with women, and she's insisted the poor King be circumcised not once, but twice.' He was overcome with a sudden paroxysm of laughter, and made a point of dragging Annette's Englishman and Angel's lodger outside, evidently to tell him of a matter much too delicate to be aired in front of ladies.

Angel had grown used to twirling again, and Annette was Annette; so not unnaturally the two women followed the men into the street to discover what the secret was. They were just in time to hear Beaupuy say, 'I do declare France will only be cured when they've taken hold of that poor fool and treated him to circumcision number three.'

'Circumcision number—?' The topic was clearly beyond Williams' bedroom French.

'Yes, Wordsworth. We're going to circumcise his head. I'm glad to inform you we at last have a machine that will perform the operation painlessly.'

There followed some talk about the Louisette or Guillotine, a subject serious enough for Annette to show an interest again, until William said he couldn't see how a device which had been executing criminals in Scotland and Halifax for centuries could possibly be adapted to cosmeticize King Louis's matrimonial shortcomings.

Impossible to know whether the Englishman was jesting, or simply deficient in understanding. Beaupuy clearly thought he was jesting, and hugged him fondly as a prelude to embracing the ladies. As he did so, the Captain announced to them both, and in both ears of them both, that he was in need of an after-dinner sleep. It wasn't yet lunchtime, or even noon according to the sundial which was the only reliable clock, but he had toasted Annette's birthday with very great enthusiasm, and it was clear that if they did not speed him on his way to his bed they would shortly have to carry him to it.

Scarcely had Annette treated any man to such a display of affection as the one with which she dispatched the grenadier officer of the Bassigny Regiment on this occasion. She was warmly loving towards Williams' friend, and the Englishman thanked her with a smile.

They watched Michel Beaupuy step purposefully indoors, walking so widely he might have had a horse between his knees. They listened to the interrupted drum-roll of his progress upstairs.

Then Angel saw Annette turn fiercely on her Williams and say, 'When does that man leave?'

The poet pulled several kinds of face at her before managing to answer, 'Why, July. The Bassigny Regiment leaves for the Rhine in July.'

Angel did not normally interest herself in run-of-the-mill military arrangements. Maps, destinations, strengths and orders of battle were beneath her interest and attention. Yet as a land-lady she was obliged to know all manner of vulgar details. 'The Thirty-Second will march on the twenty-seventh of next month,' she said. So it would, and so, miserably, would her house be empty.

'The twenty-seventh of July, then,' she heard Annette whisper to her poet. 'When that pernicious Friend of the Constitution has withdrawn his influence from Blois, you may feel more able to grant your family a little more of your attention. I judge that to be an excellent date on which to speak to mother.'

Angel was more intrigued by the manner of this speech than interested to guess at its import. She would not say her friend hissed the words, or not quite. A hiss is very like a whisper, and whispers often come out badly.

Be that as it might, Angel was surprised to see Annette depart as soon as she had delivered them. She turned weakly into her brother's house and went wearily upstairs in her turn. Angel hoped Wodswod's room was fresh and his bed orderly.

First Beaupuy who was drunk, and now Annette who was scarcely less than sober! Both of them in bed with a headache! What a way for the poor girl to celebrate her twenty-sixth birthday!

The Englishman, praise be, was a gentleman. That is he was a male divested of all the beastliness of man! He didn't follow her. He kicked boot against boot, examined his soles for wear, then took himself away across the river for a long walk in the Salogne. He stepped so briskly that Angel longed to go with him. But she was both a married woman and a bourgeois lady, and walking would never do on either count. If poor Annette continued to droop her days away like this, Angel would suggest the young Englishman borrow, hire or buy a pair of horses. Angel would ride with him. Angel would never droop.

BLOIS.
SATURDAY THE TWENTY-SEVENTH
OF JULY, 1792

This was to be the day of Beaupuy's departure from him, and waiting for it to happen left the poet feeling not so much dismal as empty. William had been educated to a mathematical view of the universe. '"Nature abhors a vacuum",' he quoted to Pardessus the younger, who did not think he was being in the least mathematical.

Nor did the second Lacaille, who also stood with them where the river road, the Eastern Road, crossed over the Rue du Pont at the city end of the bridge. Both men thought William was becoming bored, if not downright impatient.

'Ah!' smiled Pardessus the younger, 'you're quoting our Rabelais who was borrowing from Plutarch.'

'He's a thief then,' said the second Lacaille. The Lacailles were a family who shot thieves, and preferred, in general, to design guns for gentlemen of similar persuasion, rather than for doctors who made sentimental slaughter among the ducks they were in love with. There were many people the Lacailles were not in love with, almost all people if the truth were known. He sensed an air of misery seeping from the Englishman, and would quite cheerfully have shot him too.

'"*Natura vacuum abhorret*",' Pardessus the younger triumphed.

It was the sort of Latin one can understand aloud, even in a foreign accent. His two companions were grateful to him for it. The second Lacaille in particular was so grateful that he fingered the stops on his nose and blew it nostril by nostril, a barrel at the time, a full five paces ahead of him to ornament the cobbles at the centre of the street, exactly where the thousand officers and men of the Bassigny Regiment were shortly expected to tread, being overdue, being long long overdue on their march to face salvos fiercer than these. The Prussians were on the Rhine. The Austrians were on the Rhine. A vast army of émigrés was reputed to be in their van, and if none of these terrifying circumstances seemed to worry Pardessus the younger or the second Lacaille, they certainly left William with a lump in his throat. He fretted. He fretted for Beaupuy. He fretted for his bride. She hated walking, he knew, and standing was, for a young woman, much the same thing albeit without moving the legs or swinging the feet. But she ought to be here. He needed her here. They were to see off the Thirty-Second Regiment of the Line and then go and talk to her mother. The lump in his throat subsided, and became a sympathetic chill in the stomach. He hoped she was up to it.

Annette had gone to fetch Angel, and her maid and her wet nurse and the children. While she and Angel were alone – it did not happen often – she realized there was something urgent they must talk about. It struck her, all in a rush, that her sister-in-law had better be in possession of the facts before she took Williams to confront her mother. She was maturing as a strategist. No less than the secret armies that were massing in the Salogne, and in Brittany and the Vendée, she needed a safe haven to fall back upon. Her sister-in-law and friend represented one half of such a place, and her rooms were appropriately empty. Her eldest brother Jean-Jacques was, unfortunately, the other half, and his portcullis might remain lowered and his gates barred out of respect to their parent. Now nonetheless was the hour. So she told Angel straight out, and helped Angel come to a conclusion her suspicions had already brought her to several weeks earlier.

Angel embraced her warmly. What Angel said was, 'You should have come to me. I could have stopped you getting like that. There are devices.'

'"Devices"?'

'Stratagems.'

'We want a child, Angel. We want *this* child. It was intended.'

'My poor Annette.'

'We are married.'

'How can that really be possible? I know you say it is possible, but how can it *really* be possible, Annette? I mean, you have no house, and maman says you are not married.'

'How is it that you and my brother can say you are married, Angel?'

'That is a rhetorical question merely. You were there in church. You are here in my house.'

'You were married by a priest. So was I.'

'Maman does not think so.'

'Maman believes in the non-juring priesthood.'

'She believes in common sense, Annette.' Angel embraced her friend again. She seemed anxious to take the sting from her words, but she clung to Annette too long, as if she were saying goodbye to her. 'I am happy for you, very happy. If you're sure it's what you want.' She appeared to reconsider the terms of her embrace, and kissed Annette again. 'You may have need of me. And of Jean-Jacques. We are always here.'

Then the nurse came in, cradling Anne Zoé asleep on her breast. She was followed by the maid, who was also a nurse, leading little Anne Angélique. And, yes, they were always here.

For a few moments the sisters-in-law fussed over the two children, made certain of their own and the servants' clothes, and then went walking out to the trill of Anne Angélique's excited chatter. Their emotions were varied, but their principal purpose was to see Captain Beaupuy leave town.

So Annette arrived very late at the bridge end of the Rue du Pont. She stood with and among the people she knew, who were the people of note in Blois, and most obviously she stood with Williams. Blois's people of note were not ones to stare. Like all the best people they could see without looking. If they saw the way she touched Williams' sleeve, and the support he gave her, then they saved the matter for later discussion.

They had to save it for a long time. The Thirty-Second

Regiment of the Line marched late, though only those intimate with one of the Regiment's officers, people like Angel and Williams, had the least idea of when this was meant to be in the first place, and these had been offered different times, depending on when they last spoke to that officer, how senior he was, and whether he told them what was intended, what was ordered, what was considered likely, or indulged in some more cynical form of prophecy. Line officers were aristocrats or the close relatives including bastards of aristocrats, and aristocrats were betting men. The officers of the Bassigny Regiment had opened a book on their actual time of departure. Most of them had wagered early and openly and variously to support that book. Lately they had hedged their bets by an exchange of handshakes among their friends.

Before the day could begin, breakfast had to be taken. Regiments do not do this quickly before a march. Feeding their men was not normally prominent among the officers' priorities. Nor was eating breakfast the first ambition of those who had to be on parade in immaculate turn-out with weapons impracticably bright at seven-thirty in the morning as a prelude to day-long drill. Lunch, taken at four when the drill was over, lunch was the meal a soldier hungered towards, and frequently after, because lunch suffered from organizational fatigue as well, since those responsible for providing it would themselves have eaten several meals by then, at Angel's table or similar parlours of excellence, and consequently would see little need of it. They would have gone out riding or to place bets, sometimes with the ration money, or been unavoidably delayed watching their friend Jean-Jacques Vallon sever fishgirls at the elbow or shorten carters below the knee.

Before a march, matters were different. A regiment needed breakfast or the parading starvelings would rapidly become outnumbered by their shadows, and the regiment be a regiment no more. Its people had to be fed, and it needed to find enough of them to feed. Before a march an even fuller inventory of personnel was required, and some of those who were previously absent from parade with decently military excuses, such as running errands for their officers, or suffering from fevers, or both, were inevitably found to be still absent, this time without excuses and undiscoverable in their company lines or among the beds of the Regiment's women.

Williams had all this information from Michel Beaupuy, a warrior happy in everything except his citizenship, and he explained them eagerly to anyone who wanted to listen. This did not include the second Lacaille, who found his observations too obvious for comment, or Pardessus the Younger for whom they were too trivial even for contempt. Annette disdained them, because they were derived from Beaupuy, and Madame Vergez arrived midway through them and did not notice them on principal.

'Here they come!' cried Angélique Adelaïde. Madame Vergez had brought her other two daughters and tried to assemble the Vallons as an inner bastion of good taste within the rest of the town's notables.

'The gentility have eyes of their own,' Madame Vergez hissed. 'And as for our ears, we do not need to be a-buzz with your voice.'

Angélique Adelaïde's features burned for a long time, to receive such a public rebuke, but they were nothing as scarlet as the first face to process past them to the thud of an approaching drumbeat.

It had been well prepared with liquor and belonged to the Colonel of Regiment. He sat astride his horse in radiant mood, a man both proud and happy. He was proud of the Regiment, pleased to know it was moving in such strength and good order behind him, and happy at having won the bet recorded in the official mess book. He had foretold the time, and his guess had been for a later hour than was fair to the industry and punctuality of the men under his command. But he it was who gave the order to march, and he it was who had insisted on a delaying last-minute inspection of the Regiment's leather and web.

He was followed by his *chef-du-bataillon*, also mounted, and by the Regimental Sergeant Major.

Pardessus the younger began to talk about a supposed irregularity at the head of the column, but he was speaking to the second Lacaille, who had observations of his own.

Williams wanted to explain that Michel Beaupuy had lamented the lack of a second battalion, the more so as there was talk of the Bassigny Regiment becoming a *demi-brigade*, but a *demi-brigade* of what?

This was beyond his French to say quickly. It embarrassed Angel, now she realized how his time with Annette had really been spent. It must all have been in love talk, whose vocabulary is small, and in bed talk, which – even with a surgeon and scholar like her Jean-Jacques – follows no grammar at all.

William would have stammered on for ever, if Captain Beaupuy hadn't immediately ridden by, immaculately turned out from head to foot and sleek to each high-stepping hoof, but most splendidly noticeable because his hat of tall skins – and very lofty it made man and horse appear – his *bonnet à poil* was decorated with a red cockade and a gold tassel of enormous length and serpentine complexity made even more stunning by a fist-sized tassel that buffeted him nobly about the cheek and moustache, and a racket of solid gold or sun-filled brass that dangled even lower.

It was clearly a point of pride with him not to notice William and the ladies, as a parading soldier looks at nothing except the clean feet of God where they dangle from a cloud close to the horizon and a little above eye-level. As for the rest of them, Williams and the ladies excepted, he held Pardessus and the entire clan Lacaille in total contempt.

His company of grenadiers, the bomb-throwing élite of the Thirty-Second Regiment of the Line, marched smartly behind his elaborately stepping slowly advancing horse. They marched head of column because they were hand-picked men and in most regiments entitled to, and because in this case they were commanded by the senior captain. Their self-esteem was the higher for having to process behind only four horses, all of them decently nurtured on dry hay.

Six – no, eight – fusilier companies followed in four divisions. Hence Williams' incoherence about second battalions and *demi-brigades*.

Lacaille was now no longer the second Lacaille merely but one of a completely gathered ceaselessly chattering clan, each of them so similar in appearance to his cousin, his brother, his son and his son's paternal grandfather that they could have formed a parade on their own account and currently made both edges of the street and quite a lot of the bridge resemble a corridor of inwardly facing cheval mirrors. Lacaille – on the evidence of voice and cobblestone it *was* still the second or warrior Lacaille speaking – began to explain much more succinctly than Williams but just as abstrusely that a division *within a battalion* is something *totally different* from a division *commanded by a general*, which is a collection of brigades, battalions and innumerable other chess-pieces of the kind collected by generals of division to play with on their segment of the battlefield.

Lacaille, whichever one was still speaking, was delighted to find his observation was of overwhelming interest to the ladies, especially those who were highly born and had consequently come here in need of some such piece of social enlightenment, and now turned to hide their faces in awe of it, with their fans a-flutter in a ripple of excitement and with a delicate smile of appreciation so private that their men were excluded from it, even husbands and expectant fathers and Lacaille, whichever Lacaille, himself.

The Lacailles were bold but not entirely prudent. Having gained so much approval for themselves, they began to discuss matters military and martial as if they had the admiration of all ladies equally, and as if the entire populace of Blois were full of anti-Constitutional pre-revolutionary ardour. Indeed, it soon would be, as the Lacailles intended to supply guns to all hunters of Jacobins.

'They're pretty,' a Lacaille said, indicating the passing infantry, which still stepped proud, even though it was commanded by increasing numbers of horses. 'Very pretty indeed. But they can't do anything fast. Their training won't let them.'

'You think *we* can *fight* regiments of the line?' Pardessus wondered. This was still Pardessus the younger. He had been joined by his father, but the old man was much too wily to offer opinions on a pavement's edge.

'Easier than a militia,' Lacaille said. 'I've studied the matter. I've got bullets through my shadow to prove it. The militias are rabbles, but a rabble that can come swarming after you. A regular battalion is all plod. We'll just take them in the woods on horseback from the side and ride right through.'

'I've never seen a Line Battalion in a wood,' Old Man Pardessus said, expressing a fact which was neutral as far as a lawyer was concerned, and not an opinion which never was.

'Or – if we *must* meet them in the open – fire a single good volley into them and run smartly away.'

'Run away?' asked Pardessus the younger and all the Lacailles within earshot. 'What will that achieve?' Pardessus it was who finished the question, but he lost half a box of snuff in the draught of the regiment's passing or a gust of Loire wind. He was now very cross. 'How can you ever win if you run away?' His snuff wouldn't stay on the back of his hand as far as his nostril, not even with a row of women's necks to protect him from the breeze. 'Tell me.'

Lacaille had no difficulty with Pardessus's snuff. 'It means you can kill a deal of them but they never harm any of you. Ask the Englishman to explain the mathematics of it.'

'Eh?' said Williams. He was still gazing after Beaupuy's departure as if watching a hole in the air.

'That's not war.'

'Never mind war. It's winning that counts.'

Lacaille knew there was one person present who would agree with him absolutely. He tugged at Annette's sleeve, but her attention was taken by the parading ranks of fusilier companies interspersed platoon by platoon with horse-riding captains, lieutenants, sous-lieutenants, an adjutant major, and adjutants-sous-officers with their white pom-poms and gold bands. A young woman was educated to have an eye for such people, and she didn't lose it simply by becoming married.

So Lacaille was reduced to making the point to her that the fusiliers as such were not well-named as they were armed not with one of his own family's specialist rifles, which were *rare*, but merely carried the 1770 musket. 'The year I was born!' Williams triumphed to her, glad to find some kerbside chit-chat he could understand at last. He immediately regretted it.

Annette gazed at her young man, her husband and lover in adoration, now he had at last volunteered his year of birth to her, and proved how deliciously young he was. He was like a Spring flower, still resolute in the stem, with quite a bit of Narcissus about him, and something of that elusive solitariness. And yet he was so sure of himself, so learned, so wise . . .

These raptures, part Williams, part clean-smelling lightly sweating fusiliers, were interrupted by a horse *nudging* her with its nose *from behind*.

It wasn't just *her* the thing nudged. It barged most people's backs and bottoms in turn, or else breathed their ears, and nearly tipped several of Blois's finest and most important people into the path and beneath the hoofs and marching shoes of the remainder of the parade.

Horses do not walk where folk are ordained to stand, not townsfolk of note, nor nudge at their behinds. Most of those of note, especially Madame Vergez, did their best not to acknowledge the horse and certainly not talk to it.

The horse persisted. Its nose persisted. It invaded and pervaded in all the ways a horse can do, until Madame Vergez turned to reprove it round the eyebrows with her fan, only to see that Jean-Jacques Vallon her firstborn and the most noted surgeon of this place was for some reason astride it. He was not a comfortable sight. It was a borrowed horse, quite possibly a provided horse, and a long way short of civilized. His legs were clenched fidgetingly on flanks which were unfit for a gentleman's knees, being unbrushed and in several regions ulcerously scarred from the attention of warble flies which had mistaken it for the cows it clearly bedded among. It was one thing for a son to barge his horse into one's back, her hauteur tried to tell him, but for that horse to be scabbed and fly-defiled was too horrible a circumstance for it to be taken as another.

'This marching of regiments is a bold sight,' said old man Pardessus, still not recognizing the horse.

'It leaves the town without protection,' his son said.

Jean-Jacques tried to speak to anyone who would pay attention to him, his wife say, or his mother who would not hear him, but in the end communicated only to William. 'There's been a fight,' he said. 'Some men are injured.'

'Some men?'

'In the Forest, so I am told. I expect it's only one. Hysterics are never any good with numbers, especially when they can't count in the first place.'

Angel was listening by now, but totally unable to hear him above the sound of the retreating drum and a tumult of children rushing after.

'I expect it's only one, as I say. I don't suppose there's been a fight at all. A fellow's lost his fingers on a saw or dropped a tree-top on his foot. It's always happening. Well, I've got my bag.' The horse was a dirty place for a surgeon's bag to rest, and most people pondered this fact as if it existed by itself.

Williams had heard rather more of what was being said, and grew suitably alarmed. 'The Western Forest, you say?'

'Yes, the *Forest*, sir. *The* Forest of Blois.' He spoke as if it were a park, and not a nightmare William preferred not to venture in.

'Let me ride with you,' Annette heard Williams say. 'That Forest is a dangerous place.'

Annette was speechless that he should think to leave her at such a time. Was he running away from her mother? She was relieved to hear Jean-Jacques burst out laughing, 'The Forest, *dangerous*? The fine Forest of Blois. It *was* for you, sir. You got married there.'

He had come to communicate, not to argue and had scant time for both. He adjusted his bag on the horse, pressured it with his knees and lower legs and turned rapidly away from the dissolving crowd to join a group of strangers who were waiting for him. His little daughter cried after him, but Angel's attention was taken by the baby. She smiled on it adoringly and handed it to the nurse.

Angel spoke to Annette, but Annette didn't notice her. Annette was thinking how like Williams it was to want to run away with her brother to the Forest, and on such a feeble excuse. She drew him purposefully towards her mother.

'There will be trouble now that the Thirty-Second has left town,' the second Lacaille called. 'Can I sell you a blunderbuss, Madame Vergez?'

'Trouble will hardly dare make itself known to me,' the lady said firmly. 'And as for selling me a blunderbuss, if it's some kind of gun then I must tell you my bed is full of them since I took Monsieur Vergez to be my husband.'

'I am sure your bed will require no protection, madame,' said Pardessus the Younger. 'It's when you ladies walk abroad that we must worry.'

'That, I am sure, is why Sir Worswor spoke of vacuum,' said Lacaille.

Madame Vergez turned away. She wasn't interested in hearing what the Englishman could say on any possible subject. The man had invaded her daughter, twice at least to her certain knowledge. His proximity with her on an adjacent paving stone was almost more than she could bear.

As for Williams, he guided Annette into step behind her mother but otherwise took no notice of the older woman. Lacaille meanwhile tried to explain to Annette that life, if viewed according to scientific laws, was a simple matter of cause and effect. The problem, and here he agreed with Pardessus the younger, was to identify the cause. If the departure of the Bassigny Regiment, the dear old Thirty-Second, was indeed a cause, then what would be the effect?

William had heard enough of Pardessuss's Latin. He had a more homely example for Lacaille. 'When the farmer leaves the barn, the rats steal the corn,' he offered.

Pardessus didn't like country comparisons. 'I may earn my living as a lawyer, sir, but I like to think of myself as a scholar historian as well.'

'Indeed, you are.'

'History takes a long time in the making, sir.'

'A very long time.'

'So it always surprises me, as a student of it, to notice just how much of it can happen on a single day.'

By now they had reached Madame Vergez's front door. It seemed that everyone was bound there.

Madame Vergez couldn't wait to be rid of them. Once she saw the Englishman, she knew he couldn't be left alone with her daughter. She probably said as much, though not quite in as many words, to the assembled Lacailles and both of the Pardessus, also to Angel and her children.

Angel took the children to their nurses in the kitchen. The Pardessus and the Lacailles left in excellent spirits, so Annette knew her mother must have been malicious at someone's expense.

Several months had elapsed since Williams was evicted from her mother's house, and several again since the fiasco that followed her wedding. On this occasion he held her firmly by the hand, a sticky habit that earned Madame Vergez's total displeasure. Yes, Williams was absolutely staunch, completely reliable.

Yet some pieces of news are best passed between child and parent alone. 'Wait for me in papa's gun room, Williams. I'll not be long.' Annette tried to reassure him with a kiss, but was deflected by her mother's gasp behind her. She was determined to stay calm and said, 'Whatever happens, my husband, do not let them persuade you from here.' She was speaking for Madame Vergez quite as much as for him.

She led her mother towards the salon upstairs. It was empty. Even her sisters were in hiding. The room had been used to the chuckles of Old Pardessus, the whispered asides between his son and Montlivault. Not recently. Their plotting, like the rest of Blois's genteel Chouannerie, was nowadays continued elsewhere, or at least behind her back.

Vergez followed Williams towards his guns, perhaps to make sure the cabinets were locked. He very quickly joined his wife where she faced her daughter.

Annette made herself sit down.

Madame Vergez never stood anywhere, except occasionally, in the best company, on a paving stone. She sat herself calmly in the winged chair generally occupied by Old Pardessus.

'Mother, papa, I am four months with child.'

Her mother didn't say anything to this, perhaps because she already knew or guessed, more likely because it was bad news and bad news was to be disapproved of. She studied the front of her daughter's day dress. It was bound once beneath the breast, but not any lower down, with its riband bowed low on her back.

'Croup,' Vergez said. 'It's much too high for anything else. You eat at Angel's, and she feeds you wind.'

Croup lodged itself in the stomachs of fowls. In humans it

found itself in quite another place. Both of the women translated him easily and without comment.

'Shall I just run my hands—'

'No,' his wife said. To Annette she observed, 'A woman needs to cohabit before she can conceive. There's all kinds of nonsense to be gone through first.'

'I'm married, mother. Williams and I are expecting our first baby, and there's an end of it.'

'No, my daughter. If what you say is true, then it will be no more than the beginning of the beginning. The very beginning.'

'You'll be a grandmother, and—'

'I'm a grandmother already. You'll find one day that a woman's ambition to be a grandparent is much more limited than some of you suppose. Are you certain?'

'Have you missed any thingies?'

'Four.'

'That's a lot,' Vergez reflected. 'Well, it *could* be a lot. But with food being what it is. And you're young to be settled in to them.'

'I'm twenty-six, papa.'

'Years younger than your sisters. If I could just—'

'No, Vergez. I've already forbidden it.'

'Palpate her?'

'It isn't necessary. I can see from here. It will be a girl. Another daughter in a house with daughters enough already. Unless we can starve it out of her.'

'She's too far gone, my ring-dove. Unless it's croup, as I suggest. If a woman's four months gone, then it's her you'll extinguish with fasting. When a nestling's got nothing to eat, there's always the mother's bowels for it to feed on.'

His wife stood up as if to move away from him, but it was only to find herself in a more reflective chair. 'That Englishman! I should have been warned by Paul's letters about the boy.'

'Your son writes in riddles, turtle. If that was a warning he sent you, then all I can say is he's not a very scientific man.'

'You like Williams, stepfather!'

'He understands ducks, I give him that.' His eyes brimmed over. Clearly the Englishman understood them only too well. 'All I have against him is he won't drink wine with me—'

'Nor with anyone else, papa.'

'And he's poor,' Vergez muttered to himself. 'A poor man with daughters loathes poor men.' Realizing he had been over-heard, he said to Annette, 'There's nothing personal in my opinion of him, my fantail. I was merely quoting the first law of nature, little tuttle.'

The old man was addicted to waterbirds, and yet he always addressed his wife and her daughters by the nicknames of pigeons, many of the species he selected being common in num-ber and far from savoury in habit. This was often discussed by the women of his household. They had never mentioned it to him, and neither felt the need to do so now. Vergez was the master of the house, and the best way to acknowledge the fact was to ignore him.

His wife decided it was time to give him his instructions. 'I think we'd better find what that English boy's worth. We know the answer, but you may as well discover the worst of it.'

Annette now had her mother's undivided attention.

William's wait began badly. Vergez's guns were locked away. His books on wildfowl, if he had any, were in another place. So were his anatomical treatises, supposing he felt the need of any such distracting information. There was nothing for the young man's brain to feed on.

He missed Michel Beaupuy, and wondered how the days would pass without him. The idealistic officer from the Bassigny Regiment had been the only man in Blois he could talk to. True, he shared a few convivial words every lunchtime with Angel's husband Jean-Jacques, but the surgeon was always hur-rying between sickroom and sawpit and his clothes smelled of blood. The poet promised himself that he would cultivate him more carefully just the same. He was a cheerful, open man, by far the most likeable of Annette's brothers, and a lot less devious than Paul.

These were William's thoughts, and they made him very sad.

The arrival of Annette's stepfather did nothing to improve his mood. He was mourning the loss from Blois of the only man he could bear to talk with, and here, with his mirthless smile, was the one he couldn't bear to listen to. 'Ah, monsieur,' the poet said, 'maître, what have you come to say to me?'

'It's more a question of yourself, sir. You're the young man who holds the key.'

'Last time, sir, you conjured me out of the doors before I could open my mouth.'

'No, sir. Not I, I promise you. The women, monsieur. The women and their son, Paul.'

'This time, Vergez, I come here proposing to cut you in half, if necessary.'

'A duel? Professional gentlemen do not fight duels. We leave that to students from Cambridge.' He unlocked a gun cabinet and felt behind a fowling stock to find himself an unstoppered decanter of coffee-coloured liquid, then went beyond a litter of powder horns to uncover some glasses. He thrust one at William.

William saw he must drink with him or spit at him. He decided to sip. The liquid was peppery, and tasted of being locked up with gun oil, and dusted with saltpetre and sulphur.

'No, sir. We must not fight. We must *not* fight. I'm too good a shot for you, sir. I can crease a swan's forehead at a hundred paces.' He sniffed his drink at William, and added reflectively, 'My daughter has told me her news. When women tell us their news, it behoves us as men to make what we can of it.'

William looked at him and waited. The other man drank and waited. William sniffed his drink. Vergez poured himself another. He was waiting for William's proposal. William had promised Annette that he would propose nothing, certainly not to go to England for money.

'You mentioned – I go back to our first encounter, young sir – you mentioned your expectations.'

'My expectation, sir. I have just the one.'

'And what could that buy?'

'A cottage.'

'Such an item will cost money. Pounds from the English mint.'

'Yes, sir.'

'And how many of these pounds are owing to you?'

'About a thousand – say thirty thousand livres.'

Vergez allowed himself to whistle. It was a note that went very well with his face. 'Well, monsieur, that is a certain sum, as you say, a certain sum indeed. It is not, in itself, a very great lot, but it's more than a trifle and, as such, an indication. It approaches the point, if you follow me?'

William couldn't follow him at all, and the smile fell to whistling again, but this time in tune as an aid to introspection. 'My daughter speaks of a further wedding, sir, but that is, of course, out of the question.'

'I'm surprised she finds it necessary.'

'Her mother found it necessary, sir, until her daughter, albeit reluctantly, agreed with her. Now neither of them finds it necessary, because both have decided it is intolerable for them to agree with one another. We are men of science, Wodswod. As such, and as men most of all, we were created in harmony and agreement. We are surrounded by women and serpents, alas; and, situated thus, we must continue to participate in our first father's tragedy!'

William had rarely been a diplomat, and a wit never, but he smiled into the lopsided grin beside its tilting decanter and shouted, 'Thank God for ducks then, sir.'

'Yes, young sir. Thank God for ducks. They bring me to the entire point. What we require from you, Madame Vergez and I, is not a further wedding. We require a husband for that young woman's stomach and subsequent child. *Bona fide. In situ.* In Blois. Is my Latin too fast for you? In which case, be damned to the *nihil obstat*. Be damned to the legalistic niceties of the *in matrimoniam dare*. Give me the *vir fortis* with a few hundred *livres* in his pocket and I'll carve you wonders out of him.'

William found Vergez's French very clear, but its meaning once again hidden.

'If our daughter's child is to have a father, then our daughter must have a husband who will provide her with an establishment and support her there.'

'Yes, sir.'

'And – what is much more – support her honour with his continued presence at that establishment.'

'I thought Madame Vergez wanted a proper marriage?'

'No, monsieur, not at all. Your marriage was proper enough

for her. It was merely the poverty of it she objected to.' He
made to fill William's glass again, but William had been vigilant
this time: not even a genius of the meniscus like Vergez could
top it up by so much as a teardrop. 'No, Monsieur Wodswod, we
have had enough of weddings, and of priests who are suitable
and priests who are not. What we require is yourself across the
waters and returned, yourself *in person* with money in your
pocket.' He caught William by the forearm, and jolted a little
ullage into his glass. 'I mean, sir, can you do it in a letter?'

William thought – no, not of escape. He thought of seeing his
sister. He thought of gaining a temporary respite from being
told what to do by Annette and what not to do by her mother.
He wanted a little freedom from this place, this drivel, this
oppression by tongues, most of all this incomprehensible, this
endless refilling of an endless glass. He wanted a month away
from the expanding belly. A poet should never lie against one of
those, nor be told what to do with its owner. 'I think the matter is too delicate to be handled in a letter.' Never had he felt
more in love with Annette than when he spoke those words.
Love needs its broken promises, and the occasional glimpse of
freedom to start its longings throbbing once more. He ached at
the thought of leaving her for a little month or so.

Vergez patted William's sleeve as if to reassure himself of the
cloth's undoubted quality. 'Quite right, much too delicate. It
involves families. And families *are* a delicate matter. You can
never put your family in a letter.' He smiled wistfully, as if wishing he could make a parcel of his own, but then he always
smiled. 'Well, I daresay a poet could, but it would have to be a
long one.'

William's thoughts became confused, then anguished. He felt
like a bird beating against a windowpane. The glass in his hand
was empty, then it was being refilled. Then it was empty again.
Had the liquor been spilled or drunk? His dilemma, both in little and at large, was exquisite.

He was disturbed by a pounding of the cerebral arteries,
which he later diagnosed as an insistent knock at the front door,
a commotion in the street. The tiny veins in William's forehead
seemed to snap one by one like cobwebs. Briefly, for a few mad

moments, his pulse was overloud. Then he realized that more than one person was beating on the door, and that fists, perhaps sticks were being used.

A small crowd gesticulated outside the window. They implored rather than menaced. The knocking was urgent, not threatening.

Vergez hurried from the room, and William was in haste to precede him. Vergez was first to the door. He opened it quickly and closed it at once.

'Here's a thing, Wodswod. Follow me to the kitchen if you've a stomach for it. Follow me just the same. I've told them to carry it round the back.'

William followed him. 'Bring what, sir?'

'Bring what changes the matter entirely.' As they went down to the kitchen, Vergez muttered, 'No sooner does a man find one item settled than some other part of his life is in equal upheaval.' His face still offered William its unalterable smirk, but his voice was brisk with a terrible anguish. 'The women mustn't see it, sir. Not my wife as a mother, nor yours as a mother-to-be. Not as it is.'

'See what, sir?'

'Young Jean-Jacques' corpse with its head cut off.'

'With its—'

'Cut off, sir. Almost completely severed. Skin is the only difference, sir. A tissue of skin by the windpipe and the stubborn tube of an artery.'

What William remembered and Vergez perhaps didn't know was that Angel, her maid and her nurse had gone towards the kitchen with the children, and might still be waiting there for her husband's death to come sprawling in.

The kitchen was empty, praise God. Angel and her children were long since gone.

The kitchen door burst open, and some five or six men stumbled in, swearing as men always do when they carry something awkward and heavy, and not pleasant in the bearing.

They supported Jean-Jacques on his riding cloak. They held him in a bundle with his legs folded up and his head stowed under him. What could be seen, and at a glance, was that the wound was absolute. They dropped the body on to the stone floor with its head still beneath it, and it lay with its chest raised up because of the great lump of flesh between its shoulder-blades.

Vergez shook everyone by the hand, then shooed them out. They went, but not before they'd each left him with a version of what had happened, then shaken William's hand as an after-thought of politeness.

'Some say the Chouans killed him.'

'Why would that be?'

'Because he's a Vallon, sir. And a daughter of the Vallons has been seen with a Republican English Constitutionalist and friend of Captain Beaupuy. More likely, if it *is* the *Chouannerie* who are responsible, more likely because the same Captain Beaupuy boarded at this Vallon's house.'

He opened a drawer in the kitchen table and found himself some twine and a poultry needle. 'The general view – five from six of them – was that he was killed because he was a Vallon, sir. The Vallons are known to be traditionalists. Every member of the Constitutional Club wants their blood.'

He stooped, felt beneath Jean-Jacques' shoulder blades for his head, turned it face up and fitted it to its neck. 'A man can do nothing, Wozwoz. He can stand for nothing, say nothing. He can be a priest, he can be a doctor. His friends' enemies will still kill him.'

Jean-Jacques looked very lifelike in death, his expression seeming the more animated because completely still. Vergez went to gather the severed flesh together with twine and kitchen bodkin, only to find the attached piece of skin was twisted. He rotated the head carefully, untangled the skin, then began again. 'Cutting off heads is the fashion now.'

William watched the process intently, as if, being a doctor, Vergez was in some way giving the corpse back its life. 'Angel,' he said, wondering who would tell her.

'All in good time. Thanks be the older daughters are out and the maids out. The Bassigny Regiment leaving town is like a day at the fair for them, all waving and weeping.' He pulled his stitches very tight, and William understood his choice of cooking twine: 'Fishing line would be better,' the surgeon grunted, 'but I keep none, as you know. Nor will I, till they find me a good bait for ducks.' He straightened the body's elbows. The chest twitched and the head twitched with it. 'Lungs full of air, but I've no time to join up the poor fellow's belch to his windpipe. He'll just have to leak round his stitching in silence and pretend he's a gentleman.' He tugged at Jean-Jacques's knees, which were stiffening. 'Ignorant way to kill a man. Even the untutored know a fellow's dead once his head is chopped off. They have just now invented a machine in Paris to do the very thing. Did you hear that?'

'I did, sir.'

'So far they've only used it on thieves and highwaymen, and not many of them. Soon they'll set it to work on people, Wodswod, and chew us all up.' He patted the corpse's cheeks. 'They've cut your head off, Jean-Jacques. I wish you could see it.'

'What more can you do for him, sir?'

'I've done all I can do. But it will do a very great deal for his sister and his mother. Come, sir. I shall tell the one and you the other. Then we must go to talk to little Angel. Thank the Good God her house is empty of lodgers tonight.'

TIME BETWEEN DEATHS: JULY TO SEPTEMBER, 1792

He couldn't leave her at a time like this. Nor could Annette desert her family, any more than they could bear to part with her. The baby, the great news she intended to become the centre of her mother's and sisters' universe, was eclipsed almost as soon as it was uttered. Her mother had even smiled at her, once, as soon as they were alone and there were no men to consider. Then death had burst in upon them.

Jean-Jacques had been shot. He had been stabbed. Or he had suffered one or the other. Vergez was not a man to dwell upon human details. He offered a sympathetic grunt to anything his family suggested. With every grunt his stepson's injuries multiplied. Nor were the local midwives able to offer more sober advice woman to woman. Vergez washed the corpse himself, without the help of his assistants. He saw no reason to submit his surgical kitchen-stitch to the scrutiny of ladies expert at pudding bags or the closing up of fish. When the corpse lay mother-naked he dressed it in a cravat and sutured the knot. He hid the suture with a decorated pin. Jean Jacques was laid out in a cravat, and would be buried in a cravat, always with its suture and its pin.

William didn't even grunt when asked. All he could have told Annette would have been blood, lots of blood. Blood on both sides of the shirt, blood inside the cloak. Blood not so much as a Shakespearean dew, as blood in a kind of jelly. Blood as a syllabub. He saw no need to mention any of this, not once the clothing was bundled away and burnt with a stench like cindered fur or chicken feathers.

The terrible injury to the neck was accepted and forgotten. Vergez dealt with death in ways that made it easy for life to ignore. If Madame Vergez thought about her son's wounds and she never admitted to thinking – if she thought, she would have assumed that someone struck her firstborn's neckbone from behind with a sabre, or crept after him through that dreadful ornamental forest with a woodman's axe. Like mother, like daughter. So with all three daughters. So too the widow. A ruffian had taken their loved one from behind with a hatchet.

Vergez drew William aside very early. He held a finger against his nose before addressing him. In English, in the English of Cumberland and Westmorland if not of Cambridge, this meant: *listen to what I tell you. Neither repeat it nor say where you heard it.*

Seeing Vergez's lopsided smile of inquiry, still with its lips sealed, still resting quizzically against an uplifted finger, William nodded his agreement to what he thought was its question. Vergez required several nods. He needed not so much a nod as a stutter. 'Post mortem,' he said. 'That wound to the upper vertebrae and associated *longissimi*, it was delivered *post mortem*.'

'But the blood, sir?'

'From that crater in his thorax. He was bleeding from his wind, Wozwoz, hence the froth, but mostly from the main return vessel where it enters the heart. He had a lot of heart, did my stepson.'

'A member of my university, sir, has proved conclusively—'

'I won't bore you with anatomical technicalities, sir. I thank God the cadaver was lifeless before they robbed it of its head. It's a barbaric thing otherwise to lay a professional man face-down in the loam and tread his neck through with a shovel.'

'A shovel – how do you know?'

'Or a spade, sir, or some similar kind of invention. It's cut in a curve, don't you see. A chopper won't cut in a curve, nor a saw, nor any kind of cutlass. You need a blade like the end of a scoop.'

'A specially sharpened shovel.'

'Or blunt if you like, Wodswod. The blade can be as blunt as you like if there's a heavy enough boot behind it.'

'Where was he found?'

'At the end of the town. But there's a hutment in the forest—'

'The far side of the Forest – towards St Cyr?'

'You have the place exactly. That's where he was summoned to attend an injured man.'

William remembered the day of his marriage, and how the place had filled Beaupuy and himself with such foreboding.

So Annette's family kept Williams by. They didn't want him, but they saw they might need him later. Vergez described him, to wife and stepdaughter alike, as a young wine that could only improve with keeping. Madame Vergez was fond of a good phrase, and quickly made it her own, along with the images she could conjure from it. She took this one and stored it away in her armoury of calculations. A young wine, yes, a very young wine whose time was certainly not yet, and might properly be never. To this she added a further gloss. If the Englishman was to be stored, let it be in the cellar, and let him be racked. If the family should be presented with a better vintage from somewhere closer to itself – it was an improbable hope, she knew, but not incapable of fulfilment: she herself had been resourceful enough to achieve a second harvest from life's stony vineyard – *if* the family should be blessed by *une cépage plus noble*, then the foreigner could stay hidden away or be smashed.

He was encouraged to call. Annette encouraged him, and her mother allowed. He was invited in the mornings when everyone, even tradesmen, could loiter in attendance. He was invited when supper was cleared away after dark. He was encouraged to sit among grieving sisters at chocolate, coffee, or more latterly hot water and warm milk. After dark he would crouch with Vergez and watch him drink several glasses of brandy or drippings, according to the luck of the decanter. Vergez would take these glasses slowly as a discriminating surgeon does. He would take them a sniff and a sip at the time. At the end of the evening, during which period of tedium the Summer moon would have swollen a little or slimmed a fraction according to phase, Vergez would stand abruptly and down at a gulp the glass he had poured for Williams. If his grin said anything it said, 'A man must be prepared to do such things for a guest who does nothing for himself.' Annette thought that was what it said. Williams, she knew, made no attempt to decipher it. Puzzling over *that* cryptogram could lead him to drink.

So what does a family talk about when it has a son scarcely buried and a guest that only one of its number wants? Everything except itself. On the thirtieth of July the rabble Marseillais reached Paris. They spoke out about that, and in the same breath mentioned that the Théâtre Français section of the Assembly had since yesterday admitted 'passive' citizens to its constituency, people such as women – who had long since admitted themselves – and members of families without the means to qualify for the Third Estate. Other sections followed, consequently enfranchising the entire population. As Madame Vergez observed between a biscuit and her fan, they had abolished the Middle Class at a stroke. Annette didn't feel abolished. After due interval of childbirth and mourning she intended to fight. She was wise enough to point out, though only Williams applauded her, that the greatest threat to their privileges came from the fact that *all* men, irrespective of station, were on the same day entitled to join the National Guard.

'I wonder what Monsieur Gellet-Duvivier says to that,' Williams said. Any mention of the National Guard turned his tongue to Gellet-Duvivier, Annette noticed.

'They can kill us in our beds,' Madame lamented.

'So can cholera,' Vergez said, inclining as always towards the larger view. 'So can smallpox and the stickier kind of measle.'

'God gives us warning of a plague,' Madame said. 'What I seek to allude to is the highly dangerous fact that once these ruffians are admitted to the Guard they'll automatically be granted the privilege of bearing pikes.'

'They're all in the Town Guard already,' Vergez said, 'so they've been carrying muskets all year, and none of us is the worse for it. Besides, we're a surgeon's family, and surgeons are always safe.'

Angel had been mourning whatever memories she had of

Jean-Jacques quietly until this point. She had distracted herself by clinging closely to Annette and wondering how many weeks it would be before she could see her friend's stomach kick. She had only two locations for grief now, with her own family and her dead husband's family, a situation she shared with most widows. Unfortunately her dead husband's family was engulfed in Vergez, and dining with Vergez was like drinking a bowl of gamblers' soup. She didn't know which way the dice were up till she'd suffered her way down to the bottom of him. Even with Jean-Jacques at her side, she never sat near her stepfather-in-law without feeling she was listening to frog-spawn. She began to cry, not noisily but tearfully. This was unfair of her, because it took some time for the other grievers to notice, Vergez last of all, perhaps because he had less to grieve about.

He was upset at his own insensitivity, and rose to take himself across the river among the waterbirds with his longest gun.

'It's a quarter before eleven in the evening,' Annette reminded him.

'And dark as soot,' his wife protested. 'It won't be light until . . .' She let the sentence trail away. Cockcrow was not an hour she troubled to calibrate.

He shook his head sadly at these irrelevances, and left the room and the house.

'Do you suppose your husband has found another woman, mother?' The question was posed by Françoise Anne. In a time of social upheaval, even Madame Vergez's daughters could grow cheeky.

'Lots of them,' Madame said surprisingly and firmly. 'I daresay he's got lots and lots of them. And he can do what he likes with them, as far as I'm concerned, provided he shoots them first.'

Thus the ladies in the Rue du Pont were given permission to laugh, and like many people close to grief and even closer to the grape they began to laugh immoderately. Françoise Anne laughed herself breathless and Angélique Adelaïde laughed agape, showing her gums. Annette laughed more gently, sitting above her stomach as she was. Angel giggled wet-eyed, and even Madame Vergez permitted herself a smile at the stark moral force of her own joke. She was in control of her family again.

Williams didn't laugh, Annette noticed. Then he wasn't the man to be made happy by laughter, and he was close neither to grief nor the grape.

Other people's wars seemed a lot less important to him now he had a young woman ripening in his arms and sprawled about his memory. Other people's wars and other people's woes.

He too roamed at night. Sometimes Annette joined him in the evenings, prowling about lamplit lanes and starlit courtyards, but only in the safest parts of town. Often he walked alone, finishing to gaze up at her window, imagining her face against the casement like a woman in a poem.

Sleep was their daily exercise. When they tired of it they woke to loving, or to gentle adoration. They spent half of each day lying in William's bed, where Angel's widowhood lay heavily with them. Annette would cry for her brother, too. She did nearly all her crying in Williams' arms in his bed.

On some days, her mother would call, so they couldn't get up, since Angel would be re-embarked upon a lie which had already floated for a month or two, saying Williams was out walking, and Annette clearly elsewhere.

Since one of her brothers was dead and manifestly not at work, she had one less place to be. It irked Madame Vergez immoderately to think she might be walking with the Englishman, but Angel distracted her with a scheme.

'Now my poor Jean-Jacques is dead,' she said, 'I think your second son should have his place. My brother-in-law Charles Henry is an excellent man, and we don't want a surgeon's place at the Hôtel de Dieu going to a stranger, or someone from out of town, maman.'

Madame Vergez could forgive Angel for many things when she spoke to her like that, and Angel spoke in this manner often. 'The post has belonged to the family Vallon for the last three generations,' she said.

The two women agreed to do what they could about it, which meant that it was already as good as done, and the Vallon surgical inheritance assured.

Perhaps Madame Vergez heard a noise from upstairs. A house

with upstairs rooms is full of noises upstairs, but Madame Vergez's mind insisted her senses be much less vague than that. She had lived two matrimonial lives, both in the beds of scientists.

'Could it be Wodswod is back?' she asked.

Angel paused only a little before conceding that anything was possible.

'Could it be that there's a woman with him?'

'Only if he shot her first,' Angel said.

It was a tribute to an outstanding joke, and her mother-in-law acknowledged it graciously.

They fell to discussing the Hôtel de Dieu again, and the intricacies of surgical succession. Just the same, Angel thought she should warn her friend that her mother kept matters in mind.

August was it? No, it was the first day of September. William must write to his brother Richard again and demand the advance of some money. Twenty pounds should do. Twenty pounds? Yes, he could make it last. It was a thatcher's wage for two years.

His bed was empty and the day was well advanced towards noon. He walked out to find Annette.

Her casement was strangely unenlightening. Did he feel forebodings already?

It was Summertime now. He was used to shutters flung wide upstairs, bed linen taking the breeze. He was accustomed to an open front door.

What he saw was closed wood and Madame Vergez's paintwork. William advanced and tugged the bell-pull.

Nothing happened.

He swung upon the pommel. He drew it from the wall to the full length of its cord. The bell undoubtedly rang, and the cathedral gonged nearby, but still nothing of note happened.

He beat upon the door. That is he lifted the brass knocker and thudded it against its anvil with increasing violence.

He paused. He thought long and hard. He did not suppose the family had been murdered in their beds or at their breakfast table. Even in these restless times he could not really think that death would visit any of the houses in Rue du Pont *on the inside*.

Murder and rapine were for meaner streets or the shadier glades of the forest.

He went round the buildings by alleyway and covered passage. He approached the back door. There were maids astir, the discarded older woman from the Lacaille family already busy with a sauce or a soup.

William knew better than to trouble such people. A dignified man does not even let himself be noticed by them, especially when he is presenting himself as a lover.

He returned to the front of the house and came face to face with Vergez, who thought he had eluded him, and was about to cross the river with a gun.

Vergez clearly hoped not to see him. He hoped even more clearly not to be seen seeing him. He put his finger to his lip and led William up the street and away from the window.

'Why has Annette not been to see me?'

Vergez knew how to answer a question about a young woman as between man and man. He smiled and said nothing.

'I must know, sir. Where is she? Is she ill?'

Vergez touched the side of his nose.

William took this to be a renewed gesture of secrecy. He was becoming familiar with this language of finger and thumb.

'Grief, Wodswod, grief! The whole household is awash in embarrassment and our subsequent confusion.'

'Where is she, sir? Where is my wife?'

'I am not allowed to tell you, sir. Save to say she has been returned. She went unwillingly, but a neighbour's chaise had a seat, and Madame her mother was adamant she sit upon it.'

'To Orléans?'

'I am not precisely bidden to communicate anything that might be construed as information. That being said, where exactly would you say Madame's daughter has gone to for her lying in?'

'Orléans, as I suggested to you. And where in Orléans?'

'Again, sir, family discretion is at a premium when bellies are enlarged.' Vergez's finger devoted several seconds of family discretion to the side of his nose, then shared it with the front of William's jacket. 'All I can say is – supposing you are right about

Orléans – what lodgings would most readily come to mind, herself having a dearly belovèd brother in that city?'

'The Rue Poirier?'

'I am not a man who likes to stand chattering, sir. Not in a crowded place when my piece is stuffed with duckshot. A word, just the same!' He seized William firmly by the shoulders, and his grip was not to be despised, even though the fingers of his left hand enfolded a gun barrel as well as William's cloth. It had in its time pulled down countless infants with the high and low forceps, all of them issuing from the underbelly of an animal still not intelligent enough to lay duck eggs, which ooze softly along the birth canal and do not harden until they have tumbled into the sunlight from among the miraculous feathers.

William tried to break that grip in vain.

'My word is that vigorous matters are afoot in Paris at this moment. The Mob, sir. September is scarcely begun, and yet we speak of *Septembriseurs* – butchers, sir, butchers! Thousands of our sort of people are being butchered at this very moment.'

'Butchered? Who by, sir?'

'Their sort of people – who else? Take a care, I do advise.' His grip tightened, as if fearful of losing something of value. 'Take a care if you travel. We need a husband in the family, I insist, and a father when the offspring is fully hatched. We don't want a fellow with his head split any further, sir.' His grip became an embrace, and his embrace a kiss of farewell. Vergez was damp but genuine about the lips, moist beneath the nostril, and downright wet around the eye; but his hug was preferable to being held up by the ankles and slapped.

William accepted his father-in-law's drizzle of affection. His thoughts were elsewhere. They were searching for his love.

How could Vaudracour travel upriver? Only when the breeze was apt, and always against the stream.

ORLEANS.
SEPTEMBER 1793

As he travelled – and the breeze blew more and more slowly – it struck him that a young man can be plunged into an intolerable state of sickness by the inconstancies of woman. Her power to afflict him with such a disease is often his love's only attraction for him. William felt like cursing the Vallons, their mother most of all. They had turned him back into an orphan.

Orléans was like the landscape of a poem. The richly painted, offal-heaped lower arcade of the Rue Royale was as melancholy bright as Milton's Hell. It mirrored the madness in his soul down to its last particular. Its mood exactly fitted his own purposeful indecision – he was desperate to search out his love, without having the least idea of what he expected to find, or how to treat it. The place was such a pitiful correlative of his own inner chaos that he went through it without thinking, as if his own emotion had just invented it. He had composed its streets in despair. He had written them cobblestone by cobblestone.

Something was wrong with the shuttered warehouses, the barricaded shopfronts. The disturbance wasn't his own. It was outside his own buzzing head and nothing to do with him. The town seemed stunned and angry. To step among the rubbish in the arcade was like approaching the lair of a wounded animal. Orléans was reeling as if from a dart in its side.

He could personalize it in this way because it was so empty. No, not empty. A town is never empty. It was visibly full, but of people who kept to their doorways, or came out only to whisper, to huddle and be still.

Monsieur Gellet-Duvivier wasn't among the huddlers. His tongue was unafflicted, his sense of outrage unfettered by silence. 'Sir Wodswod!' he called. 'They told me to be expecting you.' He was in full scream, but mercifully not at street-level. 'I allude, of course, to your kinsman Maître Paul Vallon!' He met William from above. He perched upon his stair and hopped upwards and ahead of him like a painted bird. Had he been going in or coming out? Or waiting in one place like a toy monkey on its stick? 'They have butchered the Count Lefebvre-Desnoëttes.'

'Not *him*, father!' The Demoiselle was behind them, or ahead of them, and unable to manifest herself properly until they reached the salon. Her grey eyes were the same, or even brighter, her voice a new discovery that William was expected to gloss over, and he did, but with a gasp of wonder. There had been nine months absence for its growing. It was like a birth.

'Captain Guy, Count Lefebvre-Desnoëttes, was an officer of Cuirassiers,' he explained in his best French, glad to second her, and entranced at her speaking. 'He nearly rode me down with his horse.'

'My head, sir! My memory!' Monsieur Gellet-Duvivier knocked them both with the thumbside of his fist. 'My head is like my heart, sir, bursting with such an agony of veracity that it cannot give truth a name. I mean the Count de Lessart, Antoine de Valdez de Lessart, that De Lessart – do I come near enough, Wodswod?'

'The finance minister.'

'The *late* finance minister! The late *minister of the interior*. The very late foreign minister.'

'"God in three persons",' the Demoiselle whispered.

'A man with his honour intact and a truly noteworthy pedigree, Wodswod. A high-born unfortunate suffering the merest spasm of political affliction – a man only in need of an impartial tribunal to return him to influence and liberty. We are to have such a tribunal here in Orléans.'

'You have been waiting for it for some time, sir.'

'We are to *have* one, Milor Wodswod. They took him from

the prison, and several score more, some of them the finest flower in the land, the rest of them – even the lowest – decent enough as people—' Monsieur Gellet-Duvivier began to weep. He began by weeping all at once, and as he wept he howled, 'They have kicked their heads to bits.'

'To bits, sir?'

'To bits, Wodswod.'

'And more than their heads,' the Demoiselle put in, undoubtedly determined to remain in voice, and revealing her note to be an excellent thing in a woman, soft and low.

'More than their heads?'

'Yes, Wodswod, their bits as well.' She did not sob, nor do anything to redden those cool grey eyes. 'They have been visited with clubs and hatchets, and the poor wretches altogether chopped limb from loin.'

This was a bold speech for one so young. Her fresh eager gaze, the bright *greyness* of her looking, reminded William of trout and other mishaps of social intercourse unwittingly perpetrated in her presence. He decided he had not heard her words aright or translated them correctly. Even so they left him with a strong feeling of horror.

Gellet-Duvivier's sense of outrage was inexhaustible. 'Bourdon took them, Wodswod, and that damned American.'

William had heard of Léonard Bourdon, the self-styled Bourdon de la Crosnière, and judged him harmless. 'Could the town do nothing?'

'The town cheered. Your brother-in-law and I would have rescued the poor wretches single-handed, but – by a vile misfortune – I was without my sword.'

'Your *sword*, Monsieur Gellet-Duvivier?'

'Yes, milor. Without it. And I need an order from a higher authority before I dare discharge my musket.'

The Demoiselle turned her big grey eyes upon William. 'My father's sword was at the grinders, Monsieur Wodswod. It was being *sharpened*.'

'And polished, sir. But principally sharpened. It didn't need polish to slice through that idiot American.'

'"American", sir?'

'His name is Fournier, and he's French, in all of his quarterings. But he's called the "American" because he's been to that country and become contaminated by its politics. Being an Englishman, Sir Wodswod, you must detest America?'

'No, sir. I admire the entire nation for being free of our idiot King.'

Monsieur Gellet-Duvivier was saddened rather than surprised. He directed the remainder of his remarks towards William's Adam's apple, as if too disgusted to lift his gaze any higher. 'I thought you'd lost all such manners on your march to Paris, milor.' He grew fierce. 'Those are radical words to hear from the lips of a man who can afford such a suit, Wodswod, particularly one who has worn the mob's rope round his neck in addition!'

William did not take much notice of any of this, or very much else. Even the Demoiselle's eyes lost their allure for him. His longings for Annette – or his sense of lack – came on very fiercely at that moment, with a pain he knew wasn't hunger. He became an orphan again, an orphan in a foreign place.

So it was he heard many horrifying embellishments to the activities of the Septembriseurs at Versailles, the mutilations, strangulations and axe-bludgeoned butchery of men and women who had so recently been hurried away from this very town, and who were now a bloodied pulp, some of them hidden among their own ashes. His heart was in a similar heap of ruins. How could he suffer further, especially when he remembered his life's other missing component, his soulmate Michel Beaupuy, saying, 'Some Frenchmen will have to die, William, but not so many as will be killed by a single battle'?

The Demoiselle took over the narrative from her father and told him about the torture of Marie Gredeler at the Conciergerie and, on the same second day of September, the mutilation of the Princess of Lamballe, the cold-blooded clubbing to death of boys at the Bicêtre, and the sabring of women at the Salpêtrière by men who tore off their victim's clothing and in general found their own blood rather warmer. She was developing fast as a storyteller, the Demoiselle; but Vergez had already mentioned something of this in the morning, and a lover finds it hard to understand such matters or accommodate them to his scale of things, or he does when his arms are empty.

Remembering Vergez put him in mind of an immediate stratagem. He kissed Monsieur Gellet-Duvivier on the one cheek and then on the other, bowed towards the Demoiselle in a way they both found appropriate, and indicated his need to leave his case and depart.

'Take a care, Wodswod. There are men outside throwing stones. Every night they throw stones.'

'Why do they throw stones?' he asked.

'Because they've just discovered they cannot eat them,' the Demoiselle said. She regarded William eagerly, though not as if she could eat him, or not quite.

Just the same, her expression was entirely beneficial to his *amour propre*. He bowed again, did no more kissing, and left.

ORLEANS.
SEPTEMBER THEN OCTOBER 1792
BEING YEAR ONE OF THE REPUBLIC

She was there at the Dufours' house in the Rue Poirier, just as Vergez's crooked smile had promised him. Marie-Victorie-Adelaïde showed Annette to her Williams in the large upstairs withdrawing room then left them alone to enjoy the view or turn their backs on each other as they would.

Annette swore she had written to him, she knew she had written to him, of course she had left him at least a little note, she had left him several. Now she heard he had not seen nor even been offered one of them, the tears burst from her eyes and she too ached from the remembered loneliness of her banishment from home. The chaise – well, it was bigger than a chaise: it had more wheels, more cushions, more brakes, more horses, more springs – the chaise had been drawn up and waiting. She and the maturing crisis in her belly had been stowed aboard it, and both of them told by her mother (after prior arrangement with the neighbour, the neighbour's wife and the neighbour's wife's maid, all of them impatient people) that the vehicle could not delay its departure even as long as the cooking of an egg, no, not even the coddling of its white, while she ran up the street to her sister-in-law's house to bid farewell to her husband. She had, however, written him a note, notes, buried the salver on her mother's visiting table and then the table itself in an avalanche of missives explaining her destination, bewailing her banishment, and beseeching Williams to follow after and if possible be there before her, or – if impossible – as soon as . . . Here her subordinate clauses lost their way, and her griefs ran over. Once again, letters had been penned and Williams had not seen them. She had been in a fever of uncertainty all day. She felt no confidence in his need to be reunited with her. She was a woman with a stomach. She was fettered by weight and chain, and her cannonball was forever growing bigger.

She broke off her stream of words to be visited by horrors of another sort. Her mother was an avid reader of letters not her own. Since she was as God within her household, she expected to know all things equally and instantly. The Almighty reads her family's letters as soon as they are written, so why not Madame Vergez?

One she would have read already, for one at least had been written on a paper that lay outside the mind. In it, Annette had poured out her fears to Williams. She had spread them in a lump. She had considered the contraption she must travel in, this coach that was open to the elements though larger than a chaise, this land-carrack, torture-bed, this wrack on casters, this storm of contesting springs, and concluded her mother meant to bounce the infant from her belly via any orifice available and leave it still-born along the way. The recipe was an accepted one. It had been tried by young women's mothers before and found extremely efficacious. Annette had put all this in writing. She had also written, for her Williams' eyes only, that many English miles separated Blois from Orléans, and like all English miles they were full of potholes.

There is nothing like wet eyelashes and a torrent of kisses to effect a reconciliation. They wept and felt better for it, Williams especially. He kissed her dryly and thoughtfully, then grew philosophical about English miles. He explained to her that, according to the very best and latest theories available at his university, a road cannot be *full of holes*, since a hole is an *emptiness*, and an emptiness is a *nothing*, and no multiplication or division, and certainly not a straightforward addition, can conjure a *something* from a *nothing*. The universe depended upon the fact. Since a road cannot be a sequence of nothings it cannot be full of holes. Therefore she had nothing to fear at the outset of her journey, and her mother, who was married to a scientist, would see her

letter as the hyperbole it undoubtedly was and dismiss it as a figure of speech. Newton, who should be living at this hour, would
agree with him.

As a woman, which she increasingly was, Annette knew
Newton to be a fool. Euclid likewise. Women are always at risk
from the something that comes from nothing. They are aware, in
philosophical terms, of the nothing that becomes a something
and is nine months in the growing. As a woman, however, she
was wise and didn't mention the matter. Williams had his hand
upon it now, and if he couldn't deduce the fact from such a
straightforward experiment in physical science she saw no point
in proceeding to hypothesis. What she did say was truly
Cartesian just the same. 'A hole,' she said, 'does not merely con-
sist of its emptiness. It also consists of its edges, which some call
its rims or lips. These are what make axles bounce, and men and
horses trip over.' She had his whole attention now; he was a creature who loved finite things. 'And where men and their horses
trip, a woman may be given leave to miscarry.'

At some time during or before this conversation they had left
Marie-Victorie-Adelaïde's withdrawing room and gone up the
main stairs in search of brother Paul's lodging. Annette dwelt
within his protection now, not in a room apart.

Brother Paul's protection was less than comprehensive. When
he wasn't busy with the law, he spent his time gambling. If he felt
himself too broke to afford the table-stakes – and he was always
a lucky man – then he turned his attention towards the young
women of the city. There were many thousands of them in
Orléans, all of them difficult to bid farewell. So much for her
brother.

As for landlord and landlady – well, Annette was here by
arrangement. That arrangement implied that almost anything is
permitted in a young woman who is visibly pregnant and at
least half-married.

Her belly, which was round but entirely beautiful, had been
displayed upon her bed for Williams' reassurance. His hand
spread itself comfortingly upon the pothole of her navel, another
nothing, save for its edges, which were stretched, and the base of
the declivity or defile which were no longer as her mother and

the midwife had formed it. Lover's hands have few places to wander, yet travel always in total delight.

'I have sent for enough money to keep us until well after the baby is born,' he said, as he huddled in her belly's shadow. 'We can take a lodging for ourselves, I mean a proper establishment.' He mumbled these last few words against her, as if mouthing them to the baby direct. 'We shall be in funds until several months into the New Year.'

'Orléans is not safe for you, Williams. I had to hide you from it once.' She spoke brusquely now her tears were done. 'We cannot live that way again.' He was paying too much attention to her stomach and not enough to her. 'Blois will be a safer place, when my mother judges it discreet to return.'

'She should not have banished you in the first place. You have a husband. Your baby has a father.'

'Not a husband and father who can keep us.'

'Until well into the New Year. Until March or April say, when my capital can possibly be extended. If I'm not safe in Orléans, we shall take lodgings in Blois.' Again he made the mistake of imparting this confused piece of intelligence to her navel rather than herself. He might prove to be a very possessive father, and an inattentive husband. He might find another Beaupuy to waste his days with. She had to think of these things.

'None of my mother's daughters will ever be allowed to *lodge* in Blois. The Vallons live in houses, in fine stone houses with roofs of blue tiles. Blois is famous for its tiles. We do not live in lodgings.' Her speech was almost as laborious as Williams' own, but this was an extremely serious subject, and it was important it be understood.

'Your brother Paul lives in a lodging. He lives in this lodging here. We are lying upon a couch inside the very item.'

'My brother Paul is not a married man, and his lodging is not in Blois.'

He jumped from her belly's shade, straightened his clothing and bit his lip in annoyance. 'So I'm not allowed to live in Blois and you tell me it isn't safe to live where your mother sends me?'

'My mother did not send you, Williams. I'm very sure of that. She had no wish to tell you where I had gone.'

He turned slowly to face her, no longer biting his lip. She had pulled down the hem of her dress and smoothed it about her ankles, then returned to lying down. She was resting. Her stomach was hidden away, and so was that tiny symmetry of hair that brought his imagination such comfort. He wondered when he would be allowed to glimpse either of them again.

'You came here because you chose to, Williams. It was your decision to follow me.'

She had every domestic advantage over him, this woman refusing a home. She was bearing his child. He gazed at her uncertainly, in an anguish to know whether her migration here had really been her mother's idea, or a love challenge directed at him and calculated to test the limits of his affection. Whatever it was, she had defined his dependence on her in no uncertain terms. Or what she thought was his dependence.

Anguish can quickly become contentious. He could not afford to show anger. He bent over her and touched his lips to her forehead. If she thought his kiss was dismissive, so be it. Her own lips weren't offered. They kissed in a different language. 'I'm lodging with Monsieur Gellet-Duvivier,' he said. 'At the Coin Maugas. You know, in the Rue Royale.' He was being offensive, but he had found her after a long and unhopeful journey, and her greeting had been less of a welcome than a struggle for power.

He went from Paul's lodgings, and passed swiftly downstairs, leaving before she could unman him by showing he had hurt her.

Dufour and Paul Vallon stood chatting at the foot of the stairs. Marie-Victorie-Adelaïde was sitting between them on a visitor's chair. She had spread her skirts very wide, a woman at ease in her kingdom. William disliked encountering her in the hallway: it reminded him of the day before Christmas she told him Annette had gone away. Her gaze, as always, was amused and level.

He realized they were grouped here as – well, not quite chaperones, but so they could keep an inquisitive eye on things, or at least an ear cocked.

'You dog,' Paul said. William thought he said dog. He might have been alluding to the chains of matrimony, the yolk of parenthood.

Dufour gestured towards a decanter. It was a cheery house, as William remembered, with decanters everywhere. Unlike Vergez's, they weren't hidden.

William could ill afford enemies. He took one glass with them, before nodding his farewells.

The Rue Poirier was one of the safer streets to live in. Therefore it was one of the more dangerous ones to be out in. Cobbles had been lifted, though the trouble was not here. A great crowd could be heard a street or two to the North, in the direction of the Cathedral. It was being very noisy. There were shouts of anger, shrieks of pain, the unmistakable sounds of staves striking flesh, and of bones splintering with a wrench like teeth being pulled. Annette was right. Orléans was no place for him. The Mob had nothing to do with correctly motivated revolutionary change.

A face rose towards him from where it had been crouched in the shadows. It might have been alone. It might have been one of a hundred. There were shadows enough. It came leaning closer, threatening or beseeching, and William smashed it away with his fist.

When he reached the Coin Maugas, flames glowed in the sky. He went inside to join Monsieur Gellet-Duvivier at a sparse late supper served to them both by the Demoiselle. The soup was thin, there were no other servants, the main course was a crumbled portion of river fish in a porridge of sop. The Demoiselle took wine and smiled. Her father took rather more wine and wept. The Demoiselle reminded William of his fairy-tale about trout giving suck to piglets. William was a married man. Young women were allowed to joke with him now.

He lay down in a sulk. As a married man he found it much safer to go to bed in a rage at his wife than allow himself to be disturbed by a bad conscience about her. Unfortunately he could not fall asleep. He was troubled by much the same woes as afflicted him the last time he lay in this bed. He was confused by love. He wanted her in his arms so she could explain herself. He needed to smother her in kisses, smother her at least.

After an hour or so he'd have been quite happy for someone

to smother him. He'd forgotten how many bells there were in Orléans, and quite overlooked the fact that the Coin Maugas was near to them all. The crowd, which was everywhere, grew strident beneath his window. Several times it seemed to be inside his room. All in all, his sulk made very little progress. Dawn arrived slowly. He renewed his acquaintance with cartwheels.

He woke late, to discover the Demoiselle letting a great dazzle into his head by unshuttering the sun. He gasped in pain. His bedclothes were stripped back – this caused a joyous disturbance in the air. Then – with eyes still screwed up against the light – he felt her gloved fingers laid against his lips. She kissed him.

He had dreamed of this miracle often. Now it was happening to him he found he was in no mood for it. Still, a man and his good manners are inseparable, so he allowed himself to wake cautiously. He couldn't deal brusquely with such a heavenly visitant.

Her hair smelled familiar, her skin like most women's, a rousing moisture of pastry and toilet water. Why should this youthful angel taste any different?

The teardrop was a surprise. So was the next one. It struck his eye exactly, blinding him again. Then the phantom became a fullness, saying, 'Williams,' weeping a little, sobbing, 'Williams, my Williams!' in a voice that could only be Annette's seeking forgiveness. So much for sunshine.

There was to be no miracle, and he was grateful for the fact. There was to be no breakfast, either. He had seen the signs last night. In the absence of regimental boarders, Monsieur Gellet-Duvivier could provide very little for the Demoiselle to manage on. He wondered how Angel would fare.

The lack of breakfast was a pity. A cup of coffee and a rusk can do a lot for marriage in those mid-morning hours when a man and woman can find little else to stir the imagination. So what could they do now?

She lay beside him on the reassembled coolness of his bed. 'You poor, silly boy,' she scolded, once she was done with weeping. 'The streets are dangerous here after dark, especially if you lack a ready tongue. I had arranged for Paul Léonard and Charles Augustin to walk home with you when I had finished talking.'

Silly boy sounded like a phrase borrowed from Madame Vergez. *When I had finished talking* exhibited unwelcome symptoms of the grand manner, a disease young married women catch easily from their mothers. She hadn't come here seeking forgiveness after all. She had come to tell him off – after making sure he still loved her.

He sighed and gathered her close. That is what tears were for, he knew it now. They were to soften her changes of mood. They were to oil the axletrees.

'What I needed to say – and what you did not let me say – is that you must not wait with me a day longer than necessary.'

He kissed her. 'I shan't,' he said. Yes, it was a truly divine sensation on the lips. Marie-Adelaïde's pastry, Annette's own toilet water. 'I shan't,' he promised. A day longer than necessary was love's recipe for eternity.

'You must leave at once.'

This brought him on to his elbow and out of the bed.

'Orléans is not safe for you – nor for us as a couple. You should go to London and seek out our money. Then we can live in Blois.'

'Or in Harwich – in England – if I can arrange it so.'

'When our child is born. Perhaps.'

Her parents had sent her away, and yet she still clung to their wretched imperatives.

She smiled, sadly. 'I shall not be unattended. The Dufours will be a great strength and comfort. Perhaps one of my sisters will come to my lying-in. Vergez has promised to assist. So has my brother Charles Henry if I can send word in time. I'll be better off knowing you are safe in England. Better still if you can bring money to Blois.'

The money was almost impossible to explain to her. What he said was, 'I can't leave you. Not like this. You might die.'

'Die?' she scoffed. 'Nonsense. My family is all doctors.' She remembered her dead brother and her eyes filled with tears again. She was glad to find Williams beside her on the bed once more, but she was a woman making provision for herself. She must be resolute. 'Women from a doctor's house never die in childbirth,' she lectured. 'They suffer for their safety, no doubt.

They have to put up with all the newest tricks for their pains, and bear all manner of implements accordingly. But *die*? Who could be safer than a doctor's woman?'

'A Cumberland shepherd's,' he said briefly. 'A shepherd delivers more ewes at a lambing than most doctors or village midwives manage in a lifetime. And in fearful weather!'

She laughed at him. She was winning the argument, so why not? 'So that is why I must come to England?' Heaven forbid. 'So I may have my babes on top of a mountain?'

'That's it,' he said. 'Conceive them in the forest and bear them on the fells.'

'What's "fells"?'

'I must teach you more English.'

'I must teach you some French. At least our baby was made in the sunshine, although it was still winter.' She started to remind him of the March afternoon that illuminated his bed at Angel's, but he was in a hurry to interrupt her again.

'"Begotten in the sunshine,"' he said, '"delivered in the rain".'

He was full of such saws. She didn't need much English to follow this one. She wondered at the stuff they taught in English universities; but decided not to make a joke on the subject. She knew his mind was like the rest of him, assembled in a wilder place.

'I shall go,' he said, standing away from the bed once more.

'Go to England? Before the baby is born?'

'Yes,' he promised. 'Before the baby is born. Let's hope I'll be back in time.'

The baby was her clock.

The wrench of parting, once its inevitability had been agreed upon, was a torment to be delayed as long as possible.

It could not be deferred for more than a few weeks. Williams needed to leave France, reach London then travel to all manner of remote places in what was clearly a badly designed country. Then he had to return to her with a loan raised on the money legally due to him before it was time for her lying in.

They brooded in silence after this. They spent so much time these last days lying nose to nose in his little bedroom that speech often seemed unnecessary. Love is full of silences, and those silences can be charged with excitement. So is marriage, and those silences can not.

He had learned his silences in Cumberland, not Cambridge. What he seemed to be saying to her was that cats sometimes go a little mad before they have their kittens, and he supposed women were likewise. He made it plain, or his nose against her forehead did, that he acted on the very best advice Annette could give him, but he had absolutely no faith in it. He was not weak. Before God, she knew he was not weak, but he found it convenient to be indecisive. So he did as she wished. To do otherwise would be to quarrel with her, and she knew he saw no future in that.

This would lead to a certain amount of pacing about the room, by Williams, not by herself. She was growing too heavy for striding about. He needed to ask someone's opinion about their predicament, she could see that. Fortunately, she was the only person he could ask.

He would leave her for a little, but only in the middle hours of the morning when violence rarely happens. She forbad him walks. That is she said her baby and common sense forbad them. If he felt like walking, she made him kiss and name and bless the tiny boots that she and others had knitted for the unborn child. Kissing his baby's boots was as close to walking as a father-to-be was allowed.

She had a drawer full of such objects. He made few gurgles of wonderment, but took a polite interest in them, as young men do. These were the talismans that were to keep him from the forests across the river, the rougher streets in the poor parts of the city, and the villages at its edge. He was allowed the arcades on either side of the Rue Royale, and the first few yards of the Rue de Tabour. He rarely availed himself of these freedoms. He would rather walk his fingers through the cake crumbs on his table cloth.

The King was stripped of his crown on September the twenty-first and she was horrified at just how much this cheered Williams up. He thought it wonderful to have lived in France during the Third and Fourth Years of Freedom and now in Year One of the Republic.

A France without kings was inconceivable to Annette. It was like a world without God, or her child without a father. The idea plunged her into a strange melancholy, and she began to live in a perpetual sense of loss.

She searched about to find some item of news which she and her prisoner could agree upon. She discovered for him the disturbing fact that the cut-throats who led the Paris Mob were not content with abolishing the Royal Year and the numbered years of Christ her Lord. Far from it. They were going to have an entirely new calendar, with new names for its months, all of them specially invented by a poet who had begun by rechristening himself. The perfectly good French week which had served the country so well and so long was to be abolished, and its days counted in tens. These changes in the months sickened her almost as much as pregnancy. She was outraged to think the nation's life might be regulated according to words dreamed up by a poet. Poets were the least qualified of all people to invent new words for everyday things – she knew Williams would agree. Had a poet invented January, February, March?

Almost certainly yes, he insisted. But his mind seemed to be on another rechristening. The Louisette was now definitely known as the Guillotine. Dr Guillotine was the acknowledged father if not the actual sire, and his mechanical offspring was at last functioning in Paris. Williams felt purified to think of it. No more butchery with the labourer's adze and hammer. An end to malodorous strangulations on the lantern bracket. The new state was eliminating its old tyrants and doing so quickly and humanely with a blade that rose up and down on its pulley as easily as an English sash window. He wondered how Michel Beaupuy viewed these matters – he hoped with approval.

'I shall need to spend time in Paris,' he told her as September changed to October.

She didn't like this. It was all right for her to speak of Williams leaving. He mustn't mention the matter.

'My papers were taken during my first days in Orléans. I don't know whether I told you that.'

She didn't know.

'I might have retrieved them – I have a way with the French

common man – but you kicked the fellow down the river wall, Annette.

'He deserved it,' she said, flicking at the heavy journals of news that lay across her limbs. They were buried in atrocity nowadays. 'Look at what he's done!'

'Well, not him exactly.'

'No,' she said. 'There must be another one.'

He wondered at her humour, but concluded that pleasantries would be beyond a young woman in her condition on a sticky October forenoon.

He clung to her extravagantly. The journals were full of so many horrors and similar wonders that a thinking man could scarcely find a place in his life for sexual affection. There was such a history of lurid event that nature allowed no time for amorous dalliance to any civilized person who wished simply to keep himself abreast of the printed argument. William was heartily thankful to be married and away from all distractions of the lower parts.

No sooner were the September massacres at an end, and the Prussians unexpectedly defeated at Valmy, and Annette's belly of such an altitude as to make passion extremely difficult anyway, than here was Gorsas writing in vinegarish strophes and a style otherwise plain enough for William's understanding to prove it was necessary for the Princess of Lamballe to be paraded naked and without vital portions of her anatomy, for boys to be hammered to pulp, and aristocratic women beaten on the bare buttocks with brooms whose handles were put to a more fundamental use immediately afterwards. Such actions were less than magnificent, but they were necessary, Gorsas assured him.

William could not partake enough of these and similar intelligences. Nor, in truth, understand them at all. He dreamed of a noble freedom to be bought without blood, even though Annette told him it could never be. There was blood in the fish's mouth. There was blood in a cooked supper. Surprising that men never look.

With blood beating loud in his ears, he went to buy the news. He walked as far as The Three Emperors, hopeful that some Paris journals might have found their way here on the diligence.

They had, and the paper-seller was eager to sell them, and even the impoverished were pressing to buy.

William queued patiently among good-natured people. Surely he could live safely in Orléans? He discussed the price of bread, the taste of the wells, the stench from the river. Then he riffled among the seller's wares, till at last his coins clinked home into a hand bleary with printer's ink and road-dust, and the fellow called, 'Spy!' in a very loud voice.

William laughed his laugh. It was a good laugh; and he was always the Constitution's friend.

'Spy! I haven't seen this man before. He is clearly a most notorious spy.'

'He is. We have been warned about him.'

'Often, citizens.'

The queue became a crowd which gathered more and more closely about, summoning others who materialized from nowhere to discover William was English, adequately dressed, fatter than a skeleton, and clearly not to be liked for any of those reasons.

William had a considerable amount of French now, but not enough to argue with a crowd.

It was thickening very rapidly. He mustn't let it congeal. He spun about to face the Coin Maugas, and for the third time since coming to France he struck out, newspaper in hand.

One of his blows struck flesh. Several more struck air, but with such a breath of passing that stout men stood back from them. An old woman held her ground, perhaps being more acclimatized to a beating than men are, but William had already run round her and through everyone else.

They chased him for a thief, but he had been recently a schoolboy and a student less than a year ago, so took no offence from that. Master Tyson had told him that a man may be chased for anything the world pleases, provided he does not allow the world to catch him.

He reached the Coin Maugas almost in a bound, and Monsieur Gellet-Duvivier did allow the world to catch him.

'Thief!' they called.

'Where – in my house?'

'In your house and workshop.'

'Then I shall hang him. Hanging thieves is a habit of mine. I am well known for it. You may depend upon me.' He passed Wordsworth on the way to fetch his sword. 'They say there's a thief, Wodswod. You must protect your lady, if she's still about you.'

'I have seen no such person, sir.'

'They're imaginative fools. Protect your lady, even so.'

Annette was close to tears, especially when she saw the scuff marks in the dusty nap of his jacket, the deep injuries to his newspaper. 'You must leave as soon as it is safe, Williams. As *soon* as it is safe.'

Her tears were extremely gratifying. He kissed them one by one. 'I'll be safe enough in Paris. I have letters.' Seeing how startled she became, he said, 'Not that one. I've lost it.' It had been rained on too many times to be handed to any woman. It had been sweated on, possibly bled through. Besides, he wouldn't know where to find Helen Maria Williams now, nor what to say to her. The poetess's commentaries in support of recent events in France were so clear, his own impressions confused by comparison.

He kissed Annette's cheeks long after there were no more tears to kiss. This would be the last, almost the last time. 'I have business to complete with your brother Paul and with Maître André Augustin. Then I shall be back here for our farewells.'

'I'll come with you,' she said. Her mother had not brought her up to agree to untidy arrangements. 'You shall take me back to my brother's lodgings, and I'll wait there while you finish your business with Maître Dufour.'

Quitting Williams' room pained Annette. This was the bed where they'd first loved, and this the little table where he had read her his interminable poem that was beyond her English, and remained just as incomprehensible when he'd tried to translate it for her. Here she had failed to teach him French. As she left with him she knew this was the proper way. She needed to say her farewells in the lodging where she must suffer his absence, and by the bed on which their child would be born. Her mother had not taught her to be orderly in matters quite as vulgar as these.

Madame Vergez's sense of what was fitting rested on a much broader base. If a woman's life was tidy then its pains could be suitably accommodated, its random ecstasies ignored. Annette knew very clearly where she must say goodbye, and it wasn't here. They went outside.

The Autumn sun was due South of the river. It stood at the end of the bridge and illuminated the lower arcades of the Rue Royale in a clear noon light. If any still gazed about for Williams, then they were probably dazzled by it. The paper-seller looking down from The Three Emperors would have it directly in his eyes. Annette hurried her man towards the corner of the Rue Poirier just the same. Their progress along that road was slower. She quickly became breathless.

'Our son bears down on me,' she laughed.

'Your son's a daughter,' he said briefly. 'A boy never sits so high.'

She did not argue the point.

Paul was home at the Dufours', perhaps for lunch, more likely to make ready for an afternoon's gambling. Annette explained that Williams had some business for him and André Augustin. Paul gazed at her quizzically, then went downstairs to find Dufour.

Annette arranged herself on her bed, and watched Williams follow her brother downstairs.

The two men stood in the little hallway with Marie-Adelaïde. The three were again taking wine, and made a very similar tableau to the one William had descended towards after his last, and much more irritable, parting from Annette.

He refused the offered cup, bowed towards Marie-Adelaïde, and was again greeted by one of her smiles of appraisal, as if it was her continuing task to submit him to affectionate scrutiny on her friend's behalf. 'Messieurs,' he said briefly to the two lawyers, 'I need your help.'

'Ah!' sighed Madame. His words explained everything, she seemed to imply. Her sigh acknowledged it all.

André Augustin Dufour touched Paul's elbow, and motioned William upstairs towards the salon where William had once worked at his poem. The writing table was again littered with quills.

'Maître André Augustin, Maître Paul, you both know I have gone through a form of marriage with your sister, sir, Marie Anne. She is now, as is evident, expecting our child, and would wish you to know that nothing immodest occurred between us until we had exchanged those vows.'

'Of course, monsieur.'

Paul's silence was always to be hoped for. On this occasion he did not even laugh.

'Maîtres, you know that on several counts, not only the constitutional one, my marriage to Annette has no temporal force. It is unrecorded in any register, except in Heaven.'

'Amen, sir. I do say amen to that.'

'Amen,' Paul agreed.

'Your marriage was doubtless legal in form,' Dufour pursued, 'but less than legal in context. In fact, its context has been proscribed in law for upwards of two years. It was dealt a further blow several weeks past, in that it was rendered irrecoverable by the banishment beyond the nation's boundaries of the priest who performed it.'

'I did not know this,' William said.

'Sir, he is either banished or he has jured. If he has jured, we may find a form of words that allow him to say he has married you. But first we would need to find and then persuade the actual priest. I fancy that will not meet the present case, or not immediately.'

'No, sir. I go this night towards England to claim my marriage portion. I shall return as soon as may be. Coming back will be easy enough. It is leaving France that will present the problem. I am currently without travel documents. What I now propose should ease matters if I am delayed.'

Paul's eyebrows had climbed since their arrival in the salon – the truth was always an amusement for him. They subsided as soon as William spoke again.

'Now, sirs. I intend in the interim to make provision for the child and its mother.' He glanced at them both in turn. 'Firstly I wish one of you to draw me up a paper, which its mother's family will hold and I will sign, acknowledging the child's paternity and giving it my name.'

'In times of change, sir, there can be no more durable docu-ment,' Dufour smiled. 'Already the Republic speaks of dissolving all of our marriages retrospectively – or insofar as we may wish – and making all future bonds transitory and informal.'

Paul chuckled with delight. 'Matrimony could almost become attractive to me on such terms. I've long lived in envy of the Arab and the Turk – not to mention our red-headed cockerel.'

William was in no mood for small-talk. 'Should I not return in time for my wife's lying-in, then I humbly beseech you, Maître André Augustin, to represent me at the child's christen-ing and see that it bears my name. Monsieur Paul I cannot ask, as his sister will need her to second him.'

The two notaries bowed to him, and then towards one another.

William already knew from Annette that they made a ritual of behaving formally, though he suspected it was more of a charade as far as Paul was concerned. 'I will not, from family and friend-ship, offend either of you by offering anything in the way of legal fees. I know I may look to you, Monsieur Paul Léonard, to defray the cost of any emergency?'

'Naturally, my brother.'

'But I should like to leave this four hundred and fifty livres with you, Maître, to give to Madame to meet any of her expenses regarding my dear one's confinement.'

They shook hands. They exchanged money. They chuckled gravely. They made the necessary sounds. André Augustin bent over his writing table and scratched at a paper with an unduly noisy quill. He wrote slowly and beautifully. He had once been a copy clerk. It was soon completed, this page that gave William's name to the child Annette believed would be a son and William knew would be a daughter.

William signed it and then they took wine together, the lawyers copiously and by mouth, the poet by sniffing at it.

Then his time here was done.

So he left Annette. But he could not depart from the Rue Poirier without passing by Marie-Victorie-Adelaïde syllable by syllable at the front door. She allowed him to kiss her cheek, she inclined her head towards him and demanded it. Then she brought her maids and her children to say farewell too. The young man from England was behaving properly at last. He was leaving Annette his name on a document, and a rather more than trifling sum of money to look after her. She would have kissed him back, but he moved fast in these matters.

A small crowd was gathered in the Rue Royale. As nearly always, it had collected outside the hosier's and hatter's establishment at the Coin Maugas. William recognized Besserve and the disgusting Goulu, or a very similar head in a very similar headpiece. There were perhaps three score of them, the men growling, the women being noisy. It didn't seem at all appropriate for a person of Besserve's eminence to growl, but he was a Frenchman. He growled.

Monsieur Gellet-Duvivier scolded the crowd. He looked happy again, so he chided them without agitation. He was flanked by cavalry officers. They were drunk and propped themselves together like muskets, but they were the Madman's protection. William wondered what Beaupuy would say if he were here to see drunken aristos giggling at underfed people in the street. He would growl no doubt.

William went around them and beyond them and quickly upstairs to pack. Heavy boots followed him up. The salon became full behind him. He realized his host had lodgers again, lodgers and proxy-lodgers. It accounted for the man's bravado, the benign glow on his countenance. He had his circle of gambling imbibers. Just as last year, he had his cavalrymen. He could be himself again.

'Wodswod, Milor Wodswod!' The Madman was looking for him, hunting through room after room with his idiotic shout. The Madman found him, and clasped his hand in farewell. 'We are still alive, Wodswod. We continue to thrive. You must return one day soon. These nobility have just brought me a brace of hinds, and the Loire bursts with fruit again. It's well known that corpses improve the fish in any river.'

'Surely men pull them out?'

'Fish? No – we in the Guard won't let the town louts eat them. We must keep a semblance of order.'

William had been referring to the corpses. He tried again. 'I thought you were letting them all into the National Guard now. I thought the Constituent—'

'No, Wodswod. We'll never let fish into the Guard, nor corpses either.' He hit his thighs or some part of himself above the knees and shrieked with laughter. 'Do you remember last year, monsieur?'

'Very clearly.'

The Demoiselle was here now, and in no mood to remind him of anything. Her farewells hung about her like a cloud. She was no thicker in the blouse than last year. Only her voice had grown.

William let go of the Madman's hand and stooped towards her. Her eyes were bright enough, and the tears that fell from them were plump.

BOOK THREE:

THE TERROR AND AFTER

ORLEANS 1792.
A JUMBLE OF DAYS IN DECEMBER

Williams was still in France when he should be in England. But what was England and where was France, now her lap was out of sight, and perhaps did not exist? From above, her day gown looked wider than a writing desk.

She sat with his letter resting on top of herself, and felt much too tired to ponder what its news might mean. It said he was delayed at the Ministry in Paris. He must remain there or nearby waiting for the papers that would allow him to return to France. And then go to Rouen for papers of another kind. Too late to worry now. He would find a way. Her mind was on larger issues.

Paul made a joke about her waist. He called it the Equator. Marie-Victorie-Adelaïde spoke a kindness in her turn. Annette was too full of herself to reply. Her belly, Paul said, was more than a nation: it was a continent. She could have told him it was her globe, and had become her world. She lived as it lived. When it was calm, she wallowed in a Sargasso dullness that floated her away from any sense of anxiety. When it was wild, and hers was a restless child, then she endured its storms.

For the moment it was still. She had called it by an appropriate name, Jean-Jacques Williams Léonar, and it had grown entirely still in consequence.

Orléans was a-buzz with names at the moment. Plans were already afoot to call this sunny fourteenth day of December after an appropriate fruit and inscribe it in the final décadi of Frimaire.

Annette was less troubled by these public manifestations of ungodliness than she used to be. She was confident the Almighty would avenge them, and excuse her from troubling herself now the child was due. Little Jean-Jacques Williams Léonar was today nigh on his vintage date. He was expected.

Vergez had sent her a chart to confirm her own calculations, and Marie-Adelaïde said only just now, 'Your front has altered its shape, my Annette. I have an eye for all matters feminine, and you can believe me when I tell you your front has altered its shape.'

'What does this mean?'

'It means your front has altered its shape,' Paul said, bowing to both of them in turn and making his way from the upstairs salon and downstairs towards the front door, through which he departed.

'In what ways am I changed?'

'Yesterday you were a cushion, a lovely plump cushion. Today you are like a shelf in the kitchen.'

'I return to my question. What does this mean?'

'I think it means your child has pushed its head down and is ready to come out. Standing on its head fatigues it, so it has shot both of its legs right in front of it as square as any shelf and hooked its big toes in the back end of your navel!'

Annette blushed. Her face, which was warm, felt warmer. Marie-Adelaïde was her friend. She was also a woman. Surely it was improper to discuss intimate latitudes of the feminine cosmography – the reverse side of her own navel was a daunting example of such a meridian – with another woman? True she was a surgeon's child, but her friend was not. She was not Paul. Annette could never be mealy-mouthed, but she was growing coy of late. An enlarging abdomen had caused a considerable shrinkage of her mind.

On the other hand, the item had been named. It would seem extremely provincial to sit blushing about it, and this was exactly what she was doing. 'Ducks don't have navels,' she said for no reason at all, save she had Vergez's chart in mind. 'Their carcass has been designed with no need of such an organ. Just like a barge's hull.' Her mouth made all manner of remarks since she was pregnant.

She was saved from embarrassment by Paul reappearing. His return was quite unexpected. He did not knock at the outer door, as was his wont so the maids could run after him. He opened the house with his own key and came cringing in.

His face was cut. A portion of his left cheek was flayed open. A triangular flap of skin hung wide from its bone. The wound gaped stiffly with blood; the weather was too cold for it to bleed properly.

'A stone,' he explained numbly. 'Not a cobble, not a tile' – he spoke as if he had been rejected from a higher examination and must make do with an inferior result – 'just a stone.'

Marie-Adelaïde refused to let Annette come anywhere near his cheek in case it caused a spasm of sympathy. She gazed into the wound in detail, then sent for a maid.

'The thing missed me,' Paul went on. 'It was only a small stone, as I say, but in missing me it struck the wall of the house I was walking by and sprayed me with fragments of brick – or perhaps tiny portions of itself.' He was being very exact. He laughed. His teeth were chattering with shock, and he had to keep his courage up while first the maid, and then the lady of the house, searched out his apex of skin with a needle and darned it back into place, rather as if they were repairing a stocking.

'You'll need to grow your hair down a little,' Marie-Adelaïde told him.

'Or wear a fatter wig,' giggled the maid.

'Williams has still not left Paris, you say?' Paul spoke to unclench his teeth. The needlework was becoming painful. The wound grew warmer from the fire, and trickled.

'He says he cannot get permission to travel,' his seamstress breathed in his ear.

'Is this likely?' He spoke the question to Annette direct.

'How should I know – if he says so, yes.'

'I think he loves Paris, or someone in Paris, more than he cares for you.'

'I think it is this Revolution he loves.' There was no need for Annette to answer. Her friend could do it for her and in his ear, or to the hole in his face. 'Paris is where he thinks the new France is, and he cannot bear to tear himself away from it.'

She knew the fourteenth of December would be the day. Her body's clock and Vergez and the flight of waterbirds were all agreed on the matter. She felt a stirring she could not rein in, and watched a ripple run down herself much like the one she had seen take possession of Angel a few months earlier. It shouldn't have been, she was sure it shouldn't be, but it was instantly followed by another like clouds racing across the glass or geese skimming low over water.

'It's,' she said. 'I'm—'

'It is, and yes, you quite certainly are,' Marie-Adelaïde agreed. 'Well, I've secured your brother's teeth with a stocking stitch. It only remains for someone to put some kettles on.' She smiled encouragingly at her maid.

Her maid was a someone. She obliged by putting kettles on.

A lesser person than her brother would have sought his own room at this juncture. He had been painfully injured and even more painfully repaired, and now his small sister was about to give birth – not at once and not exactly here, but the day threatened to become a long and noisy night.

Paul took a larger view of the matter, and of his place in it. He said, 'I am a marked man now.'

'Nonsense. Your hair will grow over it, as I said, and anyway the blemish is no larger than a single smallpock.'

'You misunderstand me. That stone wasn't a random one, and it might just as easily have been a musket ball or a sabre.'

Annette hoped that another body pang would protect her from this nonsense, but she knew that the birth waves do not flow this frequently, or not early on during a first delivery. She had to say, because she was exact and a Vallon, 'I've never heard of a person actually *throwing* a sabre at anyone – not even Monsieur Gellet-Duvivier.'

'Come, little sister! You continue to misconstrue me entirely. Now that I am once again regarded as a suitable target, I may be struck down *by design*, whatever the weapon. I am seen as an enemy of the people.'

'Who says so?'

'The people who see themselves as the people. Now we no

longer have your Englishman about us, they know we are free to operate.'

'"We"! "We" is a big word,' she scoffed. Who are this "we"?'

'Not you, for certain. The people who used to trust our family before they feared Wodswod might be a spy.'

Her instinct was to rush towards him and pummel him about the chest and heart. Instead, the vileness of his accusation drove her backwards. Her fists clenched fiercely enough, but a huge convulsion wracked her. It did not flow over but through her, and unlike the earlier ones seemed to start at her very centre with a sharp pain inside. She gasped, then cried out aloud.

As she stopped, she heard Paul say, 'Saint Mary's only Son, and He alone, knows why the Englishman remains in Paris so long. And who he talks to – and what he reports!'

'Williams would never—'

'Who knows what secrets a man gives away when he cannot speak our tongue? The search for a word becomes more important than even the most dangerous truth. He has no room for wit or deception.'

These were strange words, and they stayed with her as she allowed herself to be bundled up the narrow flight of stairs that led to her bedroom. She was quite capable of walking by herself, but Marie-Victorie-Adelaïde pushed hands against her bottom and heaved her heavenwards. So did any number of maids in person or by proxy, a whole procession of busybodies with hard shoes clattering towards the attic and taking such a care she didn't tumble backwards that several times they nearly tipped or tripped her on to her face and the curiously adaptable imminence of her child.

Herself regarded as a traitor to her family and friends because she was in love with Williams and Williams might possibly be a spy? Williams couldn't possibly be a spy. Whoever heard of a spy who wasted his time with verses, and in English?

These thoughts distracted her from the loosing and lifting overhead of her day gown, and the dragging clear of her calves and ankles of everything she wore beneath it.

She had nothing within her baggage to match her friend's idea of the proprieties of the occasion, no short petticoat, specially abbreviated nightwear or suitable chemise. Fortunately Marie-Adelaïde had travelled this way several times herself, and pronounced a man's shirt — full in the chest and sleeve as it should be — an entirely suitable substitute.

Williams had left no shirt of his behind him. Even if he owned such an object in the plural, it, they would be holed and stained with old age and his intolerable striding through bogs and branches.

Another ripple distracted her — a giant affair this, much like an earthquake in a book, or one of those fabled accounts from the times of the ogres when — according to Vergez — all the mountains in the South of France blew their tops off and every time a good wife turned round a fresh hill had poked its head up. It was reassuring to know that these throbs and squeezes were no longer her own but universal cataclysms sent from God to trouble all men equally.

By now she was wearing a man's shirt, slid over her shoulders by a giggling maid — whether it came from the wardrobe of her brother Paul, or André Augustin, or had been hanging in some arcane birthing closet of Marie-Adelaïde's own, she had no way of knowing. The spasm had subsided, or begun again and subsided, and the room was now considerably less crowded.

Just then an archangel began to sing from the corner of Paradise. Or, if distracted was becoming distraught and her poor wits were slipping, then one of the luminous order of cherubim was tuning his voice-pipe somewhere closer in the ether.

Her body rearranged itself like a storm ripple wandering shoreward, and she was reminded of the naked woman dancing in a murderer's noose and continuing to undulate through her sleep from the banks of the Loire. The music persisted, as it will throughout a dream, only by now she realized it was nothing more heavenly nor infernal than her host practising his scales.

This brought her to herself with a jolt. Her body was all jolts. André Augustin used to sing before shaving. His Muse was less to do with angels' wings than the glittering passage of blades across the skin.

Here was steam, not clouds of glory but *steam* as from washing, rising about her lower limbs even now, and she was immediately thigh-deep in wetness and stickiness and suchlike unpleasantness.

Worst of all she saw the blade of a razor. It was a razor from a box of razors, and the maid who had recently stitched Paul's face now stooped towards her waist – stooped? no swooped – with this unlikely scythe.

'No,' she said.

'Sweetest Annette, it is entirely normal, as a preparation.'

'No!'

'Believe me, there are all kinds of circumstances – I do not wish to upset you by mentioning them – but *all kinds* of circumstances in which—'

'No. I will not be shaved.'

'You will be better without such an encumbrance.'

'I am content to keep what I have.' It had been with her for some dozen years now. It was not as unusual as she once thought it was, and she refused to be parted from it.

The maid left in a huff, or Marie-Adelaïde led her out in an even bigger huff in consequence of having her best advice ignored in the very nick of the *accouchement*. Or perhaps people became frightened at the earthquake which once again began in a far corner of the room, agitated the nails on the crucifix and entered Annette's body by the bed head.

She didn't care whether she was surrounded or completely alone. This was the room she scrubbed a whole year ago in hopes of receiving Williams here, and receive him she had and did. She felt her body tremble and watched the pale wooden Christ shudder on His dark wooden cross. She still did not know how many months or centuries He had been hanging here, any more than she could tell how many minutes or hours must pass before she cradled Williams' child in her arms.

She seemed to sleep – surely not that? When she opened her eyes after a long uncontrollable blink it was dark, and Marie-Adelaïde was bathing her forehead with a cloth she handed to a maid to wring out and refresh.

If she had offended her friend, she was forgiven. The spasms seemed to have been progressing during her doze, and – as she remembered from downstairs – there was a sharp pain at their centre, a tearing where no pain had ever been before. It threatened to go on and on.

Awake she gasped, 'It's going wrong. I know my baby is going wrong.'

'You should have let me send for my woman, my dear.'

'A woman is no good in matters of learning and science. Fetch my stepfather Vergez. Better – run and send for my brother!' For her dead brother most of all.

'Sweetest Annette, they are both in Blois. You could give birth to a whole family before they reach here.'

She lay in distress, rage and more and more frequent pain, for so long it seemed Vergez and Charles Henry could have hopped here or even danced. She could have cried. Several times she whispered for Williams – he had time to reach her from Paris, the agony was everlasting – but ordinary mortal men and mere poets who are not also surgeon–physicians are no good at times like this. They wait drinking together in the next room, and the next room was as far off as Paris, and Williams could not drink.

She nearly cried. Crying was beneath her. She sobbed but remained dry-eyed. Then the pangs once more reasserted themselves and took charge of her brain. Again she gazed on her crucifix. She knew she wasn't the first woman in the world to do this, nor would she be the last, any more than she was the world's first or last woman. She wished there could be some proper comfort in her martyrdom, some potions, some exercise, some blessing. Then she thought of La Pucelle, Orléans' true martyr, and felt her being burned by the English at Rouen where perhaps Williams was now, having been to England and back again, her body had strained so endlessly.

'Why don't you scream a little, Annette? Let your lungs out with a really good yell. Even the bravest do.'

She had to be worthy of trust again. She must not scream.

'Myself I make such an awful noise, André Augustin says he cannot bear for me to give birth.'

People did not trust her. She did not scream.

'He goes for a long walk, I frighten him so much. They never think of going for a long walk when they are getting us with child.'

She let a breath out, lots of it, all of it, in case Marie-Adelaïde thought she was blushing at such talk.

'No need to suffer further, my darling. His head is here already. Or the top of it is. He's as dark-crowned and hairy as your brother Paul. Or yourself, of course . . .'

The room became crowded with neighbours, maids, children, possibly a dog, anyone feminine, all of them offering conflicting advice and swallowing air. It might take a minute, it could take an hour. Best to pretend it would only be a minute.

And it was only a minute, though that minute was a long time after midnight.

The baby was a daughter, they told her. She could find very little wrong with having a daughter, even though she had been certain it would be a son.

Williams had said she was carrying a daughter. Now she could hold her at last and see how like Williams their daughter was, she felt closer to her Englishman than she had ever been.

The baby was swaddled and put to her breast. It soon slept, as if born into a great calm. Looking at her, Annette knew Williams would be back, and soon. He had roots in France now.

More important still, she could return to Blois. She was a mother, not a pregnant woman. Her family had a stake in her marriage.

BLOIS.
JANUARY SEVENTEEN HUNDRED
AND NINETY-THREE.
THE HOMECOMING.

Her mother had not chosen her usual chair. She sat in the high-backed settle that Vergez never presumed to occupy, but reserved for Montlivault or Old Pardessus. Sometimes she sat in it only briefly and from need. A few months earlier she had gone to it, for example, in order to be seen digesting the news that Annette had allowed herself to become debauched by the Englishman. Today, the prodigal had returned, and it seemed likely Madame Vergez would sit in it often, perhaps continuously, for the sake of dignity and calm.

She took no notice of her daughter, nor of her daughter's daughter. As well as a babe-in-arms, Annette had brought two pieces of paper to show her. One was a letter from Williams in London, glowing with ardour and promises, the other a document from the Cathedral in Orléans.

She waved Williams' morsel aside. Young men always write letters like that, but only for as long as they can be persuaded to write anything at all. Madame Vergez had only one ambition for Sieur Wodswod. She needed him back in Blois with a banker's draft and a new suit, or she wanted her daughter widowed and the nonsense forgotten.

The Cathedral document was far more interesting. It was less than a dozen lines of manuscript including signatures, but it seemed likely to last her quite as long as a three-volume romance. She read it through slowly, then more slowly again. Then she demolished it word by word.

First she began with the parchment it was written on. 'I have never, in all my life, seen a paper looking like this,' she said.

'Wasn't I baptized, mother? And the rest of us?'

'Not on parchment like this you weren't.'

'It's cathedral parchment. Perrin is the episcopal vicar.'

'He's a jurist, then.'

'I was *married* by a non-jurist. That was wrong, too.'

'You should have let me arrange it. I would have told you it was all quite impossible.'

'Then it wouldn't have been arranged, would it?'

'The time was neither ripe nor right.'

The babe cried, once or twice noisily, but her mother remained so calm and her grandmother became so terrifying that she lapsed into whimpering silence and then slept again, as sacrificial infants are supposed to behave when they are carried towards the wild beast's lair or spread on the fatal riverbank.

Annette sniggered nervously, in spite of herself. Her daughter opened an eye, found the sound agreeable, and slept again. Annette regained her calm. A woman with a child is a woman with authority.

'He has given my child his name, mother. Williams has—'

'Are you sure? His name appears twice. Each time it is spelled differently, on both occasions wrong. "*Williams Wordswodsth*," it says, followed in the selfsame sentence by "*Williams Wordsodth*," followed by "absent", the only word of truth in the entire document.'

'Mother—'

'Your name is not down here as Wodswod, or Wordwodsth, or Wordsodth, or any kindred thing – though praise God for that, I say. You are here as plain unmarried Vallon, like any silly girl of the parish.'

'I had to be Vallon. It is, also, the new law of the land. André Augustin and your own son Paul witnessed the deed, and they are both lawyers. They have to uphold the law. Maître Dufour – André Augustin – is *greffier du tribunal* at Orléans. He represented Williams—'

'Not only do you pick an Englishman – descended from the Scots as you are, and should hate the English – you pick an Englishman whose name you cannot spell.'

'I can spell it perfectly well.'

'No one else can!'

A small silence followed. Any silence that has a baby in it is fragile enough, but Madame Vergez was beyond babies. 'This little mite was not only falsely baptized, she was presented to God by a brute who actually records the date on her birth certificate as the Second Year of the Republic. What Republic? We still have King Louis.'

Her mother's sentiments were very much her own, but Annette was enough of a realist to know that although the nation retained its monarch, the monarch was unlikely to retain his head much longer.

Madame Vergez refused to waste time with politics. France was full of ills. So was her family. And from where she sat in Montlivault's chair, France was merely the image. Here in the Rue du Pont was the only reality. She flicked the certificate of baptism with her fingernails, as if marking out topics for future disapproval. Then she placed the paper to one side.

Annette breathed a sigh of relief. The hard part was over.

'Another female in the household. They cost money from their first breath and they can't be brought up to anything.'

'Look at her, mother.'

'I have done so already, and doubtless she will be here from time to time in the future. She must be put out to nurse.'

Annette wasn't prepared for this, but her look made clear what her answer would be.

'Yes, Annette. It's a disgusting thing that nature asks of women. I won't have it done in my house, not by you nor by anyone else. Take her to a working woman. Such people don't mind hanging themselves out in the front.'

Annette succeeded, briefly, in forcing Caroline Anne into her mother's arms, praying as she did so that the child wouldn't puke, or do anything odorous and in general unworthy of a descendant of Madame Vergez.

'Take her now, Annette. Take her and find a suitable nurse. I've had enough of grandchildren.'

'She is only the third.'

'You are forgetting your brother, Charles Henry.'

'Charles Henry has yet to marry.'

'He's much too prudent for that sort of thing. But he'll forget himself one day and his wife will bear him issue. I have already imagined them.'

Babies do not smile often, especially at ladies with underchins. Anne Caroline smiled up at Madame Vergez nonetheless.

Annette's mother was briefly impressed by the child's intelligence, but she handed her back to Annette just the same. Caroline Anne was promptly sick.

'English manners,' grandmother scolded. 'You'll have to cure her of behaviour like that if you're to bring her here again.'

It had taken some time for the awfulness of her mother's sentence to sink in. Her baby was not only being put out to nurse. Little Caroline was banned from the family house until a father could be produced for her.

There was nothing Annette could do except wait for Williams' return. She began to see that her stratagems before the birth – those against Williams and her family alike – had been too hastily, not to say madly, concocted. Were Williams here now, for example, even without money, she would not be separated from her daughter like this.

Her sisters were allowed into the upper salon at last. They had tried to enter several times before, but Madame Vergez's glare had forbidden them.

Now they came about Annette, cooed at the baby, flapped their lips at her, crooned, exclaimed, and made other embarrassing noises without embarrassment, and in general stoked up their mother's irritation.

Françoise Anne took the child, dandled her up and down, then made as if to show her to the maids below stairs.

Annette stopped her. She felt too upset to trust anyone, even the sister who had stood with her against their mother in the past. She could not bear to let Caroline out of her sight. She had once let her Williams be shut outside the room on an occasion like this; when she had tried to go to him, it was to find he had already been banished to Angel's.

'Where's Vergez?' she asked her, so seizing the baby back should not seem too abrupt.

'Across the river at an *accouchement*.'

'Across the river?'

'He's helping ducks give birth to duckmeat.' Seeing how little her mother liked this kind of jest, Françoise Anne rounded on her and said, 'You're not going to deny a home to a poor little baby – banish your own daughter's child?'

'I'm banishing the smell of milk. The sooner your sister stops nursing the sooner she'll dry up.'

'It's winter, mother. Babies are never any trouble in winter.'

Annette was grateful to her sisters for being so staunch, but her mother was not the one to retreat easily.

'It will soon be summer, and the Montlivaults will be visiting and the whole group meeting here now the Englishman no longer comes. Montlivault, Pardessus – people like that – they would not let us include an Englishman, still less an English republican. Such a man is too ready to become a spy.'

It was the same feeble slander her brother Paul had uttered. Annette held Caroline close and began to say her child's father would never betray her family, or her family's friends, in any circumstances.

Madame Vergez held up the palm of her hand, against interruption. 'It is not a suspicion that worries me,' she said grandly. 'Wodswod may be a spy, he may not.'

'What has all of this to do with Annette's milk?' Françoise said stubbornly.

'Or anyone's milk?' Angélique Adelaïde said, not following a word of the argument, but hoping to be sisterly.

'Breastmilk is a reminder of the Englishman,' Madame said. 'So is this child.'

Françoise laughed aloud. Angélique Adelaïde began, or thought she began, to entertain suspicions that their mother was becoming mad.

Annette knew better. She had argued with the lady too often and knew that whereas most people's thoughts at least try to move in straight lines as if taught in Williams' Cambridge, her mother's moved by sharper routes.

'The fact is, my children, as we have said often, your brother Jean-Jacques was probably killed because of the Englishman.'

'By one side or the other,' Annette said quickly. 'By our own people quite as likely as the Constitutionalists.'

Her mother held up her hand for silence.

'It was you who sent Williams out of this house to lodge with my brother,' Annette said.

'Angel kept lodging for officers,' Angélique put in. 'That wasn't popular everywhere.'

'Killed is killed, Annette.' Madame Vergez rarely allowed herself to perform in tears, nor did she judge the occasion demanded them now. 'All I know is my son is dead. Your brother is dead.'

Annette knew when to give her mother the day. Françoise, bless her, did not. 'I've been taught the scriptures, too, mother. I know this Englishman quite probably stormed the Bastille. But he didn't nail up Jesus all by himself, did he?'

It was a non-sequitur worthy of Madame Vergez, and it silenced the lady completely.

Unfortunately Françoise decided to go one better. 'Nor did he give our Mother Eve the apple.'

A saintly smile flittered across their mother's face, and she stood away from Montlivault's chair, a movement so intense that the baby whimpered. 'He certainly knows how to give a woman something,' she said quietly. She left them talking together while she went to make arrangements.

Annette wrote to her Williams immediately, telling him she was back home, and pouring out her heart. She already knew from his letter he was hopeful about money and had decided to ask his young sister to intercede for him. She was best placed to win his uncles round.

Annette didn't care about his uncles. Money was the key to the problem, surely? She didn't want to be that impossible thing a priest's wife, any more than she knew he wanted to be a priest.

Caroline started to cry. It is hard to comfort a crying child when the mere fact of her crying makes you nervous.

The child was right to be restless. Annette's mother arrived to her room, her face glossy. She was clearly about to announce something beyond contradiction.

Annette dried her pen, one little act she had in common with Williams.

'The Lacailles have a serving woman someone has made pregnant. Her baby is the same age as my granddaughter' – a fine diplomatic moment, that! – 'and she'll be happy to earn a coin or two for giving the child suck, and I dare say quite a few more for tending and rearing her otherwise.'

These words of her mother's were so terrible that Annette could find nothing to say to them. They certainly pleased the older woman a great deal.

It was only when she heard the girl lived in St Saturnin, that Annette burst out, 'South of the river! You can't send my baby south of the river. Why can't Angel have her, or one of her girls? You're used to arranging matters with Angel.'

'Angel is to return to her parents. Anyway, she's run out of suck, small wonder.' Her mother was already moving her and baby Caroline downstairs. 'Besides, the implication will be that the child is Jean-Jacques' child, and I'll not have my poor dead son insulted in this way.'

'Just for a few days, then, mother. Just for one week.'

'Days mount into weeks, and weeks mount up too, I'll grant you, Annette. You're a mother now. You know how to count the minutes in their passing.'

A girl of sixteen or seventeen was waiting by the kitchen door. She wore a short coat and a shawl, and the gown inside them was open. A baby was bundled against her.

'She's too young.'

The girl sulked.

'Look at her,' Madame Vergez triumphed. 'She's full of milk. She smells like a cattle-biscuit, and has several very good teeth.'

The girl continued sullen.

'She has a mother of some discretion and industry, who will oversee what is what. Vergez will pay, and one of them will bring my grandchild past the window daily – but not inside.'

'For one week, mother.'

'They'll want longer than a week, Annette. Vergez will pay more than adequately, believe me.'

BLOIS, 1793.
HER MOTHER'S JANUARY BECOMES FRANCE'S FEBRUARY. MEANWHILE TIME HAS ITS HEAD CHOPPED OFF.

Williams must come back. He must come back immediately. She wrote his name on letters. She sent him himself. She sent him his promises, which were himself. She sent him her love for him, which as far as she could determine was himself by another description. She embroidered him. She stitched him into the clothes she made for Caroline. She stitched his name often. His face was there always. Principally she kept herself busy. Without her baby to nurse she would otherwise go mad.

She carried messages for Montlivault. She was free of motherhood now. She found out what he and Old Pardessus were doing. Nothing. She found out what Pardessus the younger was about. Nothing. This was what their so secret secret was about. Nothing. Lacaille was up to something, Lacaille by whichever face, but mostly it was chipping gun flints and spitting in gutters.

The group met almost every day, sometimes at Pardessus', sometimes at the Lacailles' workshop, often at Berruet's coffee house The Three Merchants, but most usually in her mother's salon where the chairs were more appropriate. Montlivault was its leader, Old Pardessus its president. Each meeting closed with a stirring resolution to be watchful. They must wait and be watchful. So Annette carried stirring messages full of waiting and watchfulness. Only about town, of course. Only where a loaf could be carried, or a duck well concealed in its basket. A young woman mustn't step further, lest she meet with an Englishman and bear his child.

The authorities knew they were up to something. The prefecture knew, and the sub-prefect, and his secret police. Sometimes they stopped her, but the group had progressed far beyond writing letters. Its messages were so complex they could only be explained by word of mouth. The group was waiting. It was waiting for events in Paris, but most of all it waited for the certain uprising in the West. Lacaille had already been there, several Lacailles and their apprentices with a wagon-load of muskets, or a boatful of muskets, with muskets anyway, but at least they had been there. The Lacailles all in all were a different matter. They went places. They fired at the people they did not like. They boasted, but they bled.

Annette wasn't entirely pleased with them, even so. It is difficult to like a family when one of its women works in your kitchen. There was also the fact that they were no more than craftsmen, rich though their skills made them. They were not professional men, unlike the Pardessus and her father and stepfather. There's a whole world of difference between turning a lump of iron into a gunbarrel and transmuting a limb into a stump. Damascening cannot disguise the matter.

Then there was the grossness of the gunsmiths' appetites, as if blowing on hot metal all day gave rise to nothing but carnal thoughts and libidinous behaviour. She hated to think that Old Lacaille – some said the *Oldest* Lacaille – might be the father of the young woman's baby across the river. That would make the wretch father to the milk that ran in Caroline's mouth and replaced her own.

Then, on the twenty-first day of January, scarcely a fortnight into Annette's misery, the King lost his head before a large crowd and on the common guillotine.

The meeting was in her mother's salon. The Three Merchants was considered too public a place, and the Lacailles and the Pardessus insisted that matters were far too advanced for their own establishments to be considered safe. And as for Montlivault's, they never met there. 'When a man has several dwellings,' Montlivault said, 'to meet at any one of them could be construed by the authorities as suspicious.'

Old Pardessus called the meeting to order, and they sat for a few moments with their heads lowered in memory of poor King Louis the Sixteenth, twice and most recently circumcised, as a Lacaille reminded them, and now shorter by his head.

'It would have been kinder to the poor man for God to have let him suffer those cuts in a different order,' young Pardessus said.

They looked towards Vergez, amputation being a surgical matter, but neither he nor Charles Henry were here.

'Let's hope that bitch of a Queen soon joins him,' Madame Vergez said. 'She's a foreigner, a sorceress and a woman lover, and responsible for all of our troubles.'

They agreed that this was so, but thought a weighted blade was altogether too simple and quick for a woman of her sort.

A considerable amount of noise was building up in the Rue du Pont, as the news of Louis's death spread and became digested. A great number of servants, shoe menders, men who worked in boats and women who did nothing from the age of fourteen to forty-five but suckle children, most of them their own, were obviously receiving the tidings with some joy and a great deal of alcoholic abandon. The decent people, the loyal people, and in Blois this was quite a lot of people, wisely kept inside their houses.

'Now, surely, is the time?' Annette asked, tentatively. 'We are not Parisians. His death offers us the perfect occasion.'

'Not while there are people in the street,' Montlivault said decisively.

'Not while there are so *many* people,' Pardessus the younger agreed.

'What we need is a resolution,' Old Pardessus said.

'What you need is some resolution.' Annette agreed. 'We ought to be on the streets and doing something.'

'Not in a crowd.'

'This is a secret society,' Montlivault said. 'We are known to the authorities as such, so it behoves us to be extremely cautious.'

'We're not a secret society,' Annette cried out. 'You are that most dangerous thing, a *secretive* society. There are too many women among you.'

'Only your sisters and your mother,' young Pardessus said silkily.

'My mother and my sisters are the *young* women here. The rest of you are the old ones.'

'You, my Annette, are the only one among us who has been caught at it,' Montlivault said. 'And you've scarcely been busy a fortnight.'

'I still say we should be on the streets. If we sit in an upstairs salon how can we even judge the temper of the crowds?'

'We can look.' Old Pardessus spoke as if this was a proposition of extraordinary daring. He stood up and walked to the great window that looked down to the street, and after a moment of contemptuous amusement, he was joined by his leader.

'If you had done that on any one of several dozen evenings in Orléans,' Annette told them, 'you'd have got a stone in your teeth.'

'This is not Orléans,' her mother sniffed.

'Nor is it evening,' Old Pardessus said, a lawyer to the last.

'The old fellow hasn't any teeth,' Montlivault offered with a grin. 'So he can hardly get a stone in them.'

It was his last jest of the evening, or the last Annette heard from him. The unwashed were indeed down there, and in thickening numbers, and they all appeared to be facing the Vallon household as if it interested them mightily – or, worse, as if it could be expected to contain something that would.

Annette knew that look on a crowd's face; she was acquainted with the particular smell of its hunger. She had met it in Orléans outside the church of Notre Dame des Miracles when the mob had pressed forward to kill cuirassiers and smash heads. She had become acquainted with it most particularly on the firelit and torchlit faces of women waiting to see Williams stripped and hanging from a tree.

The crowd had pointed to their house. They had laughed at her mother in the window, but they weren't breaking in. They had another point of interest.

Those nearest to the house knew that they were somehow in procession, and that the real point of the carnival was somewhere further back.

With a self-effacing grimace of disgust, Madame Vergez had seen what it was. It was her husband completing his not unusual afternoon walk, burdened with fowling-piece, shoulder baskets and the corpses of waterbirds, largely ducks.

As so often on these occasions he did not walk alone. He was too heavily laden with feathered corpses to stagger more than a step or two by himself. So he had shared his load among the many urchins who used to wait for him at the far side of the bridge, having already burdened the few he trusted to be secretive enough, and sufficiently silent and invisible to the birds to accompany him to the slaughter itself.

There was never any shortage of boys. Blois was full of any number of mothers who yearned for a quick route to a poultry supper.

The crowd led his boys and the boys led their hero and benefactor to the front door of his house. The crowd worked the bell-pull for him. They hammered upon the door in a cheerful and engaging thunder.

'Pray God your servants do not answer,' Montlivault hissed. 'We dare not let them in here.'

Annette noticed that his dark face had grown incredibly grey. He lacked Williams' curiosity to encounter ordinary people at first hand.

'Amen,' muttered Pardessus the younger.

'We haven't brought our guns,' the Lacailles mentioned, in voices quieter than fear. 'I'm not even carrying a pocket pistol.'

'My maids will be terrified to answer the door,' Madame Vergez told them all. 'I can't leave the poor man outside.'

This was the first time Annette heard her mother speak well of her stepfather, let alone protectively.

Madame had meanwhile left the room to confront the mob at the street door herself, a move which filled everyone inside the house with alarm.

As Annette followed her mother downstairs, accompanied by Françoise Anne and Angélique Adelaïde, she noticed the older Pardessus opening a puncheon closet, not to take any wine out but to see if there was space to get himself in. Montlivault and the Lacailles were already searching their way upwards towards the next landing.

Annette admired the way her mother opened the door into

the crowd, advanced through it, stepped back inside and waved people in as if welcoming them to a soirée.

Vergez and several score ducks entered first, accompanied by small boys, more ducks and a frenzied clapping of hands. His wife kissed him, full on the lips. She had forgotten what they tasted like, if she ever knew, and now might be her last chance to remind herself.

The kiss was necessarily abbreviated. Good taste dictated the matter and common sense underscored it. In any event, there was soon to be no more kissing room. For where Vergez and his ducks led them, the rough people of Blois followed.

As they followed, so did they applaud. As they applauded, so did Madame Vergez applaud them in her turn, clapping her hands more largely and uncouthly than Annette had ever seen in her, and with never a glance at their footwear and its effect on her floorboards and carpets. As Madame applauded, so did Vergez and his urchins and stepdaughters present the starving populace with ducks and similar bloodied morsels, a dead duck being easier to dispense with than your own life.

In spite of the narrowness of the door – grand enough for a house in the Rue du Pont, but more like a postern than the main gate of the château – those who had ducks departed with their ducks, and promptly, while others still thronged to press in.

These men – and their women when they brought themselves – could be offered nothing. Nor should they have expected anything. Sieur Vergez and his urchins and stepdaughters had already distributed two dozen brace of ducks, snipe, coot, wood pigeon and perhaps an unlucky starling or two. Nonetheless, these people had arrived hopefully, and people who arrive hopefully do not always leave peaceably, especially when invited to do so with empty hands.

A speech from Old Pardessus would have helped, a brief address from his son might have dampened matters down even further, the one being admired, the other merely respected. A few words from Guyon de Montlivault would also have been useful. When a crowd presses through the portals of great ones, great ones are what it hopes and expects to see.

What it saw was Sieur Vergez and the women of his family,

and a woman is of very little use to the hungry. She costs money to keep and she sells for even less than a middling-sized river fish.

Fortunately the surgeon was well loved, he was a noted dispenser of fresh meat, and his women were applauding their happiness at the King's beheading and bidding them welcome. Nobody showed Annette an axe or a broom handle – it wasn't that kind of crowd – but quite a few men wearing riverboat caps and other things knitted or woollen caught hold of her and started to prance about in a sequence of steps too intricate to follow. She needn't try to pick them up – her feet rarely touched the ground.

The same men, some of them with mouths as brown as any sick spaniel's, caught hold of Françoise Anne and Angélique Adelaïde and pressed them into the same riotous dance. Most men of those who found their way far enough presented themselves to Françoise Yvon Vallon Vergez. She was the woman they wished to whirl about then hold on to, because she was the most woman of them all, plumper and taller of spirit than the other three put together. These men measured their women in three ways only. They measured them by weight and they measured them by inches. There was a third way, and this was undoubtedly more tenderly philosophical, but they were soon too breathless to explain it to her or she to hear.

As far as anyone could tell at the time this celebration did not penetrate the house any further. It stayed out of Vergez's gun room, and it did not contemplate the stairs – either down to the kitchen or up to the salon, which was a fine place for dancing except that the beetle was rumoured to have been busy in the joists. So the great adventure had to be returned to the streets.

To prance across the bridge, along the quays or up a back alley with one of Sieur Vergez's ducks in your hands was one thing, but with his wife or – failing that – a stepdaughter quite another, and not for decent men or one's own woman to encourage. So the party was again in danger of fizzing out, and again therefore in danger of danger.

It was then that Annette's mother allowed herself to be kissed – she may even have suggested it – a kiss taking less elbow room than a dance.

The dancing immediately stilled, or her area of dancing did, and her daughters were put down and otherwise returned to their feet not a breathless moment too soon. They stood beside their mother while a orderly queue of men shuffled patiently in from the street, men and some women too, kissed Madame Vergez by both cheeks, sometimes squeezed her close or treated a daughter to a similar courtesy, then returned through the door, often with a brandishing of the fists and a loud cheer.

Annette was charmed to see her mother being so reflective in her kissing and, yes, so womanly. When the door was no longer crowded – her mother was too wise to bar it – the good lady said quietly, 'The trouble with the masses, and similar people, is that in general they can't be overawed.'

Her mother paused to wipe her face with a small handkerchief, perhaps to cleanse it from the kisses of the rabble. 'The nobility and gentility are susceptible to it. The mob aren't.'

Montlivault, both Pardessus and the whole family of Lacailles had clearly been overawed, and now stole gently downstairs, with only Old Pardessus finding anything to chuckle about, 'Your husband has saved us,' he assured Annette's mother, 'he has saved us all, he serves for us all, and is doing so now.' He made no mention of her daughters. Then he was a member of the high bourgeois if not the gentility, a four-square swollen-stomached leader of the Third Estate, and like the rest of them he had been too frightened to notice the women when they placed themselves in the firing line.

They were pleased to amuse themselves at the window just the same. Vergez had been taken back into the street, not so much a captive as a prize to be fêted. It was the women who fêted him, for ducks in the past and the promise of benison to come. They celebrated their surgeon by dancing with him, hop step and slide, on the slippery cobbles. He was currently in the arms of a market girl with very little on her chest and nothing at all on her feet, all the parts of her anatomy that kicked and knocked against him being formidably large and ill-matched and out of time with the rest of her.

'Ha!' scoffed Montlivault.

'Heh! hey! hey!' coughed Old Pardessus, like a donkey demanding fodder.

The remaining conspirators laughed more moderately, like gentlemen even. And like the men they were they went on doing nothing.

The second brother Lacaille bore scars to prove he was occasionally capable of doing something. He, of them all, did not laugh. 'My understanding of kings is limited,' he said, 'but it takes me this far. France has just killed its King. There's a whole race of kings beyond our frontiers who will band together and decide they do not like us for it.'

These were terrible words, and Annette shrivelled to hear them. Lovers loathe wars, separated ones even more so. And wives and mothers who yearn for husbands overseas?

Lacaille was correct in his prediction of doom, and Annette in consequence right to dread the outcome. She did not usually take notice of the Lacailles' pronouncements, but this was Warrior Lacaille as distinct from the rest of the Firebrand Lacailles, and she felt the man should be heeded.

He was, as it happened, diametrically wrong. France declared war on England a few days after the riot, and not the other way about. Diametrically wrong is only half a turn from right, and her country and Williams' country were at war. Otherwise nothing changed. France was in conflict with nearly every other country in Europe, because the fools who ran France in place of its King thought that a France at war with the world would soon be at peace with itself.

The declaration led to immediate food riots in Orléans and Angers, and God knows what more in Paris. Annette's heart was already broken by her enforced parting from Caroline. Now its pieces became entirely separated as the improbability of Williams' immediate return became borne in upon her. She read this image of her torment in the pages of a romantic novel. The words might be flowery, but their truth was beyond argument. The pain was worse than high indigestion.

It was Madame Vergez who brought the bad news to her. To be fair, her mother bore it bravely, but the lady's opinion of Williams had been changing of late. The household held three daughters, two and a half of them still unmarried. Madame

Vergez took the long view of mathematics. She was inching towards the notion that a skinny bird in the hand might be better than a fat purse in the bush. Wodswod in a new suit and with even a thousand pounds in his belt had come to seem almost downy during the last fortnight since she had gazed upon his child and realized there was scant chance of sending Caroline back again. Besides, a granddaughter who was *her* granddaughter couldn't be all bad.

These modest hopes were dashed by the fools in Paris. She encouraged Annette to weep, and wept a little herself. Perhaps she wept for her poor Jean-Jacques, perhaps in anticipation of hunger. Vergez's popularity had been bought at a price. No one in the street required him to dance again, but a number of ladies were becoming insistent that he part with his ducks and similar fruit on a daily basis.

Françoise Anne decided to comfort her sister as well. The alternative was to join Angélique Adelaïde who beckoned with a jug of wine, but she was beginning to fear that a woman of thirty-one was not going to go very far on jugs of wine. 'Talk to Vergez,' she suggested. She wasn't joking. Talking to Vergez, which in reality meant listening to him, had become quite the family routine since he and their mother had saved their lives. The Vallons had owned him for some years, but it was only since the murder of the King, and the subsequent riots, that they realized they had a sage in their midst.

Annette was particularly keen on the old fool. He made a pleasing change from Montlivault and the rest. With the exception of her brother Paul, who could never stay serious long enough, he was the only man she knew who did not boast. Even Williams boasted, if to say he was a poet was a boast, and it probably was. French was the poets' language – everyone knew that – and he did not write in French.

Her stepfather was in the room off the downstairs hall, the room he called his gun room. He was drinking something that smelled like gun oil, perhaps because he was cleaning his gun.

He rose slowly, partly propped up by his fowling piece, his other hand clawing wildly at the air as if brushing away flies, before coming to rest on her shoulder with a touch as light as a gnat. He listened gravely. 'Don't you sob, my tuttle. Or, if you must sob, not about nations at war. I'm an old man' – he clung to her more tightly – 'an ageing man, so I've seen several wars between nations, and can tell you they've made no difference to anything at all. They certainly made no difference to ducks, for example, nor waterfowls in general.' The weight of his hand became noticeable, his gun trembled. 'When a waterbird's so minded, it flies right over a war. The war doesn't touch it. A war's only as high as its tallest tower. The rest belongs to birds and to Heaven. No more shall it touch you, my downy one.' Something was agitating him just the same.

'The war is between my husband's country and our own, stepfather.'

'They'll never fight, my darling. You need to put armies together to fight – believe me, I've studied the matter.' He trembled. Everything about him trembled. Perhaps it always had. 'The English do not have an army. They have a navy. If we could borrow the English navy for a fortnight we might put our army in England and have a very fair tangle of spurs together. As it is, we lack the means to get ourselves there, and the English have nothing of themselves to bring over here, so I should forget all about the war till your clutch has hatched.'

'Caroline Anne is already born, papa, and sent out to nurse across the river.' He looked so hurt and accused at this that she added quickly, 'France has a navy, too, full of fine ships as well.'

'French ships are like the goosander duck, my dove. Like the goosander or even the smew, both of which come here in Winter from Wodswod's England.' His grip was now a clench, but totally without meaning or menace: he seemed to have difficulty standing up. 'Goosanders are only for ornament, and as for the smew – just like our ships.' His eye gazed into and a long way through her. 'Just like our ships. Don't think about the war, think about the . . . think about the the think about the ducks and try to stay cheerful and cluck–cluck.'

'Stepfather! Papa!'

'*Cluck*!' Vergez's smile was always intense, however shy the rest of his face. Now it widened, split right open, then fell apart in a series of most alarming spasms, while his head made noises much like a goose quacking. His gun came tumbling towards her, gashing her lip with its foresight, but by now he was flat on his back and entirely still, save for a lopsided straining of the chest, his quacking and rattling in the lungs having reduced itself to a swanlike hissing along the floor from the strangely crooked throat. She could feel the draught on her ankles.

Madame Vergez was never far away when her husband was alone with one of her daughters. Now she came briskly into the room to survey the wreckage.

Annette dripped blood from her lip.

'Trust him to be untidy,' her mother said. 'There's a place for things like this, but men never seem to find it in time.'

'And where exactly might that be?'

'He's not exactly a young man, your stepfather. I do hope it will be Heaven.' Her mother gazed down at her husband's twitching form, as if realizing her words did not meet Annette's question. Compassion softened her face, followed by a concern that went almost as far as love. 'The bedroom will do for a start. Fetch your sisters to help you carry him.'

Annette was struck by her mother's refusal to let the maids touch her stricken husband — there was symmetry in the embargo, which was quite as strict as the one which had kept him from touching the maids or her own daughters, even in moments of medical *extremis* such as this.

Angélique giggled at Annette's lip, as if she'd rouged her face in a childish game, or had been dipping into the jam or other preserves. Françoise Anne leapt up to help Annette without comment — then she hadn't allowed her sister to beguile her with wine.

They hurried into the gun room, even Annette appalled at this latest view of their stepfather, who lay with gaping mouth and his eyes jammed open. One of them still tried to focus unblinkingly on a point beyond the ceiling. The pupil in the other was so wide and empty that it had swallowed the iris altogether, and seemed about to do the same for the white.

Françoise Anne gasped, and Angélique Adelaïde continued to giggle, as if she believed or hoped her stepfather was merely drunk.

Their mother was in no mood to rebuke anyone. She surprised them all by walking upstairs backwards, guiding her husband gently by the head, which would otherwise have flopped unsupported.

She waved them on past the matrimonial bedroom though, and upstairs again. 'He's a stubborn old man,' she said tenderly, 'so he'll not be in a hurry to get himself buried. I'll not want to share a room with him while he waits.'

'Nor, of course, afterwards,' Angélique said. She had stopped giggling now, though her remark lightened the sisters' mood considerably.

Annette's room was the nearest, and she was the youngest. She was to move in with Angélique, drunk or sober. They threw the wreckage of kindly old Vergez on to her bed, where he sprawled as untidily as she must have done with Williams' weight upon her. Poor man, it was the sky's weight he felt now. Her mind was full of suchlike silly images. His legs were apart and trailing, the knees up while they tucked him, still dressed, under the blankets. Madame Vergez would have no one undress him but herself.

She smiled towards Annette with a curious expression of sympathy, before turning her out of her room. 'Troubles never come singly,' she explained. 'Or not to a family with women in it.'

BLOIS AND ORLEANS AND OTHER PLACES.
MARCH 1793

Vergez lay in funereal splendour in Annette's room, but only for a day. Madame Vergez scrutinized him on the second morning, and had her son Charles Henry look in upon him as well.

He was clearly a long way outside life, but considerably short of death.

'His vital functions are unimpaired,' her son said. 'His heart beats like the pendulum on a great clock. His pulse is steady. His lungs fill themselves with air and empty themselves very tidily. Are his bowels in order?'

'Only too well,' their mother sighed.

'His brain is blown to pieces, as you can deduce.' He gazed into the old man's enlarged pupil and then into the one that still strove to focus upon the ineffable distances of angel's wings and high-flying waterbirds. 'He might just as well have taken a round shot through the forehead for all that remains to him of his cognitive self.' Madame's second son was a brisk boy, and he came to instantaneous conclusions. 'You'd better transfer him down to the main bedroom again. You'll have priests calling, and well-wishers, and all the other people who hope to take advantage of a dying man's prayers and purse strings.'

So Vergez was carried to the head of the little flight of stairs, and her mother arranged to take over Annette's bedroom.

Halfway down they dropped him coccyx first on a warped tread.

'Better below,' Charles Henry said. 'It won't be so far for the maids to carry the things that they have to carry.'

Nobody bothered to explain that their mother refused to let anyone else touch him or any part of him.

They spread him upon the great matrimonial bed, huge enough for many a pursuit and evasion, and waited while his wife changed his socks, his night-cap and his shirt. Then the three daughters and the surgical son paid dutiful homage to his bed linen.

'By the way,' Charles Henry announced. 'I propose to get married in a month or so. She's an excellent young woman, well connected, and I have most of her father's permission. May I bring her round for the family's approval?'

'How can that possibly be?' his mother asked. 'We're a family in mourning.'

'I don't think so,' the surgeon said. 'Oh – mourning for my brother, of *course*, mother! But for my stepfather? Not for many a long year, is my prediction.'

'But you say his head is dead?'

'As with most people else in Blois.'

'He winked at me!' one of the sisters screamed, probably Angélique Adelaïde, who was given to parrot-like behaviour.

'Winked?'

'Or blinked.'

'Blinked could be *very* significant,' Charles Henry said. 'It might even indicate—' He began to tap the old man about the head.

'I hope he's doing neither.' Madame Vergez sounded stern for the first time since her husband's seizure. 'I'll not have winking *or* blinking in my house.'

'Farting is the main problem when one keeps tryst with the afflicted,' her son said, kissing everyone farewell. 'I hope to bring my intended to meet you all, as I say, and I don't want him belching or farting at her.'

Several days followed before the conspirators dared to meet again. Vergez's stroke provided them with an excuse and an opportunity. They could go to the Rue du Pont to pay their respects to the stricken man, and the Secret Police with their spies from the Prefecture could do little about it. They sat by the dozen round his bed, meeting his left eye or failing to meet his right, and generally avoiding everyone else's, especially the gaze of Madame and her three daughters who were now heroines, and as such made the cowards feel uncomfortable.

Montlivault was not happy to remain a coward for long. 'Your son, Paul,' he began.

'My Paul Léonard, yes?'

'He is a key man. We must get word to him.'

Annette's first journey to Orléans had begun exactly like this all those months ago. Annette felt his gaze upon her, and decided she had other things in mind.

Montlivault considered her both as woman and as messenger before deciding to entrap her via her mother. 'He's a hero frequently attacked by the enemies of the Crown.'

'He was injured by a stone that entirely missed him,' Annette explained. She had forgotten to tell her mother on her return, and subsequent events had made her brother's hurt seem trivial.

'*All* my sons!' Madame whispered, her eyes closed tight, her face whiter than Vergez's knuckles.

'Charles Henry is risking no more than matrimony,' Angélique Adelaïde said with the giggle she always found herself with after three in the afternoon.

'Weddings are a dangerous business,' Old Pardessus agreed.

'My face is full of scars,' one of the Lacailles muttered. 'Most of them were made by women, and I don't mean their kissing and biting either.'

Montlivault grimaced at this irrelevancy. 'Paul Léonard is our halfway man for both the insurrections in the West. I think you must bake him a cake, Madame Annette.'

'My cake would grow stale on the journey. Besides, I hear of no insurrection in the West.' She challenged Montlivault with a direct stare, and saw him fidget. 'Or, rather, I've heard talk of one for over a year, but I see no evidence of it.'

'Take him your cake and there will be one, I promise you.'

These were unusually direct words.

'Who goes to fight?'

'My brother,' the younger Pardessus whispered in considerable awe at the family connection.

'Some of us have already gone.' This from a Lacaille, but there was never any counting them.

'Bake a cake, Annette.'

'I have my baby to consider.'

'A woman can have no greater disguise than a babe-in-arms.'

Better be accompanied by her daughter than a cake. Better either than this ridiculous talking in ciphers, this talk in general.

She agreed, so she could have Caroline with her.

Montlivault rose, touched the back of her hand and gave her two waxed packages. 'Both of these to your brother,' he said. 'This for him to deliver to my banker in Orléans – he will know how to proceed. The other to pass on to the usual person.'

She turned the packets over in her lap. 'These could lead me to the guillotine.' She spoke quietly.

'And me. I have not concealed my name in this. Your baby will keep you safe. Stitch them into her blanket.'

Only when the conspirators had gone, and her mother had written to her son Paul and changed her husband's linen, did the older woman say, 'You can't separate your baby from her milk. The girl will dry up, and you've none of your own.'

Annette had seen Caroline that day, looked upon her and held her. She was in two minds about risking the mite anyway; so she agreed to travel alone.

As with the end of all journeys through which she could only hurry slowly, she arrived with a terrible sense of foreboding.

It was already dark by the time she disembarked. Paul wasn't at his lodgings at the Dufours. An exchange of greetings and kisses with Marie-Victorie-Adelaïde took no more than a few minutes. She could sleep there that night. They would gossip later. She hurried immediately to the Coin Maugas, hoping to catch her brother at a game of cards.

The entire house was empty, empty of men anyway. The place smelled neither of tobacco nor of cavalrymen.

The workshop was empty, perhaps because of the lateness of

the hour. No lights were burning there, nor in the shop, which was usually the most ornate on the Rue Royale.

She went hesitantly upstairs.

The Gellet-Duvivier daughter, her Williams' breathless Demoiselle, received her as if she were some kind of expected saviour. Clearly the girl had been praying for something of advantage to manifest itself to her and she was that something.

'Praise be,' she said. 'Now you have come, reason will prevail.'

Annette did not seem to have been very successful with reason of late. No one would listen to her. Now she must listen to the Demoiselle, who was clearly distraught but adrift from herself and unable to put her fears into words now she had someone to listen to them.

Seemingly her father had gone out at least an hour ago, armed and in uniform. Other rankers and non-commissioned officers of the National Guard had come for him, but the Guard as such was not being turned out. There were detachments already posted at various of the municipal buildings, so this was a purely private foray.

Annette wanted to ask about her brother before the Demoiselle lost herself in any further convolutions of anxiety.

'Maître Vallon, yes. He is with them.'

'He has not joined the Guard?'

'No – he has gone with them to caution patience. He spent many minutes trying to stop them.'

It seemed that Grenadier Gellet-Duvivier's friends wished to second their comrades at the Town Hall and prevent an intended insult to the Guard. Grenadier Gellet-Duvivier, in his not unfamiliar guise as the Madman, intended to go further and actually kill someone. He intended to avenge the King and the victims of the Septembriseurs, he said.

There was nothing new in Gellet-Duvivier's intentions. Annette was much more concerned about her brother's involvement in them.

'Believe me,' the girl whimpered, 'I have never seen my father so determined to damage himself.'

'Who is he quarrelling with this time?'

'Deputy Bourdon.'

Léonard Bourdon, the soi-disant Bourdon de la Crosnière, was a leading Jacobin, a vainglorious liar, and held by many of Annette's friends to be a murderer. Even so, he was the Legislature's deputy for the City of Orléans. To consider an attempt upon his person was an unimaginable piece of folly. To be seen to fail would be even more dangerous than to be known to succeed. He was very spiteful. Her brother would be at risk if he was associated with the man's attackers in any way. Annette hurried downstairs.

The Demoiselle insisted on following. She gave off an incredible coolness of body, like a wraith ghosting after her.

Annette didn't wish to be accompanied any further into danger. She turned to say her farewells.

The young woman was exceptionally beautiful and quite unreal. Annette could see why Williams said she belonged in a poem. As she hurried towards the courtyards of the municipal buildings she tried to keep calm by telling herself that a poem was the place for that young lady. Preferably a poem in English.

Events in the courtyard of the Town Hall were very French. She was glad Williams wasn't here. He would have tried to stand too close to them so he could understand the debate.

The Deputy for Orléans, Citizen Bourdon de la Crosnière, was there at the head of an extremely noisy crowd of men, including the Apothecary Besserve. Mercifully there were no women, or bad would very quickly have turned to worse.

Bourdon was trying to lead his followers up the steps of the Town Hall and take possession of the building. The citizen band at his heels were largely the members of the old Constitutional Club. It had changed its name so many times, even before Annette last left Orléans, that she was no longer clear what it called itself. Many of the crowd did not know either. When challenged by the six members of the National Guard who stood on duty there they replied variously, 'Friends of the People', 'Friends of the Friends', and simply 'Friends'.

The six members of the National Guard were friends of no one. 'We can admit people one by one,' the picket commander said. 'We cannot admit a rabble, however friendly.'

'I am Citizen Besserve, and this Citizen is none other than Deputy Bourdon de la Crosnière.'

'No matter whose friends they are.'

'Then admit us one by one,' Léonard Bourdon said persuasively.

'That's four score friends you have there, if a man. No – five score. You are clearly a very popular figure, Sieur Deputy.'

'Citizen will do,' Bourdon said.

His friends applauded loudly, and then began to count one another noisily, each man adding his own count to the next man's, the way drunks do, until in their own estimation there were thousands of them.

Annette moved forward and stood to one side of the steps in the inner courtyard, much as Williams would have done, after all. A great deal of well fed, excellently wined people seemed to be multiplying in numbers all about her.

'This is, as I say, Deputy Bourdon de la Crosnière. Have I told you that? I am Citizen Besserve.'

'We know you, Besserve. Go back to your pills.'

'This citizen is not only Deputy Bourdon. He is—'

'Deputy Bourdon de la Crosnière, on an important mission to the Côte d'Azur, and he demands admission.'

'This is not the Côte d'Azur. This is Orléans.'

'I'm the Deputy for Orléans.'

'And that makes you a very important person, Sieur Deputy. You may certainly be admitted to all of the City's offices. By yourself. Accompanied by an appropriate retinue. Tomorrow. During the hours of daylight. Assuming those offices are open.'

'You fat lout, Besserve!' The voice was unmistakable, though Annette could not determine from exactly where in the Town Hall it was calling. 'You've eaten your lunch. You're all so drunk you've not noticed it's gone suppertime. Why don't you take that murderer back to your pigsty and wait for breakfast!'

This led to roars of laughter and shouts of rage in roughly equal measure, the laughter turning to rage as those who were merely drunk and happy saw they were in danger of being drunk and insulted.

'I am *not* fat,' Besserve shouted, seizing upon the debate's one irrelevancy with instantaneous clarity of mind. 'I'm a man of the people. I'm too deprived and poor to be fat. You're the fat one, Gellet-Duvivier.'

'I work too hard to be fat.'

'This is Bourdon de la Crosnière.'

'He's a cissy and a murderer.'

The Madman was as drunk as he usually was at this time in the evening. Everyone else was as drunk as he wanted to be, which was much too drunk for safety. Everyone except those of the National Guard who were properly on duty here.

Bourdon was now in no hurry to climb any steps or enter any great doors. For a start, he now had so many men at his back that he clearly felt he could raze the whole building to rubble without a moment's preparation. Much more important he was, when sober, a politician and had been, before he could afford to drink, a schoolmaster. He had a paper in his hand and a pencil, or perhaps one of his friends carried an inkhorn in the handle of a staff. He had heard the Madman's name, and he made a note of it very obviously, 'Gellet-Duvivier', spreading the item out, sucking on it, almost mouthing it aloud in his awe at his own power over any man with a name.

The Madman was not done with him. 'Tell your murdering friend I've nothing to answer for, Besserve. I've brought my lawyer with me. Maître Vallon advises me constantly.'

A chill troubled Annette at this latest piece of folly. Gellet-Duvivier was now plainly in view, centre stage at the head of the stairs. He was hatless, without musket or pike, but with his sabre drawn. He waved it about him like a Moorish pirate in a storybook. Confronted by ten or a dozen men he would be a daunting figure. Facing a hundred drunks, with goodness knows what rabble besides, he was a powerful incentive to riot.

Bourdon had already noted that tell-tale word Vallon. He now had two useful names in his pocket. He trod upon the stair and waved his followers upward, shouting that these people were his friends and shared his every right.

The National Guard had now doubled in number, possibly thickened by the off-duty friends of the Madman who gathered here to avoid an insult to the hallowed uniform and colours.

The steps were now protected by a twin file of muskets with bayonets fixed. Those files would be swept aside if the mob charged, but no one is in a hurry to confront either a musket bullet or a bayonet, especially if one marches head of column as Bourdon did.

'Kill the Guard!' The shout came from behind.

The guardsmen kept their ranks and held their fire. No one killed anyone.

In the remaining seconds of peace that the adversaries hoarded between them a disturbing event occurred. Bodies were passed overhead from behind, the way a large crowd will hand forward women and children to save them being caught in the crush. Annette had an impression of white-stockinged legs, all of them shoeless, heads stripped of wigs and in one case of hair, of a face without ears, these convenient handles having either been snatched off or severally swung upon until the man's neck and head ran with blood. There were some half dozen of these human bundles in all.

The Friends had been amusing themselves with some aristos, or supposed aristos, as a necessary prelude to feasting and debate.

A voice barked at them to stand up, or otherwise move forward. An arm shot out from the rear file of the Guard and beckoned these unfortunate through. They crept up the steps followed by raucous cheers from their despoilers.

'See,' Besserve shouted. 'The gentlemen of the National Guard will always let aristocrats pass!'

The gentlemen of the Guard were rich men indeed. They carried percussion muskets, and now made an unmistakable noise with their cocking handles.

'They'll have to discharge them now,' someone whispered thoughtfully, not a crow's flight behind Annette's ear. She moved a step or two more to the side.

The leaders of the crowd were still not minded to risk musket fire direct. Nor did they intend to disperse. Nor in all probability could they. Instead they pressed past the front stand of bayonets and took to fondling the soldiers by their jacket buttons and other regimental ornaments.

Another dozen National Guardsmen came down the steps – having presumably found entrance through the rear of the building – and thickened the front rank as well as making a third file to the rear.

Several events now took place at one and the same time. Annette was aware of Besserve staggering backwards and Bourdon clutching his own throat and then his chest, like an actor in a play or a mountebank at a fair.

Simultaneously she heard the substantial tramp of soldiery in the outer courtyard of the building or the street. Reinforcements were arriving, whether of the National Guard or the much less trustworthy Town Guard she had no way of knowing.

Bourdon continued to stagger histrionically. Besserve to drip blood. Whoever had ordered the extra files down the steps had clearly not enjoyed the sight of a revered uniform being fondled by the buttons. The files had presented their firearms with some vigour. They already had bayonets fixed, and Besserve and the Deputy had been in the way either of the new members of the front file, or of the second and third file presenting over the shoulders of the men in front.

'Stand fast!' someone commanded from the back of the inner courtyard. 'Citizens, I order you to disperse to your homes.' This was the National Guard indeed. The rioters were penned, and the riot defused. Annette could breathe again – or she could have done if the injured Bourdon were not in possession of those two names.

It was then that she saw Paul for the first time. As Gellet-Duvivier's counsel, keeper and guardian of his common sense, he had leapt through the doors of the building to restrain the Madman from further action. He was now an actor in the major scene.

The Madman had no intention of being restrained. He had practised restraint for too long, and it had done nothing but lose him his King, his wife, and his wits. He threw Paul to one side, clapped his legs together as if he still had his horse between them, and jumped his imaginary mount over the files of his on-duty colleagues that were separating his last vestiges of reason from his massed enemies.

Annette thinks he flew face first. He banged his belly on a head in the front file, and knocked a kneecap and a boot or so on several hats to the rear. Face first, teeth foremost, and proceeded by a howl of execration, he arrived behind his sword, which travelled hard in his hand in an impossible salute, parry and invitation of flying prime, all in a rasp of iron and twinkle of finely honed danger.

Its point was somehow swept aside by Bourdon's not unreasonable gesture of self-protection, otherwise it would have completed the task the bayonet so imperfectly began, split the villain open, and dropped the innards out of him like teasing the guts from a river fish. As it happened it did no more than prick him with its point, gash his rather splendid coat with its edge, and knock Besserve's teeth from his face with its finger guard, the two men standing close to one another the way great ones do, especially when hurt.

The cut to Léonard Bourdon's coat knocked him over. The Madman straddled his head with his feet, tried to position himself for a stab at his throat, but ended up by doing no more than tread on the Deputy's ears, before he was dragged off his intended victim by friend and foe alike. The friend, again making himself much too evident, was Annette's brother Paul.

Grenadier Gellet-Duvivier was a hard man for a foe to catch hold of. With a friend he was more tractable. He let Paul draw him away, and Paul allowed himself to be led, in his turn, perhaps from his shock at finding Annette in Orléans.

They passed visibly but safely up the steps, the Madman's uniform being their passport. As they did so, the fighting behind them became general until a single shot was fired into the air, and order was restored. Annette sat with Paul in the tiny family parlour in the shop at the Coin Maugas while the Demoiselle served them wine and hot water. It was a deceiving potion, intended to reassure and console. In face, it brought wetness to her eyes and quickly made the head swim.

They were secure for the moment, perhaps until dawn. The captain-commandant of the National Guard had insisted it turn out in force, and it now held the streets and the main buildings of public concern. The Town Guard was also standing to. It was without Besserve and its more socially elevated components, as these had been feasting all day with Bourdon and their fellow Jacobins. So there was no conflict between the two bodies, or not for the moment. The City was quiet, the time not yet midnight.

Monsieur, now Grenadier – he refused to be Citizen – Gellet-Duvivier was not with his comrades. He had saved them once from humiliation on the steps and in the courtyard of the Town Hall. He was not allowed to parade himself again. This was in part because the skin of his nose was broken and otherwise bloodied as a result of his long flight from on high and subsequent hawklike stoop upon the person of Bourdon de la Crosnière – he had bounced from several of his comrades' heads and quite possibly their muskets – more because he was Gellet-Duvivier, and his presence almost anywhere was held to be inflammatory.

He was on duty even so, swooping high and low, upstairs, downstairs, through stockroom, serving room, and stitching rooms, then pounding the parade ground of the grand salon in remorseless fast time, as he guarded his kingdom, saluted his gods and his goods, while making a restless inventory of his chattels.

Every so often he stopped in the little family room the others sat in. Annette had never seen it until this night, though Williams had often described it to her as the arena of his linguistic misadventures with the trout. 'Before God,' the Madman shouted every time he paused, 'I nearly killed him for you. If he hadn't been snivelling behind our rascally neighbour Besserve, I'd have sliced him up for certain.' He declined his daughter's warm water. He was drinking from his own stoneware bottle, and since the skin on his face was now as red as his skinless nose it probably held something warmer than wine. 'He's a public sewer, that Bourdon. A standing drain. A stinking cesspit. A pity he wasn't arm in arm with Fournier the American. I'd have stuck them both and avenged a lot of good men.' He surveyed Annette and his daughter one by one around his painful nasal blur, then brought them both into focus by fattening his cheeks with a mouthful of spirits. 'And women,' he added. 'They had good women killed last September. *And* otherwise ill-used.'

'Patron.' Paul dignified him by his older and more calming title. 'Léonard Bourdon is a deputy.'

'Praise God we've put his rabble in their place.'

'He has been conducted to his hotel with an escort.'

'Under arrest!'

'No, patron. Your commandant called it an honour guard. You are likely to be the one behind bars once this affair has been sifted.'

These words were a mite too direct for the Demoiselle. She went to heat more water.

'Me?' the Madman asked. 'Why me? I'm inconspicuous enough.'

'Bourdon recorded two names,' Annette said. 'He has Gellet-Duvivier and Paul Vallon in writing. Doubtless he'll be given others. But he has yours.'

It was her brother's turn to look flustered. He recovered himself quickly. 'Patron,' he said. 'It is my bet that any recorded names will be arrested. I don't propose to wait here to find out. And if I'm arrested I certainly can't help you with your defence.'

'Come to Blois,' Annette said. 'My family can hide you among its friends.'

The Demoiselle returned. 'Let us leave with them, papa. You've been very public these last months.'

These were hardly the words of an immature daughter, much more the scolding of a surrogate wife.

'I could never leave here,' Gellet-Duvivier said simply. 'Not even for a night. Your poor dead mother, that saintly miracle among women, would never forgive me. Besides, the West has risen, those fools in Paris have been given a bloody nose – why should I leave my post now?'

Annette indicated to her brother that they should go at once.

'Nobody has posted you here, patron. You should leave with us.'

Monsieur Gellet-Duvivier already had his own bloody nose. He regarded Paul balefully.

As they hurried towards the Dufours' household, Annette reproached herself aloud for being such a poor messenger.

'Nonsense,' Paul said. 'You bore packages to place in my hand, then heard I was in danger. What else were you to do? I'm touched and flattered.'

He indicated that André Augustin could deal with Montlivault's banker. Annette's other package was probably too late. The loyalist uprising was already taking place.

The Dufours were not in bed. They were worried for Annette, and then for Paul. They were also disturbed at the news from the West.

The peasants and the bourgeoisie of the Vendée had rejected the Constitution, mustered forty thousand men under arms, and now held all the land towards the mouth of the Loire. There was little firm news, though all the rumours were clear they had captured Cholet and were advancing towards Saumur and Angers. These were only names to Annette, and probably to everyone else. So, too, their leaders Stofflet, Cathelineau and the noblemen Elbée, Bonchamps, La Rochejaquelier and Charette.

'At least they're not sitting on their bottoms like Montlivault.'

'Or determined to lose their heads like Gellet-Duvivier,' Paul mused. 'I'll tell you this much – Montlivault has a most intelligent bottom. Sitting on our own is the best thing we can do at this time. The ordinary men and women of Blois and Orléans favour the Republic and the new way in general. We can't have an uprising without the mob, and that ought to be the end of it.'

'There's a more sinister consideration,' André Augustin added. 'The National Guard has been detailed to put this rebellion down. And it will do so. It is a club for royalist gentlemen no longer.'

'Only a few fools like Gellet-Duvivier insist on the old white uniform,' Paul muttered.

'The royal colours are as dead as the vestments of the mass priest.' Marie-Adelaïde had been busy trying to arrange matters domestic for Annette, but she had to get a word in now Paul made it clear they would not be staying.

'Where will you go?' she asked him.

'I know a waterman or two,' he said cheerfully. 'And I've had good winnings of late.'

'Be careful who you treat with, then.'

'I've a pair of pistols upstairs and the night merits a topcoat to conceal them.' It was a long time after midnight, and he left Annette behind him while he went to arrange their passage downstream.

She chatted with her friend and waited. The news of the expected uprising and her own view of this evening's nonsense seemed equally unreal. She wondered how different the war in the West really was from this evening's horseplay with wine and swords. Rumour is a powerful voice.

'Your friend Montlivault has deeded a great deal of money to the White cause,' André Augustin said, having looked through the package she had brought for Paul to give to his banker. 'Remind your brother I shall take care of this.'

Paul returned almost at once. He had woken some watermen and secured a boat. 'Knocking on some of those doors with the Cathedral clock gonging two and then a quarter after is the most dangerous thing I hope to do in this life,' he chuckled, as he kissed everyone goodbye. 'Those ruffians all sleep with a wine keg for a pillow.'

So they left.

Dawn was little more than a product of the fancy when Annette followed her brother and stepped once more onto the back of the interminable river. Even if the sky was in truth breaking, then it did so behind them as they drifted towards Blois and a little closer to the war. They went quickly this time. The air was still but they had the stream.

BLOIS.
THE EVOLVING SUMMER

They floated to Blois on the 19th March, not daring to rest because of the excitement on the river, and arrived home in the evening. Supper was a brief affair, with Paul even more tired than Annette. After a quick rearrangement of bedrooms they went to bed early.

Another letter from England awaited her. It was from Williams' sister Dorothy, in sparse French but full of warmth and sisterly affection like several others she had already received from her. Dorothy was younger than Williams, but a much more whole-hearted correspondent than her brother. She spoke of the cottage they would all live in together. The idea seemed bizarre at this point of excitement, but it was also full of hope. Annette fell asleep with it by her bedside.

Next morning Caroline was brought by the house early. Her sisters had been trying to bring the baby inside during her days away, but her mother had forbidden it. She was almost a widow, and proposed to deny herself nothing in consequence. When Françoise Anne argued with her, and Angélique Adelaïde giggled, she changed her argument, became immediately dry-eyed, and explained that a suckling babe ought never to be allowed in a house of imminent death.

So Annette cradled her daughter in the street, held the child against her heartbeat and let her hold her finger. Having scolded her nurse and made her a decent present of a coin, she once more parted with the baby and went inside to find her pen and fold some paper into letters.

She wrote to Williams at nine in the morning and poured her heart out. Love, in a letter, was all dash and haste. She knew that from her novels. She also knew that a lovesick woman can be excused for writing like one. She had no certainty that anything she wrote was reaching England, both because of the war and the watch the secret police kept upon her, as Montlivault had already warned.

She mentioned nothing of Paul's recent adventures, nor of her own. Williams might find them alarming, and other eyes too full of interest. Better by far to write, '*Ta soeur me parle de notre petit ménage avec un entousiasme qui me fait grand plaisir. Que nous serons heureux, ô mon tendre ami, oui on sera heureux . . . Aime toujours ta petite fille et ton Annette qui t'embrasse mil fois sur la bouche, sur les yeux et mon petit que j'aime toujours, que je recomande bien à tes soins: adieu, je t'écrirez dimanche. Adieu, je t'aime pour la vie . . .*

Her tears fell on the page as she wrote so bravely. She corrected neither spelling nor grammar. The heart has nothing to do with pedantry.

Re-reading it as far as the loving conclusion, she decided a little thought might be called for as well. *Parle-moi de la guerre, ce que tu pense, car cela m'occupe beaucoup.* Yes, she thought about the war all the time, and Williams, and the sharp pain of separation, and her fatherless daughter even more.

Deciding the letter was good she began another one to Dorothy at ten in the morning.

Scarcely had she finished writing than her brother Charles Henry arrived, followed by Old Pardessus. Charles Henry had now secured every preferment there was at the Hôtel de Dieu, and like many a person who bears excessive responsibilities he found he had more than enough time on his hands for all manner of extra tasks like calling in upon his family several times a day.

'A pity you don't learn how to shoot,' his mother observed. 'You could walk out with your stepfather's gun one afternoon and arrange us some supper.'

Charles Henry smiled brightly at her in that strange empty

way surgeons have, especially with people who love them and think that they know them. Then he went upstairs to feel the sick man's wrist.

He came down almost at once, preferring the company of his brother Paul and Old Pardessus. 'He still can't sit upright, or focus his eye, or speak,' he told them all, as if they hadn't noticed, 'but his pulse is as regular as a woodpecker. I expect him to live for another dozen years if you go on turning him and keep him clean.' He kissed his mother absent-mindedly. '*No* warming pans, though. They may over-excite him.'

He stayed a few minutes longer, chatting not to his mother or sisters, but offering measured conversation to Old Pardessus and his brother Paul. Their talk had more manner than meaning as far as Annette could judge, and was designed by the three of them to impress upon each other and principally the women just how important they all were.

Important people know when to leave. This is always soon so they can explain how busy they are as they dash through the door.

Charles Henry had an after word, however, and for Annette. 'If I were you, sister, I'd not write any letters for a while, especially to England. Indeed, I'd not write any letters at all. That's my advice to you.'

'Why, my brother?'

'Because that was a fellow's advice to me. I can't tell you *who* he was, I'm not exactly certain. I identify him by two enormous abscesses – we call them scrofulas in the profession. They were boils really, but both of them as big as carbuncles. One of these was on his tongue, the other on his scrotum.'

Annette's sisters began to laugh at this, and Old Pardessus to snigger. 'My,' he said, 'carbuncles on the—'

'*Not* in my house,' Madame Vergez said. 'Scrofulas and similar words are totally out of place at this hour, before anyone has had a decent cup of chocolate.'

'He thought he was dying,' Charles Henry explained to Annette. 'Also he couldn't pay, so he obviously felt he owed me a tiny truth in return for some extremely exact surgery.'

'But who *was* he?'

Her brother was already gone, so Old Pardessus said, 'My money is on a spy for the Prefecture, if not the secret police. My son Jean Marie is convinced the police spy on you, Madame Annette.'

Charles Henry was an excellent surgeon and clearly a physician of some acumen. Like his stepfather, he was no mean zoologist, though he preferred to capture birds with the water-colour brush rather than the fowling piece. Just the same, or perhaps because of this, Annette was intrigued to hear him likening a sick person's pulse to the tapping of a woodpecker.

Perhaps she should have questioned the image at the time, as Williams certainly would have done.

One morning soon afterwards Madame Vergez went upstairs to her husband, taking three maids with her to open the shutters and carry hot water.

The sound of shutters being opened was followed immediately by the screaming of women, and then Madame speaking sternly – she *never* screamed – and the even more melancholy note of shutters being closed and their ratchets fastened.

'I think it's stopped pecking,' Angélique Adelaïde said. It would have been the perfect occasion for her to giggle, but she didn't.

The maids were sent back downstairs at once, two of them to make lavender water, one to fetch the ancient relative of the Lacailles who always attended a family on these occasions.

The ancient lady took some time laying Vergez out, but presently she contrived to make him very peaceful, with both eyes closed and the axis of his chin at last parallel with his shoulderbones and at right angles to his neck. The stroke had obliterated, or at the very least straightened, his smile so he made an attractive corpse indeed, and one the entire family could weep over.

Jean-Marie Pardessus was a surprising first visitor to the house. He arrived even before Charles Henry had looked in to pronounce the old man dead.

Wine and appropriate cordials had already begun to circulate. Their tardiness in calling for medical confirmation of death began to tease Angélique Adelaïde's sense of whimsy. 'It's a good thing she's only laid him out,' she whispered.

Their mother had withdrawn to her own room, which was Annette's room, in order to be private; so Angélique felt she could proceed.

'I mean it's a good thing we don't as a family go in for – I mean, supposing we'd already *embalmed* him.'

Charles Henry arrived at last, and scolded them for the wine as much as the indelicacy of their haste. 'He's been tied off,' he complained. 'It's not an infallible practice, but if a man can be encouraged to pass water then we can sometimes look to get his other pumps going as well.'

'Medical talk!' Françoise Anne scoffed.

All this time, Jean-Marie Pardessus had been talking most earnestly to Paul, and paying no respect to the dead man's person at all, not even swallowing a biscuit in his honour, let alone raising a glass.

Just as abruptly he departed.

'Are you all right, Paul Léonard? Are you well?' Angélique Adelaïde was generally giggling uncontrollably by this hour, without the amelioration of death-bed cordials, but she it was who noticed that their brother from Orléans was if anything whiter than the corpse.

He had been standing alone to digest the news he had from Pardessus, and was clearly in two minds about alarming the household with it.

'Gellet-Duvivier,' he said. He spoke to Annette, since she was the only one for whom the name held meaning. 'The Madman's been arrested, Jean-Marie tells me.'

'We must see what we can do for him,' she suggested. A rescue was surely out of the question.

'Nothing, little sister. I'm afraid we can do nothing. They've already taken him to Paris, and we know what that means.'

At that moment there was a noise at the front door, a timid note on the bell-pull, then something rather more furtive than a knock.

Paul looked even more sickly, as if he had further news to impart but was frightened that events might have overtaken the messenger.

Annette went downstairs from the bedroom and found a maid at the door, and Caroline crying outside. The girl was trying to quieten her at the breast, but had disturbed her by reaching for the bell-pull. The girl had obviously been calling by in the usual manner, and intended merely to carry the baby up the street past the window as her instructions demanded. Then she sensed the quietness of the house and saw the bolted shutters. Even a servant girl from South of the river is allowed to be politely inquisitive, and anyone connected with the Lacailles would know how to intrude her curiosity.

Annette took Caroline from her. 'You must come back tomorrow and I will find you some money. Tell your mother this is how it must be. You have been satisfactory.'

The girl didn't understand, and reached for the child again.

'My baby is staying,' Annette explained to her. 'Matters are quite different here now. Caroline is going to live with her mother.'

Madame Vergez, Widow Vergez, did not let the world revolve without feeling her hand upon it, even on a day like this. She arrived at the very moment they were exchanging the child, and although Annette's mind was fully and finally made up, the girl might find it easier to obey her mother than herself.

Save that Annette already had Caroline firmly cradled to her. 'Everything has changed, mother. We must have a little talk, you as head of household and my sisters and I as something rather different from what we were.' A Caroline moreover who stopped crying.

This gathering in of her baby, her final and most absolute refusal ever to relinquish her, was the most looming event in Annette's almanac, but like much else in her recent life it was immediately swept aside by history.

Her mother's mouth was clenching shut as a prelude to a lengthy opening, when all four of them, girl, Annette, baby, Madame Vergez – and the still hovering maid – were swept aside by a soft-footed onslaught through the doorway.

Six members of the Town Guard, six surprisingly neat and clean members with muskets, had stolen down on the house from further up the hill, and were now inside.

The maid screamed. The girl screamed. Annette was grateful to them. She guessed what the men were here for, and it was important that someone should express alarm at their presence.

A tall man in town clothes stepped through the door behind them. 'Paul Vallon?' His gait was easy, and he spoke without any suggestion of an inflamed tongue, but he was obviously one of that fraternity.

'My brother has not lived here for several years,' Annette said. 'Maître Vallon lodges in Orléans with the Senior Clerk of Sessions.'

'Indeed. Well, he's not there and he's wanted in Paris. We'll look for him if we may.'

'My daughter's word should be good enough for you.'

'I have every confidence, madame. Should my confidence be misplaced, then this Vallon will not be the only one of you travelling to Paris.'

Four more fusiliers of the guard arrived to them, coming into the hallway from behind them all. Men had obviously been stationed at the back door as well.

'There's no one in the cellarage, and only women in the kitchen.'

'Search the house carefully, a floor at the time.'

They were inside for the better part of an hour, shouting at one another, slamming doors, and once causing a wincing avalanche of crockery. This brought Annette's sisters trembling downstairs. The men wore very soft footwear for soldiers, and for poor folk even more so. Clearly the Town Guard had some members who were a long way richer than ordinary.

The search party came downstairs at last. Paul was not with them.

The tall one in town clothes said to Madame Vergez, 'My apologies, madame. And my condolences for your recent loss. Sieur Vergez, I believe?'

He took snuff, perhaps against death, and offered it all round. The women did not take snuff.

'You would have saved time had you believed us,' Madame Vergez said. 'Not to mention the blasphemy of an armed presence in a house of death.' She seized Caroline. 'Not to mention this poor mite here, scarcely delivered into the world.'

Caroline began to cry, and Angélique fainted.

To faint was to gild the lily, surely? There was no need of it. No man enjoys a baby crying. The tall man in town clothes bowed, then led his ten men in double file through the front door.

Madame Vergez returned the child to her mother and dismissed the girl. 'A pity Vergez is dead,' she said. 'He'd have enjoyed seeing soldiers passing two by two through our front door like that. We must be the only house in the street with a door capacious enough for such a manoeuvre!'

Angélique still lay on the floor. It was an unusually long faint, but no one could be certain that she was drunk. Her face was very pale, if so. There had been several pale faces today.

They helped her to a chair in the gun room. Annette suggested they go there so they could have a better view of the street.

She also said, 'The three of us have been talking, mother. Caroline will stay here with me. We will all remain here with you. These are going to be hard times, but if we're to starve it will be much more convenient if we do so together.'

Madame nodded, abstractly. Her mind was on her son Paul's predicament, and did not go much beyond Vergez's funeral.

After perhaps a quarter of an hour, with Caroline again stirring, Annette said, 'I think we should go upstairs. It will be foolish for our brother to show his face by this window.'

Angélique's spirits began to revive. She did not quite giggle again, not today, nor could she or her oldest sister be very coherent about Paul's hiding place. It was plain that they didn't want their mother to hear that he had lain either beneath his stepfather's bed or under his corpse itself. Annette could not take the matter further, out of delicacy.

When they arrived to where the old man was lying as if in state they found Paul sitting quietly in the room.

There was a further ring, a funereal ring, at the street door.

'I don't think you should be seen by any of our visitors,' Annette counselled him. 'Our friends are all much too discreet to be any good with secrets.'

★

Paul moved back to Orléans almost at once. He decided that Blois was too small and too gossipy for him to be entirely safe, and the country at large impossible. New arrivals in a town or village had to report their presence, and he was in doubts about whether he could successfully assume a new identity, the Bourdon affair having become so blown up that it was now occupying as much of the Legislature's time as the Vendéen War.

Bourdon de la Crosnière had written to Paris complaining of a murderous assault by an organized gang of political assassins. Grenadier Gellet-Duvivier and Paul Vallon were among the ring leaders. Certain aristos and other prominent members of the National Guard had seconded their attempt to have him bayoneted, sabred and shot. He had been saved by what a more superstitious man could only describe as a sequence of miracles, but he was a true Jacobin and did not intend to share his voting rights with God. Metal bracelets, buttons, and lucky charms had blunted the murderous assaults upon him at a dozen points of his anatomy.

Gellet-Duvivier and eight of his supposed companions, all known to Paul, were now at the Conciergerie du Palais, waiting to be arraigned by Fouquier-Tinville and processed by the guillotine. Warrants had been issued for the arrest and transfer to Paris of at least ten other ruffians, all of them having been afforded a preliminary hearing *in absentio* by declaration and deposition, the most important testimony originating with the Apothecary Besserve.

Paul did not return to the Dufours. Annette alone of her family knew where he was in hiding, and likely to remain. The search for him at Blois was only a prelude. A further warrant for his arrest was issued on the twenty-fourth of April. On the sixteenth of June Fouquier-Tinville indicted him and ordered he be committed to the Conciergerie with the rest of them.

The Demoiselle insisted on accompanying her father to Paris and to prison. She now presented a petition explaining that since her mother's death her father's mind had been deranged, that the people of Orléans knew him to be an idiot, and that his friends, boarders and employees referred to him as the Madman. After his arrest his madness had become extreme, and his incoherent shouting of oaths, prayers and military words of command kept his fellow prisoner awake at night and enraged the guards. When she visited him he did not recognize her, called her by the name of his dead wife, relived their courtship and frequently asked her to marry him.

Fouquier-Tinville granted him a medical examination, but decided to keep matters tidy. He knew that for nine men to be condemned then one of their number reprieved would result in a painful situation for the remaining eight. He signed accordingly and the warrant was executed.

The nine men from Orléans mounted the scaffold and were despatched one by one before a large and appreciative crowd on the thirteenth of July in the Fifth Year of Freedom. One of them was in an extremely bad temper.

The guillotine was new to France, and had only been used a few hundred times, but it was acquiring a considerable folklore. The severed head was rumoured to play a trick or two of its own, rather like a badly killed chicken. Learned men were gathering to study the evidence, and a number of scientific papers had been written.

Eyes were commonly seen to roll, faces to grimace, cheeks to blush, mouths to shape words of grief and indignation. Deaf people were invited to sit near them and decipher their lips, and various and peculiar their utterances were supposed to be.

Only one head was ever reported to shout aloud, and this was on the thirteenth of July in the Fifth Year of Freedom. It bellowed so vehemently – in spite of its absence of breath – that the executioner dropped it.

There was no record of what the cry was, or whether it was coherent. But when Annette read of the story in a letter from Paul her own lips pronounced the one word '*Idiot!*'

She remembered the idiot moment she had fallen in love. She had never explained the word as an *adjective* to Williams.

FRANCE.
1793. AN OCTOBER JOURNEY HIS DREAMS WOULD NOT LET HIM FORGET.

It was most of a year since he had seen her, weeks drawn into months without news.

Did she have news of him? She complained he did not write or that his letters could not reach her because of the war.

Certainly letters had not often found their way to Dorothy or himself, even though the few they received made it clear that she often posted to him several times a week. As well as her wondrous outpourings of love, the news of his daughter, and hints at terrible events, they used phrases like 'two more to each of you before Sunday' or 'again on Monday'. She had clearly written much. Even so, a great fog of unknowing had fallen between them with a damp that might one day corrode the heart but in the meantime caused him unbelievable anguish.

What in truth could he really tell her when he wrote? His financial affairs were advancing though scarcely advanced. He had published his poem, with an earlier one, at the beginning of the year. It made him famous almost overnight in a small way. Since he intended to be famous in a large way, he saw nothing very exciting in that fact. Nor would she.

He went on a walking tour to Wales, hoping, as separated lovers must, to annihilate an otherwise unbearable interval of time. Still no news of her when he returned.

Instead, he received dismal tidings from Orléans and Paris. Largely through gossip and the letters of friends who had contacts in France, he heard of his late landlord's execution and of Paul Vallon's sentence. Poor old Madman. The poor Demoiselle. Poor Annette. Poor dear Annette. He had to find a way to be with her. Sometimes her letters had asked for no more than that.

If only he felt more like her husband he could have borne the interval. She was his wife before God, there could be no doubt of this. A priest had married them, but he was not her husband nor she his wife according to the law of either land. A long ago letter from her at the beginning of the year had urged him to return and marry her according to civil law. She called him her husband when she wrote, but suffered the ambiguities of the situation as painfully as he did himself.

His best hope was to go back to France and persuade her to return with him to England. People were reaching France by small boats, in spite of the war.

They put him ashore in the dark, among sand dunes and grass-topped runnels of mud at the mouth of an estuary. He supposed this must be the Seine, but the only one of them who would talk to him said that the names of French rivers were a matter of supreme indifference to him. He must have been landed close to the smugglers' ultimate destination, but they obviously weren't about to tell him where that was.

There were no cliffs, or the shoreline had receded from what cliffs there had been. These presented themselves to him as a dark scarp some half-a-mile inland. He climbed this easily. Its slope was gentle enough for trees to be growing on it. Behind him, and across several miles of water, he saw a large town, full of lights. He guessed it was Le Havre.

If it was Le Havre, then the river was the Seine as he suspected, and led all the way to Paris.

For a moment he thought of striking south, towards Blois, or to Orléans first for news. But he didn't know whether Annette and baby Caroline were alive or dead. There had been no word of them for months, and the last word had spoken of danger.

Lovers cannot bear to hurry towards bad news, but a young man can always be drawn to Paris.

★

She had longed to see him all year long, and to *hear* from him. Now there was this sparse note, saying he intended, however fleetingly, to come to her.

She went to hug Caroline, then to be with her mother and sisters.

Williams' return at this moment would be an impediment to her. She wanted to see him, ached for him, yet she had her daughter to bring up, her brother to save from the guillotine, her family to defend. If Williams could only return as a provider for herself and Caroline, splendid. If he could provide for her mother and sister, better still. But his few letters, and his sister's letters, made it clear that there was no money yet. He could return only as a lover. There wasn't enough food here for one of those.

She kissed the note again, and it tasted strange on her lips. She began to turn it carefully this way and that, examining the handwriting with suspicion. It was his own dear hand for certain, and yet its taste was wrong. If those ruffians in the secret police really intercepted her mail they would surely have kept examples of his handwriting?

She examined every particle of his words to her, their last little curlicue and stab. A hand does change according to the quill, the cut of the nib. And if he wrote with a borrowed iron pen, the metal could be harsh and unbending, as uncomfortable to use as a stranger's shoes.

Yes: the note had been written by Williams. He was certainly coming here. And yet . . . and yet.

As she pondered the matter, she heard a tradesman ask for her at the back door. She went down the kitchen steps to find out what he wanted. It was only a query about the cloth Widow William had ordered.

She accepted being a widow nowadays. It explained the absence of a man with considerable finality, and her mother seemed to prefer it. Widow William and Widow Vallon-Vergez were in considerable demand socially.

William was her preferred way of writing her surname now. She had caught Williams from that Helen Maria, another English poet, and she had honoured her by name long enough.

*

He had no letters of introduction this time, no wartime papers of accreditation, and little money to change in a country at war. When he sat in little inns at night he learned the true extent of his danger. All foreigners were to be imprisoned, by decree. They could be executed, or otherwise disposed of, according to the whim of local magistrates. In general they were to be treated as spies unless they could furnish clear evidence to the contrary.

Conscription had been announced half a dozen months ago, and he was of an age to be conscripted. His only hope lay in his evident poverty. Riding in diligences and any form of transport whether by hoof, wheel or riverboat, would render him conspicuous. So would sleeping in inns.

His best chance was to be a wayfaring man, and he was aided in this by the extreme shabbiness of his clothing. He sought places where there were people, slept among market stalls or under hedges, and in consequence grew even shabbier. If spoken to he answered in jerky French, harshly delivered down his nose. He shambled like an idiot man and tried to sound like an idiot boy.

Paris seemed safer to him. It was a city which was managed by lawyers but where the masses wore their dirt with dignity.

It was with an inevitable curiosity that he sought out the place of execution. The guillotine had been moved several times since it was first used at the Carrousel last year, while he was still in Blois, so he could have no certainty that this was where Monsieur Gellet-Duvivier had died. He believed it was on the opposite side of the Place Louis XV from where they had rid themselves of their King. In that case, this was almost the identical spot. At least the poor fool had ceased his struggle in a noble square.

William stood in a large crowd and asked questions of no one. If he sensed anyone watching him he fidgeted aimlessly, like the imbecile he pretended to be. Several times he thought he glimpsed the Demoiselle wistful among the bystanders, but surely she would have no stomach for such a ceremony unless her father's untimely end had left her as witless as he was? Then he was a young man who imagined beautiful faces everywhere. Several times he thought he had seen the Demoiselle in England, and once in Wales. He dreamed about her often.

Long before the condemned arrived in their demeaning cart he had heard all their names. Each was discussed enthusiastically, as if they were prize fighters or wrestlers at a fair.

He knew one face without needing a name. He had been introduced to Gorsas a day after his arrival in Paris in 1791. The man was a literary figure, much like himself, the proprietor of a news sheet called the *Courrier*. He had revolted William by defending last year's September massacres. Now, without a struggle, his life had been turned into a bloodied lump, and his head lay gawping in the basket.

William was already sickened by this judicial carnage and its attendant indignities. The executioners played very unsavoury games with the severed heads – suppose his Annette were to be treated like this? Or her brother Paul. He saw no reason for men and women to be brought to their death in an open cart.

He was older now, and wiser. He kept his feelings to himself.

Somebody spoke his name, afflicting him with immediate terror. That awkward word 'Wordsworth' was uttered with shrivelling accuracy.

It was an acquaintance called Bailey. The man asked him what he was doing in Paris and immediately told him to leave. 'The English are to be locked up,' he said. 'It will be enacted before the end of the week. We have had enough of this Tom Paine, Helen Maria Williams, John Hurford Stone. You can see what is done to scribblers, Wordsworth. We cut them short.'

William left the city that evening. It was the seventh day of October, and he had only been in France for a few days. The way between himself and the Channel was beset by menacing pitfalls. South seemed safer, or as safe. He hurried towards Blois.

Two days later, Annette received a note delivered by a stranger. Again the handwriting was familiar, if a ghost can be said to be familiar, or a shadow. Again it looked like Williams' hand – but brought to her by a stranger? and from south of the river? where people can be lured and made to disappear?

Surely this was an attempt at entrapment? Several such tricks had been tried on them all since Paul had been sentenced.

She was known as a widow to all who asked for her. She was

recorded at the Prefecture and with the secret police as a widow.

'My husband is dead,' she said, handing the letter back to the man at the door. She saw no need to offer a coin to a spy from the police. 'If his ghost is still there and waiting for his letter, tell him to walk over the water to me. It's the least a ghost can do.'

This was a blasphemy, but these were ungodly times.

The next day, Jean-Marie Pardessus was at the door. 'Madame Williams,' he said, notaries and advocates being slow to accommodate the new, whether it be in name or style, 'Madame Annette, I bring disturbing news for us all, and a worse rumour for yourself in person.'

It seemed that the Jacobins of the local guard had tired of the law's delays and were about to put several dozen inmates of the town's prison to immediate execution. 'These men will certainly die if they go to Paris,' he explained. 'But for the moment there is no sign they can be sent there.'

'You imply that I know one of these people?'

'Perhaps. Their action has been precipitated by the arrest of an English spy. If he is indeed English and indeed a spy, he may – by the law of last October, fifteenth Vendémiaire – be summarily despatched. The problem is that a single execution – according to the method chosen – is frequently as expensive as fifty.'

Annette was puzzled by all this. 'What is the chosen method?'

'That I must ascertain – since I am the advocate for many of these people. Seemingly they have been brought to a hulk on the river, just below the bridge. The problem for our local officials is whether they should be incinerated, drowned or shot.'

He went through the house door, leaving her sickened at the thought of such slaughter. There had been no political executions in Blois so far. She wondered what could be done to prevent this one from taking place.

The younger Pardessus was back and clutching her wrist. 'The Lacailles are putting some muskets together, and some people stout-hearted enough to use them. As an officer of the court, I cannot advise a rescue, but I see no other way. Still, take heart, Madame Annette. Take heart and be of good cheer.'

She was at a loss at his concern for her. Was it that her

mother and sisters were out, and that he thought compassion an exclusively feminine matter?

He sensed her bewilderment and matched it with his own, clapping his hand to his brow. 'The rumour,' he cried. 'I presented you with the facts, and – good advocate that I am – I spared us both the rumour. The spy, Madame Annette Williams, is said to be your husband. Not an imagined husband of no name, but the actual Wodswod himself, your celebrated Englishman! Could that be so?'

Jean-Marie Pardessus defended many 'Whites', 'Chouans', non-juring clergy, émigrés, and people in general who were bored or revolted by the modern state. He was not a man of extremes himself, but he protected anybody's right to be bored or revolted by anything.

His enemies loved him. Like all of the greatest advocates he constantly reminded them how orderly, just, sincere, and high-and fair-minded they were. 'The Constitution is a noble instrument,' he would proclaim, before demolishing it crumb by crumb like an old woman tearing bread for the birds.

So it was now. He presented himself to the main deck of the hulk by the bridge. The stench was pretty intolerable, as the prisoners had been aboard for the best part of twenty-four hours.

He helped himself to a measure of snuff and passed his box to those who grouped themselves about him. 'Excellent,' he said. 'Excellent. I told you that your prisoners need a change of scene. You are all to be congratulated.'

'We brought them down here to do away with them, Maître.'

'Excellent. They'll die the happier for being able to watch those gulls. The woods over there will one day be regarded as a pretty sight, as soon as mankind acquires a decent appetite for nature – mark my words.' He passed his snuff box again. 'Well, gentlemen. If we're going to cut throats may I suggest we begin at once. I'll have to lodge my reports with the prefecture and with the Directory in Paris. Once we begin to kill people, it requires such a tedious amount of writing and such a tiresome mass of sig-natures.' He smiled, in case they thought he complained. 'I do congratulate you on your determination to reduce the prison population, just the same! Now how shall we begin?'

'We are not yet ready to begin, Citizen Pardessus.'

'Are we going for the rope, the bullet or the blade?'

'We were thinking of the river, maître.'

'Providing we begin at once, gentlemen. A man has the right to die in the forenoon, according to the law. A man, or in the case of a multiple execution such as this, a proportion of men. Until I have the numbers, I won't be able to advise you upon the size of the proportion.'

'If I have my way, Maître Pardessus, and very reasonable it is, all of these encumbrances to the Constitution will die more or less simultaneously.'

'What a brave sight that will be, Captain. I can see the Mayor agrees with you.'

The Captain of the Prison Guard began to speak very rapidly. 'We're not Septembrists. We're not going to drag these poor wretches out and hack them to pieces one by one.'

'Certainly not.'

'And what shall we do once we've done it? Four score of corpses will need a lot of burying, a deal of burning. What I say is – we have the river.'

'Exactly. Here in Blois we have the river.'

'And the river is clean.'

'The Loire is, above all, clement. It provides a merciful death. This method has been used before. It is called "republican marriage", citizens.'

Jean-Marie Pardessus became keener than bright. 'You have women here?'

'Certainly not, maître. Blois enacted bye-laws against the execution of women.'

'What hawks you are for matters of law, Captain and Mayor. And doves when it comes to clemency, I shouldn't wonder. Splendid men. You *must* have women for a "republican marriage". The ceremony requires you drown women yoked to men two and two about, much as the Good God created us.' He passed more snuff.

'This hulk is rotten,' the Captain said. 'What I suggest is we forget this marriage nonsense, and simply knock a plank or two out and let them sink.'

'Not above the town,' the Mayor protested. 'Some of us drink that water. And all of us have the women of our households do the wash in it.'

'That's why the rest of us don't drink it.'

'Listen to that church,' Pardessus cried out in an aggrieved tone. 'And listen to the great cathedral bell. Gentlemen, I'm afraid it is already noon, and as I understand the law we are already too late for today.' He passed yet more snuff. 'Let me ask you a question – which I shall, of course, follow with some more. Do you have a spy here?'

'That is why we are proceeding with them all,' the Mayor said.

'They are all spies?'

'If we use this hulk a hundred will be as cheap as just the one.'

'Can you give me the name of this spy?'

'He is Widow Williams' husband from the Rue du Pont.'

'A very sinister fellow, if he is indeed a widow's husband. Can you produce him to me – I take it he has had a fair trial? Or examination taken with evidence given on oath?'

'The truth of the matter is we do not have the Englishman Williams,' the Captain reported. 'All we have is a letter. We *thought* we should have him. That is why we went to all this trouble.'

'And I congratulate you on it. I congratulate you. I do not, however, think I can recommend to the Mayor of our City that he allows this execution to continue, even tomorrow, when it might well become legal at a duly appointed hour with a duly appointed headsman.'

'There you have it,' the Mayor agreed. 'I absolutely dare not let the execution continue.'

'Since you don't have a foreigner who is also a widow's husband and also a spy and also an excellent excuse to make a summary example of the rest of them, who aren't foreigners or widows' husbands, but who are potential spies and nuisances in every other way, I don't think I can recommend a single lawyer who will second the idea!'

'What do you suggest then, maître?'

'I suggest you tow this hulk downstream and set it on fire before it causes the city's noses to rot. After you have returned the wretches down below to their dungeons.'

He closed his snuff box with a considerable snap and pocketed it. Once he was ashore he turned and said, 'I shall write a very favourable report, gentlemen and citizens. You have acted with commendable humanity here in allowing both your prison and its prisoners a change of air.' As he walked back across the bridge he could be heard calling, 'Build some better evidence against them. It's your main and perhaps your only chance.'

At the town end of the bridge, he met over a dozen Lacailles and their apprentices. They were brandishing a variety of weapons, and carried bags and baskets as if they were going duck-shooting. 'No need,' he chuckled. 'No need at all, unless you intend to rescue them anyway when they're brought back across the bridge.'

'What do you suggest?' Grandad Lacaille asked him.

'Let them return to prison. We don't want four or five score guilty men milling around the town trying to hide in innocent people's attics.'

Someone had clearly attempted to betray her Williams. And someone else had equally clearly thought the treachery successful. Praise God it hadn't been.

Williams was here now, looking no meatier than a ghost, and a terrible source of danger – though, of course, entirely welcome.

He would eat upstairs with her family this night. He could, if they all dared and if he restrained his unnatural appetite for walking, stay a day or two. A day might be preferable to two days, because she knew now – by October 1793 – that the price of love could be a severed neck. In fact, tonight would be risk enough.

Meanwhile she kissed him, and kissed him. He kissed their child, who was compact and beautiful and clearly adored him, as she would any man else who made a fuss of her.

He told her his purpose in coming here had been to take her away with him. He now knew better than to ask. She longed to be with him, but she couldn't bear to leave here, not at this time. Nor could she risk the journey.

His efforts to bring himself here had left him numb with terror. He would certainly be unable to protect her. He was a man of peace lost in a war. She didn't mind that. His fear was the most palpable quality about him. She much preferred the bravery of terrified men to the mouthings of self-proclaimed heroes. Her circle was full of them.

He had proved himself by coming to her. Her Caroline's father had proved himself to be more than a mere poet.

The meal that followed was meagre, the talk affectionate but subdued. Even her mother was kind to him. The widow, the true widow, saw that the best they could hope for from Wodswod was his continued safety. And his love for herself and Caroline had placed that in considerable doubt.

He shared her narrow bed, and she lay for one night close in his arms, with Caroline in her cradle at her bed's foot. Her mother did not object. He was her husband. Or if not quite and no longer that, he was her only love, and she was one of the four people who made the rules in the house. They talked. They should have slept. They talked instead. They had a lifetime's talking to do. A year's at least, and perhaps a whole war's.

It wasn't a night of passion. There could be no passion between them, not with so much heartache and fear. Neither of them sought anything in the flesh, even as consolation. The next day would be so terrible they lay wrapped in each other as if both were going to their own execution, as indeed they might be at any time.

Her twenty-seventh birthday had passed. Her waist had thickened, then she had starved. She had done what no bourgeoise ought to do. She had walked out in the sun. She had crouched in riverboats in the rain.

Privately, and between the legs, her baby's birth had made her a changed woman. He did not touch her there, nor did she want him to.

In the morning they could scarcely speak to one another. The closeness of parting can rob love of its words.

She watched him as he stood beside her and clad his white skin. He did not look the same, even after so few months. He was emotional, wordless, desperately lacking French, and, yes – young.

He began to tell her about his poem, of all things. She was glad to hear him talk as the dawn quickened.

He understood, and only too well, that she could not leave Blois with her family impoverished, her stepfather dead, her mother ailing and her brother in hiding for his life.

Please, please God, let him go soon. She could not bear to see soldiers again invade her house and search for someone she loved.

Their means of escape presented itself at last at the back door. Jean-Marie Pardessus had spoken to Guyon de Montlivault on her behalf, and that nobleman had sent one of his carters. Williams was to go grinding north amid faggots of wood until he was well clear of Paris. Beyond there, who could tell? Montlivault's writ did not run for ever. It mightn't even last an English mile.

They kissed goodbye. He kissed Caroline endlessly, until the child tired of his cold nose. Annette would never tire.

'Until the Peace,' he said.

'Always,' she said. Then, 'Your lips taste of paper.' His face always smelled of writing materials.

'No,' he said. 'Not paper. Vellum. I'm a sheep.'

'From Cambridge.'

'From Cumberland!'

BLOIS 1793–1796.
AGREEABLE DAYS, DISAGREEABLE
MONTHS, SOPORIFIC YEARS.

If Williams had been taken and executed, she would not have believed it. Or if she heard he had been taken, and told of his execution, she would not. His presence here was so fleeting, its circumstances so unreal, and herself plunged into such an anxiety by it, that it was all best dismissed as a dream.

Then the letters started to arrive again, not many but some. He was back in England. He had scarcely been away. How real he seemed now he wasn't here. Her husband and lover was no longer a forgery. He was as noble and remote as an exquisite poem. She heard from Keswick, early in the New Year, and then, after an interval, from a place called Lincoln's Inn in London. Then from Racedown Lodge in Dorset. She tried to look for these names in map books that had belonged to her father or to Vergez. She could not always find them. A map was so insubstantial. It was like trying to read the future in a hand.

At least he was with his sister now. A man living with his sister was a comfortable arrangement to contemplate. And a letter, even when infrequent, was often more acceptable than the man who wrote it – perhaps because it didn't seize her by the hand and rush her down the road for walks she didn't want, often with stones or bullets flying. There were stones and bullets enough, and blades in the dark, without being rushed towards them.

The Vendéen War collapsed. It was half over by the time Williams had lain like a narrow ghost in her bed. Then the

Whites fought back, defeating huge national armies, and captured vast areas of France. In a month they were obliterated, many of them shot, others drowned as they tried to cross the Loire, which was formidably wide further down. Towns were burned, children slaughtered.

In Paris a great terror was afoot. The people she detested began to execute one another. The guillotine killed aristos, émigrés, traitors, priests, Brissotins, and finally the Jacobins themselves. The Jacobins were all that were left, so they killed one another. Then there were no more Jacobins and they were replaced by people who were even worse.

That was in Paris, where life was orderly. Elsewhere, people didn't give one another labels or employ the tidiness of the guillotine. No one quarrelled about politics. Men and women simply settled old scores. For a time, townspeople didn't have enough food to maintain a long fight for anyone against anything. But there is nothing like a brief spasm of rage if a man has the ambition to pluck out eyes or stamp on children. And in the valley of the Loire, and further south, there was always enough wine for any degree of rough behaviour.

The warrior Lacaille found his way back from the Vendée. The youngest Pardessus did not. He was not known to have been killed, but as day succeeded day he became a question that was no longer asked. Jean-Marie would abruptly change the subject, and he was a mist in the old man's eye.

Montlivault lost everything, and decided to call a meeting on the subject. The atmosphere was very comfortable in the upstairs salon now the conspirators at last had something to discuss.

'The thing is this,' the nobleman said. 'I arranged for a whole party of stout-hearted men to be trained in the woods. I paid for their horses, shared money among their wives. They gave an excellent account of themselves. Now they are dead.'

He received the expected murmurs of condolence, and Annette's whispered thanks for saving one of her own. Then he said, 'The fact is that defeated Whites are coming up the Loire, not many, but some. And then there's that silly business of the English.'

Annette thought he wanted thanking a second time for

Williams' rescue, but he explained himself differently. 'For reasons I never understood, the English Fleet put twenty thousand émigrés ashore in the West as well. Perhaps they wished to kindle or rekindle the Vendéen War. Perhaps—' and here he smiled kindly at Annette – 'perhaps, being English, they simply did not think what they were doing. Anyway, they beached them in the wrong spot, on a spit of land which was easily isolated and militarily untenable. On a kind of isthmus, with a very narrow neck.'

'Caesar has a word on that subject,' Old Pardessus mumbled. 'He says—'

'Caesar wasn't there to see it happen!' Montlivault did not take kindly to interruption. 'The fact is they had to surrender. These émigrés obviously aren't up to much, or they wouldn't be émigrés in the first place.' This was a novel concept, but no one wished to argue with it.

'They surrendered decently, and in an orderly fashion, laying down their arms in accord with the normal usages of war. So what does Paris do with them? It orders them instantly shot, all twenty thousand of them, bang through the head.'

Françoise began to fidget and Angélique to yawn. Annette thought she could guess where his argument was leading.

'So that's a second band of men making their way up the Loire.'

'Not if they're shot.' Old Pardessus was not about to forget Caesar in a hurry.

'Some of them ducked,' Montlivault said testily. 'Sometimes a fellow has to reload a musket, or a man can feign dead.'

'Ah!'

'We must search these people out, pick them up and bestow them. If not they'll be butchered piecemeal. They're being butchered now.'

'We can't hide them,' Madame Vergez put in. 'And if we can, we can't feed them.'

'You find them, I'll hide them,' Montlivault said. 'I've got some fifty widows to consider, and fifty unfilled places in their beds. If not, the secret police and their spies will be out counting husbands.'

This remedy seemed less than satisfactory to Annette, though on maturer consideration it struck her that almost anything was preferable to the guillotine, or even a bullet in the head.

Jean-Marie Pardessus it was who solved the matter. He suggested the open-air feast. 'I've always wanted to take a basket full of food and a great flask of wine, invite a few friends and just go and sit in the country and watch what the birds are doing. But no one has a word for the idea, and in consequence they won't do it.'

'Lunch on the grass it would have to be called,' Annette's mother said. '*Déjeuner sur l'herbe*' would be the silly Paris title, if anyone was ever foolish enough to invent such a thing.'

'You're not suggesting we trap the poor fellows with a plate of cold meat are you?' Montlivault asked.

'In a word, yes. We must not attract attention to ourselves. And if we go sneaking about, we will. Now if we put ourselves in a couple of carriages – yours and mine, say, Montlivault – and fill them up with these beautiful Vallon ladies, all four of them with sunshades, we could have a very agreeable ride in the direction of Cheverny.'

'Of *course*,' Madame thrilled – any mention of Cheverny always revived her – 'my late husband has already invented the idea, Jean-Marie. It isn't called Lunch on the Grass at all. No one could possibly believe *that*. It's called a *shooting* party. We must take his gun.'

'And mine,' Old Pardessus said. 'We must carry them to protect our lovely women against wolves and ruffians. Nothing but fowling pieces, mind. No one ever thinks he can be killed with a fowling piece, whereas lots of people are.'

'You've killed several,' his son Jean-Marie said.

'Vergez must also have done so in his time,' his widow mused. 'But if he did, he let them lie.'

During the next month of fine weather, the shooting party became a noted part of the social scene at Blois. The Comte and Comtesse of Cheverny themselves both recorded the fact in their journals, each of them very crusty at not being invited to accompany one of these forays, perhaps with musicians.

Nobody was allowed to join except the conspirators, and this did leave a great deal of noses out of joint. Especially since the Lacailles were included, and the Lacailles were only tradespeople, and travelled to the lunches in a wagon crammed with blunderbusses and men with red faces.

Forays through the Western Forest, the scene of Jean-Jacques' murder, brought in three trembling Whites. They had been hunted all the way from the Mauges, driven by men with guns, and sometimes beaten for, like rabbits.

South of the River was the better place. The Salogne echoed with distant gunshots – perhaps they were Vergez's own, still rolling about: Annette wasn't fully acquainted with the necessary science – and hid almost as many Whites as waterbirds. They brought in over thirty, at least one a day, as well as several émigrés from the English ships. These were very well hidden, and generally didn't even know of one another's whereabouts, but the Lacailles nosed them out with their dogs.

The dogs delighted Annette. A dog is even less secretive than a shooting party. It struck her that no man who walks in the forest with a pack of hounds could ever by any stretch of the imagination be accused of doing anything secretive. Huntsmen were, quite simply, the most perfectly clandestine people in the world. No one would suspect them.

They had a bad day. Perhaps they must start earlier tomorrow and drive further south. Perhaps there was not another fugitive to find. Only the Lacailles looked happy when they at last formed up with them at St Gervais-la-Forêt for the long drive home.

'We've got one,' they mouthed.

The rule was that anyone who was found was interrogated.

'I think we should ask him some question,' Annette said.

'I've still got thirteen widows,' Montlivault said tersely. 'He'll do for one of them provided he's got enough legs.'

The others were tired and thirsty. When a day is spent on wine, fresh water is at a premium.

'We made a rule.' Annette too was cross. 'We are not the ones who impose the penalty.'

'We can't look at him here,' Montlivault said.

The wagon was hard to turn, the coaches scarcely more easy,

but they swung them round at last and moved them back into the deeper quietness of the forest.

The man was slight, and possibly starving. He'd chosen an extremely damp hiding place and been in it several nights.

'You'd think he'd pick up a bit of woodcraft on the march,' one of the Lacaille apprentices observed, 'but, I daresay, being an aristocrat—'

Annette gazed into the man's dirty face and knew she had to denounce him.

'Weeks ago, months even, this man brought me a letter purporting to be from my husband. I had no proof then that he was a spy and none now. But if he was in Blois, and roaming at large, all those weeks ago then he's not just come up from the West.'

'Interesting,' Jean-Marie reflected. 'Now what I proposed is—'

The Lacailles had already taken the fellow. After a few minutes they came back. Their faces were as waxen as candles and sweated rather more. 'They won't find him,' one said. 'Nobody will. Not out here. And if they do, there won't be a mark on him.'

Children of eighteen months have their truths as well. 'Man,' Caroline said, 'man went into trees.'

Someone had sent him. Someone was keeping an eye on them. The hunting parties would have to end.

The knocking on their door that night was particularly startling because totally unexpected. They were sitting at the family table, when a maid brought in a lad of fifteen. 'I've been told to ask here,' he said. 'We've come from the Vendée. My father has just been shot.'

Charles Henry and his bride sat at table with them. Indeed, they had brought the food, since he was in receipt of all the good things that used to come the way of his stepfather and his brother Jean-Jacques.

'Does your father need help?' he asked.

'No, sir. He's beyond that.'

'Who shot him?'

'Your Town Guard, the National Guard, the Army – who knows?' the lad said. 'Everyone shoots us.' He had a hearty appetite, just the same.

'I think we should wring his neck in a blanket,' Madame Vergez said under her breath.

'They won't use a boy as a spy,' Françoise Anne said. 'Even I know that. Besides, he's got clean teeth. Whoever saw a spy with clean teeth?'

'Equally,' said Angélique with her evening giggle, 'he's much too young for a widow's bed.'

'Your name is Lacaille,' Charles Henry said. 'I know it's not, but from henceforth it is, or we'll never be able to stow you.' He threw down his napkin and looked at the lad. 'Do you want to be a gunsmith? Well, you'd better.' He resumed his napkin and his spoon for several minutes of intense eating, pleased with his own genius. 'The thing is I'm taking on a Lacaille as a surgeon-apprentice, and looking after you can be my price to them in the matter.'

'The authorities can never keep track of the Lacailles,' Annette's mother said. 'But I still think we should strangle him in a towel.'

The trouble with these hunting parties on wheels was an ongoing one, even when the wheels stopped rolling. Hunting on wheels was a privileged pastime – all hunting was – but it caught few ducks. The populace wasn't to know it, of course, but they weren't hunting ducks. Sieur Vergez hunted ducks. Sieur Vergez was a good man, well remembered now dead, and better by far than some of his family yet living. Sieur Vergez used to share his ducks, the citizen Vergez did.

So it was they had hungry people at their door for a second time, even though they themselves were hungry.

'What shall we do, mother? Do you want us to kiss them again?' Angélique offered the idea as a serious suggestion.

'Send a maid out the back for the Lacailles.'

The Lacailles brought several dozen of themselves, men and boys and their new apprentice, together with some new muskets they wanted to try. They also brought Jean-Marie Pardessus.

Their first volley was aimed high, and fell midway across the town bridge.

The crowd thought nothing of it. Shots in the air were com-
monplace nowadays. So were shots through the hair. The crowd
also knew it takes most of a minute to reload a musket. In that
time a crowd can charge.

Crowds did not charge the Lacailles. The Lacailles brought
ready loaded muskets by the box. They brought them by the
cartful. The Town Guard arrived. That was what Jean-Marie was
for.

'Bravo, gentlemen!' he called. 'Bravo! The problem is this
way. This volunteer detachment of vigilant citizens has been
keeping things in check for you. But we're in a desperate case,
gentlemen. Almost a pickle! I doubt we could have protected the
peace a second longer. Praise God, you arrive so promptly.'

'I know you, Lacaille,' the Commandant of the Town Guard
said. 'I know you all, and I'm confiscating those muskets for a
start. You understand me?'

'Perfectly,' the oldest Lacaille said. 'You want my muskets,
then come and get them. I have to warn you they have very delicate triggers and are likely to go off. Of course, if you're saying
you want to *buy* some, then I'll readily adjust the action to suit
you.'

So do riots end in rage and laughter. The survivors are those
who can rely upon their friends. And so do the months and years
pass.

BLOIS.
INTERTWINING DATES AND
INTERWEAVING YEARS, ALL WITH
TOO MANY KNOTS FOR A WOMAN
TO HANG HERSELF.

It was a letter from England – but not from Williams. Her heart leapt and sank almost in the same instant. She had learned to expect this double knock of emotion, but she couldn't grow used to it. Letters were so rare.

She read it quickly, not even chuckling over Dorothy's French. She looked for news of Williams, greetings from Williams. But he sent none, not by this letter. He had been walking with a man called Coleridge. In Blois, and from Blois, fresh from her arms, he'd walked with a fool called Beaupuy. He was probably wearing the same funny boots. She began to laugh and then to cry. Oh and he was writing a poem, Dorothy said. He was always writing a poem. He was writing a poem in Orléans, then in Blois. He'd scribbled a poem all across France.

'Caroline,' she called, trying for the child's sake to be happy through her tears. 'Caroline, my darling. It's a letter from my sister, your Aunt Dorothy. She sends us news of Daddy.'

'Daddy's dead,' the child said gravely. 'Bad men killed him over there in the forest. Even Grandad could not save him.'

'That was your uncle, Caroline Anne. That was your uncle Jean-Jacques. Daddy is alive and in another country.'

'Daddy's dead.'

Brother and lover – the griefs were intermingled. Widow William dried her tears. She couldn't be a widow if she told Caroline her father wasn't dead.

Only yesterday she had attended a wedding in a private chapel, a wedding that had been given by a non-juring priest. Afterwards she had been asked to sign as one of the witnesses in the chapel register.

Her signature was Madame William Wordsworth Vallon. Even her brother Charles Henry had insisted on having his marriage to the Charruyau girl blessed by a non-juring priest.

Williams and his Dorothy were at Racedown now. She was glad to know her husband and his sister had a life together, irked to hear he had received several sums of money only to lend them to other people.

Not that she could be persuaded to join them in Dorset, even if peace were declared tomorrow.

If peace were declared tomorrow, she would want her husband here, where there was warmth and wine. Unfortunately, Williams did not feel the need for wine, nor probably for warmth, and his sister Dorothy, though loving, was by her own account a very frugal young woman. Bread and sops was their usual fare. Even when starving, the Vallons ate better than that.

Suddenly her brother Paul was pardoned. This good news obliterated everything from England. Paul could at last leave his hiding place in the house of Monsieur Lochon-Pettibois where he was able to do nothing except brood for two years, and grow extremely fat. A small man, scarcely taller than a donkey's tail, he had aged and become introspective with not even his gambling to distract him. And as for the company of women, he must be starving for it. He knew so many, yet for over two years had been able to see none of them. Praise God Williams was not like her brother.

Now Paul could return to his work, and live in his room at the Dufours' where he could flirt with the maids.

Jean-Marie Pardessus came to see her often, and frequently enlisted her support. Men and women were constantly being oppressed under the new régime, and Pardessus needed someone who would write a good letter to harangue the Prefect.

He went through her latest batch of documents. 'Ha!' he said. 'You strike the *exact* tone.'

'I should know it,' she answered. 'I've caught it from you.' She took the letter from him and explained, 'It is only with difficulty that I can retain my patience with Prefect Corbigny. And his servants. I've called into his office at least four times in order to gain the release into wider surveillance of that poor fellow Fonteney. He'll starve if he's put on daily report in Blois. If only they transfer him into open arrest at Vendôme, he has a living there.'

'You'll win for certain,' Pardessus said. 'Listen to you. "Forgive my last importunity, for I am determined no more to trouble you . . . nothing will make me forgo the pleasure of doing good, but I shall manage to set bounds to it." The poor Prefect is certain to surrender to you, Annette. May I?' He helped himself to some wine from the carafe on the writing table, and cleared his throat. 'Madame Annette,' he said. 'It cannot have escaped you that I call here very often.'

'You are welcome, Jean-Marie. You are a valued friend of the family.'

'I come here to see you, Annette.'

'You ask me to write letters. I write them. You have taught me a very great deal in the casting of them.'

'Madame Annette, it will take me a little time to come to what I have to say.'

'In the interval, I shall sign this letter if I may. Will you glance at the others and remind me how I style myself?'

He picked up her morning's correspondence and read it through. 'You favour the new style. You sign yourself "Wife William".'

'It is, as you say, the fashion for us married women now, Jean-Marie. That is how I propose to sign this one, and all of the many hundreds more you will surely ask me to write.'

Pardessus blushed, looked pained, said nothing.

'Thank you for helping me, Jean-Marie. Am I to assume that I, in my turn, have helped you with the speech you were proposing to make?'

He nodded, still speechless.

'Well, you honour me.'

Jean-Marie Pardessus never tried to make his speech again, but he continued to call with tasks for her. In the early Summer of

1796 he presented himself to the entire family in a state of extreme agitation. Annette was always surprised to see such a self-assured man as Jean Marie behaving like this. Sometimes, she allowed herself to enjoy the thought that he had never been perturbed about anything until that morning he had been on the verge of declaring his love for her.

'This pernicious act of the twenty-second Germinal, Year Four of the Republic,' he said.

Nobody in the Vallon household, not even Madame herself, thought to rebuke anyone's use of the Revolutionary Calendar by now.

'It makes a bad situation worse for émigrés and juring priests,' Annette said. 'Their lot was grievous already, so what of it?'

'It means summary execution,' Pardessus said. 'Local process is enough. Summary process will do. The matter need not go to Paris.'

'Nor should it,' the ageing Widow said, stern even if frail. 'Blois never used to go to Paris. Blois used to be the capital of France.'

'There are two such people in the prison this morning,' he said.

'What can you do about it?' Annette asked.

'I? Nothing. Nothing more. I tried for three hours.'

'There's no guillotine in Blois, and we don't have a headsman.'

'They are going to hang them. Tomorrow.' Poor man. He was totally unused to failing.

'Call the Lacailles,' Annette said. 'We don't need the whole group. I shall get the prisoners out tonight.'

'It will take a clever scheme.'

'Just a little luck,' she smiled. 'Not even gambler's luck. Just a little of it.'

Dawn was an inconvenience. These early days in Summer it came stark and early.

Annette went with her five fellow conspirators to the prison, which was conveniently close to the Rue du Pont, just as the sky was growing light.

A stone, wrapped in a sack to muffle it, was attached to a guide cord. This was thrown by a Lacaille – who else? – so that it struck the roofing above the high outer wall. Three times he threw it. Three times it bounced back. At each throw he angled it further along the wall. When it bounced back the fourth time it passed round one of the crenellations which formed an imitation battlement along the top of the wall.

They played out more cord and the stone sank back to hand. They fastened a rope to the guide cord, and a rope ladder to the end of the rope.

The rope jammed behind the battlement and refused to budge.

The Lacaille who was John Henry's apprentice was with them, and he was only sixteen. He was by far the lightest person in the party, except for Annette. And she was there merely to lead, not swarm up a rope.

'Climb the rope,' they said to John Henry's apprentice. 'It's a change of plan, we grant you. But it's firm enough. Look – we can't dislodge it. You can' t fall.'

'If you do fall we shall catch you,' Annette promised.

The wall was as high as the tallest house in Blois. The boy crossed himself and climbed the rope. Once on the battlement, he freed the rope, passed it round the crenellation and brought up the rope ladder. This he secured as best he could.

Three people held the end of the rope, in case he hadn't fastened the ladder well enough. The lad came back down the ladder, and joined his weight to those holding the rope.

Two men quickly climbed up the ladder, crossed themselves at the top and made their way along the top of the wall until they had rounded the angle of the roof. They found a drainpipe and used it to climb into the courtyard below.

Jean-Marie had drawn them a sketch of the prisoners' whereabouts, and apparently they found them quickly. Annette had calculated that the guards would be sleeping the sleep of the honourably drunk, and they were. They were paid very little in money, but mostly by kind. This was principally food and wine. The only liberal part of their allotment was the wine. If the keys were on a hook, well and good. If they were on a drunkard's belt, that would be where the luck came in.

Three figures appeared on the wall. One of them was a Lacaille. The other two were the prisoners. The two prisoners climbed down the rope. Lacaille turned back to find his relative, who had been left behind as a decoy in case the alarm was given.

The prisoners tried to embrace everyone. 'We were to hang at noon,' one said.

'You still may,' Annette said. 'You must follow me, please.' She led them briskly towards Pardessus' house. Pardessus would pass them to Montlivault as soon as possible.

Just then she heard a patrol approaching them. 'Walk quickly,' she said. 'But only run if they do.' She turned them towards the Rue du Pont.

The men tugging on the rope to secure the ladder stuck to their task. The chance was that they could have escaped. The two men inside could have wound up the rope ladder and waited on the roof, then looked for a way to secure it once the patrol had gone.

She heard shouts, a shot. The men outside the wall had been arrested.

Another shot. The wind of its passing plucked at her hair. They had seen her, and fired on her. Had she been recognized?

She stole home and waited with her sister.

Ten minutes later Jean-Marie was with them. He had passed the escapers on. 'Montlivault has them now. They're in some barrels on a horse sledge. No one will ever stop it, but the ride will be uncomfortable.'

Again the house was invaded by the Town Guard, front door and back door, in the way she had grown used to. The only difference was that they had to knock this time. Françoise was for leaving them outside, but Annette had too much respect for her mother's paintwork.

They searched the house only briefly. Annette had been recognized. There were some rope needles and sheets in the kitchen. Also a small piece of rope which would undoubtedly match the ladder.

'There is no need to arrest her,' Pardessus said. He handed round snuff and poured some of the Vallon wine, which the men were eyeing as if minded to help themselves to anyway. 'All you need do is charge her formally in my presence, as an official of the court. Then release her into my supervision for an agreed cognizance, which I will lodge with you later. May I suggest eight hundred livres?'

They considered eight hundred livres.

'There will, of course, be a small handling charge to yourselves. Come now, gentlemen. You can't possibly shut a young woman, with her child, into the town prison. This will ultimately be a capital matter. You'll want her to look her best.'

The beauty and composure of women as they mounted the scaffold were frequently noted. Was there not Charlotte Corday?

Annette was charged and released against the lawyer's surety.

They had saved two men from the hangman. The six of them could be *en route* to the guillotine in consequence.

'I am suing for your case to be heard in Orléans,' Jean-Marie told her.

'That means that you can't defend us.'

'True. But I can see no defence. If you go to Orléans you will face an Inquisition by Jury. You will be questioned by your peers and the matters decided by your peers.'

'We'll be brought up before the Jacobins there. They'll associate my name with my brother Paul and Gellet-Duvivier.'

'I think not. The Terror has ended, Madame Annette. Most people are sick of it, and the Orléanais have had more of it than most people. Have you done as I advised?'

'Yes. It's in the loft. Nobody found it.'

'Good. I must go and advise my other clients.'

The defence was very simple. Six people had been out very early for a walk. It was indeed early, and walking was not an exercise the bourgeoisie normally countenanced, but there was to be an execution, did the Jury recall?

It was a callous thing to admit, but the two condemned were manifest villains, and the walkers were out to glimpse for themselves where the gallows were to be erected, then leave one of their number to guard a spot while the rest went to fetch some chairs. Did the Jury understand?

The Jury understood.

To their surprise they noticed a rope ladder badly attached to the wall.

'But one of you scaled the ladder.'

'Two of us,' a Lacaille said. 'I was the first. My friends were fearful the prisoners had escaped. I said they couldn't possibly have escaped or be about to escape. The ladder was badly secured and clearly wouldn't hold them. So I tried it.'

'And?'

'It held me. So I scaled it without further difficulty. This fact alarmed me, so I walked along the wall.'

'Why was this?'

'To determine if there was indeed an escape in progress and, if so, find a responsible person to report the matter to.'

'And why did you go up?'

'My friends sent me up to bring Lacaille down. They wanted us all to walk round to the front door of the prison and tell the guard we had found the ladder.'

'Why didn't they go anyway?'

'They felt their weight was needed on the rope that fastened the imperfectly secured ladder.' The speaker gazed at every member of the Jury in turn. 'This is proved by the fact that even with the dawn patrol of the Town Guard marching very noisily towards us, none of them and neither of us attempted to run away. And very noisily that Town Guard does march.'

Here her brother Paul rose to address the Jury. He had no right before such a Tribunal, or he had every man's rights. He rose, be that as it may. 'Gentlemen, there is no evidence against any of the accused, except that they were there and did not run away, which is not denied.

'It is true that they are charged with helping two prisoners escape, and those prisoners escaped. No one saw them escape, or saw them being helped to escape. The villains themselves are not here. *They* would have told us what role, if any, these men fulfilled. But the villains, as I say, are not here. They are the only witnesses, and they cannot be produced.'

'But what of the evidence against the woman? The men are obviously innocent, but the woman is another matter entirely.'

They examined the evidence against the woman. It would obviously go badly for her. The escape had been carried out by means of a rope ladder. Fragments of similar rope had been found in her kitchen. A river chandler's had given the Watch Committee a deposition to the effect that the accused Annette Vallon, her legal name – she is also known as Wife William, Madame William, Widow William – the accused *Demoiselle* Vallon purchased twenty-seven fathoms of that same rope the day before the crime.

'Well, Demoiselle Vallon.'

'I did purchase the rope. I freely admit it. And paid good money for it.'

'Why, Vallon?'

'To make a Summer cradle for my child. I couldn't do it. It was too stiff. I cut no more than a thumbnail of the stuff, the fragments the guardsmen picked up in my mother's kitchen. The rest of it, all twenty-seven fathoms of it, is still in the loft. They didn't search the loft.'

'They didn't search the loft, you say?'

'Ask him. He was the picket commander. And that one there is the Secret Policeman – if he will own up to being such a thing. Ask them if they looked into the loft.'

They had not searched the loft.

'This matter will have to be verified, Vallon.'

'Well, send someone round to do it then. It's a huge distance to Blois, but you have messengers to command. And horses.'

It did take some time, but there was clearly no case against them, lacking evidence as they did, and witnesses other than themselves.

As soon as they were acquitted they became very drunk. Then they rode back to Blois in a carriage belonging to Berruet, the coffee-house keeper.

When they reached the Rue du Pont, the festivities began in earnest.

This was not her last escape from punishment, nor by a long way her last rescue. If she could achieve a just result by picking up her pen, so be it. Prefect Corbigny was showing himself to be a reasonable man, and he seemed to enjoy the verbal fencing with her. She knew he sent spies after her and her friends, but – rather like Williams – he was inclined to see the best in people. He obviously took everything his minions told him about her with a large pinch of salt. This could only be to her good, because some of her friends were indiscreet, and his spies must often have brought him disturbing news.

Why did she think of him as often as she thought of her husband? Was it because their letters were so similar – rare, brief and coolly to the point? He was as young as Williams, too, if not a year or two younger – at as ridiculously youthful an age for him to be appointed prefect at twenty-two as it was for Williams to take on the duties of a parent. He was a Breton, too, a man born so far away, she might just as easily think of him as an Englander, a word she had just picked up from her émigrés. They were full of such like *argot* from the Low Countries!

Poor dear silly Corbigny! She regarded him in those terms, much as she regarded Williams, because he wasted his time on pretentious and unnecessary pursuits. Just like her beloved Williams, he wrote poems and tragedies.

In spite of Corbigny, life held many tiny triumphs for her. She spent days being anxious, and whole nights aware of her sisters' terrified sleep. Sometimes the house seemed to mutter with bad dreams, as they lay fearing the knock on the door, or the tar-soaked incendiary through the window. Then the fugitive would leave his hole in the attic, the town be once more in order, and she could rejoice. Happiness, she realized, was not made by the presence of husbands. It was being calm, seeing Caroline run round the rooms and play. Most, it was having enough to eat.

The sisters' great stratagem for eating was to proclaim a feast. They proclaimed feasts on saints' days, they proclaimed them for the old-fashioned calendar months and old-fashioned Sundays. They held them spontaneously for each successful escape or piece of good news.

Then, lest the watchers became suspicious, they came to celebrate the New Calendar as well, all the way from Vendémiaire to Fructidor. They raised glasses to every décadi. One of their greatest nights of wassailing celebrated the day when poor Fabre

D'Eglantine, the poet who'd invented the Calendar, left his inspiration on the scaffold. His mouth, according to the chronicles of the guillotine, took a full quarter of an hour to die. 'Even with his head struck off,' Angélique said, 'he went on reciting rubbish.' Her giggle had grown throaty of late. Her sisters hoped it would soon sink to her chest and be swallowed up altogether. Poor Fabre D'Eglantine.

The advantage of proclaiming a feast was that people would bring them food. Jean-Marie Pardessus, the whole Lacaille family, their own brother Charles Henry – such people were more and more often paid in kind, especially by peasants, chandlers and farmers. An amputation, for example, and quite certainly a new musket, whether flint-fire or percussion, would be worth rather more kindness than an ordinary larder could hold, so the recipients could with a little flattery be persuaded to share. As Charles Henry's new wife said to them, 'It's a pleasure being related to you all in the hot weather. Otherwise my house would stink of bad meat.'

'I prefer Angel,' Françoise whispered. 'If Angel could still lay her hands on food, she would not only bring it here, she would cook it for us.'

Madame the widow merely grunted. She regarded her own kitchen still to be entirely competent, even if frequently bare.

(Françoise Anne and Angélique Adelaïde had shortened their names, after the Republican fashion. Annette's name had been shortened for her, so she felt free to disapprove of them, though she knew that modern women, as her mother called them, will always follow the latest fad.)

Once a woman's name has been suitably shortened, life can happen to her much more quickly. This was only Annette's impression, but it was borne out by coming on Françoise giggling – yes, *Françoise* – giggling with Angélique one breakfast time just after their guests had gone home, and the two were alone in the kitchen.

She seemed reluctant to continue her giggle in front of a married woman, but their mother was long since abed and Caroline not yet waking, so she said, this time without amusement, 'I've never done it before, now I seem to have it done with everyone. It's really quite feasible with wine – a bit like bob-dance, or kiss-in-the-ring. But it can't be very enjoyable for a woman when she's sober, do you think?'

They whispered together for a moment, and then it was Angélique who confessed, 'The thing is amusing enough, but it always has a man on the end of it, and they're always much too serious. Think of Jean-Marie Pardessus.'

'Think of *Old* Pardessus.'

'Or Guyon de Montlivault. He sits on himself as if he's still astride a horse.'

'I don't think I'll do it again.'

Annette gazed severely at her two older sisters. 'If you do, you could catch yourself an April Fish, the way I did.'

This was an early caution against Springtime Folly, as the month was still January, and they had just been celebrating the arrival of Pluviôse, poor silly Fabre D'Eglantine's Month of Rain. Annette was glad that her sisters already judged that rain enough had fallen upon them overnight to last them a season. She went to snuggle in bed beside Caroline, grateful to be a married woman far beyond needing men.

Ventôse was a windy month indeed for Françoise, and both of the older women were quick to be suspicious. Inquisitive sisters won't keep their hands off one another's bellies, nor in prudence or decency should they when food is short, and the fact was that by mid-Germinal one of them was clearly budding, and continued so through Floréal, Prairial, Messidor and Thermidor. By this time even their mother was asking questions, in spite of loosely tied Summer gowns, this being the Month of Heat.

'Who, exactly, is responsible for this?' she demanded.

This question had been asked of her very fiercely and very often, not least by Françoise herself, but she was completely unable to reply.

'Françoise Anne, I insist on knowing who is responsible for this.'

'Françoise is,' Angélique said helpfully. 'Françoise and a man.'

The father was never known, not for certain. He was clearly one of several, but Françoise could not even remember which several, the wine had been so strong, the dancing so robust, or

her discretion so absolute. She couldn't name a several it might
be, nor even a several it certainly was not. 'I think it was all of
them,' she confessed. 'It was certainly one of them all.'

Since there was so much confusion about its origins it was
appropriate the poor child was born on the tenth day of
Brúmaire, the Month of Fog.

'The case is far different from Annette's,' their mother had
decided as long ago as Messidor. 'Annette's Caroline has a father.'

'And Annette has a husband,' Angélique said. 'We saw them
both married.' Her giggle had sunk a long way now, and
sounded very like a scold.

The birth wasn't an easy one. When it was over, Françoise
had – but didn't have – a son. Charles Henry immediately took
the babe away from her, and placed it in the orphanage of the
hospital. The family gave him nothing but a name. He was called
Toussaint Décadi, and in his orphan name both calendars were
united.

Françoise wept a lot, and her sisters suffered with her. Their
grief did not abate, nor did they relent their determination to
part with the child. Toussaint Décadi was not another Caroline
Wordsworth. He did not have a father, either in fact or in name.

During this time of grieving their mother chose to die.

Sister Dorothy wrote the letters now. They were full of news
of Williams, a Williams who greeted his daughter as Dorothy did
her niece in phrases fastened as carefully together as a child
threads daisies.

Annette searched the letters anxiously, unpicking word from
word, syllable almost from syllable. She was looking for the
flower that spoke of Williams' love.

BLOIS AND CALAIS, 1796–1802.
OLD-FASHIONED VALUES

A few letters from Williams began to arrive again, for Caroline and herself. His sister, Caroline's Aunt Dorothy, always wrote the warmer ones, but England is a stone cold place for men, though their hearts can always be made to thaw out after a short time in France.

Apparently, just as poor Françoise was pushing Toussaint Décadi from the warmth of her body then away into the hostile world, Williams published a notorious book of poems. He had written it with an accomplice, the frequently mentioned Coleridge, who was clearly his English Beaupuy.

Beaupuy, as it happened, was dead. She had not yet given herself the satisfaction of writing this to Williams, other matters seeming more important.

The sisters had held two feasts to rejoice at the slaying of such a triple-headed contradiction as he was: an aristocratic republican who was latterly a hero of France and general of the line.

The first feast, the best one, was a mistake. It turned out to be not the betrayer himself but a brother merely who was slain by the Whites in the Vendéen War. Thoughtless of the man to have brothers, thoughtless but typically so, several of them rising to be generals of France. Brothers of the same surname were confusing to historians, and even more so to her sisters and herself who dwelled in Blois and had to content themselves with rumours.

So when he was killed properly and finally in the November of 1796 at the Battle of the Elz, and brought low not by Frenchmen but by Austrians, the sisters had to spread another table.

Poor dear Angel refused to attend either feast. The renegade had been a lodger of hers, and dandled her babies as well as helping her wind her wool. Williams had been a lodger there too, and Angel's reluctance to rejoice was a salutary reminder of the futility of mixing business with pleasure.

Then, after the second feast, Annette found herself weeping as well. She loved Angel, and hated the thought that her friend and poor dead brother's widow could find anything to moisten her eyes that she could not share in. She remembered that Michel Beaupuy had been boy of honour at her wedding. He had brought his friends to guard the bridal coach, and had arranged her night of consummation at the forest's edge. Poor brave man. Surely he would forgive the Vallon sisters their somewhat mocking wake?

She had, after all, many matters on her mind. There was Caroline, starvation, and the endless fight against the violence that threatened from everything new in France. She must try to protect the victims of the Directory, the Committee of Public Safety and latterly the Consulate. She must try to protect love against the passage of time.

Annette was thirty-five and her daughter was nine. These were wounding figures, best passed over quickly, as latterly her face in the glass. Peace was breaking out between France and England. It came shyly and uncertainly, like a meeting between friends who had not seen each other for nearly ten years. Such a meeting was what Williams proposed.

She read his letter again. Not a letter from Dorothy. A letter from him. The same hand, presumably not with a borrowed pen. They must meet and renew their acquaintance, it said. Dear friends that they were, they had many matters to discuss, one above all others.

It was neither a friendship nor an acquaintance, was it? Both of them had been lovers, and at least one of them married, even if no country but the Kingdom of Heaven recognized the fact. He did not write, in truth, as if the extension of his marriage vows was uppermost in his mind. Nor, to be plain with herself, was it at the forefront of her own.

A peace with England meant nothing to a woman who had tasks to complete in France. It meant, quite simply, that England had grown weary of trying to help her. In the time of her separation from Williams, France had been governed by the mob, then by a committee of maniacs until it had sunk to where it was now.

'Mark my words,' Montlivault said – he was terser of late, and more people listened to him. 'We are given over to the whims of a monster and two fools. How long can we expect the fools to survive?'

She couldn't leave France for Williams, any more than she ever could. And if he stayed here with her? She'd still have the same tasks to perform, the same battles to wage. It was good his latest letter did not promise much. At least it didn't threaten to alter things.

Her uncertainties were soon over. She had given everything for love in her day, and love was not dead. She packed her bag urgently but with, yes, just a tinge of fear.

As she fastened it and began to lay garments out for Caroline, she heard a clock strike, higher up the town. How often she had counted her miseries by that clock! She was more than familiar with love's war with time.

Time does not destroy love, this noon chime said, cannot conquer it, or not a love like hers. It simply moves it aside.

The road to Calais was better than she expected. At least – save for one terrible incline – it was flat.

When the coach reached the foot of this slope, the passengers alighted to walk. The way was little more than a gouged track which ran diagonally up a grass hill then skirted a precipice of chalk and rubble. Caroline scampered ahead. Meetings held no terrors for her.

Annette travelled eagerly enough. She so much longed to see Williams. She had no intention of falling under his spell again. His body would be older now. Hers certainly was. It was unseemly for a woman to gaze upon herself, unseemly but inevitable. She did not like what she saw.

Her greatest need, and her least complicated one, was for Caroline to know her father. Caroline, praise God, had a father even more certainly than she herself had a husband. The parish records at Saint Croix recorded the name of Caroline's father for everyone to see. Her sister by comparison had no such husband, even in the register of Heaven, and poor little Toussaint Décadi had no one to call father at all.

Calais was hot. It smelled of mussels and rot, and not in a way that Blois and Orléans ever did. The land was in a mess hereabouts, and finished as she knew it must but had never seen before. It piled itself into a heap then slid into the sea. The sea itself was not very remarkable. What was best about it, and what an idle person might give herself time to reflect on, was the fact that in spite of what it did it remained where it was and kept itself tidy.

As soon as she arrived there, she was shown England in the distance. It was tiny and white and chalky, she supposed much like the hill Caroline had scampered up. As she gazed, it began to fade, like teeth disappearing when a face forgets to smile.

She quickly found lodgings in the Rue de la Tête d'Or. Her landlady, Madame Avril, was someone quite outside Annette's experience. She was a person who let rooms. She wasn't a friend of her brother's like Marie-Victorie-Adelaïde, with whom one could become friends oneself and have an arrangement. Still less was she anything like poor mad Monsieur Gellet-Duvivier.

It threatened to be a strange business, this meeting in Calais. Why Calais? Why not at home at Blois, with her sisters? Williams had to travel a long way to reach here, of course, much further than she did, now he had at last been able to buy his cottage in the North of England. He was bringing Dorothy, too, and Dorothy as a traveller was a bit of a fuss, though it would be good for Caroline to meet another English relative, especially the aunt who wrote her such friendly little notes when the war let her receive them.

Presumably the Englishwoman – her *sister* in all their letters – was here to play the chaperone?

Let her watch over them as hard as she would. It showed a decent – if irritating – prudence on Williams' part. Much as she loved Caroline, and her daughter was nearly *all* her love, she didn't want to risk that kind of bother again, not even in Blois with a husband in attendance. And as for expecting a child and needing to cringe away to some rainswept cottage in Cumberland to be delivered by – what did Williams say? – a shepherd . . . Let sister Dorothy play the chaperone for all she was worth!

They arrived at last, Williams and his sister. Dorothy was handsome enough, pretty in a strange English way, with a skin that looked as if it had never seen sunshine and would melt in the rain like a bar of soap. She reminded Annette of no one so much as the Demoiselle. She needed a man to kiss her or a woman to give her a good spank. She had a lovely smile for Caroline though, but was fatigued from her journey and the sea-crossing as the fashion was, and soon summoned Williams back to their lodgings for some rest. The pair of them left Caroline and Annette with a good deal to talk about.

The next day they met over a meal, and Annette was amazed at how little Dorothy could eat, and how quickly Williams disposed of substantial amounts of food, his own and most of the meal on his sister's plate.

They both joked with Caroline, and Dorothy sang her a song in English. She had a poorish voice, but perhaps songs in English are like that. Annette couldn't understand the words, so had time to concentrate on the tune. Caroline asked her father why he hadn't learnt to speak yet. She told him that the babies at the orphanage who had no one to teach them knew more words than he did. Williams laughed and was delighted by her.

Then they all went for a walk by the sea. Williams wanted to bathe, but Dorothy wouldn't let him. It was as if she and only she had all of the rights in the matter. Williams muttered something and wrote a poem. He said it was about Caroline, and showed it to both of them, but of course they couldn't understand it.

Dorothy said it was masterly, and reminded him how pleased she was to have induced him to have a look at Milton's sonnets again, whatever they were.

This talk was not for Caroline, but she enjoyed her ball and the waves. The child clearly loved them both, and they loved her – as they should, her father and aunt.

These brief meals, these poetical walks went on for some days. Dorothy kept drawing Williams aside and urging him in English to do something. Williams preferred to wait. He'd always preferred to wait when they'd been in Orléans and Blois.

Then Dorothy said abruptly, 'William, I think you must have your talk with Annette *now*.' She spoke in French, and her accent was still very strange. She took Caroline by the hand and led her along the beach.

Annette walked with Williams for some time. He said nothing and went on saying nothing, until the silence amused her. Imagine poor dear Paul being able to take even a step and not talk!

In the end, she grew tired of waiting. Walking tired her quickly. She said, 'My husband, you are trying to find a way of saying that – much as we have been friends this past week – we cannot go back to the old way of loving?'

He looked pale, but nodded in agreement.

'Therefore it follows that you do not wish to strengthen our marriage ties, which we made before God but in accord to the laws of neither of our countries?'

Again he nodded.

'Then what about Caroline? You have, I concede, already given her your name.'

'Caroline Wordsworth is my daughter,' he said. 'My firstborn child. I can do nothing for her yet, nothing more than I have done, which is little. But when she marries – as we both pray she will – then, if my career prospers, I hope to find her a suitable marriage portion.'

She digested this news, which was heavy but not in itself hard to bear. In reality, it was much as she'd resigned herself to for goodness knows how many years.

She heard Caroline's laugh, and saw Dorothy returning with her.

'You speak of marriage, Williams, as if it is a subject on your mind.'

'I speak of Caroline marrying.'

'I think it is in your own mind, too.'

'Yes,' he said. 'Yes, it is.' He tried to hold her. He clearly wanted to cry. But Caroline was back with them now. And his sister, interrogating him with a hard, bright stare.

When somebody is about to acquire what you think you no longer want, you have to remind yourself many times over that you no longer want it. That was her first thought on her first night of not sleeping, and it led to bad dreams at dawn.

When she woke, she thought how easy it had been to be separate from him when she was sure he had no one. Now he had another woman the pain would be unbearable. Seeing them together, feeling so excluded, she had found even Dorothy's presence difficult enough. She slept again, and dreamed of Blois as if it were a fever town, of every footstep there thudding like the pulse in a delirium, her whole life poisoned by the sickness of loss.

Their separation had been a lie, so had their moments of intimacy. He wasn't going forward to another woman. He was returning to a childhood sweetheart, and this was no consolation at all, no matter how ugly her face was supposed to be.

For the first time, she was sincerely glad to have Dorothy here, however spiteful she felt towards her. She was bitterly jealous of this Mary, this plain-faced friend, who was going to lie with Williams' body naked beside her own. If his sister hadn't been here, she would have had to have him again, she was sure of it, with goodness knows what consequence.

When she was calmer, she thought how meaningless his second marriage would be. It wouldn't be made in heaven. It would be no better than a heathen contract he would make with the other woman. He would be taking a second bride with the first yet living, and bedding her like a Turk.

How sweet Dorothy was now she knew Williams had had his say. How they could all relax and chatter about nothing very much. How Caroline *loved* them.

As they settled into another fortnight of even-tempered

friendship, she realized for the first time how French she was, and noticed how much and how painfully her hoped-for husband was English. And his sister, with her strange strict ways. Neither of them would have lasted five minutes in the France she had known, this France that was surely returning to war.

Perhaps her problem went deeper. After all, Williams – must she call him William? – was a man. She, and now Caroline, were something altogether different, with a need for something deeper.

'When is Daddy coming back?' Caroline asked, as they said their farewells. 'When will he bring Aunt Dorothy to see us again?'

'I'll be back for your wedding,' he smiled to his daughter.

Peace permitting, she thought. They had just heard that Napoleon Buonaparte had made himself sole Consul of France. The monster had devoured the fools as Montlivault promised he would.

She had to tell Caroline before her daughter learned anything from her sisters. When their coach reached the top of the chalk escarpment on the way back to Paris, and they began to walk down, she drew her aside from the other passengers. 'Your daddy's going to get married,' she explained.

'Can a daddy do that?'

'Your father can do anything he likes.'

'Now he's not dead,' her daughter said, and began to skip along beside her.

'He tells me many things about this woman he intends to place in my bed,' Annette went on, as if the girl was either listening or could understand her. 'I gather she cannot speak intelligently, does not think, scarcely knows how to act. He intends to put her in a leaky cottage on a wild wet hill, and have his sister, your Aunt Dorothy, teach her manners and poetry till she's good enough for him. I'd rather stay in France and fight Buonaparte.'

'No one can teach you anything, mama. Not even Aunt Dorothy.'

AFTERWORD

Only a very few of the many letters Annette wrote to William and Dorothy survive. She addressed Wordsworth as 'my husband' and called herself 'your wife' while praying for his return so that they might be *properly* married according to the Republican law she disliked. She must have sensed, and with mounting anxiety, that the bonds of an extra-legal Catholic marriage would seem increasingly flimsy to a young man so long prevented from reaching her and their child, particularly a young man raised in an alien tradition.

At home in Blois, she styled herself Madame William or Williams, then latterly and more bleakly Veuve William or Williams. Wordsworth was a name too foreign to be entertained while their two countries were at war, particularly by a member of a household the secret police regarded as a nest of spies.

The family continued, when possible, to attend religious services conducted by 'non-juring' or traditionalist priests – men who refused to swear they accepted that the Church was secondary to the state. To officiate at such a service was a capital offence. To attend was to invite death at the hands of the mob.

On 14th July 1795, Annette was asked to witness a marriage ceremony consecrated by one of these priests, and thus similar to her own. She signed herself Madame William Wordsworth Vallon.